My HOOD Your BARRIO His BEAT

by

FULL BLOODED PIT

Published by
Tortoise Publishing

Printed in the United States of America

ISBN-13: 978-1484018439

Published by
Tortoise Publishing
www.TortoisePublishing.com

For Boggie Rose and Nu

Acknowledgements

I would like to thank my parents and my family for supporting my efforts to get back my life. I would also like to thank all my friends who are willing to put the past behind us. Thanks to Chuck at Helppublish.com and Yvonne at Magicgraphix.com for making this book possible.

Contents

Chapter 1

"It's all there, *vato*," the short, stout Mexican man proclaimed to the tall, dapperly-dressed Black man standing before him. "That's ten kilos of pure snow; same as last month, homes."

"Now you know damn well you ain't gotta tell me no shit like dat, Gordo," the Black man responded in a deep voice. "How long we been doin' bidness together, man? What, twenty years now?"

"That sounds about right, Diamond," Gordo answered with a proud smile on his pudgy face. Diamond handed his old friend and business associate a briefcase as he took the brown backpack from his grasp. "This ain't counterfeit money in here, is it, *amigo*?" Gordo asked before breaking out into hearty laughter.

"If that's counterfeit dough in that briefcase, a whole bunch of folks got a whole hell of a lot of explainin' to do," Diamond responded while checking the time on his Cartier. "Well, it's about time for me to be hittin' the road, *amigos*. I got places to be and people to see, so I'll catch you *vatos* on the rebound, homes," Diamond announced in his best *cholo* imitation. The smooth street hustler gave everyone in the room a friendly nod and then made his way out the front door.

"That fucking Diamond, he's a good *vato*, aye," Gordo proclaimed to his youngest brother and three protégés, once Diamond was out of the house. "He's the only *miyathe* that I trust enough to bring into my pad." Every teenager in the room quickly agreed with him the same way that everyone else in the *varrio* did whenever Gordo spoke.

Before anyone could utter another word, the door swung open with a loud boom. The doorknob slammed so hard into the wall that it penetrated the stucco. "Lay the fuck on the ground — right now!" demanded the light-skinned teenage boy who appeared in the doorway brandishing the ominous MAC-10 assault weapon. Two more African-American teenagers immediately made their way through the door, ordering the Hispanic men to lie on the floor.

1

One of the Mexican boys made the fatal mistake of reaching for the piece he had tucked into the waistband of his baggy Ben Davis slacks. Before he could aim his pistol, he was struck in the chest by three hollow-point slugs from the silent MAC-10. The boy's eyes slowly went blank as he slid down the wall, leaving a dark red trail of blood behind.

"Any of you other enchilada-eatin' mothafuckas wanna die today?" the stocky, light-skinned boy asked, before firing one more shot, this one directly into the head of his already lifeless target. Blood, bone, and chunks of brain oozed from the young boy's head. This prompted the other men to cooperate right away by lying face down on the floor. "What the fuck you waitin' for, Psych? Tie deez bean-bitin' son of a bitches up, blood." With a devilish grin and evil laugh, the young assailant produced a roll of silver duct tape from the pocket of his black, hooded sweatshirt.

"Don't nobody else wanna be a hero or what?" the teenager invited as he began stripping the duct tape. The first person the young gangster went for was Gordo himself.

The street lord asserted, in the toughest voice one could muster up with two guns pointed at him, "I'll give you whatever you want, homes. You don't gotta tie us up, *esse*."

The young thug quickly dropped the roll of tape onto the floor, and with his right hand he drew a chrome, silencer-equipped 9mm Desert Eagle from his waistband. He reached down, grabbed a handful of the chubby Hispanic man's hair in his left hand, and used it to yank his head backwards. Staring into Gordo's eyes with the same evil disposition as the young hoodlum who had just murdered his little brother's best friend, the teenager pressed the barrel of his pistol against Gordo's left nostril and made it clear to him who was in charge. "Check dis out, Paco," the youngster scoffed at the Mexican gang leader. "The only thing I gotta do is stay Black and rob your *ranchero* ass for every single tortilla you got up in this mothafucka, *comprende*?"

Gordo was not used to taking orders from any man, and his pride would not allow him to answer such an insolent question. His only response was to stare the young gangster straight in his eyes. "I ain't scared to die, homes, but if you kill me, you don't get nada."

After a brief stare-down between Gordo and the boy, the third teenager, who had been quiet up to this point, opened the briefcase that Diamond left behind, which had been lying on the coffee table. "It's enough cash in here for us to kill all four of y'all and be happy with," said the clean-cut robber. "It's fucked-up what just happened to ya lil homie, and I know ain't nobody else tryin' to go out like that, so just give us what we came for and we up out this dump. This shit is strictly bidness, dog."

This boy appeared to be a lot more rational than the other two hoods who looked and behaved identically evil. Even in the compromising position he was in, such respect went a long way with Gordo, for he himself had once been a stick-up kid, and just like this calm young robber, Gordo had never made his holdups personal. "Just do what you gotta do, aye," the boss swallowed his pride and spoke in a macho voice. "We don't want no more problems."

The boy in the black hooded sweatshirt tucked his pistol back into his waistband and then began taping each *cholo's* wrists tightly behind their backs. The teenager performed like clockwork, with such precision that it was obvious he had performed this task on many others before them. He taped the wrists and ankles of the three remaining teenage boys before lifting semiautomatic pistols off of two of them.

"Now, where you keep all da *clavo* at, tubby?" the heavily-tattooed killer toting the MAC-10 asked with a smug look on his face.

"Wait! Hold up, dog!" the comely, cool-headed teenager explained. "Kill all dat bullshit, Sick! Let's just get this loot and shake da mothafuckin' spot." He helped the Hispanic head honcho to his feet and demanded that he take him to the stash.

"All I got is fifty thousand cash and about ten kilos of coca in here right now, homes," Gordo warned the bandits, as if this were a bad thing. This was like music to the ears of all three young gangbangers. In fact, this was about to be one of the biggest hits they had ever pulled off. The clean-cut teenager ordered the savage teen with the MAC-10 to stay and keep an eye on the young Mexican boys, while Gordo escorted him and the hooligan in the black hood up the stairs.

3

Once they reached the master bedroom, the Mexican boss pointed to a large solid oak dresser. "Push that to the side and you will see a little rope hanging from out of the carpet under there. Just pull on that rope."

The young gangster quickly obliged this request and found a hollowed out space beneath the thick, black carpet. One by one, he reached down into the floor and pulled out eighteen well-compacted bricks of white powder before producing an Oakland Raiders gym bag. He unzipped the gym bag to find several rubber banded stacks of cash. "Jackpot!" blurted the obnoxious young criminal without making the slightest attempt to conceal the taunting tone in his voice.

Gordo could feel his blood boiling. He could not believe that he was being robbed by these three young street punks. He struggled with his instincts, attempting to dismiss the thought that his good friend Diamond had set him up like this for a few crumbs that he knew would not even amount to one week's profit. He would have gladly fronted Diamond double this if he needed it. Right then, the street boss shuddered when he came to grips with the reality of what was really going on. Just when he figured it out, his thought process was interrupted.

"Where all da guns at, fat boy? And I know you got some heavy artillery up in this bitch, so don't test my patience, aight, Pancho Villa?" the young thug demanded.

"Hey, you fucking little *putho*," Gordo responded without thinking. "There is a duffle bag under my bed with a couple of bullshit rifles and two *pistolas*. That's all there is, so take that shit and handle your business before my lady comes back with my kids."

A bulb lit up in the mind of the young hoodlum. "I think this fat piece of shit is holdin' out on us, Lil Ricky," the young savage said with a grin, realizing that he had just gained a lot more leverage over his victim.

Lil Ricky could read his comrade's mind. He was far too familiar with the demented minds of his two favorite crime partners, Psycho and Sicko. They were ruthless and relentless in their every beastly endeavor. Lil Ricky needed this balance, because he was very much the opposite.

Gordo's heart skipped a beat and then began to pound hard when he realized that he had probably just made the biggest mistake of his life. "I gave you *vatos* everything," Gordo proclaimed in an agitated voice. "I already told you guys what I had; that's it, homes."

"Well, I guess we'll just have ta wait till ya *senorita* shows up wit the little *bambinos* to find out where the real stash is at, huh, big drawz?"

Gordo dropped his head while shaking it with regret. A tear rolled down his cheek as he visualized his wife being tied up and raped while his children were bound and tortured, all due to his own stupidity. Gordo loved his family more than life itself, and he knew that his only chance of saving his family was in the hands of the teenager to whom the other two referred as Lil Ricky. With the face of a desperate man, the powerful gang leader looked the young gangster in the eyes and begged for mercy without having to say a single word.

Lil Ricky stared at the pitiful specimen that stood tied up before him. He knew of the reputation of this stout man with the thick mustache; he was a living legend on the streets of Los Angeles. As the bastard child of an illegal immigrant prostitute, he had been doomed from the day he was born. However, he was now renowned as the fairest businessman operating in the black market. Gordo had earned the name "Ghetto Santa Claus" over the years; every Christmas, he led three eighteen-wheelers packed with thousands of gifts, from neighborhood to neighborhood, passing out toys and gifts to everyone in sight. Lil Ricky himself had been on the receiving end of these gifts time and time again while growing up in his housing project.

The handsome young gangster hated himself for what he knew he was going to have to do soon. He was very aware that as good-hearted as Gordo was, he was considered among the most dangerous the streets had to offer. Lil Ricky was also aware that this powerful street don, known throughout the *varrio* as the *Llavero* — holder of the keys to life and death — had seen his face, and even worse, had heard his name. One command from the street emperor would spell certain destruction for anyone who dared cross him.

Gordo was no fool. He knew there was little to no chance of these ambitious young criminals allowing him to live to tell of his ordeal.

The kingpin's death was inevitable. His only objective was to secure the safety of his family.

Once again, Gordo looked Lil Ricky right in his focused young eyes, this time with a slight smile in his wisdom-filled eyes and an air of pride about himself that Lil Ricky found to be odd considering the circumstances. "You say this is strictly business, huh, youngster?" Gordo inquired.

"Strictly bidness, big dog," Lil Ricky replied sincerely, knowing that he had just answered a loaded question.

Gordo continued to stare Lil Ricky in his eyes with such intense concentration that the teenager began to feel like this man was somehow communicating with his soul. "What if I told you that there was two million dollars in cold hard cash hidden in this house, right now, as we speak?"

Lil Ricky could not believe his ears, but he could tell by the look on the man's face that he was serious as a heart attack.

"Two million dollaz!?" Lil Ricky's crony exclaimed, eyes wide. The young cutthroat put his 9mm back to the face of the Mexican boss. "See, I knew this mothafucka was holdin' out on us! Now, where is the mothafuckin' money at? And you better not be bullshittin' us!"

"You feel like you're a real tiger while you're waving that *cuete* around, don't you, *vato?* I bet without it, you ain't nothing but a little *pinchi gatillo.*"

The young bandit had no idea what Gordo had just said to him, but judging from the tone of the gang lord's voice, Psycho was sure he had just been insulted. Before Gordo could brace himself for the blow, Psycho slapped him in the mouth with his pistol. The gun's silencer made a loud *thump* as it connected with the mouth of his reputable hostage.

To the boy's surprise, Gordo did nothing but nod his head and smile at him as the blood trickled down his lip from his thick mustache.

"What the fuck you doin', Psych?" Lil Ricky asked in a feeble attempt to demonstrate that what his accomplice had just done had come as a surprise. Lil Ricky removed a red bandana from his back pocket and began dabbing blood from the mouth of Psych's victim,

"Yo, dog, this dude ain't gonna touch you no more. Just tell us where the money at and we up outta here, man."

Gordo looked at him with such a disdainful expression that it immediately let Lil Ricky know that the gang lord was not oblivious to the game that was being played. The Mexican don spit a large bloody loogie onto his bedroom floor while staring at Lil Ricky's crony with a look of disgust. "As soon as you guys are finished playing 'good cop/bad cop', you can tell this little boy to get the fuck out of here so we can talk like men, homes."

Psycho could not help but laugh at the crime boss' statement. "You don't look like you're in any position to be up in here negotiating and shit, José," the young thug asserted with his gun pointed at Gordo's head.

Lil Ricky reached out and pushed his friend's hand down so the pistol was pointed toward the floor and away from Gordo's head. "Yo, Psych, go check on Sicko and make sure he got everything under control. I'll be down there in a minute, my nigga."

The teenager looked at Lil Ricky in disbelief. "You can't be serious, dog! This mothafucka will try somethin'!"

"I got this, homie!" Lil Ricky exclaimed with enough fire in his eyes to let his partner know that he meant what he said. "Bounce, so we can get this cheese and get the fuck on, nigga!"

"Aight, blood, but if you need me, just holla and I'm back up here wit the quickness," Psycho promised while looking right at Gordo. The young gangbanger walked out of the room reluctantly.

Lil Ricky began talking as soon as his homeboy was out the door. "Okay, now, where is—"

"Shhhh," the crime boss cut him off. Both men listened to the footsteps going down the stairs. When Gordo was sure that the wild youngster was out of earshot, he began talking to Lil Ricky in a low voice. "Look here, youngster; I been doing this shit far too long to not know what time it is. I know I'm a walking dead man. There ain't no way you *vatos* are gonna come up in here with your faces showing and calling out each other's names and then let me escape this shit alive. It is what it is, so I'm going to make you a proposition, homes."

"I'm listenin'," Lil Ricky replied with a concerned look on his face.

"Hey, *esse,* if I show you where the money's at, I need your word as a man that you will just take it and jam as soon as you guys do what you gotta do before my *familia* gets back."

Lil Ricky stared at the street legend in admiration. He felt unworthy of putting this great man in such a dilemma. "You got my word on my grandmother's grave, big dog," the teenager responded with such an air of genuineness that Gordo believed him.

"I really appreciate that from the heart, *esse,* but there is just one more thing." Staring into Lil Ricky's eyes, the unsmiling crime boss' demeanor switched from tranquil to grim. "I lived my whole life by the code of honor, homes," the street legend informed Lil Ricky of what he already knew. "This might sound crazy, but if I gotta go, I don't wanna die by the hands of a coward." Gordo continued to look Lil Ricky right in his eyes. "I want you to do it, aye."

Lil Ricky cringed at the request. He knew that this would not be the first or the last time he would take a man's life, but it would be the most difficult thus far. He could have easily left this task to one of his grisly crime partners, but he made up his mind to respect the final wishes of this legendary man, even if it meant personally ending his existence.

"That's my word, big dog," Lil Ricky responded with candor and sincerity.

Gordo's thick mustache wrinkled as he managed to force a bittersweet smile upon his stone face. "Now, let's get down to business, youngster."

"Now you're speaking my language," Lil Ricky responded, noticeably uncomfortable with the awkward ordeal he was facing.

"We gotta head back downstairs for the rest of the *fedia,*" Gordo said, making a head gesture toward the door.

"After you," Lil Ricky said, motioning for him to lead the way. The two men walked down the stairs to find the remaining three hostages still lying down on the floor in the exact same spot as when the intruders had first taped them up. Lil Ricky's accomplices appeared to be right at home in this situation. One of them was standing over the hostages with gun in hand, while the other sat on the couch with a lit cigarette in his mouth, counting up money stacks from the recently acquired Oakland Raider gym bag. When the money-hungry teenager noticed that Lil Ricky was back, his face lit up with an evil grin. "Greed, gimme evree thang dat I need," the young thug rapped out loud the words of an old Ice Cube street anthem.

"This way, *vato*," Gordo said before walking through the kitchen door. Lil Ricky pointed at the remaining hostages and then looked at his partners in crime and gave them a slight nod, sealing the fate of the young boys, before allowing Gordo through the kitchen door. The crime boss led Lil Ricky through the kitchen to a sliding glass door which accessed the back yard. "Back here, homes."

Lil Ricky could hear the sound of dogs barking in the distance. "What you tryin' ta do? Get me ate up by some pitbulls or somethin', man?" Lil Ricky asked with a concerned look on his face.

"Nah, homes, my dogs are all in their kennel. I only let 'em out when everybody leaves the house."

The young robber drew a semi-automatic, silencer-equipped pistol from his waistband. He then unlocked the sliding glass door and slid it open. He allowed Gordo to go out the door first. Ten seconds later, when he was sure there were no dogs on the loose, he stuck his head out the door, looked around, and then followed. Gordo led the young bandit up to a built-in barbecue pit attached to a fireplace, all constructed of red brick.

"What the hell is this?" Lil Ricky asked with a puzzled expression.

Once again, looking into the youngster's eyes, Gordo reminded the young gangster of his promise. "I got your word, right, youngster?"

By now, Lil Ricky was becoming anxious. "Yeah, you got my word, big dog! Now let's get this shit over with so I'll be able to keep my word," the boy responded, unable to conceal the uneasiness in his voice.

"It's right in there," Gordo said, looking at the fireplace.

Lil Ricky looked into the fireplace and was confused when he saw nothing but red bricks.

"You gotta reach your hand deep up into that chimney and you'll feel a ledge inside of there. Once you feel the ledge, if you reach up just a little bit higher and move your hand around, you'll feel a handle," Gordo instructed. "Get a grip on it and then pull on that handle as hard as you can."

Lil Ricky followed Gordo's directions and quickly found the handle. After a brief struggle, a large suitcase came crashing down into the fireplace. The young robber opened up the suitcase to find more cash than he had ever seen in his young lifetime.

Lil Ricky felt sorry for his victim and was reluctant to complete his final task. He watched as Gordo walked over to a nearby lawn chair underneath the patio awning and sat down. The street legend closed his eyes, bowed his head, and then said a brief prayer to Saint Mary. The teenage gangster walked over shortly after, and with a single .45 shot through the top of the street don's head, Lil Ricky kept his promise.

Chapter 2

The main streets of inner city Los Angeles tell a vivid story of the inhabitants who dwell in the old neighborhoods that lie between them. Like every other major highway in South Central Los Angeles, Broadway is filled with mainly liquor stores, run-down beauty shops, and dilapidated, drug-infested apartment buildings.

More prominent than all the other buildings on the streets of South Central are the numerous churches sprawled up and down every highway. On any given day of the week, a person can drive down any South Central boulevard and spot several funeral proceedings in progress at many of the small Baptist churches.

Sergeant Curtiss Bookman had made a hobby over the years of counting funerals while driving down Broadway on his way to work. He prided himself on being able to guess the guests of honor at the funerals by the dress code and demeanor of its visitors. Funerals of the elderly were usually well organized and respectably formal, while the gangland funerals were always the direct opposite.

The gangbangers' funerals were always the same. There would always be a long convoy of hydraulic equipped low-rider cars bouncing up and down in front of the church along with several large SUVs with 24" rims blasting gangster rap music through fifteen inch woofers loud enough to shake the church's stained-glass windows. Standing in front of the church would always be a large overflow of guests who arrived too late to cram into the tiny Baptist church that was already filled to more than capacity in violation of every fire and safety code on the books. These were the people who made Bookman's little guessing game possible.

As he drove by on this particular day, he spotted several young men, all wearing matching T-shirts with a man's face airbrushed on the back of them. This was typical at gang funerals. The men also had on dark-blue khaki pants with dark-blue bandanas hanging from their back left pockets. This automatically let Bookman know that there was a Crip funeral in progress.

The sergeant could smell the loud odor of marijuana smoke in the air as he drove past the group of young adults. He spotted two pretty young ladies involved in a catfight altercation as he slowly rolled by.

"That ain't even my man's baby that you pregnant with, bitch!" one woman screamed at the other.

"The man is dead and still havin' baby mama drama," Bookman said to himself as he got far enough past the scene of pandemonium to speed up.

The Los Angeles Police Department's 77th Division is located on Broadway between 76th and 77th Streets. The LAPD's 77th Division is responsible for patrolling some of the most dangerous streets in South Central, known as the East Side, home to over thirty different reputable street gangs, most of whom are out to murder one another whenever or wherever the opportunity arises. The members of the Mad Swan Blood Family hate the East Coast Crips. The 52nd Street Pueblo Bishop Bloods hate the 38th Street Chicano Varrio. The Circle City Pirus hate the Front Street Watts Crips, who hate the Back Street Watts Crips. The Hoover Criminal Gang just hates everybody.

Sergeant Bookman was assigned to arguably the worst beat on the mean East Side streets, the turf of the Bounty Hunter Watts Bloods, a gang so big that it held down four different neighborhoods at once. There are the Block Boy Bounty Hunters, who boast over one hundred members. About a mile from the Block Boys are the Bellhaven Bounty Hunters, who are about two hundred strong. Then there are the Ten-Eight Bounty Hunters, who clock in at a little bit over fifty members all on one little street. Right smack dab in the middle of all these neighborhoods, like a massive tree trunk holding its branches together, is the heart and soul of the notorious Bounty Hunter gang, the Nickerson Gardens housing project Bounty Hunters, where it all started. They are easily one of the biggest Black gangs in Los Angeles, with over one thousand active members. The Nickerson Gardens are also home to the *Vatos Locos Muchachos* ("Crazy Boys") gang. These two gangs had managed to put race aside and work together over the years to maintain the safety and illegal commerce of their neighborhood.

Sergeant Curtiss Bookman had a long history with these two violent street gangs. Over the twenty-year stretch that he had been working the "Hunter beat", he had attended twenty-nine funerals of LAPD comrades who had fallen victim to the ruthless Bounty Hunter Watts gangsters.

Back in 1987, the young Officer Bookman had been assigned to the hunter beat as a rookie. While even the most gung-ho rookies dreaded being assigned to the Hunter beat, Curtiss Bookman could not have been happier when he received his assignment. As a turf that never slept, this beat was the job that separated the men from the boys over at 77th. Three bullet wounds, two dead partners, and 246 murder investigations later, Curtiss Bookman was still patrolling this same beat. The only thing that had changed over the years was his street savvy and his uniform, which now had stripes on the side of his shirt sleeves.

Aside from the Nickerson Gardens, Bookman was also responsible for patrolling all the other major housing projects around the Watts area. The Jordan Downs, home to the Grape Street Crips and Watts Varrio Grape *Chicanos,* the Hacienda Village, home to the Village Boy Bloods, and the Imperial Courts, held down by the PJ Watts Crips. Bookman also patrolled the Pueblo projects outside of Watts, located in another crime-ridden area of the East Side known as the "Low Bottoms". The Pueblo Projects are home to the Pueblo Bishop Bloods and Cambodian Blood Asian Gang. Along with the project communities, Bookman also patrolled a host of other neighborhood Blood, Crip, Asian, and Chicano gangs on the East Side.

Over the years, Bookman had managed to build up a good rapport with a lot of small-time gangbangers and even a few big-timers in the East Side district. He had a few guys who would point him in the right direction to find the information he needed for investigations, and then he had his all-out informants. These were usually the small-time block dealers at the bottom of the pecking order, called curb servers, and the drug addict petty thieves and prostitutes known as bass heads and strawberries. Bookman could find out the location of every crackhouse in Watts by simply catching one of these snitches with one crack rock or residue-soaked bass pipe. He knew about Big Bruno's crackhouse on 114th. He knew that Lil Scrappy was slanging PCP dipped sherm sticks in the alley behind Spades Liquor. He was aware that Big Mama ran the all-night gambling shack in the projects on 111th Street and also the whorehouse a few blocks over. In fact, Sergeant Bookman knew everything that was happening or going to happen on his beat, and as long as he continued to receive his cut of the profits, the twenty-year veteran was content in allowing nature to continue to take its course.

Sergeant Bookman arrived at the station forty-five minutes late. Third watch began at 2:00 P.M., but for Bookman there was no such thing as first, second, or third watch. The sergeant did not operate according to time constraints. He had been working these streets long enough to know that the bad guys had enough sense to know a cop's schedule better than the cop himself did in most instances. They did most of their robbing and made their biggest drug transactions when they knew that it was time for a shift change, better known as "Donut Time" to the gangsters and hustlers who operated on the South Central streets.

Bookman smashed ashes into the ashtray of his latest Cadillac, extinguishing his "Coco Puff" cigarette as he pulled into the parking lot of the precinct. Bookman's favorite guilty pleasure, known as coco puff, is a mixture of marijuana with a dab of crumbled up rock cocaine, rolled up along with plenty of tobacco to conceal the odor of the illegal substances that went along with it.

The sergeant pulled into his assigned parking space and spritzed a few squirts of Lagerfeld Photo cologne onto his uniform before sliding out of his Caddy. He slammed the car door behind him and then strolled into the station with the smoothness and confidence more like that of a seasoned pimp than a veteran police officer.

"Hey, Bookman, Cody wants to see you in his office ASAP."

The sergeant had not managed to make it all the way through the door before receiving this command from his good friend and coworker, Brenda Hayes.

"What did I do this time, Bren?" Bookman responded in a comical voice.

"Boy, I do not get paid enough to keep up wit yo job and mine, too," the heavyset jailer with the dried-up jerry curl said. "Hell, somebody got shot is all I know; what else is new?"

Bookman smiled at his overworked and underpaid colleague who was obviously not having one of her better days. "Thanks, Bren," Bookman said before walking off toward the captain's office.

Captain Benjamin Cody was very much the opposite of Bookman. Cody carried himself with an air of arrogance and the old-school "Uncle Tom" negro "I'm Better Than You" mentality. Sergeant Bookman knew that, deep down, his captain had more of an inferiority complex than anything else and used his high rank as a means of concealing his insecurities. He had grown up a navy brat, unlike Bookman who had been raised in the ghetto streets similar to the ones he was now assigned. Bookman had earned his stripes the hard way, through years of interaction with gang bangers, prostitutes, and drug kingpins, while his superior had received his position on the fast track after retiring from twenty years of service in the navy as a military policeman. Although Bookman himself had put in several years of military service, his story was very different from that of Captain Cody's. Bookman had been a United States Marine Devil Dog from the ages of seventeen to twenty-two. Although there were no major wars during Bookman's four years of service from 1983 to 1987, he'd still managed to look death in the eye in 1983 during a suicide bomb attack in Beirut which left over two hundred of his fellow soldiers dead. He had also seen his share of combat later on that year when U.S. forces invaded Grenada and dismantled the Grenadian militia that was in control of the country at that time.

"What's up, Ben?" Bookman exclaimed in a loud obnoxious voice as he strolled leisurely into his boss' office. He knew very well that his captain hated being called by his first name and preferred being called by his formal title of captain. Bookman was also aware that Cody tolerated being called 'Ben' to avoid being looked upon as uppity; therefore, the unruly sergeant planned to communicate with his commander on a first-name basis until the captain conjured up enough courage to correct him.

Captain Cody was sitting at his desk, engaged in deep concentration, while reading from the top of what appeared to be a five-inch-thick stack of papers.

The captain's office was immaculate. From the spotless, pea-green carpet to the large, polished oak desk, everything was flawless.

Bookman always found himself staring at the captain's various award plaques hanging all over the walls and the trophy-filled shelves which decorated the captain's office. He could never figure out how a pencil-pushing poot-butt like Ben Cody had been honored with so many awards. Today he stared at the largest trophy in the room. *That must be THE WORLD'S CORNIEST TURD AWARD,* Bookman thought to himself.

"Do you see all these papers, Sergeant Bookman?" the captain inquired in a slow and solemn voice without looking up from his work to make eye contact with the sergeant. Before Bookman could answer his question, the captain took a deep breath while shaking his head in an overwhelmed gesture, "Here lies four autopsy reports and a police report pertaining to what appears to have been a home invasion, two eleven, and four execution style, one eighty sevens, on July 13 at approximately eleven hundred hours."

Bookman loathed the way his captain always spoke in gung-ho police jargon. "So, somebody ran up in a house yesterday, tied up four people, then robbed and killed them. Business as usual, right?" Bookman replied cynically, having heard and investigated far more gruesome criminal acts than this.

"Wrong," Captain Cody replied in an irritated voice. "I just got a call from Chief Gordan himself, who, by the way, is up for re-election in less than a year, and he's chewing my ass out like I'm the criminal who's running around killing people. He wants this case solved — and fast — because the feds, it seems, are considering launching an investigation into our department due to the many reports of corruption and far too many unsolved homicides."

This statement immediately caused Sergeant Bookman's heart to begin pounding at a fast rate. The term "FEDS" was the only four letter word in the English language that Sergeant Curtiss Bookman found to be offensive. Bookman was involved in far too many illicit activities to have federal agents snooping around on his beat and asking questions. The sergeant had a hand in every venture, from gambling to murder for hire and everything in-between on the streets of LA, and he was sure that a federal investigation of this latest mass murder would somehow lead directly to his front porch, even though he had yet to find out who the victims were.

"So what's the scoop on our vics?" Bookman inquired as nonchalantly as he could, considering the complicated new circumstances that he found himself faced with.

"Well... let's see here," the captain said while looking at one of the pages in the report. "We've got an Antonio Banuelos, a juvy who had just been paroled from CYA two days before he was slain." The captain licked his fingers and flipped through a few pages. "Oh, here's a Jesse Medina. He was also on Youth Authority Parole for several H&S violations at the time of his murder."

"Drug dealer, huh?" Bookman inquired.

"Either that or he's a chronic litterbug. Here is a John Doe. We're waiting for dental analysis on this one, but he's a male Hispanic, approximately sixteen years of age. This last one's in our gang file. His name is Joseph Ruiz, a documented member of *Vatos Locos* with a monicker of 'Shaggy'. He was twenty-one years old and had recently been paroled from Calipatria State Prison, although he never quite managed to make it to his parole office to sign in."

Captain Cody flipped through several more pages before speaking again, "We've got one survivor in this case, but he's currently comatose over at MLK. His name is Hector Torez, a forty-two-year-old male Hispanic. He doesn't have a criminal background, so most likely the poor guy was simply involved with the wrong people and caught a bullet that didn't have his name on it."

It baffled Bookman how a man could reach such a high position by being as oblivious to his job as Captain Cody. Aside from John Doe, Bookman knew exactly who every single one of his victims were at first mention, especially the latter. In fact, every patrol cop from rookies on up knew who Hector Torez was.

"Guilty by association, huh?" Bookman asked with a grin.

Captain Cody stared at the sergeant. He was often confused as to why Sergeant Bookman always looked at him with these silly smiles in situations as serious as life and death. "Anyhow, the doctors over at King are trying to persuade the guy's wife to donate his organs. They're saying he has about a one in five hundred chance of ever waking up out of the coma, and even if he does wake up, there is approximately only a one in a thousand chance that he will not live

17

out the remainder of his life as a vegetable," Captain Cody informed the sergeant.

It amused Sergeant Bookman how his captain always acted as if he were so concerned with matters about which he did not have the slightest idea. The captain had about as much street smarts as Forest Gump.

"So what did CSI come up with?" Bookman inquired, as he shifted his brain from cynically sarcastic to cover-his-behind mode.

Captain Cody sifted through several more pages. "Let's see here," the captain said while skimming over a page from his stack, "We've recovered seven 9mm shell casings and one .45 shell casing. We found a shoe print on the front door of the house which had been kicked in, a size ten and a half, and a model of the manufacturer Nike. We dusted for fingerprints, so we'll be getting some results on that soon. We also recovered one Newport cigarette butt from the living room floor where our four DOAs were discovered. We're running those through our DNA library to see if we luck up and get any hits on that. I ordered the crime scene to be left intact, so you can go on over there and have a look around to see if you find anything they might have overlooked."

"I'll get right on it, boss," Bookman replied, as he took the stack of papers from his boss' grasp. Bookman turned around and was well on his way out of the captain's office.

"Oh, one more thing, Bookman."

Bookman turned back around to find that his superior suddenly had a look on his face that one may consider slightly mocking.

"What's up, cap'n?" Bookman inquired after a deep breath.

"As you know, we just got in our rookie graduates fresh from the academy."

"Okay, and?" Bookman quickly got on the defensive, knowing exactly where this conversation was headed.

"I'm assigning all my sergeants a ride-along in order to teach them the ropes a lot faster than a regular patrol cop would. These days we've gotta—"

"Wait, wait, wait just one minute, cap!" Bookman began to stutter in anger. "Now you know damn well I fly solo. My days of rookie training have been over for years, and I don't need no dead weight holdin' me down out there. Come on now, cap; don't do this to me," the sergeant begged.

"Well, here's some good news for ya, Bookman. This time it will only be for two days a week, but here's some bad news for you also. It's nonnegotiable. You can probably use one of these youngsters around to keep you on your toes anyway." The captain turned to his computer screen and punched in a few keys. "Marcos Felix," Cody said, as if he had not even heard Bookman's line of begging. The sergeant just stood there with a blank look on his face. "Your rookie's name is Marcos Felix. He and all the other rookies are in the briefing room. Go get yours and take him to that crime scene with ya."

Chapter 3

It was an overcast morning on the streets of Los Angeles. A light drizzle of precipitation fell, giving the outside air a pleasant scent of cleanliness. This was a breath of fresh air from the usual odor of factory and traffic created air pollution.

At the Hampton Inn, in the suburb city of Carson, the lobby was buzzing with hotel guests taking advantage of the free coffee and bagels that were set out every morning for their enjoyment.

In room 310, Lil Ricky had been up all night pacing back and forth while replaying over and over again in his head what had taken place the previous day. His two crime partners slept like newborn babies as Ricky reminisced on his past. The eighteen-year-old boy had seen more murders in his short lifetime than a seasoned war veteran. He envisioned the first man he had ever killed. Lil Ricky had only been nine years old at the time. He remembered hearing his mother screaming and then walking into her room to see this giant man brutally striking her over and over again.

"Please, not in front of my son!" his mother had begged the man in vain as he continued to pound her tiny frame like a heavy punching bag.

Lil Ricky did not understand his mother's profession back then. All he knew was that every time one of these strange men came into his home and went into his mother's room, Mommy would have money when the man left. The men were usually nice to Lil Ricky. He had seen some of them come by regularly and even bring him candy and toys from time to time.

Although the boy's father, Big Rick Rock, had been in prison for over two years by then, Lil Ricky still remembered where the old green bag was where his father kept his weapons. "I know you got my wallet, bitch. Now give it to me or I'll kill you!" the monster had exclaimed as he choked the little woman.

"Get the fuck off ma mama, nigga!"

The man looked up to find that the little boy had a chrome .357 revolver pointed directly at him.

"Dat gun is damn near bigger den you is, boy! Watcha gone do, shoot me, you little shit?" He had realized what the answer to his question was, only after half his neck had been torn off by the hollow point bullet.

From that point on, Lil Ricky had been fascinated with the power of guns and became numb to killing. Gordo was the first person Lil Ricky ever regretted killing, for even though several of the murders committed by the young man had been heinous, in his mind they were all justifiable. The previous day's slaying had been different.

There was a distinctive knock at the door of room 310 at 9:00 A.m. sharp. As soon as he heard the loud bang of metal tapping against the room door, Lil Ricky automatically recognized it as the sound of one of his uncle's various gold nugget rings knocking.

The noise triggered a flashback of a conversation that Lil Ricky and his crime partners had engaged in the night before.

"Aye, y'all, we should split this two mill between just us three. Shit, we rich, blood. We don't need nobody!"

Lil Ricky had gotten a pretty good laugh from this bold statement from his homeboy. "Shut the fuck up, Sick," Lil Ricky had responded in a comical voice, "Man, every time you smoke summa dat shit, yo ass always gotta come up wit these bright-ass ideas, nigga."

The fact was that both of the twins were heavy PCP users who usually said and did things on pure impulse. It was true that Sicko had made this statement after drinking a fifth of cheap Night Train wine and smoking a potent sherm-dipped cigarette, but unlike most other occasions, the young thug had put a lot of thought into his words before he said them. In fact, he had been trying to come up with a way to implement his plan from the very second he had feasted his eyes on the contents of the suitcase.

"Check dis out, Lil Rick Rock," Psycho Twin spoke up, "All bullshit to the side, homie, we do deserve this money. Your uncle ain't even gotta know about this. We got the shit he sent us in there to get, plus we handled what he needed us to handle, so anything else should be like icing on the cake. Feel me?" Psycho had asked.

Lil Ricky was now being double-teamed. This came as a surprise because Psycho was not usually outspoken about matters such as this one, and whenever he was, he hardly ever took the side of his twin brother over Lil Ricky.

There was no disputing the fact that Lil Ricky was the smart one in this three-man wrecking crew. After all, it was Rick Rock's logic that had gotten the gang out of life or death situations time after time, and both brains of the two-headed monster known as "The Twins" understood this fact. They were both aware that if not for their beloved childhood friend, they would both have been dead or in prison a long time ago, therefore, in most situations, Lil Ricky's logic prevailed.

"Aight, peep game, my niggas," Lil Ricky had responded. "Let's break this shit down to da bare basics. We got $140,000 out my uncle's briefcase. We got eighteen kilos of powda and over $20,000 out the dude's bedroom. Then we got the lucky Howie Mandel suitcase, right?"

"Yeah, dats right," Sicko quickly responded.

Lil Ricky went on, "So let's add all dis shit up, my niggas. Let's say twelve geez apiece for da chickens, and dats lettin' um go dirt-ass cheap. Dats $216,000 plus all dis mothafuckin' cash. We talkin' about $2.4m altogether, blood!" Lil Ricky gave his words a chance to soak in before he began to speak again, "I'm damn good at math, and according to my estimates, we talkin' 'bout somewhere in the neighborhood of $600k a hizzead. Now do we wanna bite the hand dats been feedin' us all deez years or do we wanna stay true to da game and still be ballin' the fuck outta control?" Once again, last night Lil Ricky had won.

Now, on the way to open the door for his uncle, Lil Ricky paused for a brief second, stared at his sleeping comrades, and could not help but crack a warm smile. He loved these two crazy teenagers more than life itself.

Carnell and Darnell, as identical twins, were sometimes too identical for the likes of Lil Ricky, who at times found it difficult to tell the two of them apart. Both twins had the same high-yellow complexion. Even though they had never met their biological father, it was not hard to tell that he was of either white or Hispanic descent.

Both twins had long, wavy hair that they always sported in corn rows which hung halfway down their backs. Both twins also kept a perpetual, evil grin on their faces everywhere they went. This is what made it so difficult for people to tell them apart.

Over the years, Lil Ricky had learned to identify them by their eyes. They both had tight eyes with the same cold jet-black eyeballs. This caused Rick Rock to often joke about the possibility of them being half Asian and clowning around all the time by talking to them in an Asian accent. Sick Twin's eyes were just a tad tighter than Psycho's. Psycho's voice was a little bit deeper than Sicko's. As a result, Lil Ricky had mastered the art of telling his twin buddies apart. They would often joke, saying, "As long as deez hood rats can't tell us apart in the bedroom, then it's all good." The Twins had built a reputation over the years of sharing women by pretending to be each other in the bed. They were well aware that most young ladies did not care anyway. In fact, many women found it fun to be in bed with both of the 5'9" muscle-bound teenagers at the same time.

Lil Ricky had the appearance of a young Blair Underwood. At the age of eighteen, he was already 6'3" and wore his hair in waves which always stayed cut and lined up with a barber's precision. His thick eyebrows called attention to his light-brown eyes which were the same color of his honey-colored skin. Although he was tall with long arms, no one had accused Rick Rock of being skinny for years. Just like his twin partners in crime, the years spent in and out of California Youth Authority prisons, lifting weights and doing calisthenics, had worked wonders for his young body.

Lil Ricky opened his hotel room door to find his father's youngest brother standing there. "Whaddup, Uncle Dee," Lil Ricky exclaimed when he saw his favorite uncle.

"Gimme some good news, baby nephew!" Diamond responded, revealing his perfect smile. Everything about Diamond was perfect. From his thousand-dollar Dobbs derby hat all the way down to his spit-shined Stacy Adams, this man was excessively meticulous, and judging from his everyday appearance, anyone could see that he was a stickler for details.

"It's a wrap, Uncle Dee," Lil Ricky said. "Everything is handled."

23

"*Evv-erry thing?*" Diamond asked in an obvious inquiry about the fate of Gordo.

"Everything," Lil Ricky responded with a reassuring gesture.

Diamond walked into the hotel room to find that it had been trashed. "Damn, boy, it smells like a bunch of winos is livin' up in this joint."

The two men's conversation woke The Twins up simultaneously. Psycho was the first to greet his OG homeboy and best friend's uncle.

" 'Sup. Diamond?"

"You," the dapper gangster responded. "What's up wit ya other half here? He wake up on the wrong side of the coffin or what?" Diamond asked, once again flashing his pearly white smile. Sicko appeared to be upset and failed to find any humor in the question. Without any greeting whatsoever, the teenager immediately asked Lil Ricky, "You tell um bout the suitcase yet or what?"

"Uhhh…" Lil Ricky turned red with embarrassment. "I was just about to get to dat part," he responded, caught by surprise.

Diamond's smile automatically morphed into a look of intense curiosity. "What suitcase?"

Chapter 4

What's the difference between a living cop and a dead cop?" Lieutenant McGee inquired of his newly-graduated cadets. The lieutenant stood in front of the briefing room chalkboard staring at fifteen fresh new faces, all with an air of eagerness in their young eyes. McGee always felt sorry for his new recruits, for he was well aware that as optimistic and determined to save the world as they were, out of the fifteen graduates, he would be lucky to have one good cop at the end of the year.

"I know the answer!" one rookie blurted, raising his hand high in the air.

"Lay it on me, rookie."

"The difference between a living cop and a dead cop is safety," the young man said, looking right at the word "SAFETY" spelled out on the chalkboard in bold letters.

"Safety!" Lieutenant McGee agreed enthusiastically. "We are issued bulletproof vests for a reason. We are required to call for backup and wait for that backup to arrive before moving into a potentially hostile situation for a reason. We have all these protocols in place that we are required to follow for a reason. I have always been a stickler for protocol, because protocol is what saves lives out on the beat. It may save your life, or the life of a civilian, or even the life of a crim—"

The lieutenant came to an abrupt stop in the middle of his safety speech. He could not help but notice that several of his students were not paying attention to him and seemed to have their eyes focused on something behind him. Lieutenant McGee turned around to find that Sergeant Bookman was standing in the briefing room doorway with his hand raised as if he were a pupil in the freshly graduated class of cadets. "Sergeant Bookman," the lieutenant announced, perplexed as to the intentions of the renegade sergeant.

"What's the difference between an old fool and a new fool, lieutenant?" Sergeant Bookman inquired with a genuine look of concern on this face.

"I don't know, but I'm sure you'll be so gracious as to give us the answer, sergeant."

"By golly, I think I'll do just that, lieutenant," Bookman replied. "The difference, class, between an old fool and a new fool is that an old fool has been a fool longer," the sergeant proclaimed, while pointing at the lieutenant.

The lieutenant's face instantly became red as he fought to conceal his anger, while several of the rookies got a good laugh at his expense.

Bookman said, "The difference between a living cop and a dead cop, good cop and bad cop, wining cop and losing cop, is, always has been, and always will be — instinct," Bookman said, and then he asked, "Now which one of you is Mackro Felix?"

"It's Marcos, and that will be I, sir," the handsome young Hispanic man answered while standing up and saluting the sergeant in military fashion with a goofy smile on his face.

"Let's roll, Mackro," Bookman said on his way out the door.

Marcos Felix stared out the passenger window of Sergeant Bookman's patrol car. The two cops had now been on the road for fifteen minutes, and after a couple of off-hand remarks about the weather and other small-talk subjects by Marcos Felix, Bookman still had yet to speak one word to the rookie.

Once Marcos realized that he was being ignored, he decided to just stare out the window at the city and take it all in. When Officer Felix spotted an African-American woman who appeared to be at least eight months pregnant walking down the street in rags while pushing a shopping cart, then a kid who could not have been older than nine years old standing in front of a market pan-handling, then an old toothless Mexican man sitting at a bus stop barefoot and drinking from a bottle of cheap wine, all in a one-block span, the reality of his new job quickly began to set in.

"Let me give you a scenario, rookie," Bookman said, breaking the long silence as the two men sat at a traffic light at the intersection of Century and Central Boulevards.

"I'm listening, sir."

"Call me Booker," Bookman said, stepping on the gas pedal to travel through the green light. "Let's say you're riding solo on traffic duty. You pull an old lady over on a routine traffic stop. Let's say the old bag was doing seventy-five in a thirty-five. Hell, whatever. Anyway, you're writing Grandma a citation when you happen to glance across the street and see a man running into a daycare center with an AK-47 in hand. What do ya do, rookie?"

"Wow," Marcos Felix answered with a look of confusion on his young face.

"Take a minute to kick that around and let me know when you come up with an answer."

The two cops made a left turn off of Central Boulevard and onto Imperial Highway. The sergeant drove for one block and then turned into the parking lot of an old, run-down taco stand. Bookman flashed his headlights on and off as he drove into the parking lot.

Marcos was surprised when Bookman stopped and parked in this parking lot, which appeared shady at best. He noticed several young Black men who were all dressed in bright red standing in front of the restaurant. At the gas station right next door to the taco stand were two extremely dirty men arguing over which one of them was going to wash the windows of a young woman's minivan, "I saw it first, man. I called this one!" one addict said to the other. Across the street stood the gloomy black and white Nickerson Gardens housing projects. Marcos could hear the sound of Rap and Mariachi music playing simultaneously in the distance, while the odor of barbecue and Mexican food wafted into the squad car.

"Hop out," Bookman said, opening the car door. The sergeant could not help but notice the reluctance that was written all over the face of the rookie as he stared at the gangbangers in front of the taco stand. "Oh, don't mind those guys," Bookman said with a laugh. "That's just Boss Ross, Lil Smokey, Hot Dog, June Bug, and Baby Jay Boy. And see the young lady right there sitting in the Buick Regal? That's Boss' girlfriend, Tamesha. She's got at least two ounces of crack on her and a pistol," Bookman informed his ride-along as if this were no big deal. "As a matter of fact, all six of them have guns and dope on 'em, but notice how calm they are

27

seeing my cruiser pull up. They know that Bookman ain't rollin' up in here today lookin' for nothin' but a plate of Momma Maria's fine *comida*," Bookman said while leaning toward the rookie, with his feet hanging out of the car. "You see, rookie, I do things a little different than your average cop, because this is a far cry from the average beat. The day I start rolling up on these guys, jumping out, doing sporadic pat-downs, and hauling them in on petty charges, is the day that I lose their trust. Then it won't be long before they send some fourteen-year-old kid to blow my fuckin' head off," the sergeant said with emphasis. "Now let's go get something to eat. You should try the grilled *pollo* bowl; it's off the hook."

On the way in, one of the young men in front of the taco stand began pointing at the two cops, and then he yelled, "Yo, Blood, here come the one times!" as Bookman and Felix approached.

"What's wit it, fellas?" Bookman laughed, shaking each man's hand before waving to Tamesha with a warm smile. The eldest of the gangsters asked "Aye, Booker, when you start rollin' wit a potna again, man?"

"Big Ross, you the only nigga out here old enough to remember when I was riding with a partner, man."

"Shit, I'm only twenty-three years old, motha fucka, so don't act like it was that damn long ago," the man lied.

Bookman laughed as he and his new partner strolled into the taco stand. "I usually order at the walk-up window outside, but I was afraid you might piss your pants if we did that today."

The rookie did not find any humor in the sergeants taunting joke, but he laughed it off as best he could.

"Maria, this is my new partner, Officer Felix."

"Call me Marcos," the rookie interjected.

"Hello, Marcos. Welcome to Momma Maria's," the old Mexican woman said warmly. "What can we get for you nice gentlemen today?"

The two men ordered and then sat down at one of the round, red and white checker-clothed tables. Marcos stared through the restaurant window, watching as the young men took turns running up to one car after another, making transactions while he and Bookman waited for their food. "I got it!" the rookie blurted out of nowhere.

28

"You got what?" answered Bookman with a puzzled look on his face.

"The answer to your question about the daycare center."

"Well, spit it out then, rookie." Sergeant Bookman was surprised at how confident Marcos seemed in the answer he was about to give.

"This is what I'd do, sarj. I would leave the old lady there, drive to the front of the day care center, while I radio in for backup. Next, I would get on the squad car's loudspeaker and tell the gunman that we've got the place surrounded and demand that he come out with his hands up."

The expression on the sergeant's face immediately changed from that of inquisition to one of disgust "Hell, rookie, why not just call the coroner and tell 'em to bring all the body bags he's got available, in every size, while you're at it?" Bookman said. "You've gotta understand, rookie, protocol is to cops what bureaucratic red tape is to the rest of society. I'm not telling you to always ignore protocol, because you will get ya-self fired, but extreme situations call for extreme measures. Now, here's what I would do," Bookman said before clapping his hands and rubbing them together as if he were washing them without soap. "I would leave the old geezer sitting right where she was and make a beeline across that street as fast as these forty-somethin'-year-old legs will carry me while I'm radioing in for backup. Then, I would run straight up into that daycare center with my service pistol drawn. Whatever happens after that will be a result of destiny, but I would save those kids or die tryin'. Either way, I wouldn't have any regrets, and either way, I would be a hero, dead or alive."

By the time the two cops finished eating, Marcos had counted sixteen hand-to-hand transactions made by the gangbangers outside in front of the taco stand. "Seniority says that I pay the tip," Bookman announced, tossing a two-dollar tip onto the table before heading out the door. Marcos could not help but laugh as he approached the cash register. He thought to himself, *This asshole has just ordered a meal double the cost of mine and then has the nerve to leave me stuck with the bill.*

Halfway to the cash register, Marcos realized that he had left his wallet sitting on the table. On the way back to pick up his wallet, the rookie once again glanced out the restaurant's window, right in time to see his sergeant hand one of the young gangbangers what appeared to be cash and then receive a small plastic bag back in return. "Seventeen," Marcos counted to himself.

Chapter 5

Martin Luther King Hospital is located in Compton, California, on the corner of Wilmington Boulevard and 120th Street. MLK is the county hospital responsible for handling the sick and wounded from some of the most destitute and violent areas in Los Angeles, including Compton, Watts, and South Central LA.

Over the years, MLK earned the name "Killer King" due to the many patients who died every month in the hospital. Martin Luther King is by far the number one trauma center in California and has saved countless lives from gunshot wounds, stab wounds, blunt-force trauma, and many other injuries to victims who would have faced certain death at any of the so-called "Up Scale" hospitals. MLK was known only for its sometimes imperfect triage practices, which sometimes ended up in the unnecessary loss of life. These unfortunate events added even more pressure to the already overworked doctors and nurses who truly did their best to choose between treating first the man who had just suffered a gunshot wound to his upper torso, or the young woman who has overdosed on heroin, or the little boy whose mother is not sure whether or not he has ingested rat poison, or the old lady who is suffering severe chest pains. There is never a time of day when the emergency room or trauma center of MLK slows down. It is always understaffed and filled to maximum capacity, while every patient believes that their illness is worse than everyone else's.

Hector Torez lay unconscious in his hospital bed. The life support system kept his breath flowing at a steady pace, while the heart monitor beeped in one second intervals, monitoring the rhythm of his steady heartbeat.

In the midst of Hector's coma induced sleep, he continued to have the same kind of dream which reoccurred over and over again. One dream began at a point in Hector's childhood when he lived with his Grandpa Salvatore in Jalisco, Mexico. *"Ir coger de pollo por dinner,"* Grandpa Salvatore said to little Hector. He had been taught at a young age how to nab a chicken from the backyard, wring its neck, and bring it to his grandpa, who had gotten too old to perform this task himself.

When Hector opened the door to walk into the backyard where the chickens ran freely, he found himself balancing on a high diving board, overlooking an Olympic-sized pool. Terrified of heights and never having learned how to swim, Hector looked down to see his baby brother, who had not been born until many years after his grandpa had passed away, in the water floating on a life preserver. His baby brother was looking up at him while talking to him in a distant yet comforting voice, "Jump, Hector; it's okay."

Hector had dream after dream of many different stages of his life, but one feature remained the same. At the conclusion of each dream, he always found himself in a position where his life was in jeopardy if he was to take the leap, while his baby brother coached him to jump in every single one.

Chapter 6

"**F**uck dat shit, blood!" Sicko exclaimed with fire in his eyes. "I knew we shouldn't-a told this shystee-ass nigga about the suitcase." Both twins were visibly enraged, while Lil Ricky just shook his head in disappointment, clearly shaken by his uncle's stand on how the loot from the previous day's heist should be divided.

"Check it out, young bloods; I need y'all to look at the big fuckin' picture for once in ya lives," the dapper street veteran pleaded. "You little niggas don't know what to do with all this bread. All ya gonna do is go and get a whole bunch of bling bling and a bunch of other shit that ain't worth a damn after you pay for it. You ever heard that old saying 'A fool and his money shall soon part.'? The plan is to build an empire on these streets. These two mill tickets is goin' to catapult us straight to the top of the food chain, baby," Diamond assured them. "Within one year, I promise you that two million dollaz will be chump change to every nigga in this room. We got that greedy-ass bastard Gordo out the way, so from here on out it's smooth sailin' all the way to the top of the world, and y'all are my capos in this here crime family, my generals in this street army, my—"

"Shut dat bullshit up, Diamond," exclaimed Psycho Twin, who had managed to secretly slip his 9mm out and was now pointing it at his best friend's uncle. Sick Twin immediately followed suit and pulled his MAC-10 from beneath the hotel room mattress.

"Put them mothafuckin' guns down, blood!" Lil Ricky demanded, drawing his .45 pistol from the waistband of his jeans and pointing it hastily back and forth at each of his homeboys.

Tears began to roll down Psycho Twin's face as he began screaming at his best friend, "Lil Ricky, you know dis nigga ain't right, dog!" the young gangster yelled while still aiming his pistol at Diamond's head, "Dis is me, homie. You know I don't neva go against the grain, but I ain't goin' for dis shit. Dis punk-ass nigga got

33

the nerve to give us two kilos of dope and fifty thousand cash when we da ones dat did all da work? We da ones dat took dat penitentiary chance. Now you expect us to give dis fool da millions while we walk away wit crumbs? Nigga, you gotta be out your rabbit-ass mind. We can do dis shit right or we can kill each other up in this hotel room today. So what it's gonna be?"

Lil Ricky knew his longtime partners in crime well enough to know that they did not bluff. He also knew that this ultimatum was uncharacteristic of his ruthless twin buddies who in most cases would have already had empty clips in their smoking guns.

"Alright, man; y'all win," Lil Ricky said, uncocking the hammer on his .45 and setting it on the floor. "Now it's y'alls' turn."

Sick Twin flashed an evil grin and laughed at Lil Ricky's request as if it were ludicrous.

"We ain't puttin' a gaddamn thang down, Rick Rock, so let's hurry up and split dis cash up and we'll be audi five line, blood," Sick Twin demanded.

Lil Ricky shook his head with a look of desperation in his young eyes. "Psych, Sicko, what the hell are we doin', my niggas? We ain't never had to point heat at each other before. Now let's end this stupid shit before somebody does sumthin' they will regret, heh," Rick Rock managed to produce a feeble laugh at the end of this statement.

"This game done got hella old, and we ain't playin' no more, Lil Ricky," Psycho Twin said matter-of-factly. "We been tired of ya old nickel slick-ass uncle takin' advantage of us for a long time now."

This statement caused Diamond to speak for the first time since the guns came out. "Takin' advantage? You little niggas can't be serious," Diamond said, astonished at Psycho's comment. "If it wasn't for me, y'all youngstas wouldn't have this or nothin' else! I'm the one who fed you young bucks all deez years. Ya ain't got no Daddy, ya Mama is a mothafuckin' crack monster, ya grandparents is—"

Psycho interrupted Diamond in mid-sentence, walking up and pointing his pistol directly between his eyes. "We ain't dem lil niggas no more. We got big dicks and big plans now, Unk. Now if you don't mind, go 'head and start separating ours from yours." The teenager pointed his weapon at his childhood friend, "Rick Rock, your hands is free now dat you done dropped your burner, so you can head on over there and help ya good ol' uncle dibbee up this cheese, 'cause the longer we wait, the better this money looks, and the better the money looks, the better chance of us peelin' both you niggas and ridin' out wit everything."

"What dat nigga say about our mama?" Sicko inquired, laughing about this whole situation. He made his way over to where Lil Ricky was standing and picked his pistol up off of the floor. Sick Twin tucked Rick Rock's pistol into his waistband and then pointed his MAC-10 back at Diamond, "Strip down, nigga!"

"Huh?" Diamond acted as if he did not understand the teenager's command.

"Honda? Nigga, you heard what the fuck I said. Get naked, motha fucka. I wanna see yo ass cheek dimples, punk." The young maniac walked up close to Diamond, and with an evil smile he began speaking in a calm and collected voice, "Now listen closely to me, uncle fly guy. The next time I gotta tell you ignant ass somethin' more than once, I'm gonna put a hot slug in your brain to help you think."

Diamond began unbuttoning his silk shirt and then took it off. Over his white tanktop was a chrome Bull Dog .44 magnum strapped to his left side in a shoulder holster. "Oh, I'll take that," Sick Twin said, snatching the gun from Diamond's holster.

Once again, Diamond began to speak, "Okay, you got my piece now, so do I still gotta—"

"Shut the fuck up and get in ya birthday suit, sucka," the young hoodlum demanded.

Diamond knew better than to argue with the teenager, so he quickly followed the order. Once he got all his other clothes off, he began pulling down his silk boxer shorts, exposing a freakishly long penis that hung to only two inches above his knees.

"GAWD DAYUM!" Sicko exclaimed. "Put dat anaconda back in the bushes, nigga," the young thug said with a hearty laugh.

Diamond pulled his underwear back up and then joined Lil Ricky in dividing the money and drugs. Both men got down on their knees, using the bed as a surface to complete their task. After about an hour, when everyone's cuts were separated, Psycho Twin walked over to where Lil Ricky and his uncle were kneeling on the floor. Psych pressed his 9mm against the top of Diamond's head and cocked the hammer back. "Lil Rick Rock," the young gangster announced, "this nigga has been using us for years to do his dirty work while he got rich and we got the crumbs that fell off his table."

Lil Ricky quickly began pleading for his uncle's life, "Don't do it, Psych. It ain't that bad when you look at it for what it is, homie. True, we have been gettin' the short end of the stick, but we been doin' good for some young niggas. Remember when we was the only ones ridin' on Daytons and hittin' switches in the ninth grade?" Lil Ricky could see that his words were sinking in just like always. "Like you said, we ain't dem little niggas no more, so it's time for us to take it to the next level. I'm sure Uncle D understands that now, Psych."

Psycho Twin listened intently, dissecting every word that came out of his homeboy's mouth.

"Blood, smoke dat maggot-ass nigga, Psych!" Sicko yelled. "Fuck it! Let me do it then," the teenager begged, pointing his MAC-10 at Diamond.

"Hold on, Sick," Psycho demanded. "Let me holla at my nigga for a minute. Stand up, Rick Rock."

Lil Ricky stood up and looked his friend right in his cold, wild eyes. Psycho uncocked the hammer on his pistol and then handed it to Lil Ricky.

"What in the hell is you doin', Psych?" Sick Twin asked with a look of concern on his face.

"Shut the fuck up, Sick! This is our motha fuckin' brother, and I'm gonna keep in real wit this nigga if it means the death of me. Listen, Lil Ricky, dis old-ass nigga ain't no more good to us. We can waste this fool and you can keep your cut and his too, and then *you'll* be the millionaire. I don't give a fuck! I just want it to be like it's always been. The only difference is we'll keep all of our profits. We will be the niggas runnin' the hood and not this old slick willy-ass chump."

Lil Ricky began to think hard about his options. After all, it had always been him and his two best friends since day one. They had snatched purses together as teenagers while Diamond was always the one sitting on his ass, pointing out who he wanted robbed and murdered.

Rick Rock's thought process was interrupted. "Hey, baby nephew, you gotta do what you gotta do," Diamond said. "Ya uncle will love you no matter what, boy, just like I've always loved you youngstas and tried to teach y'all da game the best I know how. I'm not about to sit here and beg my protégés to spare my life, 'cause if it's my time to go, so be da shit. If takin' me outta da game is what you feel you gotta do, then by all means, pull dat trigga. Just don't do somethin' you will regret, because once you squeeze dat trig, it's curtains for Uncle D, baby."

Diamond's speech immediately brought Lil Ricky to his senses. "I can't do it, Psych," Lil Ricky said.

Psycho Twin stared his friend in his eyes for a moment and then gave him a somber, affirmative nod.

"So this is it then, huh, Ricky?" Psych asked.

Lil Ricky could not remember his childhood buddy ever referring to him as just plain Ricky. It had always been Lil Ricky, Rick Rock, Slick Rick, or a number of other nicknames of endearment. Lil Ricky quickly came to the realization that if he refused to allow his uncle's demise that from this point on, to his best childhood friends, he would be just plain-old Ricky. "But it doesn't have to be—"

Psycho put up his hand to cut Lil Ricky off in the middle of his sentence. "You know, this ain't nothin' personal, homie, but you made your choice." The young gangster picked up the Oakland Raiders gym bag and then stuffed it full of cash and bricks of cocaine. After putting his and his brother's cut in the gym bag, Psycho turned to Lil Ricky one last time, "If you niggas got any sense whatsoever, y'all will stay the fuck out of our way and forget today ever happened. But if you can't let this shit ride, you know we ain't runnin' from a damn thang, and you also know dat we ain't hard to find."

Diamond stood to his feet and reached out his hand toward Psycho Twin in an attempt to end this awkward ordeal with a peaceful handshake. The teenager immediately spit in his palm and said, "Fuck your handshake, punk. You lucky to be breathin' right now." Psycho looked at his childhood friend one last time, "Stay up and keep it gangsta, my nigga."

37

Lil Ricky nodded at his former best friend as Psycho and his twin brother headed toward the door. On the way out of the room, Sick Twin stopped short and turned around to look at Lil Ricky. "See ya around the set, Rick Rock. One love, homie," and just like that, The Twins were gone.

Chapter 7

Sergeant Curtiss Bookman received a rude awakening. The loud ring woke him up out of a deep sleep, causing him to slap the telephone clean off his nightstand. Before picking up the cordless phone, Bookman glanced at the digital clock sitting on his dresser. "Who on earth has the nerve to be calling my damn phone at 4:23 in the god damned morning?" Bookman asked himself. He picked the phone up from off the floor and pressed the talk button, "This better be damn good," the sergeant said in a low scratchy tone.

"Good morning, Sergeant Bookman."

Bookman immediately picked up the Asian accent from the voice at the other end of the phone. "Who the hell is this?" the sergeant inquired.

The voice was alarmingly calm, sending a chill through Bookman's body, "It's not who this is that you need to be concerned with, sergeant; it's what I can do for you that may interest you."

"Look here, shithead; whatever you're trying to sell, I ain't trying to buy it, okay? So do us both a favor and fuck off!" Bookman hung up the phone. Ten seconds later, the telephone rang once again. Bookman was now furious, "Do you know what time it is, asshole?" Bookman asked as soon as he answered the phone.

"Oh, but I do, sergeant," the voice proclaimed. "It's time for you to go out and take a look inside your mailbox. I'll be getting back in touch with you in a couple of days to find out whether or not you've changed your mind about buying what I'm selling."

Bookman quickly went from upset to nervous and began to stutter, "Who, who t-the h-hell *is* this?"

The line went dead.

Sergeant Bookman hopped out of bed and retrieved his 9mm Uzi from the bedroom closet. He cocked a bullet into the chamber of his weapon and then headed straight to the front door. After glancing out his peep hole, the sergeant opened the door to find a small white package inside his mail box. Although it was dark outside, Bookman looked carefully at all the cars parked on his street to see if he was being watched. Once he was sure that whoever had left this package in his mailbox was gone, he picked the package up and headed back into the house.

The sergeant slowly opened the box to find a black VHS tape with one simple message written on its cover, 'DON'T PANIC'.

Chapter 8

As he did every Sunday, Hector Torez pulled into the church parking lot at 7:50 A.M. Hector had, in fact, been pulling into this same church parking lot every Sunday at the same time for over twenty years. He was a devout Catholic who prayed the rosary daily and made it to confession regularly.

Something seemed strange today. Hector noticed that there was only one car in a parking lot that was usually packed to full capacity at every Sunday Mass. Even though Hector had parked directly in front of the church, for some reason the ringing of the church bells sounded distant.

Once Hector exited his vehicle, he immediately recognized the only other car in the parking lot besides his own. It was his beloved mother's 1978 Dodge Dart. Hector remembered vividly the days when his mom used to pick him up from the group home every weekend. All the other kids would tease him, calling his mom's car a putt-putt. That had never bothered Hector, because on most weekends he was the only kid being picked up.

Hector became so excited at the sight of his mother's car that he left the door of his 2007 STS Cadillac wide open. He found himself running up the church steps in what seemed like slow motion. He stormed through the double doors to find that the pulpit and every pew inside of the church was empty.

Hector could feel a presence with him in the church and heard what sounded like a woman's voice coming from the direction of the pulpit. He made his way to the front of the church and then on to the stage, but still he found no one. Located on the pulpit behind a long, burgundy, satin curtain was the church baptistery.

Hector quickly made his way through the curtain to once again find himself in a life or death situation. This time he found himself ten stories up, on the ledge of a burning building. Once again, he *began to hear voices which sounded familiar to him, "Hector, ess okay. Jump down."*

Hector looked down, this time to find that his little brother was no longer alone. Now it was his little brother along with his beloved mother, both coaching him to jump, as they stood beside a giant air cushion. In a deep state of panic, Hector looked back at the window behind him only to find that it had burst into flames.

With nowhere left to run, Hector licked his fingers, and after running his hand across his body in the sign of the Cross, he kissed the rosary hanging from his silver necklace, closed his eyes, and then jumped "Granizo Mary?"

Chapter 9

Hector Torez woke up from his coma at 8:29 A.M. on a Sunday morning surrounded by his loved ones. His wife and two kids stood at his bedside, soaking him with tears of joy as they embraced him with hugs. As soon as they heard the news of their brother's misfortune, two of his younger brothers had immediately flown back to California from Minnesota where they had set up a flourishing drug empire.

Although his family was happy to see that he had awakened from his coma, Hector's first words filled the room with tension so thick that it could be cut with a knife, "Mama? Where's Mama?"

His wife Grace did not know how to answer this unexpected question and looked at Hector's two little brothers, Danny and Eddie, for support. Danny was also known as "Hefty", and Eddie was known as "Sniper". His little sister Sandy, better known as "La Smurf", was also standing by his bedside.

Hefty said in a somber voice, "Mama has been dead for over two years now, *Mi hermano.*"

"No, Hefty, I just saw Mama and Javier," Hector insisted. "They saved me from the fire."

By now, everyone in the room with the exception of Hector's younger brothers had tear-filled eyes. "They killed Javier, Hector!" La Smurf exclaimed. "He's dead! They shot him in his head and killed our little Javier!" Hector lay in his hospital bed, attempting to collect his thoughts as his sister hysterically buried her head in his chest and bawled uncontrollably.

"Calm down, *mija,*" Hector said, as he began having flashbacks of the events of the morning that left him bedridden in Martin Luther King Hospital.

The first thing that flashed into Hector's mind was the handshake and the smile of his old friend Diamond. One by one, Hector began to have flashbacks of every single detail of the ordeal that had left his baby brother and three of his little homeboys dead and had almost taken his own life. He grew more upset with each recollection to the point where he could feel his blood begin to boil. Finally, Hector began speaking to his wife, "Gracy, *mija,* I need you and Smurfette to take the kids to the snack bar to get something to eat," but his wife was not ready to leave his side.

"But Hector—"

Hector put his hand up to let her know that he meant what he said, "I need to talk to my brothers about some private business real quick. Then you guys can come back in."

More tears began to flow down his wife's face. "Hector, please don't do nothing crazy!" the woman pleaded. Hector took her hand in his and kissed it softly.

"Come back a little later, *mija.*"

Hefty and Sniper watched as their sister-in-law and little sister exited the room with their niece and nephew. Hefty walked them to the door and then closed it behind them while Sniper, who was visibly infuriated, got directly to the point, "Who did this to us, *esse?*"

Chapter 10

It was 9:00 in the morning, and Sergeant Curtiss Bookman had been up since 4:23 A.M. when he had been rudely awakened by the strange phone call. The menacing VHS tape sat on top of his kitchen table as he sipped from his seventh cup of black coffee while attempting to muster up enough courage to view the tape.

Bookman had performed enough illicit acts on a day-to-day basis to know that this tape could definitely be bad news. It could also prove to be detrimental to his career as a peace officer and even to his very freedom.

Finally, after smoking one of his soothing coco puff cigarettes and slugging back a few shots of Jack Daniels rum, Bookman managed to calm his nerves enough to face his latest skeleton.

"How bad can the shit be?" the sergeant asked himself with slurred speech. Bookman slid the tape out of its dust jacket on the way to his living room and then made his way over to the DVD/VHS combo posted at the top of his sixty-inch-screen television. The sergeant took a deep breath, "Here goes nothin'." He pushed the tape in and took a seat on his black leather couch. After staring at the remote sitting on his glass living room table for thirty seconds, he picked it up and pressed Play.

At first the scene on the TV screen was a blur. Bookman stared at the television screen as hard as he could while attempting to focus his eyes. It was apparent that whoever shot this footage had shot it from at least two hundred feet away. On top of that, it had been dark outside at the time of the taping. Bookman could barely make out what appeared to be a man sitting on a curb handcuffed. Although the scenery looked familiar to the sergeant, he could not quite put his finger on what he was looking at. It was not until the camera began to zoom in that Bookman realized what he was looking at, and contrary to the message that was printed on the label of the tape, Sergeant Bookman did indeed panic.

Chapter 11

I t was 7:30 P.M., and the sun was just beginning to set over the Nickerson Gardens housing projects. The loud sound of sirens and the glare of blue and red lights filled the evening air. Emergency vehicles flew up and down Imperial Highway as they always did in this area around nightfall.

After a long and profitable day of crack sales in front of Momma Maria's Tacos Del Exquisito, Boss Ross and his longtime girlfriend Tamesha were homeward bound. "Can you please put that out until we get home?" Tamesha asked. "I done told your ass 'bout smoking that shit around me, you sorry-ass nigga," the extremely upset woman said to her man.

"Girl, weed don't hurt the baby. It's the cigarette smoke and alcohol dat you gotta worry about," Boss Ross responded while rolling down the car's passenger-side window and waving his hand around in an attempt to fan the potent marijuana smoke from the vehicle.

Tamesha got so angry that she turned red in the face. "I don't need this bullshit from you today, Deon. I'm pregnant with your nappy-headed-ass child, and you can't even wait five measly-ass minutes until we get home to smoke your stankin'-ass weed. You don't care about nobody but yourself."

"Shut dat bullshit up, Tah Tah!" Boss Ross yelled, as he threw his freshly lit marijuana-filled cigar out the car window. "Hell, you sho don't say nothin' when ya old-ass granpappy smokes his goddamn Lucky Strikes all up in the pad all fuckin' day."

Boss Ross had spoken without thinking and quickly realized from the look on his girlfriend's face that he had made a huge mistake. The eight and a half month pregnant woman cut her eyes and began talking in a calm and collected voice, "I know you did not just say what I think you said, nucka." Tamesha pulled her Buick Regal over to the right turning lane of Imperial Highway and Central Boulevard and then stopped, holding up traffic as she continued to talk to Boss Ross, "My granddaddy raised me and all three of my brothers by his damn self in these projects. He always made sure that I had whatever the hell I wanted growing up as a child, and now that he has less than three months to live before that cancer takes his life, you can be surer than shit that I'm gonna make that man's final days in this world as comfortable as possible. And on top of that," Tamesha continued, "I'm the one that wears the pants in that house. I'm the one that got us up out ya fat-ass sister's place. I'm the one who makes sure your triflin' ass has dope to sell. And I'm the one who makes sure you don't spend all our money up on weed and Hennessey for ya punk-ass homeboys instead of paying our bills, so we don't be using car batteries to power lamps like we had to do a couple months ago when you spent all the money up at the strip club. Now get your poor excuse for a man ass out of my car and think about what I said while you're walkin' home.

Boss Ross knew not to argue with her. He grabbed his .38 special from the stash behind the glove compartment and then hopped out of the car to begin his eight block tread home to 111th Street. By the time Boss Ross got to 112th Street, one block from his home, he had rehearsed his apology speech enough times to have it down pat. He had even stopped by the candy house on 115th Street to pick up a few helpings of Tamesha's favorite pregnancy craving treats — five jumbo pickles and five bags of apple-flavored sour power candies, along with a big bag of David Sunflower Seeds.

Upon his arrival at 111th and Success, Boss Ross made the left turn toward his house. With his gang in the middle of a war with several surrounding Crips gangs, Boss Ross automatically began to caress the trigger of the .38 special concealed inside his sweatshirt when he noticed the strange, primer-gray-colored van traveling in his direction. The closer the van came, the faster Boss Ross' heart pounded. Once the van came within ten yards of him, he pulled the pistol out of his sweatshirt pocket and concealed it behind the brown paper bag full of goodies that he had just purchased for his girlfriend.

Most gang bangers lived for moments like these, but, under his breath, Boss Ross silently began to pray that he would not be forced to shoot it out with anyone today. In fact, he had not shot a gun for over eight months, since the day he discovered that Tamesha was pregnant. Five months later, after a routine ultrasound, he had found out that she was carrying a boy. He'd already persuaded Tah Tah to name the boy Junior and was now dreaming of the day when he could teach his son how to throw a perfect spiral. To Boss Ross, there was nothing in the world worth doing that would take him away from his family.

When the ominous van came close enough for Boss Ross to see who was in it, he was relieved to see that it was inhabited by two of his childhood buddies, Danny and Eddie, known now days as Hefty and Sniper. The two bald-headed Mexican men started smiling when they made eye contact with Boss Ross. He quickly slid his pistol back into the pocket of his sweatshirt.

The van came to a complete stop, and then the passenger who was Hefty gave Boss Ross a friendly head nod. Boss Ross began walking toward the van, yelling at his buddies who he had not seen in years, "Hefty, Snipes! Whaddup, y'all?"

The two Hispanic men continued to smile at Boss Ross but gave no verbal response.

Boss Ross came within spitting distance of the van, when all of a sudden the driver slammed his foot down on the gas pedal and sped off, leaving only a trail of burnt rubber behind.

Something felt very strange about this encounter, but Boss Ross quickly shook the eerie feeling off, "Them crazy-ass *essays* must be high on somethin'," he told himself, as he continued toward his home, now in even more of a rush.

Boss Ross smelled the usual odor of cigarette smoke emitting from his home as he traveled up the walkway. He tucked the bag of goodies under his sweatshirt in order to surprise his girlfriend and then opened the tattered screen door and walked into the house.

Right away, Boss Ross noticed that something was odd. The living room television was on and turned to CNN as usual, but the old, brown recliner, where Tah Tah's grandfather usually sat glued to the TV, was empty. On top of that, Boss Ross looked down to find that the lit butt of one of Grandpa Otis' Lucky Strike cigarettes was smoldering on the floor, burning a hole in the carpet.

"Tah Tah!" Boss Ross called out. He began frantically searching the house for his girlfriend. First he looked in the kitchen, only to find a pot of boiling water on the stove with a pack of unopened Ramen noodles on the counter next to it. "Tah Tah!" he called out again on his way out of the kitchen.

Boss Ross ran up the stairs and into his and Tamesha's bedroom, where his face suddenly became filled with terror. "God, no!" Boss Ross dropped his girlfriend's bag of goodies to the floor.

Chapter 12

Sergeant Curtiss Bookman and his rookie ride-along arrived at the crime scene just in time to see the empty ambulance leave as the coroner van pulled up. Bookman spotted Boss Ross sitting in the backseat of a squad car with his head down. He appeared to be crying.

The two officers made their way through the yellow tape and into the house. One of Bookman's few friends on the force, Detective Richard Houston, was standing downstairs having a conversation with two CSI detectives.

The detective turned away from his current conversation as soon as he noticed that Bookman had stepped into the room. "It's all bad up der, homie," the tall slender, blond-haired, blue-eyed detective said. He and Sergeant Bookman had shared a little game over the years, where the detective would try his best to sound like a hip Black man when conversing with Bookman, and in return the sergeant would give his best White guy imitations.

"Hey, Dick, what freakin' happened here, buddy?" Bookman asked in what he thought was a pretty good White guy voice.

"Yo yo, my man, you gotta go check dis one out fa ya self," the detective said while pointing up the stairs, "and I hope dat doggone rookie ya got with ya has a strong stomach on him, 'cause it's real ugly up der, my brotha."

Both veterans turned to Marcos and gave him an inquisitive look.

"I think I'll be okay," the rookie said, leading the way up the stairs. The two men walked into the bedroom to find a scene so horrific that it nearly caused Marcos Felix to vomit.

The first thing the cops noticed was the pregnant woman laying on her bed, stark naked, in a large puddle of blood. The woman had a pillowcase over her head, and there was what appeared to be a mop handle shoved halfway up her vagina.

Next to the bed, on the floor, was an elderly man. The old man's eyes were wide open and looked as if he had seen a monster. His hands were tied behind his back with a bed sheet, and over his head and face was a clear plastic bag which was held in place with a leather belt around his neck. He appeared to be dreadfully staring directly at the woman on the bed as his lifeless body leaned against the bedroom wall.

Bookman remained silent for a few minutes, allowing the rookie to soak in the magnitude of the situation before breaking the silence, "From the looks of things, one would surmise that the old man sat there and suffocated to his death as he watched his grandchild being aborted by way of a mop handle. You sure you wanna be a cop, son?"

Chapter 13

Sicko and Psycho had been enjoying the good life for over a month now. They had exited the doors of the Hampton Inn four and a half weeks earlier with over a half a million dollars apiece and had not looked back since. They had pulled the heist off exactly thirty-four days ago but had collectively managed to spend in excess of five hundred thousand dollars in that time frame.

The boys' first stop had been in East Long Beach, to the turf of the "Asian Boys" gang. They had been purchasing weapons from one of the gang's founders, a middle-aged Vietnamese man by the name of Lu Fam, for several years now. The twins usually showed up with no more than two hundred dollars to spend, but with Mister Fam, they always left satisfied. They had even come to the old gun dealer's pawn shop one time with only fifty dollars but still managed to leave with a .22 German Luger.

This time, the twins had come to spend some real money. As soon as Lu Fam had buzzed them into the pawn shop, Sicko had unzipped the Oakland Raider gym bag and flashed enough rubber band wrapped stacks of cash to cause the little old Vietnamese man to smile so big that it seemed as if he had revealed all twenty-eight of his coffee and cigarette-stained teeth.

The contents of the Raider bag had been enough to earn the twins a ticket to Mister Fam's secret stash. He quickly let his pawn shop's blinds down and then escorted the boys through a door behind the counter which led to a long hallway. Halfway down the hall was another door.

When Psycho and Sicko walked through that door, the boys felt a rush of euphoria equivalent to the ingesting of ten ecstasy pills. From wall to wall, the room was filled with military caliber weapons. Hanging on display were MAC-10s, MAC-11s, MAC-12s, MAC-90s, .22 Uzis, 9mm Uzis, TECH-22s, TECH-9s, .45 Calicos, twelve-gauge shotguns, ten-gauge shotguns, Chinese AK-

47 assault rifles, Russian AK-47 assault rifles, M16s, AR-15s — any kind of machine gun the young gangsters could think of was there, along with every caliber and brand of handgun known to mankind. There were also several weapons that the boys only recognized from watching war movies and the evening news.

The twins felt like two kids in a candy store in the middle of all those guns. "This is like Foot Locker, except wit guns, blood!" Sicko exclaimed.

"Oh, not only guns, my friends," Lu Fam assured the teenagers as he began opening the drawers of what looked like an oversized filing cabinet. With every drawer the man opened, the twins' jaws dropped a little bit further and their eyes grew a little bit wider. There were different varieties of grenades and small bombs in every drawer.

By the time Sicko and Psycho finished picking out weapons, they had worked out a one hundred thousand dollar deal with the old Asian gangster. The teenagers had purchased so many guns, along with so much ammunition, that Lu Fam had been forced to follow them home in his work truck to transport all the illegal weapons.

The next stop for the boys was the Cadillac dealership, where each of them had purchased fully-loaded Escalade trucks which they took straight to custom shops for state of the art wireless sound systems and chameleon styled paint jobs, along with twenty-six-inch rims that continued to spin at every stop they made.

After that were the twin Harley Davidson Roadster motorcycles, the custom built, convertible 1963, Chevy Impalas, equipped with gold Dayton rims, and top of the line hydraulic systems, plus a set of See Dew jet skis each.

On top of all that was a shopping spree where the two teenagers had managed to spend in excess of two hundred thousand dollars. The spending spree, it seemed, had led the twins to every mall in Southern California. The boys were now purchasing Avisu jeans, along with their Kaki suits, aviator lens sun glasses, and their murder one shades. The two of them had also purchased enough platinum and diamonds to appear as if they played for the Los Angeles Lakers.

Chapter 14

Unlike the newly estranged twins, Diamond and Lil Ricky immediately invested their stolen money directly into the black market. Over the years, Diamond had gained control of twelve units in the projects for which he paid rent every month in the names of twelve different people. These apartments were as good as gold mines to a street hustler.

Out of the twelve units, Diamond ran five rock houses where dope fiends could stop by at any time of day or night to purchase crack cocaine. He ran one house strictly for small-time block pushers to stop by and purchase one or more ounces of cocaine. He ran two PCP houses where he sold the most potent sherm sticks in town. Diamond also ran two gambling shacks, which also doubled as all night liquor houses for whomever felt like they needed a drink after the liquor stores closed around 2:00 A.M.

The last two houses were both rest havens for Diamond's workers. He had his male workers, mostly teenagers, who he taught how to cook, cut up, and weigh rock cocaine, and then sell it off of large flat surfaces known as big boards. The young boys worked in shifts so that all five of the crack houses were manned twenty-four hours a day, seven days a week.

Then he had his female workers. Even though what Diamond was doing with these girls, some as young as fifteen years old, was nothing short of pimping, the smooth street veteran despised being referred to as a pimp. "I'm just these young ladies' supervisor, and that's it," Diamond would often tell people.

The unit where Diamond kept his girls had to be the most plush project apartment on earth. The ladies unit was equipped with amenities unheard of in the projects, including a Jacuzzi, water beds, a Dolby surround sound system, and even a small stage equipped with a stripper pole.

One thing Diamond did differently than most pimps was pay his girls well. The girls gave him every penny they made at the end of each day, and then every week on Friday, after Diamond finished counting up all the money, he would take half off the top and then divide the remaining cash equally among his ten girls. Each girl usually ended up with upwards of two thousand dollars when the money was handed out.

With this latest windfall, courtesy of his old buddy, Gordo, and the withdrawal of the twins from their circle, it was now time for Lil Ricky and his uncle to expand. While Psycho and Sicko were out on their lavish shopping and partying sprees, Diamond and Lil Ricky's purchases had been a lot more calculated. The two men had plans of beginning a family legacy, while at the same time building a criminal empire that would span from LA, all the way down to San Diego, and back up to Northern California.

Their first stop had been to the Pales Verdes mansion of a man by the name of Simon Bolivar. This man, who had immigrated from Lima Peru over twenty years prior to being introduced to Diamond, had managed to launder millions through his lucrative flower shops that were sprawled throughout Southern California. Although Mister Bolivar's flower business was extremely profitable, he was also involved in other botanicals, the importation of pure Peruvian cocaine, to be precise. This man who had the lowest prices in California for the highest quality product was the connection that prompted Diamond to knock Gordo out of the way in order to usurp him as the undisputed underground king of the streets.

Diamond and Lil Ricky had managed to work out a deal so sweet with Mister Bolivar that Gordo himself would have considered it a steal. The two men walked away with one hundred kilos of pure Peruvian flake cocaine for the low price of five hundred fifty thousand dollars, with the promise that they would return to spend at least one million more within a three month period. This was a precondition that Diamond accepted with no problem, because the price which he paid for this quantity of pure cocaine guaranteed him and his nephew a profit of over two million dollars once they finished cutting their product with baking soda and lots of other miscellaneous supplements.

The next stop took the men to a motorcycle club all the way out in San Diego County. Diamond had done a lot of business with Wild Bill Mansfield years earlier, when the two of them met up north in Pelican Bay State Prison. While in prison, Diamond had gained a lot of respect for the 6'4", tattoo-covered White boy with the thick mustache and hair which hung all the way to his behind.

On a level four penitentiary yard full of savage skinheads, Diamond had watched Wild Bill, who was a member of Hell's Angels Motorcycle Gang, fight off several attempts on his life by the Nazis, then rise up in rank until he was calling shots for every White prisoner in "The Bay". This was something that was unheard of for a motorcycle gangster to do in any California prison, much less the most violent of them all, Pelican Bay.

In the two years that the two men had been next cell neighbors, Diamond had learned a lot from Wild Bill about how the most rich and notorious motorcycle gang in the world operated. The angels had a hand in everything from real estate to murder for hire.

Out of all the conversations they had, one interested Diamond more than any other. Wild Bill was involved in the manufacturing and trafficking of designer drugs. He had told Diamond to stop by the San Diego chapter of Hell's Angels if he ever wanted a good deal on some ecstasy pills.

When Diamond and his nephew pulled into the parking lot of the motorcycle club, Lil Ricky found himself admiring all the different hogs parked out front. The bike that he found to be most interesting was a custom chopper with high-rise ape hanger handle bars and a suicide shifter. The teenager wondered to himself what kind of idiot would be crazy enough to ride this deathtrap on wheels.

The club itself was painted jet black with a super-sized replica of the famous winged skull and crossbones logo on each wall. On the way in, the two men could hear the loud cracking sound of pool balls slapping together as the song "BORN TO BE WILD" blasted from the sound system. Lil Ricky could not believe that he was about to step foot into a building packed full of drunk, racist, and suicidal White boy outlaws who just happened to have a reputation for shooting first and asking questions later.

As soon as the two men stepped foot into the motorcycle club, every pool game, dart game, dance, and conversation came to an abrupt stop, and all eyes were on Lil Ricky and his uncle. One by one, the leather jacket sporting motorcycle gangsters began standing up and walking in the direction of the two Black men.

The next thing Diamond and Lil Ricky knew, they had reached the point of no return. They were surrounded and quickly being closed in upon. "Hold on, boys," the stout bald-headed man with the long beard ordered, "Let me have a word with these young men."

Wearing dark sun glasses in a room that did not have much light in it to began with, the old outlaw approached Diamond, stepping up so close that he could smell the whiskey and Marlboro smoke on the man's breath. The obviously drunk man lowered his sun glasses in order to look Diamond in the eyes and then began to speak in a calm voice, "I think you boys must've made a wrong turn in your pink Caddy and walked into the wrong establishment, so let me help ya out — Big Bubba's Barbecued Fat Back Shack is over on the South Side of town."

The statement set off a roar of laughter across the motorcycle club loud enough to be heard from a block away. Even though the two men had just been insulted, they both experienced a feeling of relief from the disparaging ice breaker. Diamond artificially laughed along with the crowd until the bar grew quiet enough for him to give his response, "No, sir, actually we're here to see Bill Mansfield."

The sarcasm melted from the man's face faster than a popsicle in a microwave oven. Before the man could get his gumption together enough to respond to Diamond's surprising proclamation, they were approached by a young woman.

The woman was beautiful with piercing blue eyes and long, black hair. Her dark eyeliner gave her the look of a bad girl, along with her tight blue jeans and black Harley Davidson T-shirt which she had pulled into a crop top beneath her shapely breasts, revealing a stomach that was tight and smooth. "You fellas don't look like your average everyday cops, but anything's possible these days. Are you cops?" she asked while getting a closer look at the two intruders.

There was something reassuring about this young woman. Her smile seemed sincere, and she had a strong and sensual voice that made her sound intelligent.

"No, ma'am!" Diamond quickly answered, "I can promise you that we ain't no pigs."

"So what do you want with Billy — if I may ask?"

"Sure you may," Diamond responded. "Wild Bill and me did some time together back in the day up in Pelican Bay. He told me to stop by the club if I was ever out this way."

"Wait right here; I'll be right back," the pretty woman said before walking behind the bar and then disappearing into the door behind it. She quickly came back out holding a cellular phone to her ear. She walked back up to the visitors and looked directly at the elder of the two. "Diamond?" the beautiful biker chick inquired.

"That's me, ma'am!" Diamond replied, unable to conceal the relief in his voice. The woman spoke a few more words into the phone and then clicked it off.

"Good to meet you. I'm Whisper Mansfield. My brother told me to have you boys follow me to his place."

Diamond looked surprised and asked, "You're Wild Bill's sister?"

"Well... either that or I've been lied to for the last twenty-odd years," the woman responded with a laugh. Diamond shook his head in disbelief before speaking again.

"Thank God there's no resemblance."

When the trio reached the parking lot, Lil Ricky quickly found out the answer to the question he had asked himself on the way in, when he saw his new connection's little sister hop right onto the saddle of her custom-made chopper. The idiot who was crazy enough to ride that death on wheels motorcycle, with the ape hanger handle bars and suicide shifter, was none other than Whisper Mansfield.

It took every bit of Diamond's driving skills to keep up with his old buddy's little sis, as she wove through traffic from lane to lane on her roaring motorcycle. Her long, raven-black hair blew in the wind beneath her rain bucket helmet which sat on top of her head as she constantly shifted gears and gave hand signals.

It was like poetry in motion to the eyes of Lil Ricky, watching this woman who appeared to be so delicate and beautiful, handling this piece of testosterone's offspring machinery with such ease and precision.

After about a twenty-minute ride, half of which was on the freeway traveling at what seemed like Mach speed, the two men found themselves following the motorcycle-mushing beauty queen onto a bridge.

While traveling over the bridge, Lil Ricky found himself admiring the view of the many different boats floating around in the harbor beneath them. Once they reached the end of the bridge, the men noticed a big sign with 'Welcome to Coronodo Island' on it.

After five more minutes of commuting, the men trailed Whisper into a gated community. Judging from the numerous mini-mansions with the perfect landscaping and luxury vehicles parked in front of them, Wild Bill was living a life that was a far cry from what Diamond had expected.

Finally, the young woman came to a stop in front of what seemed to be the largest and most beautiful home on the block. The house was humongous and constructed of mostly red brick, giving it the appearance of an old Western mansion. On the front lawn was a waterfall which emptied into a coy pond.

Whisper swung her bike into the driveway and parked it right next to what appeared to be the only eyesore in the neighborhood. It was an old, silver, Air Stream travel trailer that looked like it had no business anywhere on Coronodo Island.

Diamond and Lil Ricky found a parking space in front of the house, hopped out of the car, and met Whisper in the driveway.

"This is it," Whisper said, as Lil Ricky and his uncle stood there in awe.

"Well? What are we waiting for? Let's go get a tour of my old buddy's palace," Diamond said and began walking toward the front of the house.

"Hey, wait!" Whisper yelled to Diamond before he could reach the front porch. With a huge grin on her face, she waved Diamond back. "You don't gotta go that far to see Billy's palace," Whisper told him and began tapping on the door of the raggedy trailer.

in a short time, the trailer door opened and out stepped Wild Bill in a pair of old, over-worn blue jeans and a tank top revealing his massive arms that were covered in tattoos of skulls, demons, and the like. Lil Ricky marveled at the resemblance between the pro wrestler, The Undertaker, and his uncle's old friend.

Wild Bill immediately embraced his old jail buddy, picking him up in a bear hug that caused Diamond to lose every bit of air in his lungs. "So, ya finally made your way out here, huh, you big ole black-ass chicken and watermelon eatin' fucker you?" Wild Bill asked in his deep, Hulk Hogan-like voice.

Lil Ricky could not believe his ears as he listened to the two old convicts' conversation. Diamond began laughing while pointing at the large hunk-of-junk trailer, "You can take the redneck out the trailer park, but ya can't take the trailer park out of the redneck, huh, Billy?" Diamond joked. "Question, how is your big, giant, seven-foot ass managing to live in this little fucked-up trailer? And an even bigger question, who in Sam's hell is lettin' your ass park this piece of shit in front of this beautiful-ass house?" Diamond asked with a puzzled look on his face.

"Aww, well… this is one of my old lady's parents' houses. Her dad is some kinda big shot lawyer, and her mama is Richard Nixon's fucking granddaughter. Would you believe they didn't want their daughter livin' in no trailer park? And I didn't wanna be livin' up in no goody two-shoes, suburban house, so we ended up settlin' on this here arrangement."

"So then who lives in this house?" Diamond inquired.

"Well, my old lady sleeps in the trailer with me every night, but you may as well say she lives in that house since she spends every wakin' moment in the fucker. I ain't never even been up in that house, and I don't plan on ever goin' in there 'cause that stuck-up, high society dog and pony show just ain't me, brother."

From the earnest manner in which his friend spoke, Diamond could tell that this was a sensitive subject and also a serious conflict within Wild Bill's marriage. "Hey, whatever works for the big guy," Diamond said, giving his friend a few sympathetic pats on the back. "By the way, this is my nephew, Lil Ricky. He's my big bro's only child."

"Good ta meet ya, Lil Ricky," Wild Bill greeted with a handshake. "I was up in Folsom with your daddy. He's a good dude, that

Rick Rock," the biker said with a look of sincerity in his usually corpse-cold eyes. "So, can I grab you guys a beer? All I got in there is Budweiser, but they're cold."

"Not this time," Diamond said. "We actually ain't plannin' on stayin' long this time. We came on a strictly bidness trip today."

"Strictly business, huh?" Wild Bill answered. "Well... you've definitely come to the right place for that one, brother. So what can I do you for?"

Less than an hour later, Diamond and Lil Ricky were on their way back to Los Angeles with enough ecstasy pills to supply a small country.

Chapter 15

Hefty and Sniper made their way through the double doors of Martin Luther King Hospital less than an hour after the murders of the pregnant woman and the old man. They walked through the door of their oldest brother's fourth-story room to find themselves alone there. On the hospital bed where he had been in a coma only hours earlier was a small piece of paper.

Sniper immediately picked up the paper and began reading it out loud, "*Que paso, comaradas*? I had to leave from this depressing-ass hospital, so meet me over at Chito's spot. We got a lot of unfinished business!" Hefty and sniper stared at one another, surprised at the way their oldest brother had just checked himself out of the hospital. Gordo was alive.

Chapter 16

The young girl hollered in agony. She thought to herself, *This is what it must feel like to push a baby out,* as the man thrust his massive penis in and out of her seventeen-year-old body. Stormy had run away from a loving and God fearing home only one week earlier.

She had grown up in the Orange County City of Garden Grove where she had attended Christian schools from the time she had entered pre-kindergarten. Coming from a working-class family in which her father was a successful contractor and her mother a nurse, Stormy had everything a young girl could wish for growing up, all except for one thing.

Being an all "A" student who had managed a 4.0 grade point average or higher from the time she started school, her parents had dreams of sending their only child off to an Ivy League university as soon as she graduated from high school. Her mother and father had been hard-nosed in controlling Stormy's future for as long as she could remember and had never been supportive in what she wanted to do.

Stormy had begun singing before she learned how to walk. By the age of seven, she was entering and winning every talent show in school and serenading whoever would listen at every opportunity and wherever it had risen. Her voice was comparable to a young Whitney Houston in her heyday. This was a rare feat for a White girl; nevertheless, the fact that she was of European descent only managed to wow her audiences even more.

"Please slow down," the teenage girl begged in tears. She could feel the man's long dick slamming into her cervix repeatedly, as she howled like a cat in heat, "Oh, God, it's too big!"

The longer he stroked her, the wetter she got, and the more bearable the sex became.

This was not the first time Stormy had engaged in sexual intercourse. She had lost her virginity a year earlier to her boyfriend at the time, a senior and letterman football jock who attended her high school. The sexual encounters had been brief and repetitious, and she had found no pleasure in them whatsoever. Her only enjoyment had been in pleasing her boyfriend for the eight minutes or so that it had taken each time.

She had now been receiving a thrashing from her second ever sexual partner for close to an hour, and after agonizing all that time in the missionary position, she was relieved when he flipped her into the doggy style position where she was able to slightly control the depth of penis entering her body.

Aside from her natural singing ability and pretty face, Stormy also had many other talents. She had spent several years teaching herself how to play the guitar that her grandpa had given her for her eleventh birthday. She had also learned how to play the piano and to read music after three years of free after-school lessons courtesy of her junior high school music teacher, Mrs. Parker. In high school she had taken dance classes, where she learned how to dance in Jazz, Tap, Salsa, Ballroom, and Hip-Hop. She had also written in excess of one hundred songs over the years, some Pop, some Jazz, some Rock, and even a few Country songs, which she had been listening to with her mother and father since birth. But in spite of her love for all forms of music, the suburban White girl was a Rhythm and Blues writer and songstress at heart, and her parents often found records hidden in her room by artists such as Mary J. Blige, Teena Marie, and Alicia Keys.

Stormy had been involved in a major argument with her parents one week prior to meeting this man who was now draining every smidgen of innocence from her that she may have had left. After performing at a local park-sponsored talent show, she had been approached by a man who had claimed that he owned a recording studio in Hollywood. The man had handed Stormy a business card along with a CD and promised her that if she could get permission from her parents, he would produce an entire demo of her free of charge, just to have her voice on his tracks.

As soon as she made it home that night, she slid the compact disc into her stereo system and pressed play. With each track she listened to, the young girl had become more and more excited. Every track was of supreme quality, and on top of that, every beat that she heard matched perfectly with songs that she had written. She removed the business card from her pocket and analyzed it. The card simply read "J STAR PRODUCTIONS" followed by two phone numbers.

Stormy had casually brought up her encounter with the music producer that night at the dinner table. "Singing is not a career; it's a hobby," her mother had said, "and not only that, you're singing that ghetto music when that's not who you are, Stormy! We did not raise you that way!" She had handed her father the business card and told him about the man she had met at the talent show earlier that day, and the offer he had made to her.

"Let me guess," her father had said. "This big shot music producer walked up to you after your show at the corner park and promised to make you a big star as soon as you come down to his studio in LA, right?" her father looked at her as if she were mentally ill. "Wake up, Stormy! Don't be so damned naïve. You're nothing but a good piece of young White ass to a guy like this. You have a nice voice, but face it; you're never gonna be the big super star on the radio. Those are pipe dreams, Angel. College is reality."

Her father had torn the business card to shreds after giving his reality check speech, and the broken-hearted teenager had run out of the dining room in tears.

That same night, she climbed out of her bedroom window. She hit the road with two hundred and fifty dollars cash in her coat pocket, a back pack stuffed full of clothes, her notebooks containing the songs she had written, and the CD she had gotten from the man at the park — her destination, Hollywood.

She exited the bus with only one mission, to find the man who was responsible for the tracks on that disc. After six days of living in a motel room, combing through phone books, and asking around in hopes that someone knew of J Star productions to no avail, Stormy was broke. The teenage girl began contemplating calling her parents to pick her up, but her pride got in the way. The last thing Stormy wanted to do was to give her father the satisfaction of saying, "I told you so," after the less than civil manner in which he had treated her.

While sitting at a Hollywood bus stop, hungry and cold, crying her eyes out, she had been approached by a girl who appeared to be about her same age, or maybe even a year or so younger. The young Black girl had sat beside her and put her arm around Stormy in an attempt to comfort her. "It's gonna be okay, girl," the young girl had assured her. After Stormy told the young girl about her situation, the girl had promised that she knew a place where Stormy could live, make some extra money, and even be introduced to some music producers.

* * *

Stormy began to feel as if she were about to explode. Her pink nipples became fully erect as her naked body stiffened and her toes curled up from the intense feeling of pain and pleasure that she was experiencing. She let out a loud scream as a sensation swept through her young body that she had never felt before. The teenage girl thought she was urinating on herself when, all at once, it felt like she released every bit of bodily fluid that her body contained. The man continued to thrust deep inside of her in a steady rhythm. She began to shake uncontrollably as a tingling sensation spread throughout her entire body. For the next five minutes, the multiple orgasms took the young girl on a natural high that she hoped would never end.

Once she had finished climaxing, the man lured his still erect, long black shaft from inside of her. As soon as she realized that it was over, Stormy collapsed face first into a pillow beneath her and was fast asleep. The talented song writer, musician, and perennial honor roll student was now just another pretty whore in Diamond's stable.

Chapter 17

When Sergeant Bookman was awakened at 4:00 A.M. by the loud ringing of his cordless phone, he instinctively removed it from the charger and pressed the talk button, "This is Booker," the sergeant proclaimed in a low and scratchy voice.

"Ahh, good morning, sergeant," it was the voice that had been haunting Bookman constantly for the past month. Every time he had found himself enjoying a moment of peace and quiet, the man with the heavy Asian accent would pop back in his head and continue the harassment. Even though this would only be the second time Bookman would speak to the man, he felt as if he had been engaged in an ongoing conversation with him for the last four weeks.

After the man had failed to call back when he said he would, Bookman found himself in a constant state of paranoia. He played the situation over and over again in his mind. What could this person want from him in exchange for the incriminating master tape? Could it be money? Bookman was fully prepared to do whatever he needed to do to obtain any amount of cash the man would demand. He ran every scenario through his head that he could think of, hundreds of times.

"Who in the hell *is* this?" Bookman asked through gritted teeth.

"Well... if I told you that, you would have to kill me," the voice at the other end of the phone replied before breaking out in a loud, sinister laugh similar to that of a karate thug in an old kung fu flick.

"Wow," Bookman responded. "I've got a natural born comedian on my hands, aye?"

"Oh, but sergeant, we have not even begun to have fun yet," the voice replied sharply. Bookman began to shudder in his helpless anger.

"Okay, man, you've got the upper hand and the ball is in your court. How much?" Bookman's upper lip began to quiver and his hand shook involuntarily.

67

"Ahh, but sergeant, if life were only so simple to where we could place a price on our freedom, the prisons would all eventually close down, would they not?" It became apparent to Bookman that whoever this man was, he was enjoying every second of the tormenting position he was playing.

"So, if not money, then what the hell do you want from me?" The anxiety weighed down on the sergeant as if an eighteen-wheeler truck had driven on top of his chest.

"Well, sergeant, I have a few simple tasks for you to complete, all of which you should find quite easy, considering your background. You just might find a couple of them enjoyable, even. Do you have an ink pen nearby?"

"Hold on one second," Bookman replied, scrambling toward his dresser. The sergeant rummaged through one of his drawers for ten seconds before retrieving an ink pen and a small piece of scratch paper. "Okay, go ahead," Bookman announced, fully prepared to complete whatever task the man sent his way.

"Okay, sergeant, here's what I need you to do . . ."

Chapter 18

Although the Watts *Vatos Locos* and Bounty Hunter Blood gangs had shared their project neighborhood since the Nickerson Gardens housing projects had been built in the early 1950s, they had always kept clear boundaries in place. Any member of either gang was welcome to roam anywhere throughout the projects as they pleased, but when it came to drug sells, prostitution, gambling rackets, and all other forms of black market commerce, there had been an invisible line drawn to maintain a peaceful relationship between the Mexicans and Blacks who dwelled in the low-income governmental housing units.

From 107th street to Century Boulevard, and from Wilmington Boulevard to Alameda Street, was known as "Little Tijuana". It was not hard to tell when one was on the Hispanic side of the projects. There were numerous fruit trucks, tamale and corn carts, and other signs of Mexican culture everywhere. Mariachi music could be heard for blocks around, as men in cowboy hats and boots, along with giant belt buckles holding up their tight fitting jeans, sat around and chatted in Spanish. Every weekend, Maxine Waters Park would be swarming with people who were either watching or participating in the neighborhood soccer games. Maxine Waters Park is huge. It is the border which separates the Mexican side from the Black side of the projects.

On the other side of the park was the area known as the "Dark Side". In the Dark Side, you could find the same things you would find in Little Tijuana. They had a fruit truck, but instead of bananas and papayas, they sold watermelons exclusively. Instead of tamales and corn, you could purchase barbecue and soul food dinners on the Dark Side. Just like the Hispanic population, you could find the Black tenants at the park every weekend. The difference was, while the Hispanic men played soccer, the Black men would be on the other side of the park engaged in a game of basketball or football.

There are two things that brought both sides together every weekend. The first was the mutual love for low rider vehicles. Every Sunday, after the basketball and soccer games, everyone would meet in the rear parking lot of the park to show off their hydraulic equipped boy toys. Rap Music and Oldies would blast from the cars' sound systems while the men and women stood around drinking and smoking as their homeboys had low rider hopping contests.

The second thing that brought the two sides together was love. In the projects, love knew no race. Many of the Hispanic women were crazy about Black men, and despite the disapproval of their male family members and friends, close to half of the young Mexican women had born children by Black men.

This had caused a few problems over the years, but none were serious enough to call for gun play. The worse that had ever occurred as a result of these relationships was when Psycho Twin had gotten his current girlfriend pregnant. The problem was that Gina was another man's girlfriend at the time that Psycho had knocked her up.

Adam Garcia, also known as "Smiley" from *Vatos Locos*, had been with Gina ever since they were elementary school kids. Their families were very close, and every family member knew that Gina and Adam would one day be married. When Smiley found out about his girlfriend's pregnancy, he had sold his low rider and begun to gradually shake the gang life off and walk the straight and narrow path.

By the time Gina delivered her baby, Smiley had purchased everything a baby could ever need, from a two year supply of pampers, a baby bed, and everything in-between. He had rubbed his girlfriend's pregnant belly every day and wished for a little boy, so when Gina gave birth to a health baby boy, Smiley had been the happiest man in the world. Even after the first two months of the baby's life, when Little Adam's complexion had darkened to a golden brown, his nose rounded out, and his lips filled in, giving him the appearance of a young Michael Jackson before the surgeries, Smiley never questioned for one second whether or not the child was his.

On the other hand, as soon as Psycho laid eyes on baby Adam, he immediately formed a bond with the child. A few days later, Psycho had tricked Gina into stopping by his grandmother's house with him to pick up some of his "Grammy's" famous butter rolls. He knew very well how much Gina loved his grandma's baking.

Grammy loved children more than anything in the world, so when the plump little-old lady saw Gina's baby, she just had to hold him. No sooner was the child in her flabby arms when Grammy began yelloing, "Boy, dis is yo child, Carnell!" the old woman had been overcome with joy. She sat on her plastic-covered couch and began rocking the baby while looking into his tiny eyes, "I got me a brand-new grandbaby. Yes, Grammy does."

Gina automatically knew that she was knee deep in hot water. The young Mexican girl knew what she had to do. That night she confessed to Smiley her love for another man and broke the news that little Adam was not his son. Smiley had been crushed by the bad news.

The following Sunday, the young *cholo* had walked to the dark side of the park by himself to confront Psycho Twin. Smiley had run onto the basketball court with a baseball bat straight up to Psycho, who was engaged in a game of full-court basketball. By the time Smiley had swung the bat at Psycho one time, there were three guns pointed at him by the spectators on the sideline. "Kill me!" he yelled. "Just shoot me, dammit!"

"Don't bust, blood!" Psycho yelled. "This is between me and Smiley." Psycho looked into Smiley's eyes, "Do what you gotta do man. I deserve it."

The look in Smiley's eyes was long past angry; it was insane, the look of a man who was no longer in touch with reality. The young Mexican man dropped the bat onto the ground, along with his head, as he walked off the court.

Psycho Twin knew that he had created an arch enemy for life. He also knew that he would probably one day regret allowing Smiley to walk off that basketball court alive, but his love for Gina would not let him orchestrate the murder of someone who he knew she truly loved.

71

Chapter 19

Sergeant Curtiss Bookman pulled into the 77th Division parking lot unusually early. Third watch began at 2:00 P.M. Bookman usually arrived at least an hour later at around 3:00 P.M., but today he pulled his Cadillac into his parking space well before 1:00 P.M. As soon as he made his way through the station's doors, he noticed Lieutenant McGee standing in the hallway having a conversation with his good friend, Brenda Hayes.

"Speakin' of the Devil!" Brenda yelled, smiling as Bookman approached. The sergeant walked up, gave his coworker a quick peck on her cheek, and then nodded to his lieutenant before hurrying away from the two of them without a single word. His two colleagues could not help but notice the peculiar way in which the sergeant was behaving.

Bookman headed straight down the main hallway, walking briskly, until he came to a door marked 'EVIDENCE LOCKUP'. He placed his hand on the doorknob and then closed his eyes for thirty seconds in deep thought before twisting it to walk in.

Peter Kinbrew had been in charge of the evidence lockup for eight years. A White man of short stature, chubby, and balding, Pete Kinbrew fit every stereotype of the "Pencil Pusher" type of cop who worked behind a desk all day and gave the "Real Cops" a hard time whenever possible.

Sergeant Bookman was a good judge of character, and after eight years of working with Kinbrew, he was quite sure that Pete was living a lie. Officer Kinbrew had given Bookman a hard time on the day when the two had first met. Bookman had come to the evidence lockup attempting to log-in two kilos of cocaine. Peter Kinbrew had insisted on a sign-off signature from the acting watch commander, which would have spelled trouble for the sergeant, since the acting watch commander at that time had been a man by the name of Benjamin Cody. Back then, he had been a lieutenant known for leaving no stone unturned. Cody would have checked all the paper work from the crime lab and then cross-referenced it with the police report before he even thought about applying his John Hancock.

Bookman remembered the scenario as if it were yesterday. The bust had been for twelve kilos of coke, but somehow, after the dope was finished being weighed-out and repackaged, only two kilos had showed up to be logged into evidence, an amount just large enough to be presented at a trial and not raise any suspicions.

Curtiss Bookman was a master manipulator, and it had never taken much for him to locate people's thumbscrews. So when the evidence lockup cop had become highly emotional over an issue as picky as a signature and rolled his eyes while popping his neck around and yelling, "No signature, no log-in — and that's final!"

Bookman immediately knew how to handle the situation. The sergeant began talking to his colleague in a voice that a man would use to sweet-talk a woman, "Awww, Kinneebrew, why are you being so mean? What's the matter?" Bookman quickly noticed the change in his mark's demeanor.

Pete Kinbrew replied, "There is nothing the matter. I'm just sick of being disrespected and stepped on by you higher-ups, with your pretty-little striped sleeves and collars, storming into my lockup thinking you can just push me around and do anything you want!"

The man was nearly in tears, and it took every bit of self-control in the sergeant to keep himself from breaking out in laughter. Bookman had leaned over the counter on his elbows so that he was face to face and within kissing distance of Officer Kinbrew. Bookman then stared directly at him in his eyes with a look so sincere that Kinbrew had no choice but to believe every word that exited his mouth, "Officer Kinbrew, I would never, ever, even think about taking what you do for granted," Bookman had proclaimed in a flirtatious voice. "These assholes don't understand that your job is stressful just like theirs and just as important to the force."

Kinbrew had bought the flirtation and had logged-in the drugs without the required signature.

Bookman knew that today would be a cakewalk as it had been that day and every time after. As soon as the sergeant stepped foot into the evidence lockup, Peter Kinbrew's face lit up like a Christmas tree.

It was always a wonderful experience when the handsome, coffee-colored sergeant waltzed though that door. Ninety-nine percent of the time that Bookman showed up to the evidence lockup, he always seemed to need some small favor from Peter, and Kinbrew would always act as if he could not grant the favor. After a brief cat and mouse game of highly flirtatious conversation, he would always succumb to the sergeant's small wishes, while in the back of his mind hoping that one day the sergeant would fulfill his greatest fantasies.

Curtiss Bookman stormed into the evidence lockup shaking his head, with a look of extreme anger mixed with a tad bit of confusion on his face.

"Is everything okay, Booker?" Peter Kinbrew inquired, with a look of sincere concern.

The sergeant just leaned against the counter with his head buried inside his hands as if he were ready to begin crying. He remained that way without uttering a single word.

"Is there anything I can do to help, sergeant?" Pete Kinbrew had never seen the confident and self-assured sergeant behave in such a manner.

Bookman lifted his head slowly until his eyes met Peter's. With the most pitiful look that he could feign, he began speaking in a voice that was even more pitiful than the expression on his face, "I need ya, Kinneebrew. These people have got my back up against the wall this time, Pete."

Officer Kinbrew's facial expression quickly morphed from one of concern to that of sheer skepticism.

"Who's got your back against the wall?" Kinbrew asked.

"I really can't go into the details, Pete. Please just trust me on this one."

"So what can I do for you?" Officer Kinbrew knew from the strange way the sergeant was acting that he was about to ask him for a humongous favor, and the lockup cop was becoming more and more on the defensive, realizing that he just might have to deny Bookman for the first time.

"Pete, I just need five minutes alone behind that there gate," Bookman said, while pointing to the steel gate behind Kinbrew's desk which separated his office from the actual area where all the evidence was stored. "I swear, that will be the end to all my problems."

"Oh, hell no!" the short, tubby officer responded. "That would undoubtedly mean the end of my career. How do you expect me to tell Jan and the kids that we no longer have a place to live?"

Bookman moved his face closer to Kinbrew's and then took the lockup officer's hands in his, "But I promise you, no one will ever find out. It will go to the grave with me, Pete." The sergeant was now being extremely flirtatious with Peter Kinbrew. Kinbrew began to feel as if he were about to faint while he became lost in the eyes of his enchanter.

"I can't, Booker. I just can't do it. I'm so sorry," the officer forced himself to say. Bookman knew that Pete Kinbrew held all the cards inside the palms of his soft, fat, little hands, and if he did not do something fast, his very life as a free man was over, much less his career as a cop.

Bookman let go of Peter's hands and stepped back. He then headed straight for the waist-high, swinging door which separated the two sides of the counter. Bookman began walking quickly up to Kinbrew.

"Hey!" Peter exclaimed. "You can't come back here. I could get—"

Kinbrew was not able to get his entire sentence out before Sergeant Bookman approached him and dropped down to his knees. He began begging in the voice of a damsel in distress, "Paleeze, Pete, you have just got to help me out on this one. I will do absolutely anything for just five minutes in your evidence locker."

This was the statement that pushed Pete Kinbrew over the edge. He glanced down at the large bulge in the sergeant's tight fitting Levi's.

"Annny thing?" Pete Kinbrew inquired with a devilish grin on his chubby face.

"Anything," the desperate sergeant answered.

Pete Kinbrew opened a drawer behind his counter and pulled out a small piece of paper. The short and stout lockup officer scribbled something on the paper and then handed it to Sergeant Bookman,

"I want you to meet me at this address tonight at 11:00 on the dot," Kinbrew ordered, "You and I, sir, are going to get a little bit more, shall we say, acquainted with one another."

Officer Kinbrew smiled at the sergeant seductively as he handed him the paper, leaving no room for doubt of what his intentions were.

"I wouldn't miss this date for the world," Bookman said, as he folded the piece of paper and shoved it into his shirt pocket. "I can't put into words how much I appreciate this, Pete. You have saved my ass once again."

"No problem, sarj. I just hope you're ready to save mine tonight in return," Kinbrew responded and then unlocked the steel gate in order for Bookman to get into the evidence lockup.

Chapter 20

Sergeant Bookman walked out of the evidence lockup feeling optimistic about his chances of retrieving the master tape that had been haunting him for the past month. It had been a little bit more difficult than he had expected it would be, but he had managed to smuggle the items that the voice had requested out of the evidence lockup.

On his way back down the hall, Bookman pulled the piece of paper that Officer Kinbrew had given him out of his pocket, unfolded it, and briefly glanced at it. "The Starlight Motel-446 E Yukon BLVD." Bookman laughed to himself as he balled up the piece of paper and deposited it into the nearest trash can. He told himself that he would try to find a way to make it up to Kinbrew in a way that would not compromise his sexuality. However, if this proved to be impossible, then Peter Kinbrew was a bridge worth burning, considering the alternatives.

With the items concealed underneath his shirt in a plastic bag, Bookman began to feel slightly paranoid on his way back down the hall to pick up Officer Felix. He felt as if every person he passed could somehow see his secret, so instead of greeting his coworkers in his usual upbeat fashion, the sergeant began turning his head, as if he did not see the people he was passing.

Finally, after what seemed like an eternity, Bookman arrived at the briefing room. He opened the door to a warm welcome from Marcos Felix, "I can't believe it; you're on time!" the rookie exclaimed. In his paranoid state of mind, Bookman quickly jumped on the defensive.

"What do you mean by that?" the suspicious sergeant asked, realizing that he was now the subject of every rookie's laughter.

"I don't mean anything by it, sarj, except that you usually get here a little later than this. That's all."

Bookman managed a feeble laugh and ordered, "Let's roll, rookie."

The two officers had been driving for ten minutes without a single word before Officer Felix broke the silence, "Is there something on your mind, sarj? Because you sure have been acting a little strange today."

"Aww, I'll be okay, man. I just got a few personal issues I'm dealin' with. No biggy," Bookman answered, waving his hand as if it was not an important issue.

"What do you think about this situation we got goin' on out here?" Felix asked.

"What situation?" Bookman inquired with a dumbfounded look on his face.

"You mean you aren't aware of what's going on with the VL and Bounty Hunters?"

"Oh, that," the sergeant retorted, caught off guard by the rookie's question. "Of course I'm aware of what's goin' on," Bookman lied. The truth was, the sergeant had become so engulfed in his own problem that he had begun to crawl into his shell like an endangered turtle.

He quickly saw evidence that something was not right when he pulled into the parking lot of Momma Maria's. Instead of seeing Boss Ross and his young crew of hustlers, he saw four other familiar faces in the parking lot where they usually stood. It was Flaco, Little one, Conejo, and Rafa, all members of *Vatos Locos*.

When Bookman and his ride-along exited the police cruiser, the sergeant walked straight up to the eldest of the *cholos*.

"Fucking Bookman, aye!" the slim, dark-skinned Mexican man yelled to his homeboys as the sergeant approached.

"Whaddup, Flac," Bookman said, reaching out to shake the man's hand.

"Oh, well... you know... business as usual around these parts," the *cholo* answered.

Bookman's eyes darted around the parking lot and into the restaurant. He saw no sign of any Black people around. "It's hard to just sit here and stare at this giant elephant in the room and not say anything about it," Bookman said. "Where the hell is the usual crew?"

Flaco stared at Bookman as if he had absolutely no idea what he was talking about.

"What crew, aye?" Flaco inquired.

Bookman struggled to hold back the anger that had begun to build up inside of him.

"It's hard to play dumb when you're already a fucking idiot," the sergeant said with a cold smile on his face. "Where's Boss Ross and the rest of the *miyathes?* As you guys say it."

All the young Mexican men began laughing.

"Oh, them!" Flaco blurted. "I don't know, aye. Looks like they went on vacation or something, homes."

This statement set off another outpouring of laughter amongst the young *cholos.* Bookman laughed right along with them.

"Ha ha ha, that was a good one, homes, but do you wanna see somethin' *really* funny? Watch this." Bookman's face quickly changed from a smile to a grimace, while his eyes filled with a cold rage. He grabbed Flaco by the back of the neck and slammed his face into the hood of a nearby parked car. "Now *that's* funny, asshole."

The other young men began walking quickly in the sergeant's direction, so Marcos Felix drew his service pistol and aimed it in the direction of the *cholos* and yelled, "Get your fuckin' asses on the ground — now!"

They were reluctant and only cooperated halfway. They all dropped down to their knees and put their hands behind their heads.

"Get all the way down on the ground!" the rookie yelled.

The men were slow to react to his command.

"Do what I said or I swear to fucking god I will blow your asses away. Prone the fuck out all the way — now!"

Finally, the young Mexican men followed the rookie's orders. Officer Felix kept the *cholos* at bay as he watched his sergeant brutalize the leader of the small pack of men.

With his handcuffs on the man as tight as they could possibly fit, the sergeant lifted the man's arms forcefully toward the back of his head.

"Aagh!" the *cholo* screamed from the excruciating pain he was experiencing.

Bookman was now calm and collected in his actions. He put his face right next to his victim and began talking in his ear, "Oh, the shit ain't funny no more, huh, Flac?"

79

Flaco could feel the sergeant's hot breath against his ear.

"What you got on you today, man? Can I haul your punk ass in or what?" Bookman began thoroughly searching the *cholo*. He emptied all the contents of Flaco's pockets onto the hood of the car. First he pulled out a large stack of cash from his right pocket. "Okay, you've got two one hundred dollar bills, five fifties, about thirty twenties, close to fifty tens, and I don't know how many fives and ones. This is clearly drug money, stupid." Bookman then lifted a cellular phone from out of the man's left pocket, "Well looky here; you've got a digital sting operation in your pocket. I'd bet that if I answered this phone all day, I'd make about a hundred busts. What do you think, funny man?"

Flaco remained silent with his face pressed against the hood of the car.

When Bookman began patting the slim Mexican down, he noticed a large bulge when he got to his crotch area, "Damn, *esse,* I thought only Negros had dicks this big." The sergeant reached his hand down the man's pants and came out with a clear plastic bag containing what appeared to be at least three ounces of crack cocaine. "Now you're under arrest, Flaco, and with your record, you're gonna be gone for a very long time. Don't you already got *dos* strikes?" The sergeant smiled at the *cholo* as he stood there in agony, "Go on; say something else funny. Tell us another joke, Mister Comedian."

Flaco remained silent.

"Now I can haul your punk ass in, or you can tell me what the hell is going on out here with y'all and the Hunter Boys, so I can go get my *pollo* plate and be the fuck up outta here."

"All I know is the big man called the shot. He gave us the green light to kill the Bounty Hunters and take their dope spots. I don't know why, and I don't ask no questions, homes. I would think that it had something to do with the big man getting shot and the little homies getting smoked."

Everything began to come together in the sergeant's mind. The murder/robbery, the brutal slaying of Boss Ross' girlfriend and her grandpa, and the VL's posting up slanging their drugs in front of Momma Maria's.

"So you're telling me that the Bounty Hunters had something to do with the shit that took place at Gordo's house a month ago?"

Flaco shook his head as he watched his little homeboys witness him snitching to the cops.

"Look, homes, I told you all I know. Now you can take it or leave it."

Bookman shoved the large sack of rocks into the crotch of his jeans and then uncuffed the *cholo.*

"Consider this dope your bail money, funny man." The sergeant patted the front of his pants and smiled, "Only a brotha can get away with a bulge this big anyway."

Sergeant Bookman turned to Marcos Felix, who still had the other three men laid out at gunpoint, "Let 'em up."

Felix looked at his sergeant in disbelief, "But aren't we going to—"

"I said let 'em up, rookie! That's an order!"

Officer Felix uncocked his service pistol and placed it back into his side holster. "You're free to get up," the rookie said reluctantly.

"Now let's get something to eat," Bookman commanded, as he walked toward the entrance to Momma Maria's.

Bookman strolled up to the restaurant counter with a big smile on his face, "*Buenos tarde,* Maria!" the sergeant greeted the restaurant owner.

"May I take your order?" Maria asked.

Bookman immediately noticed the change in his old friend's demeanor. He had been a loyal customer for well over fifteen years now and could not remember the last time he had been greeted in such a manner.

"Sure!" Bookman responded. "I'll have the large *pollo* plate with extra onions and two tortillas, also an extra large *horchatta.*"

"Will that be all, sir?"

The sergeant could not believe how short the sweet little-old Mexican lady was being with him. His feelings would have definitely been hurt, had he had any.

"Yup, dat'll do it, ma'am," Bookman responded.

"That will be $7.82," Maria said while holding out her hand.

For many years now, Bookman had not paid before he ate, but he quickly took out his wallet and paid for the food as if this were the normal routine.

"Next," Maria announced, looking at Officer Felix.

Marcos Felix stepped up to the counter and stared at the menu.

"Hi, *Mijo*," the woman greeted Marcos with a warm smile on her old face.

Sergeant Bookman could not believe his eyes and ears. He began thinking to himself, *After all the years I've kept this tortilla flippin' hoe from being robbed and extorted, this is the motha fuckin' thanks I get?* "Can you please bag that to go, ma'am?" Bookman asked the restaurant worker. "Grab my food for me, rookie. I'll be out in the cruiser."

The sergeant walked outside and crawled into his black and white. He reached into the glove compartment, pulled out a cell phone, and began dialing. After three rings, an answering machine picked up, "No one is available at this time. Please leave your message at the tone," blared the computer voice.

"Yo, Diamond, this is Dinosaur, man. It's imperative that you get back to me ASAP. I'm over at Momma Maria's taco spot, and it looks like we got a serious problem out here. Get back at me." Bookman clicked the phone off and immediately began dialing another number.

"*Ola*," the voice at the other end of the phone answered.

"Put Gordo on the phone," Bookman commanded.

"Gordo ain't here. Call back later," the man with the heavy Spanish accent responded.

Bookman's temper once again began to flare up. "Look here, *amigo*, I'm not calling back. You tell Gordo that Dinosaur called, and if he doesn't get back at me real fast, then all bets are off." Bookman clicked the phone off.

Not long after Bookman's second phone call ended, Marcos Felix strolled out of Momma Maria's carrying two white bags. He crawled back into the black and white and handed Bookman his bag. The sergeant quickly tore into his food like a wild beast, while Marcos ignored the bag containing his Number Two Combo and just stared out the window at nothing in particular. Halfway through his *pollo* plate, Bookman noticed that Felix still had not touched his food. "Somethin' wrong, rookie?" Bookman inquired, realizing that his partner had a gloomy look on his face.

"What do you plan on doing with the dope, sarj?"

A sly smile spread across the sergeant's face. "What's this? I'm being interrogated by my own fuckin' ride-along now?" Bookman was clearly amused by the question.

"No," Marcos answered, "I'm just saying that you need to do the right thing with it; that's all, sarj."

Bookman shook his head in disbelief. "Look here, you stinkin' rookie. You are as square as a pool table and twice as green, so you don't have any goddamn clue of what the right thing is yet," the now upset sergeant proclaimed while pointing in his ride-along's face. "I been workin' this beat since you was a pamper-shittin' crumb snatcher, and after all these years of puttin' my ass on the line out here, I wish to hell that I would let a dick-head punk like yourself tell me what to do. Now enjoy your meal, boy, and mind ya own damn beeswax."

Officer Felix shook his head in defeat. He knew that he could go to Bookman's superiors, but then he would be labeled as a snitch in the department. He could try to threaten the sergeant, and maybe he would turn in the drugs, but then he would be risking his life, because, after all, he was at the mercy of Sergeant Bookman in these dangerous eastside streets. Without touching his food, Felix tossed his bag out of the squad car and continued staring out the window with a look of extreme concentration on his face.

"I ain't sayin' nothin' 'bout you littering, now am I?" Bookman asked, in an attempt to kill the awkwardness which had now filled the squad car.

This only managed to make the rookie even more upset. "Okay, Mister Big Shot, veteran Sergeant, if you've been doing this shit so long, and you're such a street-smart cop with all these credentials, then why haven't you made lieutenant yet?"

Once again Bookman broke out in knee-slapping laughter, "Lieutenant, huh?" Bookman asked. "You mean like that pencil pushing maggot, Jason McGee — lieutenant? No thanks." The sergeant continued laughing. "Look here, rookie; I'm a street nigga at heart. I gotta be hands on with this shit, and sergeant is as high as it goes before they start askin' a mothafucka to do all kinds of behind the desk shit. I keep the peace out here and do all the dirty work that makes them pencil-neck punks you're speakin' about look good. They know what's necessary to keep shit from hittin' the fan, and that's why they turn a blind eye to certain things when it gets ugly out here."

Officer Felix looked at his sergeant in disgust, realizing that he was not talking to a cop. To the contrary, he was conversing with a ruthless thug. "Do you think they'd turn a blind eye to one of the sergeants being a coke head?" Felix inquired, wishing he could take the question back.

"I don't know," Bookman answered. "Why don't you run and tell like a little bitch and we'll find out."

Marcos Felix knew he was engaged in an argument that he could not win, so he remained silent.

Bookman said, "Let me put you up on some game, rookie. In the twenty years I've been a cop, I've had six poot-butt ride-alongs like yourself. Five of them are presently officers, two of them already decorated. You do the math."

Bookman tossed his trash into the restaurant parking lot and started up his car. "Oh, and by the way," the sergeant said, "Captain Cody calls me into his office two weeks in advance of every 'random' drug test and hands me a screening report with the results of my last test and the date of my next 'random' drug test written on the front page clear as day." Bookman made air quotes both times he used the word random. "So put two and two together, and it equals you betta know who you're fuckin' with."

On the way out of the parking lot, Felix could not help himself; he had to ask the question that was burning inside his belly, "So what happened to the other one?" Felix inquired.

"What do you mean, the other one?" Bookman asked.

"The sixth rookie," said Felix.

Bookman leaned his head closer to Officer Felix without looking at him and then began to talk in a whisper, "He got himself killed," Bookman replied.

Right at that moment, Marcos Felix realized that the best thing he could do to ensure his safety would be to request a transfer to another ride-along supervisor. He made up his mind to simply inform Lieutenant McGee that he and Sergeant Bookman shared too many personal differences.

Chapter 21

After more than two months of splurging, Psycho and Sicko were close to being broke. For the past seven weeks, the teenage boys had lived like Rock stars, squandering their newfound riches on everything from gambling to strip clubs, where they had earned a reputation for themselves by "Making it rain", a term used for when a man takes two handfuls of dollar bills and tosses them into the air so that they rain down on the stripper while she is in the middle of her stage performance. However, the twins made it rain with *one-hundred-dollar bills — daily*!

Once the clubs closed for the night, Psycho and Sicko would rent lavish hotel penthouse suites, where they would engage in wild orgies with the exotic dancers. The sex parties were fully stocked with cases of Cristal or Dom Pérignon Champagne, pared with several different types of the highest quality drugs that money could buy.

Sick Twin did most of the spending, while his brother, who was older than him by about ten minutes, just sat back and enjoyed the ride. When Psycho happened to look into the foot locker safe where the boys stored their cash, he nearly suffered a heart attack. "Eight thousand *dollas*!?" he screamed in a high-pitched voice.

"Uh, oh," the youngest twin brother responded with a dumbfounded look on his baby face.

"What the hell you been doin', Sick?"

The question caught Sick Twin by surprise, "Nigga, what kinda stupit-ass question is that?" Sicko Twin responded, visibly upset, "Anything and everything I did, you was right there doin' the shit right along with me and havin' a good-ole mafuckin' time doin' it, so don't blame a gaddamn thang on me, Psych."

His brother was right. Psycho was aware that they were blowing a whole bunch of cash, but for some reason, in his mind, he thought they had come across enough money to live that lifestyle forever.

"Well we ain't 'bout to sit here and point fingers and play da blame game all night. We need more bread, and that's that," Psycho said with authority,

"Yeah, and I know exactly how we gonna get it, too," Sicko Twin responded with his signature evil grin.

"And how's dat, nigga?" his skeptical twin brother asked.

"Remember dat move we had been scoping out in Gardena before we discovered the lucky suitcase?" A devilish grin quickly spread across the face of the elder twin.

Chapter 22

Stormy had been living in Diamond's whorehouse for over two weeks now and still had managed to avoid turning a single trick. All of the young girls had automatically taken a liking to Stormy. Her witty personality kept the young prostitutes laughing constantly, and whenever she was not joking or being silly, she would be serenading the young ladies and getting their opinions on the new songs she would write. One of the older girls in the house had even surprised her with an old acoustic guitar that she had picked up from a pawn shop. Stormy would also keep the place spotless and do all the girl's laundry in an attempt to earn her keep by making herself useful around the house.

Stormy's only problem in the house was the woman who all the girls referred to as "Big Mama". If Diamond were a pimp, then Big Mama would definitely be his number one whore. Her real name was Radmillia Jearman, and over the years she had gone from being Diamond's puppy love, when she would distract the corner store owner while he stole candy for the two of them, to his high school sweetheart, where she doubled as his getaway driver in small-time robberies and drive-by shootings on rival gangs, to adulthood, when she became Diamond's all-out whore. She would mostly just attract the tricks and then lead them into cheap motel rooms where she would get them stark naked and begin to sexually arouse them, leaving the door unlocked so that Diamond could storm in and pull off the easy robbery by catching the tricks with their pants down.

Radmillia had even spent several years in prison on Diamond's behalf following a botched jewelry store robbery where a police unit had pulled up behind their getaway car before they could make it out of the parking lot. Diamond had jumped out of the car and escaped on foot, leaving Radmillia holding the bag. The district attorney's office had offered her pure immunity from any punishment on the condition that she give up the bandit. Radmillia had remained solid for Diamond, and as a result she ended up accepting an eight year plea bargain, five years of which she spent in prison.

Although the many years of hard ghetto life had taken their toll on Big Mama, who was now over forty years old, she was still an attractive woman who exercised daily to maintain her tight and thick figure. Big Mama even held onto two loyal customers who she turned tricks with a few times a week, but her main objective was to keep the young prostitutes in line and teach them the ropes about how to think and behave like real hustlers.

She had known from the moment she laid eyes on Stormy that the payroll would increase by at least ten grand per week once word got around that there was a piece of young Caucasian ass for sale in her brothel, but after two weeks of counting basically the same profits as before, the new teenage White girl had turned out to be nothing more than a big disappointment.

Big Mama's patience was beginning to wear thin. It was not a problem for Stormy to attract customers, in fact, every single trick who laid eyes on the young White girl wanted a piece of her. She was regularly sought after by men offering as much as ten times more than the most highly paid girl in the house was receiving for her services.

The girls had all taken turns hiding Stormy in upstairs bedrooms for hours at a time and giving her money in an effort to make it look as if she were turning tricks. Today, Big Mama busted in after watching Stormy enter a room five minutes before a young whore and her john. Big Mama opened the room door only to find the young whore naked in the bed, straddled on top of the trick in the rodeo position, hard at work while riding him. When Big Mama walked into the room, the young dark-skinned girl turned around and gave her a brief glance but then kept on tending to her date without missing a beat. Big Mama made her way to the closet door and opened it, where she found Stormy sitting on the floor, listening to an I-POD.

"I don't know where you think you at, but this damn sure ain't *Star Search*, baby," Big Mama snarled at the teenage girl. "Now you gonna have ta come up off of summa dat tighty-Whitey little pussy of yours, or get the hell out from 'roun' here, sweetie."

"But, Big Mama—"

"But, Big Mama, my achin' black ass," the indignant house mother interrupted. "I already knew what you was doin', child. I been watchin' ya for the last two days. You gonna learn one thang about Big Mama, hun; you can't outsmart me or outslick me, 'cause I know ya kind, you lil heffa you. You thinkin' you gonna charm your way into a free stay in a hoe house. Well, I got news for you; it ain't not that much charmin' in the whole world. Any and every bitch eatin', sleepin', and shittin' in this house is gonna be suckin' and fuckin' on some dicks," Big Mama said while pointing at the sweaty young chocolate-colored prostitute in the bed with her customer. "Big dicks, little dicks, and middle dicks, it's yo job to handle 'em or get the hell out. Now what it's gonna be, lil lady?"

"Well I- I- I-" Stormy stuttered.

Big Mama cut her eyes at the young girl, "You betta tell me somethin' fast, or you gonna have to pack your—"

"Okay!" Stormy shouted.

"Okay, what?" Big Mama responded with a contemptuous look on her face.

"Okay, I'll have sex!" Stormy exclaimed, as the tears began to flow from her eyes.

"That's what Big Mama wants to hear. Now wipe ya little face off and get ya mind right, 'cause I got a special customer comin' through in the mornin' and he all excited 'cause he expectin' some young White pussy, so don't let me down, ya hear?" Big Mama threatened as she turned to leave. She leaned on the bed and slapped the busy young whore on the butt on the way out of the bedroom.

Chapter 23

The sun was just beginning to fall from over the streets of Los Angeles, making way for yet another full moon. It had been a bright and shiny full moon for three days now, and Flaco and his *Chicano* crew had been enjoying control of the drug trade in front of Momma Maria's for just as long.

The parking lot was proving to be even more profitable than the young Hispanic men had expected. To Flaco's surprise, they were easily running through about four ounces a day, one rock at a time, and the half pound of marijuana they sold daily was the icing on the cake. "Aye, homes, I can get used to this shit," Flaco bragged as he counted his large roll of cash. "Guess what, aye, I was counting my *fedia* last night, right? I got enough money to get the Chevy out of the hydraulic shop, plus get the sounds and upholstery hooked up, and still have the cash to go to the big guy and re-up the *clavo*."

"Damn, homes, maybe if you paid us like we deserve we can all get a Chevy," Rafa replied. Flaco popped his little cousin in the back of the head.

"You're fourteen fucking years old, *esse*; you should be playing with video games and hooking up low rider bikes like I did when I was your age. The only difference is, I wasn't getting a hundred dollars a freaking day to do it."

As the young men laughed and played around, Lil One noticed the car of one of their biggest customers pulling into the parking lot. The charcoal-grey Lexus always stirred up competition between the three elder *cholos* to get to the car first, because the little fat White guy driving that vehicle had never spent less than one hundred dollars since they had been occupying the parking lot.

"I got this one, homes!" Lil One yelled.

"Fuck no, *esse*. You got him earlier. It's my turn," Conejoe replied.

"Fuck this shit, aye. Let my little primo take care of this one," Flaco demanded, "and you can keep all the *fedia* taken, Rafa, since you say I ain't paying you right, *pinchi covrona*, I'm giving you a bonus."

To the disappointment of the other *cholos*, Rafa walked up and softly knocked on the tinted window of the Lexus. As Flaco looked upon, he could not help but notice the peculiar way that the little fat guy was behaving today. He would usually be in a big hurry to shove the cash out the car window, take his rocks, and be gone.

It seemed as if Rafa had been standing at the car window for a full two minutes now, "Get away from that car, Rafa!" Flaco yelled, realizing that something was not right. Rafa quickly turned and began to walk briskly away from the car, but it was too late. The three men watched as bright sparks of light began flashing inside of the car and holes appeared in the dark, tinted windows.

As they ducked behind a parked car, the men heard a slew of loud consecutive clapping sounds and watched Rafa fall to the ground, riddled with gunshot wounds. The other three *cholos* never realized they were under fire from a different location besides the Lexus, until they noticed a big, red wet spot in Conejoe's white T-shirt. Flaco drew his .38 caliber revolver from his waistband and emptied it in the direction he thought the shots were coming from.

All at once the shooting came to a stop, as a man dressed all in black ran from the back of Momma Maria's restaurant and hopped into the Lexus. The vehicle quickly burned rubber out of the parking lot, and just like that — the attackers were gone.

* * *

Dozens of people of both Hispanic and Black persuasion had walked from the projects across the street to watch from behind the yellow tape as the coroner zipped up two more ominous black body bags containing the fresh corpses of yet two more people. Lil One had watched Flaco leave an hour earlier in an ambulance with a gunshot wound to his rear end, and now, as he sat handcuffed in the backseat of a police cruiser, he watched the coroner's van drive off with two of his best friends wrapped inside body bags.

Bookman and Marcos Felix arrived at the crime scene to find Detective Houston interviewing several potential witnesses who he had detained in the parking lot. It was always a relief for Richard Houston when he saw the ornery sergeant pull up to a crime scene such as this one, because unlike the blond-haired, blue-eyed White detective, the smooth, fast-talking Black sergeant always managed to get results in these types of situations.

"How's it hangin', Dick?" Bookman asked with a wry smile on his face, "You get it? How's it hangin', *Dick?*"

"Yeah, I get it, my nizzle," Detective Houston replied with a laugh, "You must've been saving that one fa me, wodee."

"Yup, that was my ace in the hole, buddy, but seriously, what we got goin' on here, Dick?" Bookman inquired.

"Well... basically we've got two bodies and one victim of a GSW to his rear end. He got carted off to King about an hour ago. I've got nine potential eyewitnesses, all of whom are being held for questioning right there to your left, so I'd say it's the usual run-of-the-mill situation."

Bookman looked around the parking lot and quickly noticed a familiar face sitting in the backseat of a squad car.

"Here's what you need to do, Dick," Bookman announced with his usual cockiness. "Head up into Momma Maria's right there and order a large *pollo* plate with extra onions and a large *horchatta*. Scratch that — make it a medium *horchatta*. I've gotta watch my figure. Handle that for me, and in the meanwhile, me and Officer Felix will work our magic out here and make you look like a real detective."

"No problem," Houston responded, reaching his hand out for Bookman's lunch money. The sergeant slapped the detective's hand and then turned his palm up back to his colleague in a "Gimme five" gesture. "You ain't shit, you know that, Booker?" Dick Houston declared before he made his way into the restaurant.

"Aight, rookie, grab your notepad and go get a statement from everybody over there," Bookman commanded, pointing toward the nine witnesses being detained in the parking lot. "Get all their ID cards, and if they ain't got no ID on 'em, just get their names and addresses and a statement on what they saw out here, and then tell 'em they're free to go."

Marcos Felix looked at his sergeant in disbelief.

"but, sarj, those aren't even our—"

"Just do the shit," Bookman interrupted. "I'm gonna go have a word with our *vato* friend sitting over there in that black and white."

Richard Houston walked out of the Mexican restaurant to find Bookman and his rookie sitting on top of his police cruiser laughing and joking as if it were simply a fun day at the park. As he approached his vehicle with a white plastic bag in hand holding the sergeant's food, he quickly noticed that something was wrong.

Bookman slid off the hood of the police car and pulled the detective to the rear of the vehicle for a sidebar out of earshot of the rookie, "Check this out, Dick; the suspect's vehicle is a small, charcoal-grey Lexus with dark, tinted windows. As of now, it's got several bullet holes in it's windows, and it's usually driven by a short, fat White male, approximately forty-five years of age. Also, one of our suspects is a Black male, about six feet tall, with a mustache and goatee. He was last seen wearing all black. They made a right turn out of this parking lot and were last seen traveling eastbound down Imperial."

"So where the hell is my suspect?" the detective inquired.

"What suspect?" Bookman asked with a dumbfounded expression.

"Um, that would be the one who was sitting in the backseat of that there police cruiser when you drove up."

"Oh, him!" Bookman exclaimed. "You call that a suspect? Come on, Dick; I had you pegged as a whole lot sharper than that. I told that dude to get the hell outta here."

Bookman turned around and began yelling to Officer Felix, "Hey, Rookie, throw me your notepad."

Marcos quickly cooperated, removing his notepad from his left shirt pocket and tossing it to the sergeant. Bookman thumbed through the pad, ripped out several pages, and handed them to the detective. "Here's ya witness statements."

Detective Houston flipped through the small pieces of paper and briefly glanced at each witness statement.

Gilbert Serano DOB 2-11-55 address 111 South Grandee Ave, Compton, CA. Statement: "I don't know nothing."

Amerique Phillips DOB 5-18-89 Address 1353 ½ 115th Place, Watts, CA. Statement: "I didn't see nothing."

Jason Christianson DOB 9-26-70 Address 16938 Brazil St., Compton, CA. Statement: "Why should I help you? Do this mean I'm gonna get half of your paycheck?"

Michael Hightower DOB 7-12-74 address 2194 Town Court, Carson, CA. Statement: "I just got here after the shit was all over, so I don't know why y'all are detaining me."

Shawntwain Cannon DOB 9-9-76 Address 447 East 169th St. Gardena CA. Statement: "I ain't seen a damn thing."

Belinda Pearson DOB 11-17-51 Address 906 Lucein St., Los Angeles, CA. Statement: "I have no idea of what you are talking about."

Cory Blair DOB 10-1-90 Address Homeless. Statement: "I didn't see shit."

Askari Thompson DOB 9-5-71 Address 1204 Ardmore Ave., Los Angeles, CA Statement: "I was inside the restaurant when it happened."

Clifton Dradon DOB 6-5-47 Address 520 Millmont Dr., Lake Wood, CA. Statement: "I didn't see nothing."

"Wow, a whole lot of help this is going to give me. Thanks, Booker," the frustrated detective announced, handing Bookman the white plastic bag containing his lunch.

"Hey!" Bookman blurted out after he removed the Styrofoam tray from the bag, "I thought I said a large *pollo* plate and medium *horchatta*, you idiot."

"You've gotta watch that figure," Detective Houston responded with a sly smile, as he removed his radio from his chest holder, "25 to dispatch."

"Go ahead, 25," the female dispatcher answered at the other end of the radio.

"We've got an all-points bulletin on a dark-grey Lexus with dark, tinted windows, model unknown, but it is of the shorter variety, there will also be several bullet holes in the windows. The vehicle was last seen traveling eastbound on . . ."

Bookman listened to the detective for a moment. He then gestured to his rookie that it was time to leave and made his way back to his car. The sergeant started up his vehicle and then flashed a peace sign at Detective Houston who responded with a middle finger as Bookman drove out of the parking lot.

The sergeant had not made it halfway back to the station before the call glared over the radio, "Dispatch to number one."

Bookman gave Marcos Felix a puzzled look before picking up his radio, "Yeah, this is number one. Go 'head, Steph."

"We have a suspect's vehicle located in the Nickerson Gardens, a dark-grey Lexus in the second parking lot of 112th Street."

"Ten four, we are en route."

Bookman made a quick U-turn and was on his way back to the projects. They arrived at the second parking lot of 112th Street to find that several black and white units had beat him there and parked in the lot and all up and down the street. Officers were scrambling from door to door, questioning anyone and everyone they came in contact with. Bookman squeezed his police cruiser through the makeshift cop car barricade and drove right up next to the grey Lexus which was surrounded by officers.

He exited the vehicle to the greetings of Detective Houston, "So, we meet again."

"Yeah, that was quick, wasn't it?" Bookman answered.

"Well, here's our grey Lexus, and here are our tinted windows, and here's our bullet holes," the detective announced while pointing to everything he mentioned as he spoke.

Bookman examined the bullet holes in the window and said, "Looks like the tinting held the glass together and prevented this whole window from shattering." The sergeant walked to the windshield, which was the only window that was not tinted, and inspected the inside of the car. "What you guys find in the trunk?" Bookman inquired.

"We haven't even checked the trunk yet, or anything else, for that matter. We're waiting on CSI to arrive," Detective Houston replied.

"Aww, fuck that shit. Go get me a crowbar outa my trunk, rookie," the angry sergeant demanded.

Marcos quickly followed the order and came back with a black crowbar. Bookman approached the trunk of the Lexus with the crowbar in hand, and after about a minute of grunting and struggling, the trunk popped open. "Well, would ya look at this crock of shit," the sergeant announced.

Detective Houston approached the trunk to find a male Caucasian laying face up with his eyes wide open and staring into space. In the center of his forehead was a small bullet hole.

"So much for our little, fat suspect," Bookman announced.

Chapter 24

The past two months had proven to be busy for Lil Ricky and his favorite uncle. For Diamond, it was pure bliss to see his illegal businesses, which he had put so much time and effort into over the years, begin to sprout deeper roots and flourish like never before. Lil Ricky was jubilant because he was now counting *real* money.

Every since the altercation in the hotel room with The Twins, Diamond had learned to look at his nephew as a grown man and had begun to teach him the ins and outs of the black market. Diamond now looked at Lil Ricky as a business partner, rather than a mischievous teenager out to make a quick buck, which he once was. As a result, Lil Ricky was now seeing twenty percent of every dollar from every single business his uncle was involved in. Within a two week span, between the cocaine, marijuana, PCP, and ecstasy pill sales, paired with the gambling shacks and whorehouse, the two men together had raked in a profit of over four hundred thousand dollars.

It was eleven P.M., and Diamond was sitting at the living room table of one of his safe houses on the outskirts of the projects. On the table was a digital cash-counting machine, along with several tall cash stacks of which Diamond was busy loading into the machine one at a time. The old-school hustler could never have imagined himself getting tired of counting money, however, the last few days had proven him wrong. He told himself that he would just have Big Mama come handle this time-consuming task from now on, after he pressed the start button for the machine to begin counting and realized that he had loaded a stack of twenty dollar bills into it while it was still on fifty dollar bill counting mode. This was the third mistake tonight, and Diamond had to just sit back and take a deep breath to keep himself from throwing the machine into the living room wall.

Just as he began to get his faculties back in order, the cell phone on his hip began to vibrate. Before answering, he took a look at the caller ID screen, which read 'Blocked Number'. This usually meant that he would not answer, but the fact that he had not talked to Lil Ricky all day prompted him to answer, "Who dis?" Diamond answered after pressing the talk button on his Hi-tec mobile phone.

"Where in the hell have *you* been?" a hostile voice at the other end of the phone asked.

"I been busy, mothafucka, and since when do I gotta report to you?" Diamond had automatically picked up Bookman's voice.

"First of all, I haven't received this month's payment from you, so you are damn right you gotta report *something* to me," the upset sergeant proclaimed. "Secondly, I've bagged up thirteen bodies over the past two months in the projects alone, so you better tell me what the hell is going on."

"Look, man, it don't take no twenty year LAPD veteran to see that for whatever reason my little homies are at war wit deez hat dancers in the 'jects, and furthermore, that shit is puttin' a hurting on my profits. Shit, bidness is slow right now," Diamond lied. "But as soon as I get mines, you'll get yours. Ten geez ain't no chump change, Booker, so just let your boy get his cheese right."

The phone went silent for a moment and Diamond thought his phone had dropped the call, "Hello?"

"Yeah, I'm here," Bookman answered. "So, you mean to tell me that you have absolutely no fucking inkling of what's going on out here, right?" Bookman asked.

Diamond was now beginning to become uncomfortable with the conversation and tried to divert the topic, "Check dis out, Booker; I'm gonna keep holdin' up my end of our deal just like I always have. Matter fact, I'm gonna pay you another three months in advance just like I did last time, but as far as that other shit you askin' me about, man, I can't be a criminal and a pig at the same time 'cause that just ain't how shit works 'round here. Can ya dig it, brotha?"

This snide remark managed to get under Bookman's skin so deep that he was surprised at himself for how much it affected him. "Nigga, you ain't had no problem doing police work all these years up to this point, you two-bit, street-hustling snitch. Now all of a sudden you're using words like 'pig'? Well, guess what, you fucking rat, you better have this pig's dough by this day next week, or you might end up sleepin' with the fishies. How's dat for animal talk?"

"Oh, so now you're threatening me, Booker?" Diamond asked, but the line went dead, so he got up from his chair and began pacing back and forth around the room. He found it hard to believe that he had just been threatened with violence by a man who he'd been doing business with for so long, in order to stay out of prison. But tonight, that man had not threatened him with jail time, but instead, he'd chosen the thug's route. Diamond was now being extorted by means of force.

* * *

It was 11:15 A.M. and Gordo was already sloppy drunk, when his old, out-of-date cell phone rang. For the past three months, since he had walked out of the hospital, Gordo had been drowning the pain from the .45 bullet wedged in his brain with bottles of Tequila. Not only did he use the alcohol to numb the physical pain, but Gordo also used drinking as a crutch to deal with the sorrow of losing his baby brother in *latrocianio* that he could have prevented had he never lowered his guard and trusted that stinking Black *Diamante de ceniciento.*

On top of all that, Gordo was also feeling the pressure beginning to rise from below. He began to hear a lot of gossip floating around regarding a few ambitious characters in the *varrio* suggesting that due to his weakened condition he should step down from his position as *Llavero,* boss of the *varrio.* Gordo was even beginning to doubt himself. After all, it was, in fact, his misjudgment that had led to the current state of chaos the gang was now in. Maybe he *should* step down. Maybe there *was* a younger *vato* out there who was stronger and could do a better job *gobierno* than he could.

Gordo pressed the talk button on his cellular phone, *"Ola, de puto.* Who the fug ees this," Gordo asked with slurred speech.

"What's up, Gordito? This is—"

"Aggh, fucking Bookman," Gordo interrupted. "How'd you get dees number, aye?"

"You gave me this number over a year ago. Are you okay, man?" Bookman inquired with sincerity.

"I'm all right, but wha you won, man?" Gordo slurred the question.

"We need to holla, Gordito. I think I may be able to help you, but I need you to be sober when we talk. I need you to meet me somewhere tomorrow at 10:00 A.M. sharp. That should give you plenty of time to shake your hangover. Go grab a pen so you can jot down these directions."

Gordo followed the sergeant's orders, and with much difficulty he wrote down the directions on a pad.

"Don't bullshit me, Gordo. This is some important shit I need to discuss with you."

"But I don't got you money yet," Gordo said.

"Be there!"

The phone went blank. Once Gordo had clicked the phone off, he closed his eyes tightly for a moment in deep thought. As a result, he was able to conjure up a brief but sober enlightening moment of clarity. Meeting with this *miyathe marrano* tomorrow could not possibility make things any worse than they already were. The wounded street don made up his mind. His last chance to make a stand could very well lie in the hands of this crooked Black cop.

Chapter 25

A loud buzzing sound came pouring out of the hotel room's cheap alarm clock speakers at 5:00 A.M. sharp. Psycho Twin popped up from the comfort of his soft pillow and quickly reached over to the small table which separated his twin bed from that of his brother's to push the "Off" button. "Sick, get up!" Psycho yelled to his brother. "We ain't got much time. We gotta get goin' if we want everything to go right."

"I'm up. I'm up," Sicko assured his brother and partner in crime. After ten minutes of face washing and teeth brushing, the twins were both dressed and ready to go. They walked out of their hotel room at 5:12 A.M., and by 5:15 they were driving out of the parking lot in separate vehicles. Psycho drove a rented black 2008 Chevy Malibu, while his brother drove a white U-Haul conversion van that the men had rented the night before under an assumed name.

As the two teenagers drove toward the parking lot's exit, Psycho pulled up on the side of Sicko's van and began yelling out of his passenger-side window, "Make sure you got your radio on, dumb dumb."

"Oh!" Sick Twin yelled, realizing that he had almost made a crucial mistake. He quickly turned his radio on. "Can ya here me now?" Sicko asked in a joking voice.

"Yeah, I can here you now, funny man," the elder twin responded. "Now be sure not to talk into this thing until it's completely necessary, and you know when that is," Psycho ordered.

"Roger, over and out," Sicko answered, and the two men were off. Psycho Twin made a quick right onto Albertoni Boulevard, traveling westbound, while his brother went in the opposite direction, headed toward the 91 freeway where he entered the on ramp.

Psycho's trip was fairly short. After a right turn on Broadway, he traveled northbound for five miles until he reached Rosecrans Boulevard. He then made a quick right and pulled into the parking lot of an old abandoned factory, where he parked his rental car behind a large trash dumpster on the loading dock, out of view of the traffic which flowed up and down Rosecrans Boulevard. He then lit up a cigarette, got out of his car, made a forty-yard trek back toward Rosecrans Boulevard, and there it was, the pot of gold that was about to put him and his twin brother right back on top of the world. The bright sign read 'First National Bank of California'. The twins, along with Lil Ricky, had been scoping out this hit for well over five months now, the longest they had ever taken to size up a single heist, so Psycho knew that if everything went according to plan, this would be just another profitable cake walk.

*   *   *

After driving down a twenty-five mile stretch on the 91 Freeway, Sick Twin came to a large sign that read 'Now Entering Orange County'. One more mile and he arrived at his exit and got off of the freeway on Beach Street. He made a right turn and then traveled southbound on Beach, past Knotts Berry Farm amusement park, and further down, until he came to a street by the name of Harper Court. It was still dark outside with no sign of sunrise when Sicko made the left turn onto Harper Court and found himself in the beautiful quiet neighborhood which he had gotten so acquainted with over the past five months. After traveling one block on Harper Court, he came to a small street by the name of Joel Court and made a left turn.

Things looked exactly the way they had looked the morning before, when Psycho and Sicko Twin had performed a ritualistic final walk-through. Thanks to Lil Ricky, they had made it a habit at a young age of always scoping out their hits and practicing all kinds of different scenarios to ensure a smooth outcome. The only difference now was that Psycho Twin was forced to take on the roll of coach in this two man team, when it had always been Lil Ricky who called the plays. Although Lil Ricky had taken part in the planning of this operation early on and had participated in the laying of some of the framework, it was ultimately Psycho Twin who ended up having to work out all the kinks.

Sicko drove halfway down the street and began cursing under his breath when he noticed an old work truck occupying the ideal spot where he had planned to park the van. It was a good thing that he and his brother had already planned for this scenario. He then drove down to the end of the cul-de-sac and made a U-turn before driving back up fifty feet to his secondary parking spot. The only difference with this spot was his view of the front door of his targeted yellow house. After making sure that he was parked perfectly, not too close or far away from the curb, he turned the van's ignition switch off and picked up his walkie-talkie, "We got the ball on the twenty yard line, coach," Sicko proclaimed into his radio. "I repeat; we do have the ball on the twenty. Do you copy?"

"That's a copy, QB," Psycho answered. "All systems are go, over and out."

Sick Twin checked the time on his black Movado wrist watch; it was now 5:42 A.M., which meant that within the next five minutes, if everything went as planned, he would be watching a man get into the Chrysler PT Cruiser that he was currently watching and then leave in a hurry.

"Bingo," Sicko said to himself after two minutes, when he saw the middle-aged White man come from inside the house with a black briefcase in his right hand, while checking the time piece on his left wrist. He hopped into the cockpit of the PT Cruiser, and within a half a minute, he was turning off of the street. Once again, Sicko picked up his walkie-talkie and began speaking into it, "The ball is in the air, coach. I repeat; the ball is in the air. Do you copy?"

"Ten four, QB," Psycho responded. "Over and out." Once the PT Cruiser was out of sight, Sicko once again checked his watch. The time was now 5:46. He lit up a cigarette, and for the next three minutes, he took long drags of smoke and concentrated on the task at hand.

At 5:49, Sicko started up the U-Haul van. He put it into drive and then drove straight up into the driveway of the yellow house the man had just left minutes earlier. With the van still idling, he put it back into park, exited the vehicle, and walked up to the keypad mounted to the wall on the left side of the garage door. He then lifted the keypad's cover. After punching in a five digit code, the garage door began to rise. The young bandit ran hurriedly back to the van, hopped back into the driver's seat, and shoved the vehicle into drive. He managed to squeeze the van into a space right next to the Mercedes Benz SUV that he had watched leave the house so many times, by or before 6:10 A.M. Sick Twin jumped back out of the van in a hurry and bustled up to the garage door controller mounted to the wall beside the door which led into the home. He pressed the button, then drew and cocked his Glock 9mm pistol as he watched the garage door go down and close him in from the outside world.

"Here comes the fun part," Sicko mumbled to himself while reaching into his back pocket. The young bandit pulled a pair of brown work gloves from the pocket of his black Dickies work slacks. After sliding on the gloves, the adolescent intruder slowly twisted the doorknob. He opened the door a crack and peeped into the victim's home. He could hear the sound of cartoons playing on a television in the distance, but nothing else. After about a twenty-second wait, the young robber entered.

With gun in hand, he began creeping down a hallway in the direction of the location where he heard the cartoons playing. After walking all the way down the hallway and through a den-like area, he came to the kitchen. Sicko looked through the kitchen to find that there was a living room on the other side of it. In the living room, he spotted the back of a little boy's head. The kid was sitting on the couch with his back to Sicko while caught deep in an episode of *Sponge Bob Square Pants*. Sick Twin tiptoed past the kitchen and living room area and headed down the hall to the back rooms. One by one, he peeped into each room until he heard the sound of running water coming from a location near the end of the hallway. With gun still in hand, he began moving swiftly toward the direction of the running water. At the end of the hallway was what appeared to be the master bedroom, and Sicko realized that this was where the sound was coming from.

He made his way into the room and immediately noticed an open bathroom door on the other side of the room. He began tiptoeing through the dark bedroom on his way toward the light in the bathroom. Halfway to his destination, the young robber tripped over a pair of high heeled shoes, making a slight noise.

"Johnny, what are you doing?" came the woman's voice from the bathroom. "Put your cereal bowl in the dish washer and get your backpack on. Mommy's running late," the voice from the bathroom proclaimed. With his back up against a mirror-styled closet, Sicko played possum right outside the bathroom door while contemplating whether he should run into the bathroom or allow his prey to come to him.

Before he could make a decision, the running water shut off and he heard the sound of cabinet doors slamming and drawers closing. He quickly slid open the door of the mirror closet that he was standing next to and backed in, leaving just a crack in the closet door. Before long, he saw the lady who he had been watching for five months walk out of the bathroom wearing nothing but a pair of pink bikini panties with little red hearts on them. He watched as the topless woman crawled over the king-sized bed to turn on a lamp sitting on the nightstand at the other side.

As Sicko stood in the closet stalking his prey, he could feel the bulge in his trousers begin to grow. This White woman's perky C-cup breasts, with the pink nipples, along with the rest of her tight body emitting the smell of sweet perfume, was almost too much for the teenager to bear. Finally, he was able to focus his perverted mind on what was at stake and shake off the lust which he knew would definitely complicate his mission.

He watched as the pretty blonde woman opened her dresser drawer and pulled out a bra which matched her panties and put it on. She then walked toward the bedroom door and out of the sight of Sick Twin. He now realized that he had made a mistake, wishing that he would have just barged into the bathroom and caught his victim by surprise. Sicko's heart began to pound, and he almost fired his weapon, when, all at once, the closet door slid open. The woman's eyes immediately opened wide with fear as she struggled to take a deep enough breath to scream.

"Don't you dare scream, woman, or you and little Johnny are dead," Sicko promised through gritted teeth while pointing his 9mm at the woman's face.

"Please don't hurt my son. You can take anything you—"

"Bitch, shut the fuck up and lay face down on your bed, now!" Sicko demanded. The woman cooperated right away. Sicko took a couple of seconds to admire the way the lady's tight buns looked and how the little crevice ran down the center of her panties in-between her butt cheeks. He pulled a roll of silver duct tape from his black hoodie sweatshirt and began taping her wrists tightly behind her back. "Now look here, Connie," the bandit referred to her by her real name. "You got two choices today. You can give me your full cooperation to make this thang go smoothly, and the shit will be over before you know it. Or, you can pick choice number two and try somethin' stupid or hesitate or try any other kinda dumb shit with me and watch me blow your little boy's brains all over the place then snatch those cute little panties off ya tight little fanny and shove this big old Mandingo thang up in ya, which I really wanna do anyway."

The woman was now in tears. "I promise I won't try one thing. Just don't hurt us, please," the woman begged.

"Please don't *make* me hurt you," Sicko replied firmly.

Still laying face down on the bed, the woman cringed when she felt Sicko's hardness against her rear end as he crawled over her in order to grip the other side of the bedspread.

"Oh, don't worry," Sicko assured the woman. "As long as you don't give me a hard time, I won't give you nunna dis hard dick."

The young gangster grabbed the corners of the bedspread and pulled it over the woman's body so that she was totally wrapped up inside of it. He then stood her up and began wrapping tape tightly around her neck and then down to her waist and ankles so that she was totally submerged inside the blanket.

"I would've let you put on some clothes instead of wearing this bedspread, but I'm runnin' low on time now 'cause of your crying and wasting time," Sicko informed his hostage. "Besides, I think this blanket looks good on ya. Now just lay right here and think about how you're not gonna piss me off today. I'll be right back to get ya."

"Please don't hurt my son," Connie begged.

"Please don't hurt my son," the young thug mocked in a woman's voice as he walked out of the bedroom.

When Sick Twin arrived at the kitchen, he looked through to the living room on the other side of it and once again found little Johnny trapped deep in a trance while watching his cartoons. Sicko stripped a long strand of duct tape from his roll and began creeping up behind the little boy until he was standing behind the couch within arms reach of him. In a split second, Sicko managed to get the strip of duct tape over the boy's mouth, preventing him from screaming. The rest was easy. With the kid's backpack still on his back, Sicko gripped his shoulder straps and used them to pull him over the top of the couch. Unhindered by the resistance the little boy attempted to put up, Sicko managed to hog-tie the third grader without a struggle.

"You're gonna be okay, little fella. Just calm down," Sick Twin said, as he carried Johnny into the garage. He placed the young boy in the back of the U-Haul van and taped his hands to a dolly before going back to retrieve his mother.

When he got back to the master bedroom, he found his hostage laying in the exact same place he had left her, "Good job, Connie. Now that's what I call teamwork."

"I can't breathe in this thing. Please just uncover my head."

"You shole do beg a lot. I'll take it off once we get in the van."

He picked his hostage up, carried her to the garage, and heaved her into the back of the van. Once he had thrown her in the back of the van with her son, he quickly untaped the blanket and pulled it from around her, leaving her hog-tied in her panties and bra, "I don't wanna hear you complainin' about bein' cold neither."

"Thank you so much," the desperate woman said as she crawled toward her son. "Everything's gonna be okay, Johnny," she promised.

Before boarding the driver's seat of his van, Sicko ran quickly up to the Mercedes Benz SUV that was parked beside it and opened the driver-side door. He reached into the vehicle and retrieved the garage door opener which was clamped onto the sun visor. "Mission accomplished," Sicko said to himself, as he started up the van and hit the button for the garage door to begin opening.

*　*　*

Psycho Twin looked into the sky and automatically became nervous when he saw the sun beginning to rise on the horizon. He checked the time on his watch only to become more worried when the digital face on his stop watch read 6:47 A.M. He knew that his mark would be pulling up any minute now, with his usual briefcase and cup of Starbuck's coffee in hand.

Time and time again, he had watched Mister Beckett walk up to that bank door, set his briefcase down with his right hand, and fumble through his blazer coat for his keys. He knew that Mister Beckett would lock the bank door behind himself and then go straight into the vault to get the cash to load up each teller drawer, along with the money transfer cart known as the "Cash Cow". He also knew that it would be at least 7:45 before the next employee arrived, which gave him ample time to get in and get out with the day's take. His only problem now was his leverage, which just so happened to be the responsibility of his sometimes unpredictable twin brother. Psycho had made up his mind to strike without him if worse came to worse.

The young robber's anxiety was quickly turning into panic when his walkie-talkie beeped at 6:49. It was a relief to hear the voice of his younger brother beam through, "QB to coach. We have an interception. I repeat; we did get the interception, so we are at the fifty-yard line about twenty minutes from the end zone, and both safeties are in position," Sicko proclaimed over the radio.

"Let's go in for this touchdown. Stand by," Psycho replied with a slight tinge of relief in his voice. Everything was now in place and going exactly the way Psycho had planned. At 6:50, he ran across the four-lane highway and positioned himself behind the north wall of the bank in a blind spot behind a neatly-trimmed hedge. He knew he was at a close enough range to where he could reach his victim fast enough to shock him into submission. Psycho pulled the ski mask from his back pocket and slid it on. It was now just a matter of time.

* * *

Sick Twin had abducted his hostages and was barreling down the freeway in record time. Little Johnny had not shut up since the second Sick had tied him up. Connie Beckett tried hard to comfort her only son as the muffled screams from beneath the duct tape caused Sicko to become more upset with every whimper, "Shut dat little crybaby up before I tape his nose up too!" Sicko threatened, visibly shaken by all the pressure he was under.

"He won't stop crying until I take the tape off his mouth," exclaimed the fretful mother.

"Fuck dat shit. If I let you do dat, then the little fucker will really be screamin' my ear off."

Johnny continued his muffled screams as Sicko's patience continued to run thinner.

Connie knew that she had to do something or this lunatic would soon hurt her baby boy. With her hands still tied behind her back, she began unzipping her son's book bag in search of anything she might be able to use in order to cut the duct tape from her wrists and ankles.

As soon as Connie reached into the pocket of little Johnny's book bag, her hands came in contact with something that she wished she would have remembered much earlier. It was her son's cellular phone, the phone she had not wanted to buy him, but Johnny had been so persistent in his begging that she had purchased it against her own discretion. This little cell phone which she had been so adamant about not allowing a nine year old to have was now possibly a lifeline and her only hope of getting her son and herself through this ordeal alive.

With her son still screaming from beneath the duct tape, and her hands tied behind her back, Connie quickly removed the phone from the book bag's pocket and set it on the van floor. She turned around to memorize the way that the buttons were set up on the key pad until she believed that she had it down pat enough to operate the phone with her back turned to it. With her back turned, working strictly from memory and a sense of touch, Connie Beckett pressed the 9-1-1 digits and then the 'TALK' button before covering up the earpiece so that there was no chance of her captor hearing the voice of the emergency operator.

Connie counted silently from one to ten, put her mouth to the phone's receiver, and in a low but insistent and steady voice she began repeating the words, "Help! Me and my son have been kidnapped!"

By this time, Sicko had begun merging over to the off ramp of the freeway. Once he exited the freeway, there was less traffic to drown out the sound of the crying boy in the back of the van, "Shut dat little shit up, now!" Sicko demanded.

"I told you that you have to let me take the tape off of his mouth. That's the only way I can stop him from crying."

"Bitch, just do whatever you gotta do, but I promise you, if dat little woozy keeps on screamin', I'm gonna shut him up myself, and you won't enjoy watching the way I do dat."

Connie explained to her son the magnitude of the situation, "Johnny, settle down now, honey," Connie said in a calm voice. "Mommy's going to take this tape away from your mouth so that you can talk, but you can't talk too loud or the man will get upset. Okay, baby boy?"

Johnny nodded his head to show his mom that he understood.

"This may sting just a little bit, but I will be careful," she promised, as she pulled the tape from her son's lips as carefully as she could with her hands tied behind her back.

Sick Twin made a left turn onto Avalon Boulevard and then a quick right onto Albertoni. As he traveled westbound down Albertoni, the scenery began to look familiar to Connie Beckett. "Guess what, Johnny boy?" Connie said in an attempt to put her son at ease.

"What, Mommy?" the boy asked.

"We are close to Daddy's job, in the city of Gardena," Connie said with her mouth only a few inches away from the cell phone.

"Are we going to see Daddy?"

"Not right now, but we are going to see him later. Okay, honey?"

"Okay, Mommy."

Sicko continued to travel down Albertoni until he reached Figuroa Street, and then he made a right turn.

"This is Figuroa," she snuck in, "but Daddy's bank is on Broadway."

"Okay, that's enough talking," Sicko demanded. "It's quiet time now, gaddammit!"

Sick twin continued northbound down Figuroa until he came to a large building and turned into the parking lot.

"Billy's Easy Storage?" Connie announced in a loud voice. "Why are we going in there?" the scared mother asked with her mouth inches away from the cell phone.

"Stop asking me all deez damn questions, lady," Sicko snapped. "I'll tell you everything you need to know without you asking."

At that moment, Sicko's radio beeped, and his brother's voice came through, "QB, are my safeties in position for the next play?" Psycho inquired.

"Gimme two minutes, coach. I'm almost in position right now, so stand by."

Sicko drove up to a tall wrought iron gate before turning the van off. He removed the keys from the ignition and then walked up to a laser operated scanner and swiped a card past it that he had attached to his keychain. He hurried back to the van as the large gate began to roll open. Sicko proceeded through once the gate had rolled all the way open, and then made a left turn, a quick right, and drove past a series of storage garages on a narrow road until he arrived at garage number 824, and here he stopped.

* * *

Psycho's waiting game lasted less than ten minutes. Like clockwork, Lawrence Beckett drove into the bank's parking lot and pulled right into his usual space at 7:05 in the morning. He got out of his PT Cruiser and began strolling leisurely up to the bank's doors. Once he reached the bank entrance, facing the double doors, the banker set his briefcase down and reached into the right pocket of his suit coat to get his keys.

As soon as Lawrence Beckett inserted his key into the keyhole, before he could turn the key, he was startled by a clicking sound coming from close behind him. He quickly turned around and was blinded by the glare of the infrared beam into his glasses that Psycho Twin was aiming directly between his eyes.

"Now listen up, and listen very closely, Mister Beckett," Psycho Twin announced in a calm and collected but firm voice. "First of all, take your hand off that key right now, 'cause I know that once you unlock that door, you have exactly sixty seconds to punch in your security code on the keypad inside the bank before the cops are alerted to come out."

Lawrence Beckett followed the young bandit's orders, leaving his keys dangling from the lock. Mister Beckett then put his hands above his head and began speaking in a shaky tone, "Please don't shoot me, man. I'll give you whatever you want, and I promise you, I won't try anything."

"Dat's real good to hear," Psycho replied, "but I'm pretty sure dat you would try somethin' stupit, being the big shot veteran banker that you are. I'm sure you know all da tricks of the trade, so I had to put a little insurance on this gig."

Mister Beckett had no idea what the robber was talking about, therefore, he just stared at the ski masked criminal with a confused look on his face.

* * *

When Connie's kidnapper had gotten out of the van to open up the storage garage, she managed to plead a few more words into the cell phone and then sneak it back into little Johnny's book bag without being detected. To the anguish of his hostages, Sick Twin carefully backed the U-Haul van into the empty storage garage.

"Why are you taking us into this garage?" Connie inquired, visibly petrified about having been taken to the second location.

Once Sicko backed all the way into the garage, he once again exited the van. The young gangster walked up to the garage door and pulled it down, closing it from the inside. He then climbed back into the van with his hostages.

"Please don't hurt my son," the woman begged, realizing that it was now just her and her son in the seclusion of this dark garage. "You can do whatever you want with me, and I mean *whatever*, but please just leave my son alone."

"Shuddup, lady," Sicko demanded while pulling a piece of folded paper from his back pocket, "This ain't even about you." He turned on the van's overhead map light and then crawled into the back of the van with his walkie-talkie and the piece of paper he had removed from his pocket. "Now, as soon as I tell you to, you're gonna read the words on this paper exactly how it's writted down. If you add one little word or leave any word out, I promise you the inside of this garage is the last thing you and your baby boy will ever see."

Connie scanned the paper, studying its contents carefully. She then agreed to the bandit's terms.

* * *

Psycho held Lawrence Beckett at gunpoint for only thirty seconds before his radio beeped. With his chrome .45 still pointed at his latest victim, Psycho Twin used his left hand to retrieve the walkie-talkie from his black, hooded sweatshirt. He was happy to hear his brother's voice come through.

"We have arrived at the five yard line, coach. I repeat; we have arrived at the five yard line. It's third and goal, over."

"Cue 'em in, QB," Psycho replied. He then pointed his walkie-talkie at his victim, along with his pistol.

Terror swept through Lawrence Beckett's body like wildfire. He felt his knees begin to give out when he came face to face with his worst fear.

"Lawrence, this is your wife," Psycho told him.

Connie's voice began to transmit through the walkie-talkie's speaker, "Please give him whatever he wants, and do not try anything slick or the next time you see me and Johnny, it will be at the morgue."

Lawrence Beckett could hear the fear in his wife's voice, causing him to feel more and more helpless with every word.

She continued, "Please don't get us killed. We don't want to die. I love you."

"I love you and Johnny too, honey. It's going to be okay. I promise!" Lawrence Beckett yelled toward the walkie-talkie which Psycho had extended in his direction.

"She can't hear you unless I press this here button, Larry, and there ain't no reason for me to do dat 'cause you'll be talkin' to her face ta face very soon 'cause you ain't gonna gimme no problems, now is ya?"

The banker found himself unable to talk through the lump in his throat. He simply nodded his head in agreement as he struggled to keep the tears in his eyes at bay. Psycho clipped his walkie-talkie back onto his belt and began explaining in detail everything Mister Beckett needed to do to ensure the safety of himself and his family.

* * *

Back at the storage garage, Johnny had begun crying again after hearing his mother read the short note over the walkie-talkie. "Mommy, what is the morgue?" the nine year old asked as he wept. "Is he going to kill us, Mommy?"

Connie Beckett tried hard to comfort her son as she sat in the back of the van still bound with duct tape and wearing nothing more than her pink bra and panties with the little red hearts on them.

Sick Twin could feel the bulge in his pants rise every time he glanced into the back of the van. Sicko began to rationalize in his mind all the reasons why raping his pretty little White hostage would be okay. After all, up to this point he had completed every task required of him with flying colors. She had already read the note to her husband, so he really had no more need for her aside from keeping her for collateral reasons, and he had that part under control as well. Besides, she probably wanted it anyway. That's why she kept saying that he could do anything he wanted to do to her. She was practically begging for it. Her old White husband wasn't satisfying her in the bedroom. She needed some real dick in her life. The only problem was her little crybaby son. Sick Twin climbed into the back of the van and began untaping the little boy's hands from the dolly.

115

"What are you doing?" Connie inquired.

Sicko opened the van's rear doors and began dragging the screaming child out of the van.

"Where are you going with him?" Connie cried, as she attempted to use her body to block the hoodlum from taking her son.

"I'm about to take you up on your offer to do *anything* I want with you. Don't worry; little Johnny will be aight. I just need the kid to wait outside while me and his mommy do some grownup thangs inside this van."

"Mommy, please don't let him take me," Johnny begged.

"It's going to be okay, honey. Mommy just needs to talk to the man in private, so you just have to wait outside for a few minutes, okay?" Connie said in a shaky voice as the tears began to pour down her face.

Sick Twin pulled the boy from the van and taped him to the front bumper so that he would not be able to witness what was about to happen to his mother. Before Sicko could re-enter the van, he paused for a second when he heard the sound of a helicopter hovering close overhead. He stood there for a moment in deep concentration before dismissing the thought. "There ain't no way in hell," Sicko said to himself as he climbed back into the van.

* * *

Psycho Twin could not believe how smoothly everything was going. Not even Lil Ricky had ever carried out a heist of this magnitude. Had Rick Rock stuck with the team, this would have been his first time seeing the inside of a bank vault. Instead, Psycho Twin was handling the hit all by himself, and everything was going exactly the way he had pictured it, as he loaded stack after stack of cash into the Brinks Armored Transfer money bag he had retrieved from inside the vault. He had planned on dumping his victim's briefcase out and using it to carry his loot, but the cash sack had proved to be more convenient.

"Not those. Leave those stacks alone," Lawrence Beckett said, as he watched the young bandit's every move.

Psycho Twin looked at the banker as if he were insane. "What the hell you mean? Leave these stacks alone? They look just as good as all the rest to me."

"Yeah, that's just the thing," Lawrence Beckett answered. "They have the same Ben Franklins printed on them, and they are just as green as the rest with the same money wrappers around them, but the difference is that as soon as you leave the parking lot, they will explode with ink bombs and destroy all the money in your bag."

"Wow!" Psycho responded. "I'm surprised you warned me about dat. You is a smart man."

"I love my family," Mister Beckett proclaimed with a look of disdain in his eyes. "Go for those right there," the banker suggested while pointing at a particular shelf. Psycho quickly followed his advice and continued stuffing cash into his sack until there was no room left. He then placed the bag's strap over his shoulder and drew his pistol, pointing it directly at the banker.

"Sorry, my friend, but your services are no longer needed," Psycho announced with a crooked smile on his face. "Now lay face down on the floor," the young bandit demanded.

Mister Beckett cooperated without hesitation, realizing that he had reached the end of the road. There was nothing short of a miracle that could save his life now. As he stared at the floor beneath him, Lawrence Beckett prayed to God that the fate of his wife and son would somehow turn out better than his. His only hope now was that his execution would be fast and painless.

As the banker lay on the floor with his eyes closed tight, anticipating the inevitable gunshot that would end his life, he cringed when he heard the loud bang. Lawrence Beckett looked up to find that the loud noise was not the gunshot which he had braced himself for, but the sound of the vault door slamming shut. The young thug had exited the vault and locked him in. "He didn't kill me," the banker reassured himself as he sat on the floor in disbelief. "I'm alive."

* * *

Sick Twin's penis was fully erect by the time he crawled back
into the van. Just the thought of penetrating the helpless White
suburban housewife was enough to make the pre-cum begin to drip
from the head of his sex organ. Once inside the van, he removed
the pistol from his waistband, placed it on the floor behind him, and
then untaped the woman's wrists.

"You gonna wanna squeeze the hell outa me once I get all dis
up inside of you. Just please don't dig your fingernails into my
back," the cocky young criminal said. He unsnapped his victim's
bra and pulled it off, revealing her perky C-cup breasts. The hostage
shuddered as her kidnapper put her pink nipples into his mouth one
at a time until they became stimulated to the point of hardness.

"You like that, don't you?" Sicko asked as he began to pull her
pink, heart-covered panties down. "Ooh… I love it when a woman
leaves a little hair on the monkey," Sicko announced, as he stared at
his victim's pubic area in awe. He grabbed her legs and attempted to
spread them apart but was met with resistance.

"Please don't rape me. I have a husband who loves me. Please,"
the woman begged while looking deep into her tormentor's eyes in
search of the smallest trace of sympathy.

"Bitch, if you don't open your legs right this second, I'm going
to make you watch me choke your baby boy until his fuckin' eyes
pop out," Sicko threatened, visibly upset by his victim's resistance.

Connie Beckett cooperated, opening her legs wide, while closing
her eyes tight and attempting to close her mind and emotions along
with them. With his middle and index fingers, Sicko Twin spread
open Connie's pussy lips to reveal the hot, pink flesh inside of
her. He began massaging her clitoris with his fingers, giving her a
sensation that she had never experienced before from her husband.
The helpless suburban woman tried hard to fight the feeling, but her
wetness began to flow even though she attempted to imagine that
she was somewhere else. At work, at home washing dishes, in hell,
anywhere besides the back of this van being pleasured by this gang
banger while her son lay on the ground tied to the bumper.

Sick Twin removed his hand from her vagina, causing Connie to
open her eyes for a moment to see what he was up to. The young thug
began unbuttoning his pants as his victim watched in terror. He pulled

his khaki pants down along with his boxer underwear, allowing his long, rock-hard penis to pop up and stand at attention. Connie's eyes opened wide as she stared in utter shock at Sicko's thick, firm dick.

"Yeah, girl," Sicko said with an evil grin. "I bet you ain't neva seen one like dis up close, have ya?" He began scooting closer to his victim, and with his hardened penis in his hand, he began rubbing it against Connie's vagina which was too tight for him to penetrate. He began kissing on her neck while speaking softly into her ear, telling her what he was about to do to her. Connie Beckett felt herself begin to get sick to her stomach when Sicko once again began trying to shove himself inside of her. He barely managed to force the head of his dick in when his walkie-talkie beeped.

"Dayummm!" Sick Twin exclaimed, as his brother's voice came through the radio.

"QB, it's fourth and goal, and I'm comin' in for the touchdown. Are you ready to break this huddle?"

Before Sicko could reach into the front seat to answer his radio, in an instant, the garage lit up bright with sunlight. He heard the young boy scream, "He's got my Mommy in that van!"

Sicko struggled to pull his pants up and retrieve his pistol, but it was too late. The van's back doors swung open and the young bandit quickly came face to face with the service pistols of two different cops.

"Freeze!" both of the officers screamed in unison. One of the officers immediately grabbed the pistol from the floor of the van.

Sick Twin snatched his naked hostage up into a choke hold and started yelling at the cops, "I'll break dis bitch's neck. I swear I will," the young criminal threatened, as he watched a dozen officers storm into the storage garage and surround the van. Both of the van's front doors flew open as Sicko looked around, darting his head back and forth in a panic.

"Close the motha fuckin' doors or I will kill dis bitch. I ain't playin' wit you pigs."

All at once, Sicko felt a sharp pang in the back of his neck and then in his side. His body shook violently as the two police officers pumped him full of electricity from two different taser guns.

* * *

119

Psycho Twin automatically knew that something had gone wrong when his twin brother failed to respond on his walkie-talkie. The two brothers had already agreed to assume the worst if this situation should arise. Instead of making the left turn onto Figuroa to meet his brother, Psycho continued straight down Rosecrans to the 110 Freeway where he entered onto the northbound ramp. Although Psycho knew in his heart that his brother had run into trouble, he still kept his walkie-talkie on in hopes that Sicko would beam through and say that he was just taking a leak or something of that nature.

* * *

It took Lawrence Beckett approximately twenty seconds to get his faculties together before he stood to his feet and headed straight for the panic button, which he would have tripped much earlier had his family not been in danger. He knew that it would be no more than five minutes before the cops arrived with the vault key and combination to let him out.

It took only three and a half minutes before Lawrence Beckett heard some activity outside the vault. A minute later, the vault door swung open and Mister Beckett was met by several LA County Sheriff's deputies with their guns drawn.

"I'm the manager of this bank. They have my family. They kidnapped my wife and my son."

"Calm down, Mister Beckett," the White, dark-haired cop said while returning his pistol to its holster. "Your wife and your boy are safe. They are headed to the hospital as we speak," the deputy assured him.

"Now what happened here?" inquired a sergeant who had just arrived on the scene, noticing that there was cash all over the vault's floor.

"What do you think happened here? I've been robbed," Mister Beckett responded.

"What does our suspect look like?" the tubby, little redneck sergeant asked. "What kind of car is he in? Did you get a look at it?"

Lawrence Beckett began to turn red in the face, feeling bombarded by the rapid manner in which the pushy sergeant was firing questions at him. "Look, the guy was wearing a ski mask, plus long sleeves and gloves, but he was about five foot eight and weighed about one hundred and eighty pounds. I'm pretty sure he was African-American."

The sergeant stared at Mister Beckett inquisitively, "Now how would you know that we're dealing with an African-American man, sir, if the guy had on a ski mask and—"

"That doesn't matter, sergeant," Mister Beckett replied. "What matters is the robber is somewhere, not very far from here, with a sack full of cash containing at least two tracers."

"Oh shit! Well why didn't you tell us that a long time ago?" the redneck sergeant inquired. "Are you sure he has the cash with the tracers in it?"

"Yes, I'm sure. I told him which stacks to grab."

The sergeant looked at Lawrence Beckett as if he did not believe him. "Well... if he let *you* tell him which stacks to grab, he ain't the brightest bulb in the box, now is he?"

Mister Beckett did not entertain the question with an answer, "You have to call our security company, and they will give you the exact location of our robber, or at least our bag of money."

* * *

Psycho Twin had just transferred onto the 105 Freeway when he noticed the helicopter in the sky hovering over his rental car. "Oh shit!" Psycho exclaimed before he began praying, "Lord *please* don't let them be lookin' for me. Please, God, I promise I won't neva rob nobody else as long as I live. Please, in Jesus name, please!"

After driving for about a quarter mile, Psycho realized that his prayer would go unanswered, when he saw the blue and red flashing lights of several police vehicles approaching quickly from behind. As he came closer to the Central Boulevard off ramp, Psycho could see the Nickerson Gardens housing projects beneath him in the distance from the freeway.

"So close, yet so far away," Psycho said to himself, as the police cruisers arrived at a close enough distance to where he could hear an officer shouting commands from over his loudspeaker.

"Driver, stop your vehicle!"

Psycho knew that he was about to go to prison for a long time. He began thinking about his girlfriend and his baby boy, hating himself for the life he had chosen to live.

"Driver, pull over! There is nowhere to run!" came the voice from over the loudspeaker.

Just then, Psycho had a thought. He pressed his foot all the way down on the gas pedal and then stuck his hand out of the window high into the air with his middle finger extended. He pushed the play button on his radio, turned the volume up to full blast, and then lit up a cigarette as the voice of Tupac Shakur roared from the speakers, "*I won't deny it. I'm a straight rider. You don't wanna fuck with me . . .*" proclaimed the late, great Tupac, as Psycho Twin exited the freeway on Central Boulevard and made a left turn.

With the fleet of police cars still following close behind, along with the police helicopter, now joined by two news helicopters, Psycho Twin ran through the light on Imperial Boulevard, made a right turn on 114th where he tossed his cigarette out the window, and headed straight into the projects. Psycho knew this would be the last time for at least a decade that he would see the neighborhood where he was raised.

The scene in the projects was the same as always. Crack heads and prostitutes were walking up and down the streets in search of their next hit. Gang bangers dressed in bright red clothing huddled up on every corner, some involved in large dice games, some competing for the next marijuana or crack sale, and others just standing around drinking from paper-bag-covered bottles.

The loud sound of sirens and helicopters echoed through the projects, as the police cars followed closely behind Psycho. He made a quick right and then a left onto 115th Street where the project unit that he and his twin brother had lived in for so many years was located.

Psycho reached into his backseat and grabbed the loot-filled bag as he approached a pack of kids playing basketball in the middle of the street. The young project-bred gang banger pulled up right next to the children and began tearing the money wrappers off of the cash stacks and slinging one hundred dollar bills out the car window.

The kids immediately swarmed the cash while the police yelled over their loudspeakers, "Touch that money and you will be arrested. I repeat; if you take any of that money, you *will* go to jail!"

The children ignored the cop's threats and continued to scoop up the cash as others ran from all over the street in order to get in on the action.

When Psycho came to the end of 115th Street, he made a left turn onto Success Street and continued slinging cash to everyone in the vicinity. By the time he pulled his vehicle over, Psycho had managed to drive down every street on the dark side of the projects, tossing out cash to any and every person he saw. Once the young gangster had thrown out every single bill in the sack, he pulled to the side of the road and got out of the car with his hands up.

Chapter 26

At 9:00 A.M., there was a knock on the door of unit 169 in the Nickerson Gardens projects. The scene on the inside of the old black and white building was the same as it usually was this early in the day. Most of the young whores were still sound asleep, while a few primped themselves, gossiped over their cellular phones, or both.

All of the young girls knew the schedules of their johns better than the johns themselves did. Traffic usually began flowing in and out around lunchtime and flowed steadily until 6:00 P.M. when most of the tricks were due home from work. They would start to come in again at about 8:00 P.M., after a little bit of quality time with their families.

Stormy had not managed to get a wink of sleep since her heated conversation with Big Mama the day before. She had been up all night pacing back and forth in a panic while her roommate tried her best to put the rookie's mind at ease, "Calm down, bitch. It's gonna be okay. We can just do the same shit we did last time, remember?"

Stormy had been in this situation once before when Diamond himself had personally referred a client and sent him her way with the promise of some brand-new White flesh. When the man arrived asking for Stormy, he had been intercepted by a girl named Luscious. The young girl's name was an understatement when compared to the beauty that the nineteen-year-old professional possessed. As a mulatto with dyed blonde hair, she was the closest thing to White in the house besides Stormy herself. The only thing that could reveal the teenage girl's true ethnicity was the semi-nappy hairs which grew in her underarms and pubic area, however, Luscious kept a fresh Brazilian wax in those spots at all times.

When the trick asked for Stormy, Luscious had claimed to be her and led him to an upstairs room, where, with a big smile on his face, the trick had begun undressing, revealing a fat belly and breasts almost as large as the girl who he was preparing to mount. He was very dark-skinned with long, greasy Jerry curls.

"Gurrrl, I'm 'bout to tear da lining out of that sweet little White pussy!" the man shouted, right as he was dropping his drawers. Luscious' eyes opened wide, and she could not help but let out a small snicker when she caught a glimpse of her customer's penis, or lack thereof, which appeared to be about two inches of uncircumcised foreskin.

"Damn, big daddy, I don't know if I can handle all a dat. You know I'm new at this." The girl had managed to disguise her brief laughter as an amatory giggle. She undressed in front of the trick, causing his two inches to become erect before pushing him down onto the bed. "Oooh, I can't wait to feel you deep inside of me, daddy," she had proclaimed while posturing her body into a position where she could crawl on top of her customer in order to ride him.

She could smell the cigar smoke emitting from his disgusting body as she crawled closer. Luscious had almost managed to outfox the trick, when, all at once, the expression on his face changed from that of pure bliss to one of absolute fury, "Hole on, bitch," the john said while staring at the tattoos of tiny paw prints which ran up Lucious' inner thigh. "Diamond told me you had a smooth body like a virgin and didn't have no tattoos or stretch marks or no scars."

Luscious had attempted to talk her way out of the situation by saying that maybe Diamond had simply overlooked the tattoos, but the trick slapped her across the face and pushed her off of him, "I'm about to get to the bottom of this shit," the rotund trick promised. "I'm the wrong nigga to be tryin' to play like this here."

Lucious listened to the trick while he complained and made threats. At the same time, she had been watching the bedroom door open behind him as Stormy and her roommate tiptoed in.

"Well, I guess we'll just have to make this up to you then, big daddy," Lucious said while gesturing toward the new arrivals. Stormy had begun stripping as she walked toward the trick, leaving a trail of clothes behind. She was down to her bra and panties by the time she got close enough to touch the blob of a man who wanted a young White girl so bad.

"You ever been involved in a foursome?" Stormy asked before dropping to her knees and gripping the trick's small organ between her thumb and index finger. She began moving her lips closer to the man's penis until she was close enough for him to feel the warmth of her breath.

"Yeah, baby, that's what I'm talkin' 'bout," the man said while leaning back in anticipation of Stormy's warm lips on his dick.

All at once, he saw a bright flash of light. He looked up in time to see the girl who had entered with Stormy run out of the room with a disposable camera in her hand.

"Bitch! Come back here with that goddamn camera!" the trick yelled as he reached desperately for his pants, but it was too late, "What the hell kinda game is you hoes playin' up in here?" the man asked while pulling the cell phone from his pants pocket. "I'm callin' Diamond right this minute."

"I think you betta think twice before you do that, Reverend Hawkins," Luscious had said, while pushing the man's hand down with the phone in it. She saw the surprise in the preacher's eyes even more then when he had seen the flash from the camera. Luscious had began rolling her eyes and neck and snapping her fingers as she spoke, "Now I would be willing to bet my ass that Sista Hawkins and the rest of the congregation over at Double Rock Baptist Church of Compton won't be at all too pleased when they see the picture of they husband and pastor about to get his itty-bitty, teensy weeny wienie sucked on by this underage White girl. What do you think, *Reverend?*"

The girls had never seen the preacher at the house again after that ordeal.

Today was different. Stormy explained to her roommate how tired she was of sneaking around and using all the other girls to help her weasel out of her duties as a resident in the house. She expressed her appreciation of the offer and all the trouble they had gone through for her up to this point, but she had made up her mind, and she was going to begin earning her keep the same way as the rest of the girls. No matter who the trick was that Big Mama sent over, no matter how repulsive he was, no matter how bad he smelled, Stormy made up her mind to have sex with him, and there was no turning back.

When Stormy heard the 9:00 A.M. knock on her door, she was fresh out of the bathtub. She looked beautiful in a tight pair of Apple Bottom jeans and a V-neck shirt which complimented her smooth cleavage. She wore just a tad of pink lipstick to enhance the fullness of her lips, along with a dash of Trezor perfume spritzed onto her neck.

"I'll get it!" the teenage girl yelled as she headed down the stairs en route to the front door. She looked out the peephole before opening the door as she had been taught from her first day in the house in order to avoid opening the door for any cop who was not a known customer. Stormy stared through the peephole and was surprised to see a handsome, young Black man standing on the porch who appeared to be her age or at most a year older.

A smile spread over the young girl's face, while in the back of her mind she was praying that this was the customer who Big Mama had sent her way. She shook it off, telling herself that it was too good to be true. There was no way that her first official trick could be a man who she found this attractive. No — attractive was not the word, this damn fine. Things like that just did not happen to her. With her luck, this was someone who had wandered to the wrong apartment.

The teenage girl opened the door just wide enough to poke her head out, "Yes?" the young girl asked after answering the door.

"Hi, is Stormy in?"

Chapter 27

"**S**ince when did you start trickin', Lil Ricky?" Luscious asked, walking from the kitchen with a bowl of Cap'n Crunch cereal just in time to see the teenage boy step through the front door.

"Awww, girl, you know I ain't neva no trick. I'm just doin' Big Mama a favor; that's all," the young gangster responded with an uncomfortable smile on his face, revealing perfect, white teeth. Stormy found herself infatuated with the presence of her visitor. Lil Ricky walked with his head held high and an air of confidence about himself that was not arrogant. She found herself admiring his dress code. He wore a pair of sharply-creased black 501 Levi jeans with a silver and black Darren McFadden Raiders jersey, along with a black pair of 310 sneakers on his feet. Around his neck, Stormy could see the remnants of a modest-sized Rolex chain which disappeared under his jersey. She could smell the slight scent of Polo Sport Cologne on him, one of her favorite men's fragrances. Everything about him was simple yet showed a masculine sense of style, which in Stormy's opinion was exactly the way a man was supposed to be.

"So, you must be Stormy," Lil Ricky proclaimed after a long moment of silence.

"Yeah, Stormy is me. I mean, yes, I'm her," she replied clumsily.

After another moment of awkward silence, it became apparent to Luscious that these two were both like fish out of water in this environment.

"Why don't y'all go get something to eat or something?" Luscious suggested.

"Yeah, yeah, food, eat... that sounds good to me. How 'bout you?" Lil Ricky inquired, feeling as though he had just been thrown a lifeline.

Stormy hesitated for a brief moment before responding, "Well, sure, I could go for some breakfast right now, but I don't think I should, because Big Mama told me—"

"Awww, girl, that's my auntie you're talkin' about," Lil Ricky interrupted. "She ain't trippin'. Let's get up outta here," the handsome young gangster commanded before making a U-turn and heading straight back out the door.

Once Lil Ricky had walked out of the house, the two girls just stared at one another with smiles on their faces as if they could read each other's minds.

"Gurrrl..." Luscious said, "you betta go 'head wit yo bad self."

Stormy giggled as she walked out of the house, feeling like she had just been picked up by her prom date. Once she made it out of the house, Stormy spotted Lil Ricky. The scene reminded her of something right out of a rap video as Lil Ricky leaned against his big, silver Yukon Denali SUV with the big, shiny twenty-six inch rims on it in this project parking lot.

Like a real gentleman, he opened the passenger-side door allowing Stormy to get in the vehicle first. For a brief moment, the teenage girl forgot about her situation and felt as if she were a prize to be won rather than a whore to be bought.

She jumped with surprise when Lil Ricky turned on his truck's ignition and Fifty Cent came roaring through every tweeter, woofer, and six by nine in the truck, *"I got a fully loaded clip. I be on that shit. I got, I got a fully loaded clip,"* came Fifty's voice as the bass from the system pounded. Lil Ricky quickly turned the radio down and apologized to his date for startling her. He even allowed her to flip through his CD case and pick out what she wanted to hear. Stormy was surprised and impressed with Lil Ricky's CD collection, which held some of her favorite CDs by some of her favorite artists. She flipped from Keshia Cole to Erykah Badu, past Ray J and Alicia Keys. *The boy's got some good taste*, Stormy thought to herself as she continued to thumb through his case. She ended up settling on Fantasia's self titled sophomore CD, because she knew that the themes of her songs would be perfect for the moment.

The first song in particular was a perfect testament to the way she was feeling. She hit the PLAY button and the soulful voice of Fantasia began to flow through the crystal clear sound system, "*I need a hood boy, yeah, yeah, I need a hood boy*" sang, Fantasia. Stormy sang along under her breath as they drove out of the parking lot.

For a moment, Lil Ricky listened intently as she sang, and then he complimented her on her voice, giving her the confidence to sing a little bit louder. By the time the next song came on, although a bit more mellow, it again expressed how Stormy was feeling at the present moment. She sang the song out loud to Rick Rock word for word, "*You're always on my mind. When you come around I get shy. When I see you, when I see you.*"

Song after song came on as the two teenagers loosened up and became more comfortable in each other's company. Lil Ricky informed Stormy that she had selected his favorite CD in the collection.

Before she knew it, they were on the freeway and Stormy did not bother to ask where they were going, and as long as she was with the handsome young man, she did not care. Lil Ricky headed east down the 105 Freeway until it came to an end.

Stormy looked out the window to see a massive 747 jet flying in the sky with its landing gear out. It seemed as if the plane was close enough for her to reach out and touch as it disappeared behind a building.

Lil Ricky kept on straight until Stormy spotted sailboats floating on the horizon and getting closer as Lil Ricky navigated his SUV. It seemed as if they were headed right into the Pacific Ocean. Lil Ricky made a left turn onto Pacific Coast Highway and then drove southbound down the coastline. After driving for a quarter of a mile with the beach by his side, Lil Ricky opened his ashtray and pulled out a perfectly-rolled Philly blunt.

"What is *that?*" Stormy asked with a curious look on her face.

"It ain't nothing but a cigar, Lil mama. Relax," the young thug answered with a wry smile on his face.

Once he lit the blunt, Stormy quickly realized that this was not the average cigar. She twisted up her nose and began fanning the smoke away with her hand. "What kind of cigar is that?" Stormy asked, already knowing the answer to her question.

"Oh, this right here is the love of my life. Her name is Purple Cativa," Lil Ricky answered, as the smoke drifted from his nose and mouth. Stormy had been around marijuana a few times before but had always been afraid to try it. After a few long drags, Lil Ricky attempted to pass the cannabis-filled cigar to Stormy.

"Oh, I'm okay right now," Stormy said nervously.

"Gurrrl... you ain't neva hit no weed before, have you?" Lil Ricky asked, visibly high off the blunt.

Stormy found her infatuation growing with every passing second as her date sat there with a dufus smile on his face and his eyes as tight as a Chinaman's from the effects of the marijuana.

"I *have* smoked that stuff before," Stormy blurted, realizing how naïve she sounded only after the words had come off of her lips.

"I *have* smoked that stuff before," Lil Ricky mocked in the same valley girl manner that Stormy had spoken, "Go 'head; just try it one time," Lil Ricky urged, flicking the ashes in the ashtray and then extending the cigar back in Stormy's direction.

"No, I'm okay," she insisted. "As a matter of fact, should you even be driving in this condition?" Stormy asked.

"Pleeeze?" Lil Ricky begged, ignoring her question while still holding the blunt up to her face.

"Oh, alright, but just one time," and Stormy broke down to peer pressure and took the cigar from Lil Ricky's grasp.

"You better hit it hard, too, and hold in the smoke as long as you can," Rick Rock instructed.

"Boy, I know how to smoke bud," Stormy lied with a smile on her face, as she put the blunt to her lips. She took a deep pull as Lil Ricky had instructed. She managed to hold the smoke in for ten seconds, before, all at once, she began coughing and choking uncontrollably.

"Now dat's da bidness!" Rick Rock laughed, snatching the blunt back from Stormy as she hacked nonstop.

Lil Ricky continued cruising down Pacific Coast Highway, enjoying his blunt as Stormy continued coughing. After a ten mile trip, they drove up to the Redondo Beach Pier, and Lil Ricky pulled into a space with a parking meter. In front of them was a sandy, white beach where children and adults were running around. Some built sandcastles while others sunbathed or caught waves on their surfboards and boogie boards.

Stormy was still coughing so hard that Rick Rock began to worry about her, "Damn, girl, I shoulda warned you what dat chronic can do," Lil Ricky said, as he began patting the teenage girl on her back. "I know exactly what you need right now," the young gangster announced while opening up his truck's driver-side door. He headed to the back of the vehicle, opened the rear door, picked up a brown paper bag from the floor, and then headed back to the front seat. Lil Ricky pulled a bottle of Hennessey out of the bag along with a plastic cup. He quickly opened the bottle and filled up the cup. Still choking uncontrollably, Stormy did not realize what Lil Ricky was doing until he handed her the cup.

"Drink this down; hurry up," Rick Rock demanded with such a sense of urgency that Stormy rushed to down the contents of the cup. She drank the cognac so swiftly that she did not realize she was drinking alcohol until it was time for her to breath out. Her eyes instantly opened wide and she began sucking and blowing air in and out of her mouth as if she had just swallowed a flaming-hot jalapeno pepper.

"Boy, what are you trying to do, kill me?" Stormy asked, barely able to speak.

"Well, you ain't coughin' no mo, is ya?" Rick Rock responded with a serious expression on his face.

Stormy could not believe the audacity of the teenager and immediately became upset by his little trick. It was time to give this jerk a piece of her mind. She turned to Rick Rock with an ugly frown on her face and looked him right in his eyes to let him know that she meant business. Never afraid of a good fight, Lil Ricky glanced back at her with an equally challenging glare.

Stormy was not able to get three words out of her mouth before she busted out laughing. The effects of the herb and cognac both hit her at the same time, and now she was laughing so hard that tears began to flow from her eyes. Her laughter was so cute to Lil Ricky that he found himself beginning to chuckle from the contagious mood of his newfound friend.

Lil Ricky turned on the air conditioner and changed the CD, turning on E-40, an artist who he loved to smoke weed to because of his stimulating lyrical content and creativity. For twenty minutes, the two teenagers just laughed and joked while clowning around and dancing to the music.

"Aight, now let's go get something to eat," Rick Rock announced.

"Yeah, I got the munchies. Where we eatin' at?" Stormy asked with a smile, feeling loose and liberated by the weed and alcohol.

"Right there," Lil Ricky responded, pointing to the El Torrito Mexican Restaurant & Cantina built right over the water.

The two of them made their way onto the pier and into the restaurant, where they were escorted to a table overlooking the beach. Lil Ricky started off by ordering a couple of cocktails. He ordered an "Adios Motherfucker" for himself and a "Sex On The Beach" for his date, winking at her after he ordered the drink. This caused another round of laughter as the two red-eyed teenagers sat and joked like a pair of buffoons.

Over brunch, the conversation became a bit more serious as Stormy told Lil Ricky of her dreams and aspirations. She also told him about the events that had taken place to land her in the projects whorehouse. Stormy even reminded Rick Rock of what he had said earlier that day about doing Big Mama a favor. He told her that he was not supposed to reveal that information but explained that Big Mama had asked him to help break in one of the new girls who was having trouble getting started. Big Mama told him that his uncle had tried but that the girl had not caught on as they usually did after a session with Diamond.

They laughed and joked about how Stormy had managed to duck and dodge her way out of turning a single trick after staying in the house for weeks. Lil Ricky was finding that he liked everything about the young girl, from her pretty smile to her quiet feminine characteristics and ladylike mannerisms. She was also drop-dead gorgeous and came from a world that Rick Rock had never tapped into, the suburbs. He had been with White girls before, but they were all the ghetto type. Stormy was different, and in Lil Ricky's opinion, she belonged nowhere near his uncle's whore stable.

Once they finished eating, the two teenagers went for a walk along the pier and continued talking. It was Stormy who was doing all the talking, still under the influence of the potent substances that Rick Rock had introduced her to.

Lil Ricky listened closely to every word that the young girl spoke, offering just enough feedback to keep her talking. He knew that she was telling the truth from the way her words flowed, and he also knew that she was under the influence of the two strongest truth serums known in the ghetto.

Stormy told him how she had grown up singing and how her parents did not like her singing R&B and other forms of African-American music. She also came clean to Lil Ricky about the only two sexual partners she'd ever had, one of them unfortunately being his uncle. By the time they finished talking, Stormy had unknowingly told the young gangster her entire life story. Lil Ricky made his mind up that he would soon become part of that story.

Chapter 28

When the ringing of the cordless phone on the stand next to Curtiss Bookman's bed awakened him at 4:30 in the morning, he was not surprised. In fact, today Bookman was relieved by the ring and anxious to pick up the phone and press the talk button.

"You sure do operate during some strange hours," Bookman said into his cordless phone.

"Well, you know what they say about the early bird, sergeant," the man responded in his heavy Asian accent.

"And I'm guessing that I'm the worm, huh?" Bookman inquired.

"Well, sergeant, I never thought of it that way; however, I guess you *would* be considered such a creature in this little relationship we have developed," the voice answered. "So what dirt have you managed to dig up for me, Mister Worm?"

"Look, man," Bookman responded forcefully, "I got the shit you asked me for, but how do I know that once I put my ass on the line and give it to you that you're gonna give me that master tape?"

"Well, sergeant, that's where the trust comes into play."

"How in hell do you expect me to trust a man I've never seen in my life? A man whose name I don't even know?"

"Well, as I see it, sergeant, you have two choices here," said the Asian man. "You can trust me and believe that maybe, just maybe, I will surrender this tape to you once you have completed everything I've asked of you, or — you can choose the alternative and possibly wind up in prison for the remainder of your life."

Bookman felt helpless. He began to contemplate, *I could skip out of the country, maybe to Belize or some other nonextraditing Third World country. After all, how many more fiery hoops will this man, this voice at the other end of the phone, have me jump through before I'm safe?*

After a few moments of deep thought, Bookman made his mind up, and he asked, "Where do you want me to deliver the goods?"

The sergeant wrote down the location to where the items he had lifted from the evidence locker were to be delivered.

Before Bookman could hang up the phone, the voice at the other end gave him another assignment. This new task made the first one look like a walk in the park and was met with the utmost resistance by the sergeant, however, after a few more threats, Bookman reluctantly accepted the challenge with a promise from the mystery man that this would be the last mission he would have to complete.

Chapter 29

Gordo awoke in high spirits. Although the past few months had proven to be catastrophic for the street don, he had been filled with a new sense of hope from the conversation he had engaged in with Sergeant Bookman. To have the crooked *negro policia* on his team, no matter how dishonorable a maneuver it was, could definitely put him back on top in the nick of time. After all, everything was fair in love and war. His old friend Diamond had proven this to him months earlier with the failed attempt on his life and the slaughter of his baby brother and his three little homeboys.

This effort by Diamond had managed to, at best, cripple the *Vatos Locos* gang and, at worse, threaten the gang's very existence. In a four-month period, Gordo had witnessed his *varrio* dwindle from a flourishing street empire to a pack of small-time thugs barely surviving. On top of all that, he was in the middle of a bloody war, and even though the casualties were just about even, the fact that the Bounty Hunters had far more soldiers on the battlefield than the *Vatos Locos Muchachos* placed the *Vatos Locos* on the losing end of the street war. Something had to be done quickly to save his gang from extinction. Diamond had initiated the bloodshed; therefore, a truce was not an option. Gordo needed nothing short of absolute victory, and the street legend was fully prepared to do whatever it took to reach that goal.

Today was the day he was to meet with Sergeant Bookman. They had originally planned to meet up at a restaurant in Long Beach, but Gordo had received a late call from Bookman changing the time and location of their rendezvous.

Gordo exited the 101 Freeway on Lacienaga and made a right turn. He drove northbound for about five miles before he spotted the big sign that Bookman had told him to look for. When Gordo saw the sign, which read, 'The Stinking Rose', he turned into the parking lot and got out of his car, throwing the valet his keys.

When Gordo entered the restaurant, he felt underdressed upon seeing most of the men and women in the highbrow Italian restaurant dressed in formal attire. In the foyer, he was met by Bookman who alerted the attractive young hostess that his party had arrived. They were escorted to a table in the middle of the dining room and then seated.

"Damn, homes, you could have told me that we would be meeting up at this snooty restaurant. I would have dressed for the occasion, *esse*," Gordo said with a smile, sporting a Nike sweatsuit and sneakers.

"What, you ain't never heard of the Stinking Rose?" Bookman asked. "I thought that *you* of all people would know about this spot, being a big baller and all."

"Stinking Rose? Hey, *esse*, that sounds like the name of some good *yeska* to me. The most smancy joint I eat at is the Sizzler, aye," Gordo asserted with a smile.

Before he changed the subject, Bookman explained to Gordo that Stinking Rose was simply another name for garlic.

Bookman asked Gordo to give him every detail of what was happening on the streets between his gang and the Bounty Hunters. Gordo explained all the events leading up to the street war and made it clear that he intended to pay his monthly tax, but he let Bookman know why he could not afford to do so at the moment. Bookman informed Gordo that he and Diamond had fallen out because Diamond had refused to pay his monthly tax on time. Gordo promised that he would have no problem paying Bookman twice his old monthly tax if he could only get Diamond and his crew out of the way in order for him to reclaim his throne.

By the time the two men finished their food, they had shaken hands on an agreement that would result in Bookman receiving payments of fifteen thousand dollars every month, with a fifty thousand dollar balloon payment due at the time of Diamond's downfall. In the meantime, Bookman promised to do everything in his power to cramp Diamond's profits on the East Side streets, while at the same time making it easier for the *Vatos Locos* to operate.

Both men exited the restaurant with the fresh feeling of a new beginning, and both men were in a hurry to get to work.

After the meeting, Bookman drove straight back down Lacienaga Boulevard and entered onto the 101 Freeway traveling eastbound. He got off on Central Boulevard, made a right turn, and then drove until he came to 52nd Street. Bookman parked his Cadillac at the hamburger stand on 52nd and Central and walked down 52nd past the Pueblo projects for a block until he came to Ascott Street. He checked his watch and realized that he was right on time, so he sat at the bus stop and waited.

Ten minutes later, Bookman heard four quick honks from a car's horn. This was the sound he had been instructed to listen for. He looked up in time to see a line of cars at the stoplight and then stood up and waited. The light turned green ten seconds later, and a green BMW pulled up near Bookman, cracking its tinted passenger-side window just wide enough for the sergeant to drop the plastic bag inside containing the items he had stolen from the evidence locker. Bookman did as he had been instructed by dropping the bag inside the car, but then he tried to take a quick peek at the driver but to no avail. The window quickly went back up, and then the car sped off and was gone.

Chapter 30

I t had been a week since Psycho and Sicko had been nabbed from the streets of Los Angeles following their botched robbery. Both twins had been transferred to the Lynwood Sheriff station to be held until arraignment. The sheriff's deputies made sure that the men were housed in different areas of the substation to ensure that the twins could not formulate a story together in order to combat their upcoming trials.

Both twins had gone straight for the phone as soon as they arrived in their cells. Psycho Twin found out that he was being held on bank robbery and felony evading charges, with a bail of one hundred thousand dollars, while his brother was charged with two counts of kidnapping. Sick Twin's bail was set at two hundred thousand dollars.

The twins were able to communicate with one another by calling people and having messages delivered to each other. They were careful about the things they said over the phone, and Psycho had sent a message to Sick through his girlfriend Gina telling him not to talk to the detectives. Five minutes later, Sicko's cell door opened.

"Moss!" the jailer yelled.

"What!" Sick Twin replied.

"Darnell Moss, the detective would like to see you."

"I ain't talkin' to no mothafuckin' Dick Tracy, blood. Get the fuck outa here," Sicko replied.

"Well, you still have to come and tell him that you are refusing to talk to him and sign a waiver."

Sicko was escorted to a small room containing only three steel chairs and a shabby old desk. The room's walls were white and covered with graffiti.

"The detective will be right with you," the jailer announced before walking out of the room and closing the door.

Sicko sat there and read the graffiti on the walls where he spotted the writing of a few of his own homeboys. Most of the writing, however, was that of *cholo* gangs — *Vatos Locos Muchachos*, Florencia 13, Harpy's 13, Mara Salvatrucha, and it went on and on.

"Gad Damn *essays* love writin' all over shit," Sicko said to himself.

Moments later the door opened, and to Sicko's surprise his brother walked into the room. The two men quickly embraced in a bear hug and agreed that the jailer must have made a mistake after realizing that they had been brought in by different people.

With their voices significantly lowered, they immediately began discussing ways in which they might be able to get out of this mess they had gotten themselves into. They also agreed to call Lil Ricky in order to try to get him to bail them out.

After the two teenagers finished talking business, they began teasing one another about getting busted. Sicko told Psych about his adventure with the little crybaby kid and the pretty White woman. Psycho got upset with his younger brother when Sick Twin told him about the near raping of his hostage. Sicko laughed hard when Psycho told him about his trip through the projects where he flung thousands of dollars out the window. Both twins refused to talk to the detective when he arrived and were escorted back to their respective cells where they both contacted Lil Ricky.

To both twins surprise, their childhood friend was happy to hear from them and was willing to put up the thirty thousand dollars cash it would take to get them out of jail. The problem was that the thirty thousand was useless without the collateral to back it up. Psycho contacted Gina and requested that she ask her grandmother to put her house up but was turned down squarely by his girlfriend who told him that he should never have tried to rob a bank in the first place.

The twins' last hope was in the man whom they had turned their backs on a few months earlier, their OG homeboy and best friend's uncle — Diamond.

"Oh hell, motha fuckin', naw," Diamond replied to Lil Ricky's request for assistance in getting his friends out of jail, "Dem evil little bastards held you and me at gunpoint, robbed us, and then went on a million dolla shoppin' spree while we bit the bullet and hustled hard to get where we at. I told dem little niggas, Ricky, and they went and did the exact shit that I said they would do. Tell they ass to put dem Escalades and dat hunned-thousand dolla bling-bling shit dat ain't worth shit after they done paid for it up for collateral. That's what they asses get!"

Lil Ricky realized that it was a lost cause.

* * *

On the morning of the arraignment, Psycho Twin went to Lynwood Municipal Court in the same building where he was being held. Even though Sicko had been captured not far from where his brother had been nabbed, he was put on a bus to Orange County where his crimes had originated.

Both twins received grim news during their municipal court arraignments. The district attorney in Psycho's case added the charge of evidence tampering to his bank robbery and felony evading charges, and as a result, the judge raised his bail to five hundred thousand dollars.

Sicko received even worse news at his court hearing. The DA in Sick Twin's case amended his two charges of kidnapping and placed a special circumstance of kidnapping for purposes of ransom on him along with a new charge of rape. Sicko was now facing three life sentences with a bail of one million dollars.

Chapter 31

It was ten in the evening. Sue Nguyen had just finished counting up the day's profits and placing all the cash into the safe stashed beneath her working quarters. After locking up the beauty shop, she got into her Toyota Camry and headed home. Her hair and nail shop was located at the corner of El Segundo Boulevard and Avalon, which left her a choice of which route she would take home from day to day. Whenever she went home during rush hour, she would take Avalon all the way down to Slauson and then make the left turn to the Pueblo projects. The seventy-eight-block trip was much faster than fighting bumper-to-bumper traffic on the freeway. Since Sue had been the worker designated to close the shop tonight, she was leaving far after rush hour, therefore, tonight the freeway would be her best route.

She was exhausted after a long day at the beauty shop and also in a hurry to get home, since she still had to pick up her son from his baby-sitter and then go home and cook dinner. Sue made a right turn out of the parking lot onto El Segundo Boulevard headed westward toward the 110 Freeway. Ten minutes later she entered the freeway headed north. After she had traveled about two miles, Sue glanced in the rear view mirror and noticed that she was being tailed from close behind by a police car. She instinctively looked down to make sure she was wearing her seat belt and glanced at her speedometer. She was under the speed limit and driving with the flow of traffic with both hands on the steering wheel. She continued to drive as normal. Once she began to approach the next freeway exit, which was Century Boulevard, the police car's blue and red lights began flashing behind her. She merged over to the right shoulder of the freeway to stop her car.

Once she got all the way over, she heard the voice of the cop come over the squad car's loudspeaker, "Pull off of the freeway."

Sue followed the officer's directions and drove down the Century off ramp.

Once they reached Century Boulevard, the voice again gave an order. This time the cop told Sue to turn off of Century onto a side street adjacent to the freeway. When Sue followed this order and realized how dark and deserted the street was, she began to get nervous.

Once she had come to a complete stop, she rolled down her window and turned her vehicle off. She watched in the side view mirror as the cop walked slowly up to her car.

"Good evening, officer," the woman said in a heavy Asian accent with a lump in her throat.

"Step out of the car, ma'am," the police officer ordered.

"Did I do something wrong, officer?" Sue inquired, reluctant to get out of her car.

"Ma'am, I said step out of the car," the cop demanded.

This time Sue followed his instructions.

The officer immediately pushed her to the hood of his squad car and cuffed her hands tightly behind her back.

"But what did I do wrong, officer?"

The cop gave the little Vietnamese woman no response. He shoved her to the rear door of his squad car and opened it up.

"Get in," the cop ordered.

Sue's eyes filled with tears as she got into the backseat of the squad car. Once she was secured, the cop walked around the car, got back into the driver's seat, and pulled off, leaving Sue's car parked on the dark side street beside the freeway.

Before Sue knew it, she was back on the freeway headed in the opposite direction.

"Officer, why am I going to jail?" Sue asked over and over. "What did I do wrong, officer?"

"Shut the fuck up!" the cop demanded. They continued southbound down the Harbor Freeway until Sue noticed the ocean. She saw numerous bridges and boats floating around in the harbor as they continued rolling.

The cop drove all the way to the end of the freeway and then made a left turn onto Gaffey Avenue. He drove up Gaffey, passing several shopping centers, gas stations, and restaurants, until, little by little, the street became more empty. Soon, Gaffey turned into a residential street.

They drove up a big hill, and Sue could once again see the ocean when they arrived at the top. The officer made a right turn and drove down a dark street with nothing but cliffs to the left of them and hills to the right. Soon, the cop pulled off the street onto a dirt cliff overlooking the ocean.

Sue began to beg, "Please don't hurt me! I have a little boy! Please!"

Without turning off his engine, the police officer exited the vehicle and headed directly to his trunk. A moment later, Sue heard the trunk slam shut and then saw the cop emerge with a rubber hose in his hand. He rolled the front window of the squad car down just enough to shove the rubber hose inside and then rolled the window back up just tight enough to keep the hose from slipping out. The officer then walked back to the rear of the car. He leaned down and connected the other end of the hose to the vehicle's exhaust pipe.

After completing these tasks, the police officer lit up a coco puff cigarette, leaned against the car, and checked the time on his watch. Ten minutes later, Sergeant Curtiss Bookman opened the back door of the squad car, removed his handcuffs from the woman's wrists, and then removed her limp body from the backseat and threw her over his shoulder. He walked to the edge of the cliff and tossed Sue Nguyen's body into the ocean.

Chapter 32

Stormy had been living in a Holiday Inn hotel room in the City of Inglewood for the past two days. After her date with Lil Ricky, he had checked her into the hotel room and paid for one week in advance. Rick Rock had instructed the teenage girl to leave all of her belongings behind and start fresh. He promised to stop by the whorehouse to pick up her guitar and the backpack that contained her notebook with her songs.

She had been surprised when Lil Ricky had not attempted to have sex with her during the day they spent together. Although he did make it clear to Stormy that he was attracted to her by the constant playful flirtation he maintained throughout the date, he never propositioned or reminded her of the circumstances under which he had picked her up earlier that day.

The teenage girl was beginning to get restless, having been left at the hotel room with one hundred dollars and the clothes she arrived with. Lil Ricky promised Stormy that he would be back tomorrow to take her shopping and apartment hunting, but tomorrow was now yesterday and still there was no sign of Rick Rock.

"He could've at least had the courtesy to leave me his cell phone number," Stormy said to herself as she began to think that this whole thing was just part of a plan for Big Mama to kick her out of the house.

The previous evening, before going to bed, Stormy had bathed, washed her panties and bra in the hotel sink, and then hung them up on the shower curtain rod. She walked into the bathroom and found everything to be dry, so she removed the cheap white hotel robe from her naked body and put on her underclothes. After putting on the rest of her clothes, Stormy felt her stomach begin to growl. The teenager realized that she had not eaten anything since the Jack In The Box chicken sandwich and fruit smoothie she had consumed for lunch the day before. This prompted her to become even more upset.

She grabbed her purse and cursed Lil Ricky under her breath as she headed for the door.

Stormy opened the hotel room door to find Lil Ricky walking in her direction right on cue with her guitar and backpack in hand. He immediately noticed the perturbed look on the face of his newfound friend, so he quickly extended the backpack in her direction and began buttering her up, "Gurrrl... have I got a surprise for *you*," Lil Ricky exclaimed as Stormy snatched her backpack from his grasp. "I know you're mad at me for not coming through yesterday, but let me tell you what happened."

Stormy remained silent with her eyes cut in an unmistakable display of anger. Although she had forgiven Lil Ricky the moment she laid eyes on him and just wanted to melt in his arms, the teenage girl was determined to stick to her guns. If Lil Ricky genuinely cared for her, he would tolerate her unsettled mood and find a way to make it better.

"Okay, if you wanna be all mad at ya boy and give a nigga the silent treatment, then fuck it, I won't even tell ya mean ass what these go to," Lil Ricky said with a wry smile while producing a key ring from his coat pocket with two keys hanging from it. Stormy's façade quickly disappeared, and her face lit up with excitement. She hurriedly screwed her face back up in an attempt to conceal her gratification. Rick Rock approached the pretty girl and began tickling her. The young thug then began dangling the keys in the air and teasing her in a childlike manner.

"Guess who got her own a-part-ment. Guess who owes Lil Ricky an a-po-lo-gy."

Stormy couldn't hide her joy any longer. She now had a smile on her face that extended from one ear to the other.

"You did *not!*" the astonished teenager exclaimed. Before she could give it a second thought, Stormy wrapped her arms around Lil Ricky and engaged him in a passionate tongue kiss. The young gangster wasted no time returning the kiss with equal the intensity that Stormy had initiated the smooch with. For a brief moment, Stormy backed up and looked her unexpected knight in shining armor in his eyes. The next thing Rick Rock knew, he was being pulled toward the hotel room.

Inside the room, he quickly realized from Stormy's awkwardness that she was an inexperienced lover. He automatically took charge, gently laying her down on the bed as he began kissing softly on her neck. He took a second to remove his coat and toss it onto the floor beside Stormy's guitar and backpack. Stormy began helping him remove his white T-shirt and tank top. The teenage girl was impressed once she got a look at Rick Rock's body. His arms were massive and cut to a tee, with his chest protruding and chiseled, complete with a six-pack stomach underneath. Once Lil Ricky was shirtless, he began to kiss on Stormy's neck again.

He then softly asked her a question in her ear, "Are you ready for this?"

Stormy did not speak. Instead, she answered his question by gripping the back of his neck and pulling him closer.

Lil Ricky slowly lifted her shirt over her head and then unsnapped her bra, admiring how her perky white breasts popped out and blossomed at his disposal. The young gangster took his time sucking on each nipple while enjoying the sound of Stormy's moans. He looked down to find that she was unbuttoning and unzipping her pants. She lightly raised the lower half of her body into the air in order to wriggle out of her skin-tight jeans and G-string panties.

Gradually, Lil Ricky made his way down from her breasts and began kissing softly around her stomach. The lower he went, the faster Stormy breathed. Rick Rock made his way down and began kissing her inner thighs while making a trail up to her moist vagina.

Once again Stormy found herself receiving pleasure which she had never experienced before, as Lil Ricky spread her pussy lips and began massaging her clitoris with his tongue. She found herself naturally humping with the rhythm of Rick Rock's tongue as the intensity of her pleasure grew. Stormy began rubbing and gently pinching on her erect nipples, while he continued eating her out until she felt herself about to explode with pleasure.

Just as she felt herself about to climax, Stormy pushed Rick Rock's head gently away from her vagina and gripped him under his arms, pulling him up toward herself. He raised up on his knees to unbutton his pants, while Stormy pulled his pants down. She quickly found out that large sexual organs ran in Rick Rock's family when his rock-hard dick stood at attention. Stormy laid back and closed her eyes, bracing herself for what was next to come.

The sex lasted for over an hour, and both of them enjoyed every second of it. By the time it was over, they found themselves laying in a large puddle of wetness. After the sex, they hopped in the shower together, and while washing one another they joked about how good the lovemaking had been.

"Dat wasn't nothing but dat thug passion, baby," Lil Ricky proclaimed with a laugh.

Chapter 33

Approximately twenty-four hours after Gordo and Bookman met at the Stinking Rose, the LAPD received several faxes from the Los Angeles County Criminal Courts Building. In total, Bookman held seventeen search warrants in his hand, all of which directed him to housing units within the Nickerson Gardens housing projects. Over the years, Sergeant Bookman had built up a good rapport with several Los Angeles County judges after testifying in thousands of criminal cases; therefore, he could get a search warrant to any vehicle, residence, or business upon his slightest whim.

A team of LAPD officers began executing the search warrants at four in the morning when they knew that it was likely they could catch the street hustlers by surprise. By the time 9:00 A.M. rolled around, they had raided all seventeen units. During the operation, the police officers made twenty-three arrests and confiscated large amounts of cocaine, PCP, ecstasy pills, and marijuana, with an estimated street value of over seven hundred thousand dollars.

Diamond was at one of his safe houses outside of the projects when he received the bad news through an early morning call from Big Mama. It did not take long for the street veteran to realize what was going on. He quickly hung up the phone with Big Mama and began scrolling down on his cell phone until he reached the name "Dinosaur" and then pressed the talk button.

After what seemed like the longest two rings Diamond had ever heard, Sergeant Bookman answered the phone, "Whaddup, Dee?" came Bookman's voice through the phone, as if he were answering a call from one of his best buddies.

"Whaddup, Dee, my achin' black ass! What the fuck is goin' on, Booker?" Diamond inquired, "Why in the hell did your flunkies just hit me like this, man?"

"Nigga, you tell me why," Bookman replied. "I got a little saying for you, Diamond, and I want you to listen and think about this long and hard, brotha, 'cause this is one of my father's old sayings, and it's a good one. You ready?" Bookman asked.

"Lay it on me, Confucius," Diamond answered.

"Cheap shit always turns out to be damn expensive," Bookman proclaimed. "You wanted to be Mister Slick Willy and not pay dat rent, so instead of the few thousand or so that you would've paid me, you ended up making me look like super cop with a million dollar bust."

Diamond knew that he was in no position to argue with the pompous sergeant. He also realized that maybe for the first time in his life he had been wrong.

"So what can I do to rectify this situation and get back on track?" Diamond inquired in an attempt to cut his losses.

"Well... I don't know, brotha, 'cause now I don't even need you no more. Plus, how do I know that once I do blow air back into your lungs that you ain't gonna fuck around and get too big for ya britches again?"

Diamond explained to Bookman that he had learned his lesson from the morning's reality check and that he would never cross him again. By the time the conversation was over, Diamond had agreed to pay his ten thousand dollar tax at once with the understanding that Sergeant Bookman would call off his hounds. The conversation ended on a civil note, with the two men agreeing on a time and a drop-off spot for their transaction. Once Bookman hung up the phone with Diamond, he immediately dialed up Gordo's number.

Chapter 34

"**O**rder in the court!" demanded the tall, stocky, White bailiff before the judge began to speak. The pink-faced judge with the full, white beard thumbed through a few papers and then proceeded, "This is the time and place set forth for the preliminary examination in the case of 'The people of the State of California versus Edward Ong' who is present with counsel Jim Starcevich, Attorney at Law, case number TP08421. The People are represented by Deputy District Attorney Arthur Moody. Are both parties ready to proceed?"

"Yes, Judge," the tall, White lawyer standing right next to the young Asian man in the blue LA County Jail jump suit answered.

"Uh… Your Honor," said the prosecutor, still sitting at the table examining his notes, "Your Honor, there seems to be a problem. It turns out that our eyewitness who is key in this trial was found dead washed up on the beach yesterday. On top of that, Your Honor, the only two pieces of physical evidence that we recovered in this case have mysteriously disappeared from the evidence lock-up over at 77."

The judge glanced down from the bench to find that the defendant now wore a smug grin revealing his satisfaction, "I see," said the judge as he stared at the defendant.

"Your Honor, the defense moves for immediate dismissal of this case on grounds of insufficient evidence. My client should not be held in lieu of circumstances which are beyond his control," the defense attorney asserted emphatically, knowing that the judge's options were limited.

"Well, I don't know how much control your client did or didn't have in this series of events." The judge then directed his attention toward the deputy district attorney, "However, as much as I would like to detain the defendant, Mister Moody, I can't hold Mister Ong without evidence. Is there any shred of evidence with which you may be able to provide this court? Because if not, then we have no choice but to grant the defense's motion to dismiss."

"Your Honor, this is an extortion case as well as a homicide," the deputy district attorney explained, "We had a murder which took place inside a beauty shop full of workers, but nobody wanted to come forward and testify against Mister Ong with the exception of Miss Nguyen, who has now obviously been murdered. We do have one more eyewitness who would be willing to testify in this case, but she has refused to step foot in this courthouse until she is granted full witness protection status with relocation funds for herself as well as her family."

The grave expression on the judge's face quickly morphed into one of relief. "Whatever we have to do to continue this matter is fine with me. I'm going to hold an in-camera hearing right now which will be sealed. So we will proceed in judge's chambers to iron out all the details."

After a twenty minute session in the judge's chambers, the defense attorney re-entered the courtroom followed by the prosecutor and the judge.

"We're back on the record," the judge announced. "We are going to put this matter over until we get this witness protection issue in order which will be longer than a week. If the prosecution is not prepared to proceed after this time period, then this case will be dismissed after the duration thereof." The judge banged his gavel.

Chapter 35

Boss Ross pulled into the deserted alley behind Spades Liquor at exactly 12:55 P.M. Since the death of his girlfriend and unborn child, the thirty-five year old had quickly begun to move up in rank on the Bounty Hunter ladder. He was now answering to Diamond himself who was providing him with enough crumbs to stand out above most of the other neighborhood thugs.

When Boss Ross was not cooking up crack or making sales, he acted as Diamond's gofer. His mission today was to simply meet Sergeant Bookman in this project alley and hand him a paper bag full of cash.

He parked his new Chrysler 300 C beside a graffiti-covered wall, turned his car off, and lit up a marijuana-filled cigar. After Boss Ross had smoked up his entire blunt, he glanced at his built-in dashboard clock which read 1:06 P.M. He leaned back and enjoyed his high for a while before looking at his clock once again. It was now 1:17 P.M. and still no sign of Bookman. He decided that it was time to go. He would get out of the car and take a leak, and if Bookman had not arrived by then, he would phone Diamond to let him know that the sergeant was a no-show.

Boss Ross opened up his car door, releasing a large cloud of chronic smoke into the air. He got out of the car and stepped to the passenger side of the vehicle between his car and the wall. He unbuttoned and zipped his pants down, pulled out his dick, and began peeing on the wall. In the middle of his urination, Boss Ross began hearing loud clapping sounds which he dismissed as being distant enough to not pose a direct threat to his safety. He continued to pee on the wall, and in an instant, the bright-red University of Wisconsin hat which was sitting on top of his large Afro flew off and was now laying on the ground eight feet in front of him.

Boss Ross instinctively ducked down and took cover in front of his car. He looked through the car's windows to spot two masked men in the alley about one hundred yards away moving in his direction. Both of them were shooting at him with rifles. Boss Ross ducked back down in front of his car and removed the seventeen shot .40 caliber pistol from his waistband, as his back window along with his windshield shattered from the impact of one of the rifle bullets being fired at him.

Boss Ross looked up again to find that the masked assassins were closing in on him. With both hands on his pistol, the same way a veteran police officer would hold the weapon, Boss Ross began returning fire. With nowhere to take cover, the riflemen both dropped down to one knee and continued their assault. After three shots from the Forty Glock, Boss Ross saw one of the masked men fall backwards and lay on the ground. This prompted the other shooter to immediately drop his weapon and begin dragging his counterpart back out of the alley.

Boss Ross kept firing upon the second man until he fell to the ground. He then ran from behind the car and fired more shots into both men as he approached them. Boss Ross kicked the AK-47 dropped by the second man away before reaching down to remove the men's masks.

"Hefty and Sniper?" Boss Ross announced in shock. Two final shots, one into the head of each shooter, ensured that they would never again shoot another gun. Boss Ross backed his Chrysler 300 C over the corpses of both of Gordo's younger brothers on his way out of the alley.

Chapter 36

When Peter Kinbrew arrived at the 77th Precinct, he strolled into the building carefree as usual. After checking his mail slot, he greeted a few colleagues and then began his daily tread to the evidence lock-up. Everything seemed normal to Pete Kinbrew until he stepped into his office to find Lieutenant McGee behind his desk with a young female officer.

"What are *you* doing here, Kinbrew?" the lieutenant asked. "You don't work here anymore."

Peter Kinbrew was shocked. He found out that the attractive young woman was being trained to take over his position and that he had been placed on administrative leave pending an investigation due to the missing evidence in case number TP08421. Peter Kinbrew quickly left his old domain en route to Captain Cody's office.

Chapter 37

Psycho Twin's first week in the Los Angeles County Jail proved to be turbulent. During his eight-hour intake process, he experienced the bad luck of running into a few members of his project's worst rival gang. He ended up getting jumped by three Grape Street Crips who took advantage of the fact that he was the only Blood on the intake line. After that, he was sent to an eighty-man dormitory where he kicked off a melee with the Hispanic inmates. There were only two working phones in the entire dorm, and Psycho did not approve of the fact that they were both occupied by Mexicans who were an overwhelming majority in the dorm. That, along with the fact that Psycho was already in a bad mood, prompted him to go to his bunk and break down the razor he had been issued in his hygiene kit. Two minutes later, there was a full fledged riot.

When Psycho got out of the hole, he was sent to a cellblock where he was finally able to make a phone call. The restless young thug could not wait to talk to his girlfriend. After the past week, he was anxious to hear the sweet voice of his son's mother.

To Psycho's surprise, Gina's grandmother answered the phone and informed him that Gina was not at home and had not been there for three days. Worried, Psycho hung up the phone and immediately dialed up Lil Ricky who had forwarded a landline to his cellular phone so that the twins could get in touch with him at all times. Once Rick Rock accepted his collect call, Psycho wasted no time in asking him to place a three-way call to Gina's cell phone. The phone was answered after a few rings.

To the relief of Psycho Twin, Gina's Mexican-accented voice came through the phone, "Hello?"

"What's up, baby!" Psycho screamed through the phone, knowing that the girl would be happy to hear his voice.

"Who is this?" Gina asked, as if she had no idea who she was speaking to.

"You know who the hell dis is, girl, so quit playin'," Psycho demanded, not in the mood to play. Shortly after, he heard a click, and then there was no one left on the line except for him and Lil Ricky.

"What happened, homie?" Psych asked.

"It sounds like she hung up on us, Blood. Hold on; I'm gonna call back," Lil Ricky clicked over and then came back on the line with the phone ringing.

Once again Gina answered the phone, "Hello?"

"Gina, this is me, Carnell. What the hell is going on?"

After a brief moment of silence, Gina began to speak, "Don't call me no more, okay, Mister Bad-ass Psycho?" Gina announced. "You cared about your cars and your money and your homeboys better than you cared about your own son. So now you just have to deal with it."

Psycho could not believe his ears. He never imagined that his girl would ever change on him one iota, much less leave him for dead in a situation as crucial as the one he was currently faced with.

"Oh, so that's how you feel, huh?" was the only words that Psycho could bring himself to speak.

"Yeah, that's exactly how I feel," Gina said with no trace of regret in her voice. "You made your bed up, so lay in it, Carnell."

"Click her off, Rick Rock."

Chapter 38

After two weeks of what seemed like heaven, Lil Ricky realized that he was falling deeper in love with each passing day. In the short time he had been seeing Stormy, he had already taken her to pick out furniture. He had bought her a brand-new wardrobe complete with the highest names in fashion. He had even consulted with a few of his Hollywood connections in order to track down J Star, the music producer whose music had made such an impression on Stormy that she had run away from home to search for him.

Lil Ricky was building his life around Stormy, and as a result he began to clash with his Uncle Diamond frequently.

Diamond had told Lil Ricky a few days earlier, "Neph, you done went and turned into a tender-dick, Captain Save-a-Hoe. You ain't only wasting a gold mine that the bitch got inside her panties, nigga, but you payin' for it too!"

There was nothing that Diamond could say to change his nephew's opinion about Stormy. As a result, the street-smart project veteran decided to back up and allow his brother's son to learn the hard way. Diamond prided himself in knowing a whore's nature, and in his mind Stormy was a natural born prostitute; therefore, it was only a matter of time before the young White girl would show his nephew her true colors.

Despite Rick Rock's love life, he continued to handle his street duties without ever missing a beat. As second in command, he ran the projects with an iron fist. The young gangster was responsible for doing everything from collecting debts to ordering hits, and the teenager was good at what he did.

At 9:00 A.M., Rick Rock dropped Stormy off at J Star's studio as he had been doing every morning since locating the music producer. This was a perfect arrangement for Lil Ricky. He would pay J Star one hundred dollars a day to record Stormy's songs and also teach her how to operate the studio equipment. This gave the young hustler plenty of time to handle his business in the projects, but even better, it limited the time in which he had to participate in activities that were unproductive, since he had to be back in Hollywood at the end of the night to pick up his girlfriend.

The first thing on Rick Rock's itinerary today was to stop by Momma Maria's to drop off four ounces of rock cocaine to Boss Ross and his crew who had managed to regain control of the parking lot after the brief takeover by the VLs. When Lil Ricky exited the 105 Freeway and made the right turn onto Imperial Boulevard, he instinctively drove past the restaurant without slowing down when he noticed three police cars in the parking lot.

As Rick Rock drove by, he spotted Jay Boy and Hot Dog being frisked with their hands on the hood of one of the black and whites. He kept going straight and then made a left turn into the projects at the next light before retrieving his cellular phone from the side console of his SUV. He scrolled down his phone screen until he got to the name "Boss" and then hit the TALK button.

Boss Ross answered on the first ring, "Whaddup, Hunta?" came the voice of Lil Ricky's comrade.

"What's the bidness, dog? I just pushed past the taco spot and saw the homies in the parkin' lot gaffled by the one times."

Boss Ross explained to Lil Ricky that it had been that way every since the projects had been raided a couple of days earlier. He told Rick Rock how the cops would show up every time they arrived at the parking lot and how the police would show up only moments after they pulled up. He also explained how Momma Maria had been behaving oddly lately. Boss Ross felt strongly that the Mexican lady was calling the cops in an effort to shut down their parking lot operation.

This whole situation did not sit well with Rick Rock, since that parking lot had proven to be a big money maker over the years and a trap that the Bounty Hunters could count on even when other avenues failed to produce. He got off the phone with Boss Ross and immediately dialed up his Uncle Diamond.

Chapter 39

Boss Ross had been on the road driving toward his mother's house in West LA while he conversed with Rick Rock on his cell phone. As soon as he hung up with his homeboy, he noticed that he was being followed by a cop car. The fact that Boss Ross had a hiding place built into his car where he kept his pistol stashed and was not carrying any drugs at the moment prevented him from panicking when he spotted the police vehicle.

When the police cruiser's flashing lights popped on, Boss Ross pulled his car to the side of the road and placed his hands on the steering wheel. Boss Ross relaxed as he watched the two cops approach his car.

"I see you got your windows fixed," Sergeant Bookman said once he reached Boss Ross' driver side door.

"I don't know what you're talkin' 'bout, Booker," Boss Ross responded as he watched Officer Felix bring up the rear.

"You got anything in the vehicle that I should know about?" the sergeant inquired, while doing a visual sweep over the inside of the vehicle.

"Nah, man, I ain't got *nothin'* you should know about up in here."

"Okay, then you don't mind if we have a look around," Bookman said as he opened Boss Ross' driver side door. The sergeant gave his rookie ride-along a nod and then handcuffed his detainee and patted him down.

As Officer Felix searched the car, Bookman escorted Boss Ross to the police cruiser and placed him in the backseat while he ran his license for warrants.

"I thought we was way better than this kind of bullshit, Booker," Boss Ross asserted through the grill which separated the front and backseats of the squad car.

"Aww, well... shit was all good up until you niggas' daddy got to smellin' himself," Bookman responded.

161

"Fuck you, punk," Boss Ross responded, visibly upset by the sergeant's comment. "If I had it my way, you would've been patrolling the streets of hell by now, you Uncle Tom-ass nigga!"

"I already am," Bookman proclaimed as he exited his squad car.

"He's clean," Officer Felix announced, as he walked back toward the squad car. Bookman ordered Felix to sit in the squad car and wait on dispatch to respond while he took one more look inside Boss Ross' car. After two minutes, Bookman came walking back to the cop car with what appeared to be a large rock of cocaine in his hand.

"Well, what have we here, Ross?" Bookman inquired with a crocodile smile.

Chapter 40

After accommodating over four hundred guests, Saint Andrew's Cathedral was just about empty. Gordo had held a double funeral for his two younger brothers five days after their murder, and now car after car turned out of the church parking lot and followed the escort motorcycles and two hearses in a long line as they headed toward the cemetery.

Gordo had not spoken much after receiving the news of his two brothers' demise. He had issued a command to everyone in the *varrio* to stand down their retaliation efforts until the conclusion of his brothers' funerals. This order did not prevent the *Vatos Locos* from warning the streets of the violence to come through the massive amounts of graffiti that had begun to appear on the project's walls. Sprawled all over the walls were the words 'Rest In Peace, Hefty And Sniper' and the words 'Bounty Hunter' with a line through it to demonstrate the VL disdain for the co-occupants of their housing project. The words, 'Nigger Killer' even appeared on many walls within and on the outskirts of the projects.

The long convoy pulled into Inglewood Cemetery and drove to the middle of the burial grounds to park beside the grave sites. Gordo had purchased side by side plots right next to his youngest brother Javier's grave to ensure that all three of his brothers would remain together for eternity.

A large crowd of mourners stood by for the grave-side burial ceremony with their heads bowed as the priest gave his final benediction and then allowed several funeral goers to pay their respects by speaking kind words about the fallen brothers.

Soon after, the caskets were lowered and several members of the *Vatos Locos Muchachos* gang took turns with a shovel. Every member of the gang, including Gordo himself, scooped a shovel full of dirt and threw it on top of each casket.

Once the ceremony was complete, every gang member in the cemetery was excited to hear the voice of their leader cry out, "*Estuvo Raza!*" The gang had patiently waited for this moment, and now the green light was on. It was time for the killing to begin.

Chapter 41

The week following the funeral of Gordo's last two brothers proved to be the most deadly seven days the Nickerson Gardens projects had ever seen. There were multiple injuries and fatalities on both sides, which was apparent to anyone who drove through the neighborhood. Candlelight vigils began to appear in droves, some only a few feet from others.

Gordo had instructed his soldiers to fire upon any Black person — man, woman, or child — who they caught on the Lil Tijuana side of the projects. Shortly after, the *Vatos Locos* armed with assault rifles had opened fire on two young Black girls who just happened to be riding their bikes on the wrong side of the park. As a result, all of the remaining Blacks still living in Lil Tijuana began migrating back to the dark side of the projects, taking up residence any place they could. Hispanics in the dark side began moving to Lil Tijuana, cramming into housing units at a rapid rate. Soon, everyone in the projects knew their boundaries, and it became unusual for a member of either entity to be caught out of bounds.

Still, the violence continued at a steady pace as the Bounty Hunters and *Vatos Locos Muchachos* went back and forth taking turns attacking one another in a vicious blood feud.

The dastardly tactics of the *Vatos Locos* were beginning to take their toll on the Bounty Hunter gang. Not only was the Mexican gang murdering innocent Blacks on a regular basis, but they were also snitching on any Bounty Hunter who they could identify in any attack. This was another tactic approved by Gordo to equalize the numbers advantage which the Bounty Hunters held in the street war.

* * *

Diamond was losing soldiers at an alarming rate. He quickly began to realize that he had made an accidental declaration of war upon a formidable enemy. It began to seem as if he was outmanned and outgunned on the project streets. At least three times a day, every day, Diamond answered his phone to receive news of miscellaneous acts committed by the VL to victimize members of his gang along with innocent bystanders who were frequently being caught in the wrong place at the wrong time.

The war had forced Diamond out of retirement. Along with his role as Bounty Hunter Commander In Chief, he was now forced to play the role of front line soldier on the battlefield. He and Lil Ricky began working hard to find the location of Gordo's hideout or any other location where they could hunt down and kill the street don. At the same time, they planned and carried out ambushes on any member of *Vatos Locos* who they caught off guard.

Unlike the cowardly tactics which Gordo chose to use in the war, Diamond insisted on playing by the old-school rules of the streets. There was no way he was going to have his little homies out on the streets killing women and children or cooperating with police detectives and the district attorneys office by pointing out rivals in an effort to get them off the streets.

Although Diamond's pride would not allow him to stoop to such levels, he realized that he was losing the war and knew that he had to come up with a plan to swiftly put the Hispanic gang out of commission. He came up with the first part of his plan while in the middle of an early-morning bowel movement in the bathroom of one of his safe houses, "Why the hell didn't I think of this a long time ago?" Diamond asked himself before flushing the toilet.

Chapter 42

For what seemed to be the fiftieth time in the last three months, Officer Curtiss Bookman was rudely awakened from his deep sleep by the sound of a ringing telephone. By now he was somewhat adjusted to the early morning calls, and he automatically knew who would be at the other end of the phone when he answered it.

"What now?" were the first words Bookman spoke into the telephone once he pushed the TALK button.

"Ahh, Sergeant Bookman," came the voice. "You sound as if you are not happy to hear from me, old pal."

Bookman was not amused, and as a result the sergeant cut right to the chase, "Lemme guess; this is just a final call for you to congratulate and thank me for a job well done, right? Because the last time we spoke, if my memory serves me correctly, you promised that the last mission you sent me on would be a one and done."

"Well... yes, sergeant," the Asian voice replied. "I admit that I did mislead you in our previous conversation, and I do extend my sincerest apologies to you and beg your forgiveness; however, due to the occurrence of events unforeseen, it looks as if we will require your services one last time."

Overcome with anger, Bookman quickly sat up in his bed, and with all the might he could muster, he threw the cordless phone into his bedroom wall causing it to shatter into several pieces. After two minutes, the other telephones in his house began to ring. Bookman made his way to the living room where he picked up the old rotary phone given to him long ago by his grandmother and put it to his ear.

"Do you have an ink pen handy, sergeant?"

Chapter 43

J ay Boy and Hot Dog's money was once again rolling. After being jacked up by the police in the parking lot of Momma Maria's several times, the young gangsters realized that their welcome had worn out. Someone, most likely Momma Maria herself, wanted them out of that parking lot. This prompted the young hustlers to migrate to the parking lot of the gas station next door to set up shop. They immediately built up a rapport with all of the gas station attendants by establishing a rent of two hundred dollars a week for the supervisor of each shift. The six hundred dollars was chicken feed when compared to the cash they clocked on a day-to-day basis without the worry of police interference.

Soon, all of the customers from Momma Maria's parking lot knew where to find the young dope pushers. By 11:00 A.M., the two teenagers had made over a thousand dollars. This kind of spending was typical at the beginning of the month when users received their social security and welfare checks.

By about noon, Jay Boy and Hot Dog had run out of marijuana. Without weed, the teenagers could not function. The only way they usually maintained the patience to sit and wait for dope sales all day was to stay high off of marijuana and tipsy from 40oz bottles of potent "Old English 800" malt liquor which they drank back to back. They were now fresh out of both. The young gangsters agreed that Jay Boy would go into the projects to pick up a quarter ounce of herb, while Hot Dog stopped by Spades Liquor to grab a couple of 40ozs and a box of Phili Blunt cigars. They would meet back at the parking lot in a few minutes.

The first one to leave was Jay Boy who burned rubber out of the parking lot and then made a quick left turn into the projects. Once Hot Dog started up his 1977 Cadillac Coup De Ville, he noticed that his gas gauge was uncomfortably close to pointing at the big red "E". He drove twenty feet from where he had been parked and stopped his car next to the closest available gas pump.

As soon as he exited his vehicle, he was approached by one of his customers, "Let me pump dat for ya, champ," the filthy African-American man in the old, dingy flannel shirt requested. He stepped to the back of the Cadillac, pulled the license plate down, and then began unscrewing the gas cap, while Hot Dog walked up to the gas station window. Once Hot Dog paid the fifty dollars it would cost to fill up the gas guzzler, he began to walk back toward his Caddy. The old dope fiend had locked the gas pump's nozzle into the car's gas tank so it would pump automatically, and when Hot Dog approached his car, the man was busy spraying and washing the windshield.

Knowing that the crack head would be coming to buy dope with all the money he made washing windshields and pumping gas, Hot Dog decided to cut straight to the inevitable. In broad daylight, with a gas station full of customers, the young gangster reached down the back of his pants and removed his dope sack from between his butt cheeks. He walked up to the crack head and pulled a large cocaine rock from the plastic, and with his thumbnail, Hot Dog chipped off a five dollar piece of crack and handed it to the junkie.

"Aww, man!" the happy crack head exclaimed. "That's good lookin' out, youngsta."

The dope fiend headed toward the gas tank while Hot Dog shoved his dope sack back between his butt cheeks.

Hot Dog was waiting for the man to finish with his car and get out of the way, when out of nowhere he heard a loud voice scream in the distance, "Fuck your set, *esse*!" He looked up just in time to see a low riding Chevy Impala full of bald-headed Mexican men. In a split second before his brain could tell him the next move to make, Hot Dog watched his life flash before his eyes when two of the *cholos* hopped out of the Chevy, one armed with a pump-action, twelve-gauge shotgun and the other with a rifle that Hot Dog did not stare at long enough to identify.

The gunfire erupted simultaneously as Hot Dog dove behind his big gold Cadillac for cover. He wished that he had not left his pistol in the car as he squatted behind it listening to the sound of gunfire along with the whistling sound that the bullets made as they whizzed past. Hot Dog noticed a figure out of the corner of his eye and glanced over to see the dope fiend who had just finished washing his windows laid out on the ground bleeding from his head. There was no sign of the gunfire letting up, and Hot Dog knew that if he continued to squat behind his car like a sitting duck, he would soon end up like the junkie who was now stretched out only a few feet away in a puddle of blood.

He heard the sound of glass shatter as he crawled beside his car in an attempt to get to his vehicle's driver's side door. Hot Dog opened the door of his Cadillac and dove into the car, immediately reaching underneath the dashboard where he kept his Taurus 9mm pistol stashed. The gunshots paused momentarily while Hot Dog laid low in the seat and cocked his weapon.

The second that the young gangster sat up, he realized why the outside gunfire had paused. The two gunmen had managed to creep up while he was not looking and were now standing outside his passenger side window at point-blank range. The two *cholos* once again opened fire, this time with a range that made it impossible for them to miss. Hot Dog was struck in his shoulder by a rifle shot and in the face, neck, and chest by buckshot pellets from the shotgun as he attempted to dive back out of his driver's side door. The two *cholos* continued to fire at the young Bounty Hunter, leaving no room for him to return fire.

As Hot Dog squatted on the ground beside his Cadillac, bleeding profusely, he began to come to grips with the fact that his life would soon come to an end. The two Hispanic gang members were now shooting over the car in Hot Dog's direction. All at once, he heard a loud clink come from behind and felt a cold liquid begin to spray him in his face. He realized that one of the shooters had accidentally fired a round into the gas pump.

There was no mistaking the odor of gasoline, and all Hot Dog could do was watch as the gas sprayed from one side while the gunshots continued to ring out from the other. The young gangster knew that the next decision he made would be his last, but he made up his mind that if he had to go then he was going to take his enemies with him.

Hot Dog reached into his pocket and pulled out a red cigarette lighter. As the gas continued to spray from the gas station's pump, he closed his eyes tightly and then sparked his cigarette lighter.

Five minutes later, Jay Boy turned out of the projects to find the entire gas station engulfed in flames.

Chapter 44

"**A**ttention in the unit," came the voice from over the PA system loudspeakers, causing all of the inmates in module 2600 at Los Angeles County Jail to pause from whatever activity they were engaged in for a moment to pay attention, "Inmate Moss, number 1260165, roll up your property for release."

Psycho Twin could not believe his ears and knew there had to be some kind of mistake. But the young hoodlum did as the voice had told him and quickly snatched the sheets off his bunk, threw all his property inside the sheets, and wrapped everything into a bundle. Psycho Twin was standing at his cell door when the voice once again came through the loudspeaker, "Abel eleven, watch the gate. The gate's opening. Inmate Moss, step out," the cell door rolled open and Psycho stepped out with his property.

* * *

Sick Twin was once again in the hole where he had spent most of his time since arriving weeks earlier at the Orange County Jail. This latest trip to the hole was a result of a fight that Sicko had engaged in only two days before. He had been on the recreation yard doing push-ups when the big skinhead Nazi walked past him with his shirt off. Sicko was used to seeing things such as swastikas and portraits of Hitler tattooed all over the bodies of White inmates, and it was no big deal to see such things. But this time Sicko spotted a tattoo on the White man's chest that sparked his curiosity. He just had to ask the skinhead about his interesting tattoo.

"Hey, Wood," Sick Twin called out. When the man acknowledged him, he asked the burning question, "What's that supposed to be on your chest?"

The big White man smiled at the young Black gang banger for a second, sizing him up before responding, "Oh, you mean this?" the Nazi asked while pointing directly between his nipples to the tattoo of the figure with the rope around it's neck.

"Yeah, dat," Sicko answered.

"Oh, that's just a nigger hangin'," the White Supremacist answered right before Sicko's first punch landed.

The jailer came up to Sicko's tiny one man cell and ordered him to pack up his things and get ready for release. Just like his twin brother, Sick Twin was surprised to hear that he was being released. When he arrived downstairs to the release tank, Sicko found out that he had been bailed out.

Sicko exited the jailhouse doors and walked down the steps. Upon seeing his twin brother's Cadillac Escalade parked next to the sidewalk, he thought he must be dreaming. The even bigger surprise was when Sicko realized who was sitting in the passenger seat of his brother's truck.

"Whaddup, homie!" Diamond yelled out of the window as Sick Twin approached.

On the way back to the projects, Diamond and the twins had a long conversation about the events currently taking place in their neighborhood. Diamond explained to the twins that he needed their help in the street war, but in spite of all the money he had just spent to bail them out, if they chose not to get involved, it would be okay with him.

Both twins gave Diamond the response he expected, "Nigga, just shut up wit that dumb shit, Diamond," Sicko responded with a snicker. "You already know da bidness."

"On Bounty Hunta Watts he know," Psycho agreed.

Once Diamond was sure he had regained the loyalty of his young homeboys, he hipped them to all the new obstacles and traps which they would face in the projects. He warned them of the danger of going to the opposite side of the park. He let them know how Momma Maria was now calling the cops at the first sight of any Bounty Hunter attempting to hustle in her parking lot. He also informed the twins of Gordo's new tactics of killing innocent Black civilians and giving his gang the green light to snitch on Bounty Hunters who attacked *Vatos Locos*. After he ran everything down to them, Diamond gave the twins permission to do anything and everything in their power to achieve victory in the street war.

Chapter 45

Within a two week span, the time that had elapsed since the funerals of his little brothers, Gordo had managed to regain his title of undisputed overlord of the *varrio*. His desperate tactics had proven to be effective, and thus the stout Mexican man was beginning to look like a genius and also a messiah to the *Vatos Locos*.

With the assistance of Sergeant Bookman and a few other key players, Gordo was once again generating big revenue for the *varrio* and also punishing his enemies from across the park in a manner that would make Poncho Villa proud. With the new confidence and respect Gordo had earned with his soldiers, he had come up with a plan to gradually move Lil Tijuana across the park and eventually take over the entire Nickerson Gardens housing project. With Sergeant Bookman constantly kicking in the doors of Diamond's money spots and seizing cash, guns, and drugs, there was no way the Bounty Hunters would be able to sustain this war much longer.

Gordo had just finished weighing out and separating the ten kilos of cocaine he had scored the night before when his telephone rang.

"*Buenos dia*," Gordo said into the receiver after picking up his phone. The line was quiet and without a sound, so Gordo spoke once again, "Hello? Who the hell is this?" When there was no answer he hung up the phone. After a moment the phone rang again. This time Gordo checked his called ID screen, which read 'Blocked Number'. He answered the phone once again, "Who is this? Stop playing on my phone, putho."

Two seconds later, Gordo heard a loud crash at the front door of his hideout. The door flew open and several federal agents began swarming into his project apartment, "Freeze! FBI!" one of the agents yelled out while brandishing her badge and gun. Gordo knew that he was caught red-handed and also that ten kilos was far too much for him to flush down the toilet. With all the bagged-up snow on his kitchen table, along with the scale that was still covered in cocaine residue, the Mexican don knew that there was only one thing left to do. When the agents emerged, Gordo quickly laid down on the floor in a prone position. Soon after, the leader of the *Vatos Locos* was cuffed and on his way to jail.

Chapter 46

For the third time in two weeks, Sergeant Curtiss Bookman arrived early at the 77th precinct. With the suspension of his colleague Peter Kinbrew, the arrest of Gordo, and the latest order from his telephone dictator, Bookman was now working against the clock. The only bright spot in all of this was that his rookie ride-along had been reassigned and he was operating by himself.

When Bookman walked into the door, his first order of business required the assistance of his old friend Brenda Hayes. The sergeant approached the jailer's desk armed with a box of Crispy Cream donuts and two large Starbuck's strawberry frappuccinos — two things that he knew Officer Hayes loved.

"Aww, hell, you must need something," the chunky, little, brown-skinned woman announced at the sight of Bookman's offerings.

"Now why do a brotha got to need somethin' to hook his favorite comrade up?" Bookman asked. But Brenda Hayes stared at the sergeant with a look on her face that quickly let him know he had better hurry up and get to the point, "Okay, Bren, the thing is... I received some orders from Cody awhile back, and at that time I had my mind occupied on other things, so as a result I wasn't really paying attention at that particular moment in time to what he was trying to convey to me right then so—"

"Oh, cut the shit already, Booker, and tell me what you need before my grandchildren grow up!" Brenda interrupted.

"I need to get into Cody's office to review a few things," Bookman said as he stared at his colleague through puppy dog eyes.

"After you," Brenda Hayes said while motioning for Bookman to lead the way. The two of them made their way down the hallway and then stopped at the door marked 'CAPTAIN'S OFFICE'.

"You got ten minutes," Officer Hayes warned before removing her large ring of keys and swinging the door open, "and if for some strange reason you get busted up in here, I don't know a damn thang."

Once she shut the door behind him, Bookman quickly made his way over to the captain's computer and turned it on. After the minute it took for the computer to boot up, Bookman began pushing buttons until a series of folders popped up onto the computer screen. He took hold of the mouse and began maneuvering it past the folders. He stopped at the folder which read 'WITNESS PROTECTION PROGRAM' and double clicked the button on the mouse to open the selected file.

Chapter 47

As soon as Psycho Twin managed to shake his brother and Diamond, he headed straight for the Lil Tijuana side of the projects. The last time he talked to Gina, she broke up with him over the phone and hung up in his face. In jail, and feeling helpless at the time, Psycho vowed to kill the mother of his son as soon as he made it out of prison. Now that he had temporarily dodged the big house, his mind frame had changed and he began to see Gina's point of view.

After all, it was he who had chosen to leave his family behind by taking part in the dangerous kidnapping robbery. Gina had begged him many times to calm down on the life of crime he was leading. She never complained about him hanging out with his homeboys. She did not care if he sold drugs. All she wanted was for her man to stop robbing and killing, but this had been too much to ask. Psycho Twin told himself that he was who he was and that Gina knew exactly who he was when she had begun carrying on a secret relationship with him. If she could not handle the gangster mentality that came with him, then it was okay, but no matter what, she *was* going to let him visit with his son.

Deep down, the young gang banger knew that he was using his son as an excuse just to see his child's mother. Psycho was sure that once Gina laid eyes on him, the animal attraction would be too much for her to resist and she would once again be in the palm of his hand.

Unimpressed with the things he had heard about the VL attacks taking place on any Black who dared drive through Lil Tijuana, Psycho Twin did not give it a second thought as he drove through the Mexican side of the neighborhood in his Cadillac Escalade with the sound system in his truck pounding so loud that it set off the alarms on several cars parked on the side of the road.

Psycho pulled into the parking lot where Gina's apartment was located and stepped out of his truck caressing the HK .40 pistol concealed in his waistband. He noticed a pack of *cholos* hanging out in front of Gina's building who had stopped what they were doing to focus on him as he approached. The young gangster smiled at the VLs with an evil grin and then walked right past them.

He strolled up to Gina's unit and knocked on the door. A few seconds later, Gina's grandmother opened the door.

"*Uh oh,* ess *el Diablo,*" the old woman said. "*Gina! Bajar la puerta, presto!*"

"*Ola, abuela,*" Psycho said to his son's great grandmother as he waited for Gina to come down the stairs.

"I not your grandma," the old Mexican woman snapped.

Soon after, Gina came down the stairs. Shocked to see her son's father at the door, her first words were, "What are you doing here? Oh, my God, how did you get out of jail?" Gina quickly walked outside on the porch, closing the apartment door behind her. Psycho did not manage to get a word out before she continued talking, "Carnell, you cannot be over here. It's dangerous now. They will kill you. You have to leave right now."

Psycho ignored everything Gina said and smiled at her with a flirtatious look in his eyes. He opened his arms in an attempt to hug his son's mom but was pushed away.

"I told you on the phone — it's over, Carnell. I can't keep going through this with you."

Psycho could tell from the way she looked at him and said his name that she was still in love with him.

"Aww, *mija,* can I just have one hug? And where is my son?"

"*Our* son," Gina corrected, "and he's sleeping right now. I will make arrangements for you to visit him somewhere safe, okay? Now please get out of here before you start some trouble."

A moment later, someone attempted to open the apartment's front door, but Gina was holding the doorknob so that it would remain closed. "Just go, Carnell!" she yelled, as the person on the other side of the door struggled to get it open. Gina's strength was no match for the person on the other side of the door, and soon the door swung open. Standing face to face with Psycho Twin was his old friend Smiley. For a brief moment, Psycho's eyes reflected the surprise of seeing Gina's old boyfriend, and then they filled with the fury of betrayal.

Psycho yelled, "Oh, so this is why you want me to leave so bad, huh? You little nasty-ass bitch!"

"Hey, homes, don't be talking to her like that," Smiley demanded while feigning a feeble attempt to get around Gina who was holding him back.

The young Mexican girl stood in front of her boyfriend while she continued to yell at Psycho, "See? That's why I don't wanna be with you no more, Carnell; you are so disrespectful to me and I can't have my son growing up seeing that!"

Psycho was visibly disgusted, "You mean you would rather him grow up to be a punk-ass coward like ya little boyfriend here or what?" Psycho asked while pointing at Smiley. Before the Hispanic man could respond to the insult, Gina's grandmother appeared in the doorway.

"Get out of here, Carnell, or I gonna call the cops on you!" the old lady exclaimed in her heavy Spanish accent. "You are no good for my Gina *or* my grandson, so you stay away from here, Carnell!"

As upset and hurt as he was, Psycho decided not to make matters worse by arguing with the great grandmother of his son. His facial expression morphed back into his signature evil grin, which he wore most of the time.

He decided to say one last thing before he departed, "Hey, Smiley, Gina told me about your little uncircumcised peter," Psycho announced with a taunting laugh. "Do you got a beanie on your weenie, homeboy?"

After asking the insolent question, the young gangster turned around and walked off laughing.

Before Psycho could get halfway to his truck, he heard Gina scream, "No!" followed by a loud clapping sound that came from behind. He turned around to see Smiley with the .38 revolver still smoking in his hand. He felt his legs go numb before he dropped to his knees and then laid all the way down on the ground.

Hysterical, Gina ran quickly to his rescue, jumping on top of Psycho's body and acting as a human shield to prevent Smiley from firing any more shots into him.

"I'm sorry, Carnell!" Gina cried as the tears flooded from her eyes. "I love you; please don't die, baby!" Gina's pleading was the last thing Psycho heard before everything went blank.

Chapter 48

L il Ricky arrived at his usual time to pick Stormy up from the studio. He was surprised to see her in the parking lot waiting for him to pull in, since he usually had to honk and then wait five minutes for her to come out. Today, she ran up to the truck and began tugging at the passenger side door handle before Rick Rock could manage to come to a complete stop.

"Guess what, Daddy," the young beauty queen said with a big smile.

"What? What?" Lil Ricky responded, automatically excited about whatever his girlfriend was going to tell him.

"I got a record deal, baby!" Stormy announced.

Lil Ricky could not believe his ears. "You lyin' to me, girl," the teenager said, wanting to be assured about this wonderful news.

"Baby boy, if I'm lying, then I'm dying. I just met Billy Milton from View Point Records, and he loved my voice *and* my songs. J Star surprised me with the meeting, and now he's having the contract drawn up so I can sign it sometime this week."

At that point, Lil Ricky's business sense kicked in, "Well, you ain't signing a damn thang until we have a lawyer look at the contract. You can't be so happy to have a record deal that you sign a fucked-up contract. You betta look at what happened to TLC and Toni Braxton, and—"

"Okay, Daddy," Stormy cut him off. "I just wanted to enjoy this moment and celebrate the good news, baby; we are about to be rich!"

Rick Rock was slightly relieved to hear his girlfriend use the word "we" in the same sentence as the word "rich".

"So where do you want to go celebrate, Lil Bit?" Rick Rock asked, prepared to take her to the moon if that was where she wanted to go.

Stormy scooted closer to her man and then put her hand down his shirt and caressed his chest, "Oh, you already know where Lil

Momma wants to go celebrate, don't ya, Big Daddy?" Stormy asked in a flirtatious manner.

Lil Ricky could not help but blush at his girlfriend's aggressiveness. "No, not really, baby girl. Why don't you tell me?"

Stormy scooted even closer and snuggled against him, and then, with her face inches from his, she kissed his neck.

"I want to go home to *my* house," and she kissed his neck again before speaking, "and go into *my* room," and again she kissed her man softly on his neck, "and get into *my* bed," another kiss on the neck, "and make love to *my* man," kiss, "all," kiss, "night," kiss, "long."

"Say no more," Lil Ricky said with a smile before putting the peddle to the metal. The two teenagers were halfway home, still driving on the freeway, when his cell phone began ringing. He turned his sound system down and then clicked his phone on and raised it to his ear, "Who dis?" he asked.

Stormy could not help but notice the quick change of her boyfriend's facial expression, while Rick Rock exclaimed into the phone, "Blood, don't tell me dat!" His mood had changed from chipper to somber right before Stormy's eyes, "I'll be through there in about thirty minutes, dog," Lil Ricky promised before clicking his phone off. He slammed his cellular phone down into the side console of his truck and then banged his hands hard against the steering wheel.

"What's wrong, baby?" Stormy asked while scooting back toward her man in an effort to comfort him. Lil Ricky pushed her away without answering her question.

For the remainder of the ride home, the truck was quiet without a single word from either teenager. When Lil Ricky pulled up to the apartment building, instead of pulling into the underground car port like he usually did, he stopped on the street next to the curb in front of the complex. Without a word, Rick Rock reached over Stormy, opened the passenger side door, and gestured for her to get out.

Realizing that her man was going through a serious personal issue, she only spoke one sentence before exiting the vehicle, "I love you, baby. Please be careful."

She closed the door behind herself, and Lil Ricky pulled off, burning rubber.

Chapter 49

The first thing Sergeant Curtiss Bookman did when he awoke at 7:00 A.M. was to contact the precinct dispatcher to let her know that he would not be coming into work this morning. After his morning coffee and cigarette, Bookman turned on his personal computer. He sat down and waited for the modem to connect him to the Internet, went to the key-word section at the top of his computer screen, and typed in the words MAPQUEST. COM. Seconds later, a web site popped onto the screen instructing him to type in the address of the destination he was trying to reach along with the address from which he was departing.

The sergeant followed the web site's instructions, and five minutes later he hit the print button and watched the printer spit out his personal map. Along with the map was the estimated time that it would take Bookman to reach his destination. According to the printout, it would take the sergeant approximately seven hours and twenty-six minutes to get there.

Chapter 50

Lil Ricky was rudely awakened when the miniature soccer ball struck him in the side of his head. He watched as the little Mexican boy ran to retrieve the ball and threw it back in the direction of the little Black boy who he was playing with. As usual, the emergency room at MLK Hospital was packed from wall to wall with sick and wounded people along with friends and family who had brought them here. Every chair in the waiting room was occupied, and laying all over the floor were the people who were not fortunate enough to find seats.

Lil Ricky had dozed off an hour earlier while waiting to hear some news on his friend Psycho Twin who had been in the middle of surgery when he arrived several hours earlier. The teenager looked across the room to find that Sick Twin was still pacing back and forth only a few feet away from the door where the doctor or nurse would come out and give him an update on his twin brother's condition. Every time the door opened, Sicko would harass whatever employee appeared in the doorway. He questioned nurses, doctors, janitors, and security guards alike. Nobody in a uniform was exempt.

Shortly after Rick Rock woke up, the emergency room door opened and the nurse who had been updating Sicko stepped out. The attractive young nurse said a few words to Sick Twin. Then he turned around and gestured for Lil Ricky to come. Lil Ricky and Sick Twin followed the nurse through the open door and down a hall. She led them to a hospital recovery room where the teenagers saw an empty bed. Beyond it was a large curtain hanging from the ceiling. The nurse led them to the other side of the curtain where they found Psycho Twin laying in a hospital bed.

"Whaddup, my niggas!" Psycho exclaimed as soon as he saw his brother and his best friend. Sick Twin did not smile. Instead, with a serious look of concern on his face, he carefully examined his twin brother the same way a doctor would, while Rick Rock shook Psycho's hand and started up a conversation.

Sicko cut the men's small talk short, "The nurse said there was some bad news but that she would rather you break it to us. So, what's the bidness?" Sicko asked, staring at his twin brother.

"It ain't nothing, Sick. They just said I might not walk no more," Psycho informed him.

A tear ran down Sick Twin's cheek and a lump formed in his throat preventing him from speaking again.

Lil Ricky inquired, "They say you was definitely paralyzed, or is it just some temporary shit, Psycho?"

"Well... I can wiggle my toes. The doc said that's a good sign. You know me, Rick Rock; if there is any way, any chance for me to walk again, then I'm gonna walk, blood," Psycho promised. "Plus, my dick still get hard, so I'm bool for now until I get back on my feet."

Even Sicko had to laugh at this statement from his brother.

"I'll tell you what though, blood," Psycho revealed. "That motha fucka Smiley did this shit to me in front of Gina's house when I went to visit my son."

"Say no more, dog," Lil Ricky said.

"Oh yeah, Smiley-ass is a walking mummy; you can believe dat one, my nigga," Sicko added.

"I hope so, 'cause if y'all don't get him, then I will. Wheelchair or not, my trigger finger still works just fine," Psycho proclaimed.

Rick Rock was beginning to grow uncomfortable with the conversation. When it came to violence, he was a firm believer in the concept of all action and zero talk.

"So when you gettin' up out of this hospital, dog?" Lil Ricky asked, changing the subject.

"Aww, well... they say I will be here for at least another three weeks or so, and then they supposed to be transferring me to Rancho Los Amigos Hospital in Downey for rehab. That's where they teach niggas how to walk again. Either dat or learn how to play dat wheelchair basketball," Psycho said.

Lil Ricky laughed.

"Yeah, well, we need yo crazy ass to hurry up and go to rehab so you can get back on the move," Sick Twin announced.

After a few more minutes of conversation, the attractive young nurse walked back into the room, "Sorry, guys, but we have to run some tests on him, so I'm going to have to ask you guys to come back later," the nurse said while neatly setting several needles onto a steel tray beside Psycho's bed.

"That's understandable, and we do appreciate the little time that you *did* allow us to spend with this knucklehead," Lil Ricky said with a smile. "Thank you so much."

Before the two men walked out of the room, Sick Twin leaned down and whispered in his twin brother's ear, "By the time you get out of this hospital, I promise you dat punk motha fucka will be laying six feet below a plaque with his name on it. That way you can piss on it as soon as you come home."

The two young gangsters twisted their fingers into a capital "B", flashing their gang's sign to Psycho as they made their way out of the room.

Chapter 51

After three days in the LAPD 77th Division substation, Boss Ross was transferred to the downtown criminal courts building for his arraignment. Once he was shackled up and escorted into the courtroom by the bailiff, he spotted his mother and two of his aunts sitting in the audience. They all waved and smiled at him. He also noticed a young Mexican woman who looked familiar sitting away from his family on the other side of the audience. The young woman was staring directly at Boss Ross, causing him to feel slightly uncomfortable.

When the assistant district attorney read off his charges to the judge, Boss Ross found out that his charge had been amended from simple possession of controlled substance to possession of a controlled substance with intent to sell. This news crushed Boss Ross' hopes of bailing out, because a more serious charge meant a higher bail. Prior to court, his bail had been set at thirty-five thousand dollars.

After pleading, "Not Guilty," to the charge, Boss Ross cringed when the judge began to speak. "Okay, Mister Ross, you have two 'Possessions for Sale', one as an adult and one as a juvy. I'm seeing a pattern here which tells me that you like to sell drugs. We are going to bring you back in two weeks for a preliminary hearing. OR is denied and bail is hereby set at eighty-five thousand dollars, cash or bond," and the judge slammed his gavel.

After court, Boss Ross was put on the big black and white Los Angeles County Sheriff's bus headed to the county jail. All the fresh off the streets "Fish" inmates were escorted from the bus in chains into the county jail. Boss Ross braced himself for the grueling intake process, which usually took about eighteen hours.

In this intake process, a new inmate was shipped from room to room in order to be processed. One room would be the classification room; the next would be fingerprinting, and after that would be clothing, and then the medical triage. The process was never-ending, and each room took an average of two hours to complete. On top of that, the deputies made matters worse by loud talking and using intimidation tactics to keep their inmates in line. It was not unusual to see several deputies storm into a room, drag a prisoner out into the hallway by his hair, and then commence to beat him for any reason — or no reason at all.

Boss Ross had been through this process so many times that he was immune to it. In the midst of all that was going on around him, he just traveled nonchalantly from room to room and waited for his name to be called.

He was in the medical analysis room three and a half hours into his intake process when, to his surprise, the female voice called his name over the loudspeaker, "Inmate Ross, I repeat, Inmate Ross, report to the release desk."

Boss Ross thought to himself, *This is impossible.*

He had not even managed to make a telephone call since entering the county jail, and the only person he had been able to reach while in the substation was his mother. Boss Ross loved his mom dearly, but due to her crack addiction there was no way he was going to tell her where he had his money stashed, because he knew that there was little to no chance of the cash ever reaching a bail bondsman. As he headed past the deputies and new arrivals on his way to the release area, he figured that Diamond must have bailed him out.

"What's your booking number?" the crabby female jailer at the release desk asked with a hint of impatience in her voice.

"5643801," Boss Ross responded.

The jailer typed his booking number into her computer.

"Ross," the woman announced as if Boss Ross did not know his own surname. "You made bail. Go wait in tank nine, and my trustee will be bringing you your clothing shortly."

Boss Ross headed to the dirty holding tank and was happy to find that it was empty. He headed straight to the pay phone and picked it up.

"Damn!" he exclaimed, realizing that the telephone was out of order. After twenty minutes, the trustee brought his clothes to him and instructed him to go to the property counter to pick up his

189

belongings. At the property counter, a deputy handed him his car keys along with the jewelry he had been wearing at the time of his arrest. After that, he was released to a waiting area and instructed to go to the cashier's counter outside the jail to claim any cash he may have had on his person. Boss Ross' cash had been booked into evidence upon his arrest, therefore, he did not bother approaching the money counter but instead headed straight to the pay phone.

After several attempts to reach his mother on the phone, he realized that he was going to have to find another way home when she failed to answer. He thought about taking a cab and then jumping out and running once he made it to the projects, knowing that no cabby in his right mind would chase him through the Nickerson Gardens; however, Boss Ross quickly dismissed this thought, not wanting to end up right back in jail before he could make it home.

Following a few moments of contemplation, he decided to do the right thing and jump on the Metro Rail. Although he had no money on him, he would still be able to ride the train legally due to the county jail policy. All he would have to do is show his release papers to any metro officer who might detain him, proving that he had been released from jail within the last twelve hours.

Boss Ross set out on his eight-block trek to the Metro Rail station. He once again fought the temptation as he walked past the long line of taxi cabs parked in front of the county jail waiting for the freshly released prisoners. There were also a lot of people just loitering in front of the jailhouse waiting for their loved ones to be released. Boss Ross was hoping that he might get lucky and stumble upon someone he knew but realized that it was not going to happen once he reached the corner of Beauchet and Vignes Boulevards.

For some reason, he began to feel strange as he crossed the street. A faint voice in the back of his mind told him that he was being watched. He looked around but saw nothing out of the ordinary, so he quickly dismissed his sudden paranoia as being unfounded. He continued his walk toward the Metro station, passing by several run-down bail bond businesses, liquor stores, and donut shops. Without a cent in his pocket, Boss Ross decided that he was going to have to find someone to bum a cigarette off of before he got onto the train.

He walked into the parking lot of a mini-mall with a bail bond place with bright neon lights that read 'Bad Boy Bail Bonds'. From many prior experiences, Boss Ross knew that the bail bondsmen were on his side and decided to walk into the building to ask for a cigarette. He was greeted by a large biker-looking man who right away removed a pack of Marlboro reds from the top pocket of his dingy button-up shirt and handed Boss Ross three cigarettes and a business card. Boss Ross thanked the man and then headed back out the door.

As soon as he exited the building, he noticed something that struck him as being peculiar. When he had crossed the street only five minutes earlier, during his episode of paranoia, he had glanced at every vehicle that was waiting at the light as he crossed. One of the cars he saw had been a late-model charcoal-grey Mercedes Benz 190 model. He could not forget this car because he himself had owned a 190 Mercedes Benz years ago as a teenager. Once Boss Ross had crossed the street, that Mercedes, as well as every other vehicle at the light, had driven off and disappeared into the horizon. Now, when he stepped out of the bail bonds building, Boss Ross once again spotted the Mercedes, this time backed into a parking space all the way on the other side of the parking lot as if attempting to hide from his view. Boss Ross began to think that his mind was playing tricks on him. Curious as to its occupants, he began walking briskly toward the Mercedes. To his surprise, the car started up and then burned rubber out of the parking lot as he approached. This confirmed Boss Ross' suspicions, and now he was sure he was being followed.

Under the protection of broad daylight and being only a few blocks from the county jail, he knew the chances of someone trying to attack him were slim. This had to be some type of undercover cop following him. Nevertheless, Boss Ross decided to play it safe by walking only on the main boulevards en route to the Metro Rail station.

Now only a few blocks away, with a renewed sense of alertness and an eye out for the old charcoal-grey Mercedes, Boss Ross set back out with the awareness of a stray cat.

After walking past several more bail bondsman buildings, Boss Ross found himself power walking past an alley. He instinctively looked down the alley as he crossed and exhaled once he passed it. One more block to go and he was home free. Boss Ross reached the last main street that he would have to cross which was Ceasar Chavez Boulevard. He walked up to the light and began pressing the cross walk button over and over again several times as if that would somehow make the light change faster.

Ceasar Chavez Boulevard was busy as usual with cars, trucks, and buses traveling up and down the street, to and fro in downtown Los Angeles. After what seemed like an eternity, the light finally changed. With a long line of vehicles waiting at the light, Boss Ross quickly stepped off the curb and began his trek across the street.

He was relieved to reach the other side without incident and was now within one hundred yards of the Metro station. After another minute, Boss Ross found himself walking through the parking lot of the station. The parking lot was filled to capacity with the vehicles of people who would park at the station every morning and then ride the Metro Rail to their destinations in order to save time and money by avoiding traffic congestion on the California freeways.

Boss Ross was now at ease, as he strolled through the parking lot in the direction of the stairs leading up to the train tracks where he would have to board. He laughed to himself, realizing that he had jumped to conclusions a few moments earlier by believing that someone was following him. After all, who was he for someone to be following? He was nothing but a small-time drug dealer.

He was halfway through the parking lot when he heard the sound of a car's engine starting. Boss Ross looked around but paid it no mind as he continued to walk. He glanced toward the top of the steps to the platform and saw a few people waiting at the Metro stop. This let Boss Ross know that he had not missed the train. He also noticed that one of the people waiting for his train was a nice-looking young lady. The caramel-colored woman was standing on the platform with a tight blue-jean outfit on, holding a book bag in her right hand. "Dayummm…" Boss Ross said to himself. "I can see all dat ass from way down here." He told himself that this young lady was definitely a prospect, as he stared at her backside while approaching the curb that marked the end of the parking lot.

Boss Ross had about fifteen more steps to go before he reached the curb, when out of nowhere he heard the loud roar of a car engine followed by the unmistakeable sound of screeching tires. By the time he could take his eyes off the woman's derriere on the platform and look to see where the threatening sounds were coming from, the charcoal-grey Mercedes Benz had barreled out from behind the shelter of a large Ford F250 pickup truck.

Boss Ross immediately turned around and began a desperate spring in the opposite direction but was quickly overtaken by the vehicle and struck in the back by its front bumper, sending him tumbling to the asphalt. The Mercedes then backed up ten feet. Laying on the ground, Boss Ross looked back over his shoulder at the Mercedes to see the passenger-side door swing open. He saw the Hispanic man step slowly out of the car and begin walking in his direction with a large-caliber revolver in his hand. Boss Ross' mind told him to get up and run, but in complete shock, his body was not able to react to this urgent message from his brain. He was able to build up just enough strength to rise up to a crawling position on his hands and knees, but by that time the Mexican man was standing directly over him. Flaco aimed the gun at the back of Boss Ross' head and squeezed the trigger. After two shots to the back of his victim's head, the young *Vatos Loco* discharged the remaining four bullets into Boss Ross' back. In no rush at all, Flaco tucked his weapon into the waistband of his brown Dicky slacks and returned to the car.

"Good job, homes," Gordo's little sister La Smurf congratulated him while putting the car back in drive. She stepped on the gas peddle of the stolen Mercedes, and just like that they were gone.

Chapter 52

After five and a half hours of traveling northbound on the 5 Freeway, Sergeant Bookman spotted a big green sign that read 'FAIRFIELD — NEXT FOUR EXITS'. He had been traveling between ninety-five and one hundred miles per hour the whole way, and as a result he was making good time. The next sign that Bookman saw had a list of the next three exits. His was the last of the three, which was Travis Boulevard three miles ahead. He continued driving at ninety-five miles an hour but soon noticed the red and blue flashing lights close behind.

"Fuck!" Bookman yelled as he turned his John Coltrane CD down and began to merge over to the shoulder of the freeway. Not only was the sergeant in a hurry to reach his destination with no time to spare, but he also could not afford to get a ticket in this hick town, as it would definitely make his mission a lot more complicated than it had to be. The sergeant's mind began to race at a higher speed than he had been driving. He had to think of something fast.

Bookman came to a complete stop on the side of the freeway and then rolled his window down to allow the cool air from the AC to escape while the hot, arid, outside air engulfed the inside of his Caddy. Soon after, the sergeant was staring up at a California Highway Patrol Officer.

"License and registration, please," the Highway Patrolman requested. In a quick, analytical sweep, Bookman looked the cop up and down in an effort to gain a little bit of stereotypical leverage over him in the imminent conversation. The first thing that the cunning sergeant noticed was that the officer's name tag read "DOMINGUEZ". The name in itself told Bookman most of what he needed to know. Secondly, he focused on the state-issued cowboy style Highway Patrol hat and Rayband shades that the officer was sporting, typical of a conformist doing what he could to fit in. This told Bookman that he was dealing with a gung-ho individual. Next, the sergeant noticed how crisp, creased, and new the cop's uniform appeared to be. This had rookie written all over it.

"This should be easy," Bookman said under his breath as he reached into the glove compartment to retrieve his registration. While his hand was in the glove box, Bookman purposely grabbed his badge and placed it on top of his registration card. He then fumbled around for a moment inside of his glove compartment until he felt the patrolman's eyes begin to burn a hole in his back.

"You okay in there, man?" the officer asked, beginning to grow impatient.

Bookman turned around and noticed that the officer was now bending over with his head halfway inside the driver-side window. It was time to make his move. All at once, Bookman pulled his registration card out and dropped his badge onto the passenger seat of his Cadillac while making the fumble look like an accident.

The patrolman looked over his registration, and then the bright-eyed officer pointed at the badge and asked, "What's that?"

"Oh, that's just my shield, sir. I'm a sergeant with the Los Angeles Police Department," Bookman announced.

The Highway Patrolman's guard quickly went down. Before he could say another word, Bookman spoke once again, "I know I was kind of flying back there, but you know how we roll, comrade. I just came out here to swoop my daughter up because her and her mom are having some serious problems. You know how those teenage girls can get with their mamas. Then I gotta be back on the beat before the sun comes up 'cause they got me on first watch all this month, and I'm sure you know how much that sucks."

The sergeant followed this statement with a phony laugh while the patrolman reciprocated, and then he handed Bookman his license and registration back. "Enjoy your day, Sarj," the Highway Patrolman said, then, just like that, he was headed back to his patrol car.

"I knew you was a team player, son," Bookman mumbled to himself as he watched the young cop re-enter his vehicle.

Less than five minutes later, Bookman exited the freeway on Travis Boulevard. The sergeant made a right turn and traveled northbound on Travis for eight lights before he arrived at the next street, the one he was looking for. He made a left turn on San Lucas Road and found himself driving through a residential neighborhood. Closely following his map, Bookman made a series of right and left turns through the neighborhood before he ended up at Sundial Way, the street where the home he was looking for was located. He drove down the long street, watching the addresses get lower until he reached 331. The sergeant had found his destination and was now anxious to do what he had to do and jump right back onto the freeway headed south.

Bookman parked his car, reached into the backseat, and grabbed an outfit that was fresh from the cleaners still on hangers with the plastic around it. He stripped down to his underwear, removed the plastic from over the clothes, and slipped into them.

* * *

Daisy Kim had been under the witness protection program for only one week now. The little Asian woman had been given strict orders not to open the door for anyone unless it was law enforcement or someone whom she knew and was expecting. Daisy was the solo witness in a capital murder case, therefore, the district attorney did not cut any corners with regards to her protection. Until the conclusion of her testimony in trial, she was only allowed to reveal her location to two of her closest family members in order to minimize the risk of her being sniffed out by the defendant's hired goons the way the last witness had been.

Daisy had been working in SASSY GIRLS hair and nail salon when the young Asian gangster known as "Tick Tock" came in on the last Friday of the month at his usual time when the shop was closing. Lucy Fam, the shop's owner, had been paying extorted rent to Tick Tock and his gang known as The King Cobras for as long as Daisy had been working at the boutique. On that day in particular, it turned out that Lucy had been short on her payment as a result of a slow work month. She had tried to explain to Tick Tock that people were just not getting their hair and nails done as often, due to the high gas prices, the rising price of groceries, and other by-products of the looming recession. The Asian man had been infuriated about the situation and insisted that Lucy was lying about that month's take. He had become even more upset when the shop owner showed no remorse about shorting him on the rent and simply told him that there was no way she would pay him and that she did not even have enough money to pay the rent on her shop and home.

That had been the moment when Tick Tock drew his pistol demanding that Lucy open her safe. After she refused to open the safe, the Asian gangster promised her that if she did not open the safe by the time he counted to ten, he would blow her brains out. Tick Tock had counted to two and pulled the trigger.

Before leaving the shop, he had sworn to the remaining workers that they would meet the same demise unless they kept their mouths shut.

* * *

Daisy Kim had just gotten off the phone after a long conversation with her older brother when she heard the doorbell ring. All alone and not expecting company, she immediately grew nervous as her mind began to race. She had just hung up the phone from talking to one of the only two people who knew her location, and the other person who knew was due at work right now all the way back in LA. She was living in the house under an alias, so there was no way of anyone knowing where to find her with the exception of the cops and the district attorney.

Daisy walked up to the front door of the house and looked out of the peep hole. Standing on her front porch was a Black man who appeared to be between the ages of thirty and thirty-five wearing a brown UPS uniform with a clipboard and large cardboard box in his hands. Daisy knew there was no way the package was for her, so she assumed that it must be for the people who had lived in the house before she moved in.

Daisy yelled through the closed door in her heavy Vietnamese accent, "I no expect package. Thank you!"

"Oh, ma'am, sorry to disturb you, but this package is a rush delivery for your next door neighbors. It requires a signature;

however, they are not home at the moment, and they've got the 'Please Leave With Neighbor' box checked on this order."

"But I just move here. I not same neighbor here before," Daisy responded.

"Well, ma'am, it doesn't matter. All we require is the signature of any neighbor," the man proclaimed.

Daisy thought for a moment. She had met the neighbors the day she moved in and talked to them a couple of times after that. They told her that if she ever needed anything not to hesitate to come over, and she promised them the same hospitality in return. The welcoming Samoan couple seemed like nice enough people, so the last thing Daisy wanted to do was make enemies of them. After all, it was only a UPS man, so how dangerous could he be? Against her better judgment, Daisy Kim unlocked the door and twisted the knob. Before she could open the door wide enough to fit her head out, Sergeant Curtiss Bookman shoved it open, causing the door to slam hard into Daisy's small frame and knock her to the floor.

Five minutes later, Bookman slid into his Cadillac, quickly pulled off the bloody UPS uniform, and then wrapped it in plastic along with the bloody "Rambo" styled survival knife which he had just used to complete his task. Just like that, the sergeant was en route back to the freeway. On the way back to Los Angeles, Bookman made a detour through Malibu and dumped the hot plastic bag over a cliff and into the Pacific Ocean.

Chapter 53

At 6:00 P.M. in the evening, the normally upbeat dark side of the projects was unusually gloomy. The parking lots from 111th to 115th streets, which were ordinarily crowded with Bounty Hunter gang members, were all empty. All of the crack heads in the Nickerson Gardens were scrambling throughout the projects in an effort to locate their pushers, but to no avail. Every single crack house was closed, and all of the curb servers were mysteriously missing in action. The whole atmosphere on the project streets was comparable to the calm before a storm.

Deep inside the hallway of 110th Street Elementary School, out of sight from onlookers and outside traffic, over two hundred members of the notorious Bounty Hunter gang were gathered, listening closely as some of their highest ranking members briefed them on the new plan of attack.

"This shit has got way out of hand wit these god damn hat dancers, y'all!" Diamond exclaimed while standing in the middle of the quiet crowd. "We done lost too many soldiers to these weak motha fuckas, and you know why?" Diamond looked around for anyone who might dare stick their neck out by answering the question.

"Shit, it's too many niggas that ain't riding for the cause, blood," responded Lil Stretch Dog who happened to be one of the coldest killers in the projects.

"Thank you, Stretch!" Diamond said with an appreciative nod to his young homeboy. "Out of the two hundred plus homies out here and the hundreds of homies that ain't here right now, how many niggas is actually putting in work? I would say thirty, give or take. But how many of yall is makin' money in the hood by gettin' off crack sacks and weed and shit? How many of you niggas is hangin' out enjoyin' the safety that too many real niggas done got life in prison or died for? Too many of you are, and I can say that with confidence."

Diamond got quiet for a moment and just stared at his homeboys. Some he looked at in disgust, and others he gave an affirmative nod. "All the soldiers out here know who they are, and everybody out here knows who they are, so I ain't speakin' on them. On the other hand," Diamond paused for a moment and pointed at several individuals in the crowd and continued, "all yall niggas out here gettin' a free ride is who I'm talkin' to, and just like the riders know who they are, yall motha fuckas know who yall are and so do we. This neighborhood was established on violence. It was *my* gee homies who initiated the Watts riots back in the sixties. Lot boy niggas did that, not no motha fuckin' Mexicans. It ain't nothin' but Huntas who dump on the cops and kill them son of a bitches every time they get out of pocket. Some of the homies are on death row, as we speak, for this shit. How yall think they would feel after sacrificin' they life for these projects knowin' that we lettin' some Mexicans give us problems?"

Diamond became choked up and paused for a brief moment, and then he said, "Holla at these niggas, Sicko," and Diamond stepped from the middle of the crowd, allowing Sick Twin to take the floor.

"It's like this, my niggas," Sicko began. "The big homie said it better than I can say it. If it was up to me, a lot of you niggas would get ran up out the set. Those motha fuckas paralyzed my brotha two days ago, and since then I done dropped one of them, and I ain't even close to bein' finished. I know damn well that I'm gonna hold up my oath as a Hunta, and I know that Lil Ricky will too. Even Diamond's old ass came out of retirement to go out there doin' dirt."

This comment set off a round of laughter among the many young gang bangers standing around at the pow wow.

"My purpose for being here today is to stop all the excuses," Sicko said, as he walked up to several duffle bags next to a wall and began dragging them into the middle of the hallway. After dragging all the bags forth, one by one, he began unzipping them. He pulled three large wool blankets from one of the duffle bags and unfolded them neatly on the ground. Next, Sicko began pulling guns out of each of the bags and displaying them on the blankets. By the time he was finished, he had laid out enough guns to invade China and asked the crowd, "See all these heaters, Blood?" Sick Twin looked around at his fellow gang members and promised, "I'm giving all this shit away right motha fuckin' now!"

This statement automatically sparked a buzz of quiet conversations throughout the crowd. Many of the gang members began smiling while pointing at the guns they wanted the most.

"Yeah, y'all like dat, don't ya?" the smiling young gangster asked. "Well, ain't nothing free. There is a catch, my niggas," Sicko said and reached into his back pocket and produced a piece of paper. "It's time to separate the riders from the hood ornaments," Sicko announced while unfolding the sheet of paper. "With the help of a few homies, we made a list of every VL we could think of. It's over one hundred names on this list. With the help of me and my brother and Diamond, we have rounded up a gun for each name on this list, and they are all right here."

Sicko paused for a moment to stare at every man in the circle to place emphasis on what he was about to say. "Every nigga who picks up one of these burners will get a name assigned to him, and it will be your job to hunt dat bitch-ass donkey down and put his ass on a slab in one of them freezer drawers over at the city morgue. Now where my volunteers at? Raise ya hand or something. Let me know ya wit this bidness."

In a first-come-first-serve manner, Sick Twin passed out weapons to his homeboys one by one while instructing them to pick out a name on the hit list of *Vatos Locos* and sign their own names next to that name. Soon, every gun was gone and there was a signature next to every single name on the list.

"One last thing," Sick Twin announced. "I want every nigga out here to know that if you committed yourself to this shit, then failure is not an option. Me and Rick Rock got a list with three names each on it, and we already done knocked patches out those hat dancers. I made my brother a promise that I intend to keep. Now y'all can do like Lil Ricky and me and work in teams, or, for my loner niggas, y'all can handle the shit solo bolo. As long as we get these names crossed off this list, then I don't give a fuck how it get done. Now, if ain't nobody else got nothing to add, this meeting is a wrap. Me and Rick Rock got a appointment over in Lil Tijuana."

With a heavy gangster limp, Sick Twin walked off while folding the sheet of paper. After a round of handshakes and hugs, all the rest of the gang bangers began jumping over the fence and leaving the school grounds, determined to wipe the entire *Vatos Locos* gang off the map.

Chapter 54

Sick Twin exited the school grounds and entered the passenger side of the silver Yukon Denali truck.

"How was your meeting, Sun Tzu?" Lil Ricky asked, teasing his friend about the new battle strategy he had implemented after going to jail and reading *THE ART OF WAR*, a book by the Chinese author Sun Tzu.

"Nigga, you would know how the shit went if you wasn't too good to attend the motha fucka," Sick Twin replied. Rick Rock started up his truck and put it into gear.

"It ain't my job to be telling a bunch of grown-ass men what to do," Lil Ricky said before stepping on the gas peddle. The two young gangsters drove straight to their parking lot on 115th Street and pulled in beside a new-model Ford Taurus. Lil Ricky had paid one of his young homeboys, a thirteen-year-old kid, two hundred dollars to steal the car the night before.

The two teenagers got out of the truck and looked around before entering the stolen vehicle. After entering the car, Sick Twin immediately reached underneath the passenger seat to retrieve the guns they had planted there, two silencer equipped, fully automatic Uzis. Lil Ricky reached underneath the driver's seat and produced a medium-sized flathead screwdriver and shoved it into the ignition to start up the engine. Neither man spoke on their way to Lil Tijuana. They had already discussed their plan in detail the night before, so now the only thing left to do was carry out the mission.

Once the two young killers came within view of the park, Sicko reached into the backseat and then handed Rick Rock a long dreadlock wig along with a pair of aviator lens sunglasses. Sicko placed a long, fake beard onto his face and placed a dirty, blue trucker hat on top of his head over the black doo rag he had used to tuck his braids under. Both men were already sporting brown work gloves on their hands along with bulletproof vests beneath their black, hooded sweatshirts.

As the two young assassins pulled into the parking lot where Gina's project unit was located, they quickly spotted the same thing that Psycho Twin had seen when he had entered the parking lot days before. Four members of *Vatos Locos* were standing on the sidewalk a few yards away from the walkway to Gina's apartment. There were also several innocent bystanders, including children, standing around and engaged in everyday activities.

Lil Ricky spoke for the first time, "Once we get out of this car, it's full speed ahead, Sick. We take care of them four and then head straight into the pad."

Sick Twin cocked his Uzi and stated, "Let's do this shit, blood."

In an effort to go unnoticed, Lil Ricky parked the stolen car in a parking space approximately fifty feet away from the *cholos*. As soon as he turned the car's engine off, Sicko reached for the door handle but was quickly halted when Rick Rock placed his arm around his shoulder. Lil Ricky could see the fire in his homeboy's eyes, therefore, he knew that he had to calm down in order to get him into the correct frame of mind to carry out this complicated hit.

Lil Ricky began speaking in a calm, cool voice, "Sick, you can't be in a rush, homie," Rick Rock said slowly, while holding his homeboy tightly in his grasp. "Now here's what we gonna do. We gonna tuck these burners into our waistbands and cover 'em up with our hoodies. Then we gonna get up out of this car nice and slow. Then we gonna close the doors nice and soft. Then we gonna walk at a regular pace toward our vicks until we get within about ten feet."

Rick Rock paused for a moment to grab his weapon and cock a bullet into its chamber, "Then we gonna pull deez thangs out and chase 'em down then chop 'em down like old grass." At that moment, Lil Ricky saw the anxiety and emotion melt from Sicko's face, which let him know that his homeboy was ready. "Take a deep breath, homie," Lil Ricky said. "On the count of three we push. One two three — let's move."

The two teenagers exited the vehicle in a normal fashion and began their approach toward the Mexican gang members. Dressed in their disguises, the two young gangsters followed their plan closely, walking slowly to prevent the enemy from noticing them. They arrived within ten feet of their targets without alarming the *cholos* and out came the guns.

Everything began to move in slow motion for Rick Rock as he aimed at his targets with tunnel vision. One of the *cholos* spotted the two men approaching with guns pointed at him and his crew. He tapped one of his buddies on the shoulder, pointed at Rick Rock and Sick Twin, and yelled, "Look out, homes!"

The two young gangsters could see the fear in the men's eyes as they began squeezing the triggers of their fully automatic, silencer-equipped assault weapons. One by one, the men fell to the ground bleeding. The first *cholo* to spot them somehow managed to escape by running between the project buildings, however, Lil Ricky was sure he had shot him in his stomach a couple of times, so he would not get far.

By the time Rick Rock and Sicko had mowed down the other three victims, they began to hear screams coming from all over the project parking lot. Knowing that the police would be arriving soon, Lil Ricky was having second thoughts about going into Gina's apartment, but when he spotted Sicko running up to her building, he quickly realized that there was no turning back. The only thing left to do was to get the hit over with as swiftly as possible.

With Lil Ricky close behind, Sick Twin headed for Gina's front door, and as soon as he arrived he kicked it hard in an attempt to storm into the building, but the door did not budge. With Uzi in hand, he continued to kick hard on the door until he heard a loud popping sound and was struck in his bulletproof vest-covered chest by something that temporarily knocked him backwards. Sicko noticed two bullet holes in the door and realized that he was being fired at by someone inside the house. He aimed his weapon at the front door and fired five shots through it and then began kicking hard on the door again. After two more kicks, the door flew open.

With their weapons aimed straight ahead, Sick Twin and Rick Rock made their way into the apartment, but they saw no one. At that moment, Lil Ricky tapped Sicko on his shoulder and pointed to the floor where there was a fresh trail of blood leading back toward the kitchen area. Without saying a word, Rick Rock motioned for

Sicko to go up the stairs while he followed the trail of blood. Lil Ricky watched Sicko until he saw him reach the top of the steps, and then he began following the bloody trail. The drops led him down the hallway and into the kitchen area. He continued on the trail past the refrigerator and old potbelly stove. The trail continued all the way through the kitchen until he came to another small hallway which would prove to be a blind spot. Rick Rock was reluctant to peep his head around the corner; however, he knew it was necessary if he wanted to track Smiley down. The young gangster took a deep breath, then, all at once, he jumped into the hallway with his weapon aimed. All he saw when he entered the hallway was a wide-open back door. Smiley had escaped.

As soon as Lil Ricky turned around to meet back up with Sicko, he heard screams coming from upstairs, "Please don't, Darnell! Please!"

Rick Rock immediately recognized Gina's voice along with the sound of a baby crying.

"Sick!" Lil Ricky yelled as he began to spring toward the stairs. By the time he got halfway up the stairs, he saw Sicko emerge from a room and begin his trip back down the steps.

"Ain't nothing up there for ya," Sicko told Rick Rock as he ran past him on his way back down. Rick Rock immediately turned around and followed his homeboy.

Still dressed in their disguises, the two teenagers made their way out of the apartment and began a spring back to their getaway car. Halfway to the car, Lil Ricky and Sicko began to hear gunshots. Not knowing where the shots were coming from, they continued running in the direction of the getaway car and were fortunate enough to make it without incident. Lil Ricky had left the screwdriver hanging out of the ignition when they had set out on their mission minutes earlier in an effort to make the getaway process flow as smoothly as possible. He quickly twisted the screwdriver forward, starting the car's engine, slammed the gear shift into reverse, and backed out of the parking space. The gunfire continued and both teenagers could hear the sound of metal clanging as the bullets struck their vehicle. Lil Ricky threw the car into drive and then stomped on the gas peddle, putting it all the way to the floor. The tires screeched as they burned rubber out of the parking lot, leaving a long line of black tire marks behind.

"Please tell me that you didn't do what I think you did, Sick!" Lil Ricky yelled as he whipped the car around a corner en route back to the dark side of the projects, "Talk to me, Sick!" Lil Ricky exclaimed after he received no response to his first question.

Sick Twin's silence alone was sufficient to answer Rick Rock's question.

Chapter 55

From the moment La Smurf and Flaco committed their first murder together, they had become obsessed with the art of blood spilling. In fact, over a two month span, the unlikely duo had emerged as the Bounty Hunter gang's most formidable adversaries. The difference between La Smurf and Flaco when compared to the rest of the *Vatos Locos* were the tactics they used to take out their targets. Every move was well thought out and calculated to ensure the certain deaths of their victims.

In the parking lot on the Lil Tijuana side of Maxine Waters Park, La Smurf's head bobbed up and down as she leaned over the driver's seat of her car giving Flaco a blowjob. With his seat back and him enjoying the head job he was receiving from his home girl, Flaco felt his climax beginning to come, so he quickly put the crystal-meth-filled pipe which he held in his left hand to his lips and then put the blue cigarette lighter in his right hand up to the glass pipe and lit it. The pipe crackled and sizzled as the *cholo* inhaled, filling his lungs to full capacity and holding his breath. With a mouth full of spit, La Smurf continued to suck hard on Flaco's dick until he could take no more. All at once, Flaco blew a cloud of smoke into the air as the semen shot from his penis, allowing him to feel the rush from the crystal meth and the ejaculation simultaneously.

"That's the best fucking feeling in the world, aye!" Flaco yelled while smiling at La Smurf. "A straight up two for one, homes."

La Smurf removed a napkin from her glove compartment and used it to dab the leftover spit from the side of her mouth. Then she looked at her watch, "It's 2:50, *vato,* time to go monkey hunting," La Smurf announced. Flaco laughed out loud as his home girl started up her car. La Smurf and Flaco knew exactly where they were going when they drove out of the parking lot.

* * *

At Locke high school the bell rang at the stroke of 3:00 P.M., prompting its students to flood from out of their classrooms in droves. After the murders and arrests of several of his closest friends, Smokey Deuce had decided that he did not want to become another one of those unfortunate young Black men who landed in the losing column of life's statistic sheet. With a little help from his aunt, the teenage boy had checked into school and had not looked back. He always knew growing up that he was a lot faster than all of his friends, and as a result, whenever the project kids played football at the park, Smokey was always the first person to be picked.

When he tried out for the high school team, Coach Collins had been blown away by the raw talent the youngster possessed. In his entire twelve years of coaching high school football, the coach had never seen a kid run a forty-yard dash in 4.2 seconds until Smokey came along. Coach Collins instantly knew that the teenager would be a perfect fit at the running back position and would also serve the team well as a punt and kickoff returner. The only problem was Smokey's grades. He had not attended school since two years earlier when he was in the eighth grade, and he was unable to produce a report card with proof of the required 2.0 grade point average required to participate in extracurricular activities. The old, White, beer-bellied coach wanted Smokey on his team so bad that he bent the rules in order to get him. He promised the teenager that if he proved on his ten-week progress report that he was maintaining a C average, then he would be on the team. As a result, Smokey Deuce had begun spending less time running the streets and far more time staying home studying.

While all of the other students at Locke High left out of their classrooms walking briskly in a rush to reach their next destination, Smokey moved along with a leisurely stroll. Although he had a new lease on life and was determined to get himself together, old habits still die hard and gangsters do not walk fast. He strolled out of the school's double doors with book bag in hand at five minutes after three to begin his two and a half mile walk to the projects.

* * *

209

La Smurf knew exactly where she was headed when she drove out of the parking lot of Maxine Waters Park, because she and Flaco had been trailing Smokey from afar during his walk home every day since one of their young VL homeboys had told them about the young Bounty Hunter member who had recently checked into his school and who may have had something to do with Flaco's little cousin Rafa and their friend Conejoe's recent deaths in the parking lot of Momma Maria's.

By now they knew that Smokey took the same route home every day. First he would walk down Avalon for five blocks to 114th Street. Once he got to 114th, he would stop by Astro Burgers on the corner of Avalon and 114th to purchase a large drink of some kind. After that, he would walk straight down 114th beside the train tracks and then across Central Boulevard and into the projects. La Smurf and Flaco were aware that most of Smokey's walk was through the turf of the Bounty Hunters, which left them with only a small window of opportunity to catch the teenager off guard.

* * *

Smokey walked out of Astro Burgers with his mind on algebra. He had been struggling with the subject since his first day of Mister Valdez' third period class. Mister Valdez had proven to be a patient educator and took his time to go through each problem with Smokey step by step whenever needed. It did not hurt that he was an avid football fan and also an assistant coach for the Locke High Predators.

Mister Valdez was a middle-aged Mexican man who sported a thick mustache and wore his hair slicked back, giving him the appearance of a *veterrano,* an old school *cholo.* He was aware of Smokey's situation, and Mister Valdez was doing everything in his power to help the young man make the transition from gang banger to high school athlete. He often told Smokey the story of how he grew up in a gang-infested neighborhood and flirted with the gang life at a young age himself growing up but made the change when he realized where that road would lead. These pep talks motivated Smokey so much that he was now introducing himself as Mister Washington to his teachers and as Percy to his fellow students.

Now that he had gone from the gang life to the life of a civilian, Smokey was growing more oblivious to his surroundings and more careless with every passing day. When the ex-Bounty Hunter gang member started out on his walk through the hamburger stand's parking lot, he was not on the lookout for enemies, because in his mind, when he decided to leave the gang, he was leaving behind everything that went with it. Smokey had taken ten steps when he came to the back of the restaurant en route to the sidewalk that would lead him home. When he arrived at the back of the restaurant, in a split second, he was approached by a man with a familiar face.

"Whaddup, Flaco?" Smokey asked as if he had just run into an old buddy.

"What do you think is up, tar baby?" Flaco answered, drawing his chrome .357 pistol from his pocket and pointing it at Smokey's face while looking around to make sure there were no witnesses watching. To Flaco's surprise, Smokey did not attempt to run and did not appear to be afraid of being shot.

Smokey told Flaco while holding up his book bag, "Hey, Flaco, I know what's up with you guys and the Bounty Hunters, but I don't even fuck around no more. Look, dog, I'm going to school. I ain't out here tryin' to bang. Do you really think I would be slippin' in these streets like this if I was? I ain't got no problems with the VL." It was obvious that Smokey was sincere about every word he spoke. These actions and statements caught Flaco off guard. He had been sure that the teenager would try to run for his life just like the rest of them had, but instead, Smokey faced him like a man. This left Flaco with a difficult choice to make, as the naïve teenager just stood there staring at him in his eyes.

"Smoke that fool and let's get the fuck out of here, *esse!*" La Smurf yelled out of her car window.

With his gun still pointed at Smokey, Flaco turned to look at his home girl for a moment and then right back at Smokey who was now slightly squinting his eyes and cringing in anticipation of the coming shots.

Flaco could not bring himself to pull the trigger, and to Smokey's surprise, the *cholo* slipped his revolver back into the pocket of his Dickey slacks.

Smokey exhaled in relief once he was sure that his life would be spared, when all of a sudden, he heard two loud popping sounds from behind. He quickly turned around to find La Smurf pointing her small caliber pistol at him. Not yet knowing that he had been shot, all the feeling in Smokey's body left, leaving him in a state of numbness. The teenager felt as if he were dreaming when he heard the distant sound of two more shots echo through the air as everything went black. The last sound Smokey heard was the sound of running footsteps before his young body succumbed to the gunshot wounds and set his spirit free.

Chapter 56

Gordo had spent the past two days in a downtown Los Angeles federal jail. The first time he was able to get to a telephone, he contacted Mister Major Sanford, his personal bail bondsman, who he had been paying a retainer fee once a month for over ten years now. In return, Mister Sanford would bail out whoever Gordo wanted him to whenever he asked; all Gordo had to do was give him the name. This time Gordo himself needed to be bailed out.

When Mister Sanford got Gordo's call, he used a three way to contact the federal jail in which Gordo was being detained. He was told by a receptionist that Mister Hector Torez was indeed an inmate in the jail, however, he had yet to be charged with any crime. Gordo also found out that the feds could hold him up to seventy-two hours without charges before they had to release him and that it was not unusual for them to hold a person until the last minute. That statement gave Gordo a good laugh. The fact that he had just been busted with ten kilos of cocaine left no doubt in his mind that he would be charged with a crime. Before getting off the phone with Gordo, Mister Sanford informed him that the guy he had his sister call yesterday to request bail for, Mister Deon Ross, had never showed up to sign his paperwork.

"Deon Ross?" Gordo asked, baffled by the bail bondsman's statement.

"You mean you didn't okay bail for a Deon Ross?"

"Oh, now I remember," Gordo lied.

Ten minutes after he got off the phone with his bail bondsman, Gordo's cell door opened. "Torez," the jailer announced, "follow me," and the young officer led Gordo to a small interrogation room where he was greeted by a middle-aged Hispanic man sitting behind a desk sporting a suit and tie.

The man stood up when Gordo entered the room and extended his hand, "How are ya, Mister Torez?" the man asked while shaking

Gordo's hand. "I'm Detective Montenegro with the FBI. Please have a seat," the detective said while sitting down himself. "Can I get you anything, Mister Torez?" the officer inquired.

Gordo smiled wryly, "Yeah, homes, a beer would be nice right now." After laughing the statement off, Gordo realized that the detective had not found any humor in it.

The FBI detective waited for Gordo to make eye contact, and with a serious expression, he asked, "Do you really want a beer or what?"

The gang leader stared at the detective in disbelief and replied, "Oh, hell yeah," Gordo answered, realizing that the man was serious. The detective stood up and walked to the door. He opened it and then turned around before walking out of the room.

"You want anything else, like popcorn or potato chips? Do you smoke?" Detective Montenegro asked.

Gordo put in his order, and before closing the door behind himself, the detective told him he would be back in ten minutes. Ten minutes later, the detective walked back into the room holding a large paper bag in his arms. He set the bag on top of the desk and closed the door. As promised, the detective removed two six packs of Corona Extra from the bag along with a jumbo-sized bag of pork skins. Before sitting down, the detective grabbed one of the Coronas for himself and opened it, "I can't kill too many of these with you, homes. I gotta drive, aye," Detective Montenegro said in heavy *cholo*-styled lingo. Both men sat back in their chairs and Gordo popped open his first beer. The two men then began to converse leisurely.

"How 'bout them Raiders?" The detective had hit the jackpot with that question. He was aware that most Mexican gang members were die-hard Raider fans, and Gordo turned out to be no exception. For the next fifteen minutes, Gordo went on bragging about how good the Raiders looked this year. He talked about the powerful arm of quarterback Jamarcus Russel and how he had a new weapon to throw the ball to now that Javon Walker had come over from the Broncos. He spoke about the running back situation and how the Raiders already had a strong running game with Justin Fargas and how the acquisition of Darren Mcfadden and Michael Bush in the draft was overkill. He bragged about the defense and how the Raiders now had the strongest secondary in the NFL with Nnamdi Asomugha and Donte Hall. By the time Gordo finished bragging about the Raiders, he had already managed to knock down three beers, and the detective could see that he was feeling a bit loose.

Next, Montenegro switched the subject to low rider cars. This was another subject that he knew most *cholos* were passionate about. Once again Gordo started his boasting. He talked about his cocaine-white 1982 Cadillac Coup De Ville with the gold Dayton rims and how he had put a European front end on it and got it cut into a convertible. He discussed the differences between his 1963 and 1964 Chevy Impalas and the reason why the 1963 was better equipped for hydraulics. He told the detective about the differences and similarities of his 1948 Buick Road Master and his 1950 Buick Sedanette and why these were his two favorite vehicles in his collection.

Gordo was now working on his fifth beer, and by the loud manner in which he was speaking, along with his slurred speech, plus the perspiration that was beginning to build up on his forehead, Detective Montenegro could tell that the Mexican street don was now past tipsy. It was once again time to change the subject.

"So, they busted you with ten kilos, huh?" the detective asked.

Gordo had been on cloud nine up until this statement by the detective, which sent him on a free fall back to reality.

"I don't know, *esse*. Is that what they told you?" Gordo was now on the defensive, and his level of comfort with the detective quickly began to dwindle. Montenegro knew that if he was going to accomplish his feat with this detainee he would have to think fast.

"Look at me, homes," the detective announced, as he began pointing at his tan skin. "You and me are the same, El Gordo."

Gordo looked at the detective with a puzzled expression.

"Yeah, I know who you are, *esse*," the detective said. "I got a cousin from your *varrio*. You know us Mexicans always got a big-ass family. I got *familia* from a whole bunch of different *varrios*, from East Los all the way down through the Harbor Area, and I ain't better than nobody, homes." Montenegro could see Gordo's guard begin to go back down. "The only difference between you and me is I never got busted, aye. I'm brown and proud just like you, *esse*, and I will do everything in my power to help get you out of this because you are looking at a lot of *tiempo en la penta*, and I can make it so you will walk out of here today, but you gotta be willing to give me something to work with. That's the only way I can help you, homes."

Gordo looked at the detective with a new sense of hope. "So, what do I gotta do, *esse*?" Gordo asked.

Realizing that his fish had swallowed the bait, Detective Montenegro flashed a fox-like smile.

Chapter 57

One day after the brutal attack on the *Vatos Locos* and the botched murder attempt on Smiley, Sick Twin and Lil Ricky walked into the lobby of MLK Hospital on their way to report the news to Psycho. A minute later, the two teenagers walked into Psycho Twin's hospital room to find a nurse fussing at the young paraplegic gang banger, "You cannot smoke in this room, Mister Moss. There are oxygen tanks in here. What are ya tryin' to do, kill yourself?!" yelled the overweight, pink-faced White woman. When she noticed Lil Ricky and Sicko standing behind her, she began to walk toward them on her way out the door. "He's trying to set this whole room on fire," the nurse said on her way past the teenagers. Before she walked out of the room, she paused for a second but then spoke once again while looking at the youngsters with disdain, "I hope you guys aren't the ones bringing him cigarettes and lighters," the nurse said and walked out of the door.

"Cigarettes?!" Sicko exclaimed. "Shit, it smell like sherm up in here. Let me hit something, nigga," Sicko requested while looking at his twin brother. Psycho reached underneath his pillow and produced a pack of Newport cigarettes along with a small brown bottle containing a liquid substance.

"Go 'head and dip you one, but wait till you get outside to smoke it 'cause I ain't trine to hear that woman's mouth no more today," Psycho said while handing his brother the items.

"Where da hell you get some loop from anyway?" Lil Ricky asked. "I know damn well you ain't got it from us."

"The home girls Jeanna, Brandi, Dionna, and all dem came up here to see me. They bought a nigga a fifty-pour and a fifth of Henny," Psycho announced, holding up the large cognac-filled 7-Eleven Big Gulp cup that was on the stand beside his bed.

"You a fool, blood!" Lil Ricky said before snatching the large cup from his friend and taking a drink from the straw.

217

"Nigga, don't be drankin' out my straw!" yelled Psycho Twin. "The home girl Tweety told me about yo ass. You one of dem coochie eatin' homies getting all kinky with those bitches."

Lil Ricky stared at his homeboy with a look of guilt while both twins laughed at him, and he said, "Nigga, who wouldn't eat Tweety's poom poom? Dat bitch fine as hell, homie!" Rick Rock exclaimed, "Plus, the alcohol kills all the germs, so you ain't got nothin' to worry 'bout."

Psycho removed the top from his cup along with the straw and threw them in the trash can on the floor beside his bed.

Lil Ricky shook his head, "I don't believe that bitch is runnin' around puttin' my bidness in the streets like that."

This statement caused the twins to laugh out loud once again.

"We got some good news, some not so good news, and some news that I don't know how you gonna handle," Sicko announced. "The good news is we spilled about five *Vatos Locos* in one day. The bad news is that ya baby mama's punk-ass boyfriend got away." Sicko could see the disappointment in his brother's eyes and added, "He did get hit, but we don't know how bad."

"Shit, if he got shot, then he prob'ly layin' up in one of these hospital rooms as we speak. I know his name and everything, so we'll find out today."

"I didn't even think about that; that's a good idea," Lil Ricky said.

"Yeah, it's only a couple a floors separating the hospital rooms from the hospital morgue," Sick Twin agreed.

"So, what's the other news that you don't know how I'm gonna handle?" Psycho asked while staring at his twin brother.

Sicko hesitated and could not bring himself to speak.

"What the hell could it be that you don't wanna tell me?" Psycho inquired after a long moment of silence.

"You tell him, Rick Rock," Sicko requested. Lil Ricky looked at him as if he had no idea what he was talking about.

"Hey, man, whatever you talkin' 'bout, I ain't had nothin' to do with, and that shit is between you and yo brother, so leave me up out of it," Lil Ricky insisted.

Psycho focused his attention back on Sick Twin, "Darnell, what's the bidness?" he inquired once again.

Sicko knew that he had to man up and answer his brother's question no matter what the answer might do to their relationship. He looked into Psycho's eyes and spoke slowly, "Your baby mama is no longer with us, man," Sicko informed his brother.

With an intense look of confusion on his face, Psycho stared at his twin brother. "No longer with us?" Psycho asked as if he did not understand what the statement meant.

"Yeah, man," Sicko responded in an annoyed manner, "no longer with us, done deal, two new holes in her head that wasn't there at first." Sicko stared at his brother after clarifying this statement.

Psycho laid back on his pillow with a blank look on his face, staring into the air.

After a minute, Sicko placed his hand on his brother's arm and began to explain his reason for doing what he had done, "Carnell, look man, I had on a disguise, but Gina knew who I was because she called out my—"

Before Sicko could finish his sentence, his brother busted out laughing, "I'm fuckin' with you, nigga!" Psycho yelled. "You think I give a fuck about that stank-ass beyotch!?" Psycho asked in the middle of his laughter. "I'm glad dat hoe is dead, but what about my son; is he alright?" Psycho asked.

"Yeah, he bool. I didn't kill *him*," Sicko joked. "He saw his mama get sparked though, so he may be a little traumatized for a while. Other than that — he all good."

"What about her old-ass granny?" Psycho asked.

"The old bag wasn't home," Sicko answered.

"That's good shit, homie. So there is still somebody out there to take care of my seed until I get back on my feet."

"So I guess all is well in Crazyland then. We ought to giddy yup," announced Rick Rock. "You need anything before we bounce?"

Psycho thought for a moment, "Yeah, my nigga. I had mama go get my truck out the impound. I need y'all to get my keys from her before she starts selling my rims and radio and shit to buy dope with. Plus, I need my cell phone out the glove compartment, and bring it to me if she ain't clucked it off yet."

Sicko agreed to take care of his brother's business before the two men shook Psycho's hand. Then they turned around and headed for the door.

"Oh, one more thang, y'all," Psycho requested.

Lil Ricky and Sicko turned around and walked back toward the bed. Psycho Twin reached over to the stand at the side of his hospital bed to grab an ink pen and a napkin. He wrote a name on the napkin and handed it to Rick Rock, "I need you to call up to this hospital and find out if this fool is up in here, and if he is, I want you to call me right away on this hospital phone. Just ask for Moss and say my room number, and it will ring straight to me. Say that punk motha fucka's room number backwards, just in case somebody is listening."

Lil Ricky immediately pulled his cellular phone out of his pants pocket as he nodded his head in affirmation. The two teenagers then twisted their fingers into a "B", flashing their gang's sign as they walked out of the door.

Ten minutes after Sicko and Rick Rock left the hospital room, the phone beside Psycho Twin's hospital bed rang.

"Yeah," Psych said into the phone after picking it up and putting it to his ear.

"Your floor, seven oh three," came Rick Rock's voice through the phone before it went dead.

Chapter 58

"**O**rder in the court!" demanded the pink-faced, white-bearded judge before slamming his gavel down. "Once again we have all parties of interest present in case number TP08421. The People of the State of California versus Mister Edward Ong." The judge glanced down from his bench once again to find the same smug look of satisfaction that the defendant had shown on his face the last time he'd stood before him. The judge sensed that once again he was about to receive some bad news pertaining to this case. "If my memory serves me correctly, the last time we were here we had an evidence problem that needed to be solved. I think there was a witness protection issue that we needed to take care of—"

At that moment, the judge was interrupted by the obnoxious laughter of the defendant along with the chuckling of his attorney, so the judge requested, "Mister Starcevich, I fail to see any humor in anything that has been said up to this point, so maybe you can enlighten this court as to the joke?"

The lawyer and his client abruptly ended their laughter, "We apologize, Your Honor. It was just an attorney client thing," Mister Starcevich assured the judge.

Without accepting the lawyer's apology, the judge continued, "The conclusion we arrived at in our last proceeding was that the State would produce some sort of evidence incriminating the defendant by the deadline, which happens to be today, or in the alternative, we would drop this case."

The judge directed his sole attention to the district attorney, "Mister Moody, considering our conversation in chambers last time we were here, I would expect that the State is prepared to prosecute. Would I be correct in this assumption?" the judge asked.

Along with his client, Mister Starcevich stared at the district attorney in anticipation of the answer they knew would follow. Both men appeared to be suppressing their laughter as they waited for the

DA to respond. Mister Moody just sat at the table beneath the judge's bench, scratching his head with a look of defeat. Mister Starcevich and his client knew they had won, and it would not be more than a couple of hours before Edward Ong would be back on the streets.

All at once, Mister Arthur Moody smiled at the defense and stood to his feet. The look on his face changed from that of humiliation to one of borderline cockiness, "Your Honor, I regret to inform you that there has been another attack, this one on the last material witness we had available in this case," Mister Moody announced to the dismay of the judge. Judge Marshall could see the relief on the faces of the defense after the brief scare. "However," Mister Moody went on, "the good news, Your Honor, is that this time the witness has survived."

Edward Ong and his lawyer could not hide their surprise as they stared at the deputy district attorney in shock.

"Our witness is recovering in an undisclosed medical facility as we speak and will be fully prepared to testify on whatever date this court chooses to set trial for," Mister Moody assured the court.

The judge looked confused as he flipped through a stack of papers, "But how could this have happened? I thought we made arrangements to place our witness under State protection."

"We did indeed place her under State protection, Your Honor, but somehow our witness was tracked down and brutally attacked, sustaining multiple stab wounds. This, too, is now under investigation, and I will be happy to discuss the details with you off the record."

"I would appreciate that," the judge responded. "I trust that the witness is safe now?" the judge inquired sarcastically.

"Yes, Your Honor," Mister Moody replied, "and as a matter of fact, we have installed twenty-four hour police protection around her for the duration of this trial."

After consulting with his court clerk, the judge set the trial date at the earliest opening on the court's calendar. With the eyewitness who would undoubtedly seal his fate ready to testify against him whenever needed, Edward Ong would stand trial in less than two weeks.

Chapter 59

After Diamond and Sick Twin passed out weapons and ordered their soldiers to sign on the dotted lines of the hit list, it took the Bounty Hunter gang less than forty-eight hours to bring Lil Tijuana to its knees. Eleven murders in only two days was a record for even the notoriously violent Nickerson Gardens housing projects.

The Bounty Hunters had even managed to kill a veteran LAPD officer who had driven into the dark side of the projects in pursuit of one of their members following a drive-by shooting. As a result, both sides of the projects were now crawling with patrol cops twenty-four hours a day. Even this effort by the LAPD failed to deter the Bounty Hunters who were now determined to wipe the *Vatos Locos* off the map. The Bounty Hunters were just a bit more careful when they went on missions, ducking and dodging the cops on their way to make corpses of their Hispanic rivals from the other side of the park.

It was not hard for Gordo to see that the killing had quickly become one-sided. This fact made it even more pragmatic and beneficial for the *varrio* boss to complete the mission which he had agreed to carry out. Gordo removed the cell phone from his pocket and dialed a seven digit number. After two rings, Diamond answered the phone.

Chapter 60

Lil Ricky had been missing in action for two days before Stormy became too worried to fight the temptation of calling him. To the teenage girl's anguish, every time she called her boyfriend's phone it was answered by an answering machine. Stormy left message after message on Rick Rock's cell phone, calling several times an hour. The last time she called him, Lil Ricky answered the phone. He had been furious about Stormy's constant calls.

"God damn, Stormy, you know I'm busy out here. Stop callin' me every two minutes and get a motha fuckin' life!" the young gangster told her.

Stormy's feelings had been hurt bad as a result of Lil Ricky's statement. She had moped around the apartment feeling sorry for herself for several hours before her sorrow turned into anger. Soon after, her anger turned into determination, and that is when she decided that the best thing for her to do was to continue her quest to stardom.

Stormy picked up the phone and dialed a number. This time the phone was answered by J Star who quickly agreed to pick her up every morning and bring her to the studio. Before hanging up, he took down the directions to Stormy's apartment and let her know that he would be there in about forty-five minutes.

Stormy hung up the phone and got right into the bathtub to wash up. Once she finished bathing, she dried off and applied lotion to her body. Then she pulled her make-up bag from the cabinet beneath the bathroom sink. She took twenty minutes to apply her make-up, carefully putting it on so that everything came out just right. She was unusually liberal in applying her eyeliner, and once she finished, she stared into the mirror for a moment to admire her sexy reflection. Next, she put on her perfume. She usually spritzed two squirts onto her neck, but today she spritzed four. She also sprayed around her breasts and pubic area. Stormy then walked into her room and opened her underwear drawer. She selected her red, lace Victoria's Secret push-up bra along with the matching g-string panties and slipped into them. After putting on a black, tight-fitting Christian Dior dress and matching open-toe stilettos, Stormy was ready to go.

Chapter 61

It was 6:00 in the morning when Sick Twin was rudely awakened by the sound of several screaming voices, "Freeze! Don't fucking move, asshole!" yelled the voice.

Sicko opened his eyes and right away recognized the five cops with guns pointed at him as gang detail officers. Instead of the regular brown button-up shirts that patrol cops wore, every one of the officers who were now in his bedroom sported green T-shirts with collars. This uniform was the reason why everyone in the projects referred to the gang unit as "Green Shirts".

Once Sick Twin was cuffed and led downstairs, he spotted his mother sitting on the living room couch with her head down. She looked up as her son passed, "I didn't let them in, baby! I swear, when I opened the door they just pushed me out of the way and rushed in with dem guns," Sicko's mom claimed.

Sicko paid his mother's statement no attention. At this point, it really did not matter how they'd gotten in. The cops did not bother to let Sicko get dressed. Instead, they escorted him out of the house barefoot and in his underwear and then put him in the backseat of a waiting squad car.

Chapter 62

At 1:35 P.M., Lil Ricky, along with several young members of the Bounty Hunter gang, were hanging out in the parking lot of 115th Street. Never the one to hang out in crowds, Rick Rock had an ulterior motive for standing around with his homeboys while shooting dice and smoking marijuana. The getaway car that he and Sicko had used in their killing spree two days earlier was still parked in the lot, now with a car cover over it to hide the fresh bullet holes that were in the trunk area of the stolen vehicle.

Now that Sick Twin had been busted, it was urgent that Rick Rock get rid of the car before the cops found it. His plan was to drive the stolen car to an area in the City of Carson controlled by the Center View Pirus, a fellow Blood gang whose turf was right off the Avalon exit of the 91 Freeway, which made Lil Ricky's mission convenient. Located right outside that neighborhood were several abandoned factories, and this was an ideal place for Lil Ricky to torch the car, eliminating any DNA or other evidence that might still be in the vehicle.

Rick Rock's only problem was getting the car out of the projects that were still swarming with cops as a result of the ongoing violence. Every day at the same time, between the hours of 1:40 and 1:55 P.M., the police officers would clear out to make way for the third watch shift which began at 2 P.M. This left a fifteen minute window for Rick Rock to get out of the projects and onto the 105 Freeway.

After a two-hundred-dollar bet, which he crapped out on, Lil Ricky checked the time on his black Movado wrist watch. It was 1:43 P.M.

"I gotta shake this spot, blood," Rick Rock announced as he began to walk off from the crowd.

"Don't run away now, Rick Rock," taunted the teenager who had just scooped up his cash. "Let ya boy win summa dat good money."

Lil Ricky ignored the teasing of his friend and began yelling across the parking lot to a group of young women who were congregated together while putting each other up on the latest neighborhood gossip.

"Midget!" Rick Rock called out as he approached the stolen vehicle.

"What, nigga?" the pretty young lady yelled back.

"You ready or what?" Lil Ricky asked, obviously annoyed. After a few laughs, the girl hugged her friends, headed over to Rick Rock's silver Yukon Denali truck, and entered into the driver's seat.

Operating with a sense of urgency, Lil Ricky removed the beige car cover from over the stolen Ford Taurus, folded it, and threw it into the backseat. Once he finished that task, he entered the driver's seat. Lil Ricky removed the screwdriver from beneath the seat, started up the car, and pulled out of the parking space. He drove the stolen car to the parking lot's exit and looked from left to right, surveying 115th Street carefully. Once he saw that the coast was clear, he made a right turn and headed toward Success Street. With his homegirl following close behind in his truck, Lil Ricky pulled up to the stop sign on 115th and Success Street. The young gangster came to a complete stop and took a moment to put his seat belt on and adjust the rearview mirror to his liking. Once he was sure that everything was in its proper order and that Success Street was clear for takeoff, he let off the brake, allowing the vehicle to drift slowly onto Success Street before he stepped on the gas peddle. As he traveled toward Imperial Highway, Rick Rock looked into his rearview mirror to make sure that Midget was trailing close behind. He had gone out of his way to emphasize to his friend how important it was for her to follow closely behind the stolen car in order to hide the bullet holes in the rear of the vehicle. Lil Ricky was satisfied with what he saw behind him. Midget was wearing her seat belt and was driving with both hands on the steering wheel.

With his focus still on the rearview mirror, Lil Ricky noticed something traveling fast in his direction coming from in front of him. He took his eyes from the mirror to focus on the object that was closing in on him. It was a large, black SUV traveling full speed in his direction with no sign that the driver planned to slow down. Rick

Rock slammed hard on his brakes and watched as the SUV drove right up to his bumper and came to a screeching halt.

Rick Rock's mind began to race as he looked around for an escape route. Before he knew it, another large, black SUV closed in on him from the side. He put the stolen car into reverse and then looked back and motioned for his home girl to back his truck up, but she failed to move one inch due to the third SUV that had boxed her in from behind. Before he could react, Lil Ricky was being approached by several police officers with guns drawn. Once the teenager realized that there was no escape, he threw his hands up in a gesture of surrender.

Chapter 63

"**O**rder in the court!" demanded the court bailiff, silencing several conversations that were taking place simultaneously inside the crowded courtroom. Judge Marshall emerged from his quarters and took his seat behind the podium.

"Court is now in session," the bailiff announced right before the judge began to speak.

"We are back on the record in case number TP08421," the judge announced. "The People of the State of California versus Mister Edward Ong. I trust that all parties are present in this matter?" The judge took the time to look around, confirming that all parties were indeed present.

*   *   *

The trial had been unusually short since the prosecution had hung its hat strictly on the testimony of one single witness; however, the shortness of the trial had not managed to dilute the potency of that lone witness. Every person in the courtroom had paused in silence, and several people, including a few members of the jury, had covered their mouths in a gasp as Daisy Kim entered the room.

Not only was the tiny Asian woman being pushed to the witness stand in a wheelchair, but she was also wearing bandages on her face and neck, almost giving her the appearance of a mummy. Her wheelchair's pusher also drug along an IV stand, which held the tube that was protruding from her arm. The fact that she was confined to a wheelchair made it impossible for Daisy to take the witness stand; instead, she was forced to testify from her chair which was wheeled up next to the stand. In order to make the microphone accessible to the lone eyewitness, the court's bailiff had to detach the mic from the witness stand and plug an extension cord into the back of it so that it would reach Miss Kim's wheelchair.

First up to question the witness after the dramatic entrance was the prosecutor. Assistant District Attorney Arthur Moody spoke in an overly careful and comforting voice as he began conversing with his witness, "I am so, so sorry to hear about what happened to you, Miss Kim, and I thank you so, so much for having the courage to come out and testify after this horrible and senseless attack."

"Objection, Your Honor! This is irrelevant," exclaimed the defense attorney.

"Sustained," the judge said as he turned to the jury, "You are to disregard what you have just heard," the judge ordered the jury.

After planting his first seed into the minds of the jury, Mister Moody cut directly to the chase and began questioning the career manicurist. In a weak and scratchy voice, Daisy Kim whispered into the microphone, giving a long and detailed answer to each question she was asked. She talked about how the Asian gangsters had been extorting the nail shop where she worked and every other Asian-owned business in the area for as long as she could remember. She talked about how every worker in the beauty shop would have to donate a percentage of their income at the end of each week in order to cover what they called the "Snake Tax".

The highlight of the trial came when Mister Moody asked Daisy Kim to tell the jury what had happened on the night in question. Miss Kim gave a vivid recollection of how her boss had been murdered in cold blood after standing up for herself and telling the Asian gangster that she was unable to pay him his entire fee for that month. Afterward, Mister Moody asked her if that man who she had witnessed murder her boss was present in the courtroom . When she replied, "Yes," Mister Moody asked her to point the man out. Once the little Asian woman pointed him out, every member of the jury began looking at Edward Ong as if he were a monster.

* * *

Judge Marshall flipped through a few papers before he began to speak once more, "I understand that we have reached a verdict in this case," the judge proclaimed to the jury's foreman.

Eddie Ong knew that he was doomed from the moment he found out that Daisy Kim had survived the attempted assassination. All that was left now were the formalities leading up to his life sentence, or, his death sentence, depending on how the jury ruled. At this point, the gangster was hoping for the latter.

"Yes, Your Honor," the foreman responded, handing a stack of twelve sheets of paper to the bailiff, who in turn took them to the judge. Judge Marshall took his time to carefully examine each individual page before he handed them back to the bailiff. Once the bailiff returned the stack of papers to the jury's foreman, the judge turned to face the jury.

"What say you?" asked the judge.

The elderly Hispanic man began speaking, "In case number TP08421, the People of the State of California versus Edward Ong, we, the jury, in the above entitled action, find the defendant, Edward Ong, guilty of violation of section 187 of the penal code and fix the degree as murder in the first degree. The jury also finds that a firearm was used in the murder in violation of penal code section 12022(A)(1). This jury also finds the defendant Edward Ong guilty of the special circumstance in the commission of the crime of robbery, in violation of section 211 of the penal code, as alleged in the allegation of special circumstances within the meaning of penal code section 190.2(a)(17-I)."

The judge found it hard to conceal his satisfaction with the verdict, and a thin smile appeared as he began to speak, "Ladies and gentlemen of the jury, is this your finding?"

"Yes, Your Honor," the jury's foreman replied.

"And would either counsel like the jury polled as to any verdict or finding in this case?" Judge Marshall inquired.

"I don't, Your Honor," Arthur Moody answered with a smug grin on his face.

"That won't be necessary, Your Honor," Jim Starcevich replied.

"Well, in that case, let's proceed," Judge Marshall said. "Ladies and gentlemen of the jury, having found the special circumstances true as to the defendant, we will have to take up the second portion of this trial. This is the part of the trial often referred to as the penalty stage. As you are all aware, this first degree murder, along with the special circumstance finding, makes Mister Ong eligible for a death sentence. It will be your job to deliberate on whether or not you will hand that sentence down. So I will set this matter over and we will be back here in a week. I ask that you not discuss this matter with anyone. And when I say 'anyone', I mean just that — not your spouse, your best friend, your priest, your dog — nobody!"

The courtroom erupted in laughter, but Eddie Ong just sat at the defendant's table with his head down.

Chapter 64

Two days had passed since Gordo placed the phone call to Diamond, and there had not been a single gunshot on either side of the projects since their conversation. Diamond had been choked up the moment he heard his old friend Gordo's voice. He immediately began apologizing for what he had done and explained to Gordo how he'd allowed greed and blind ambition to get the best of him. The two men spoke in depth about how much money they both had lost, and were still losing, as a result of this street war. Gordo admitted that he had held a monopoly on the drug trade for years and understood that the hit was strictly business. He also promised Diamond that he would be willing to put the past behind him as long as it meant that all the killing would cease and the projects would be safe once again.

Gordo had also informed Diamond that he needed a big favor due to the loss of several kilos of cocaine which he had been fronted and was not able to pay for. Diamond automatically recognized this request from Gordo as a velvet hammer demand for retribution. What had seemed to be a sincere exchange of words relieved a large amount of pressure from the shoulders of Diamond, and as a result, changed his playbook substantially. In fact, he was now ready to continue his business with Mister Bolivar. Although he would end up having to slightly tweak their prior arrangement, Diamond was sure that these slight alterations would be welcomed by Mister Bolivar as long as the end result remained the same.

When Diamond got hold of Simon Bolivar, he was pleased to hear the eagerness in the Peruvian man's voice. Mister Bolivar had been expecting Diamond's call and quickly agreed to meet up at his Palace Verdes mansion at 1:00 P.M., which was approximately an hour and a half away.

After hanging up with Mister Bolivar, Diamond dialed up Big Mama and told her to pick him up from his safe house in thirty minutes. He also told her to drive the undercover, which was a code word for the incognito mini-van which she often drove Diamond around in when he transported large amounts of contraband.

Exactly twenty-five minutes later, Diamond heard the honk of the van's horn coming from the driveway of his safe house. After a quick breakfast at Denny's and a thirty-minute freeway drive, Big Mama and Diamond found themselves cruising through the upscale Palace Verdes neighborhood. As they traveled through the residential district, Big Mama found herself admiring every mansion they passed while fantasizing about a day when she and Diamond would live together, just the two of them, in a home similar to the ones that she was passing by every few seconds.

When Diamond spotted Mister Bolivar's home, he directed Big Mama to pull into the long driveway. Big Mama followed his orders and slowly drove down the driveway leading to a tall, black wrought-iron gate. Once the van had come to a complete stop, Diamond exited the vehicle and looked up into the surveillance camera mounted on the top of the gate. Seconds later, the gate began to slowly roll open, and Diamond motioned for Big Mama to drive through. Once she had driven through, Diamond followed on foot and the gate closed behind them. Big Mama parked the mini-van next to a Rolls Royce Cornish, a Bentley Phantom, and a few European sports cars whose names she probably could not pronounce if she wanted to.

She exited the van and found herself in awe. The backyard was huge, equipped with a tennis court and sparkling Olympic-sized swimming pool with a step-up Jacuzzi right in the middle of it so that the only way to get to it was to swim. The landscaping was beautiful, with perfectly-groomed Saint Augustine grass and flowerbeds holding exotic flowers of every color in the rainbow.

After a brief moment, a sliding glass door slid open and Simon Bolivar emerged, "Hello again, my friend," Simon announced in a loud and happy voice as he walked toward Diamond with a smile on his face and his hand extended. Diamond greeted him back with a smile and a firm handshake, "Is this the Misses?" Mister Bolivar asked, referring to Big Mama.

"Well, if you believe in common law, I guess you can say that," Diamond answered while smiling warmly at Big Mama.

"Hello, *Mija*," Mister Bolivar greeted and took Big Mama's right hand in his and kissed the back of it softly. "Let me introduce you to my wife. She is inside preparing some special Peruvian coffee. I know you will enjoy it." Simon slid the glass door open and then motioned for Big Mama to follow him into the house. Big Mama made sure to make eye contact with Diamond, gaining his approval before she followed.

After a moment, Mister Bolivar returned and the two associates got right down to business. Diamond explained to Mister Bolivar the reason why he was not able to totally live up to his end of the deal that they had made awhile earlier and also how he planned to rectify the problem. Diamond was surprised at how sympathetic Simon was to his explanation.

"Shit happens, my friend," Mister Bolivar said. "I'm just happy to see you facing your obligations head-on instead of running from them. You could have just as easily disappeared and never talked to me again, so I respect the fact that you are here with something."

Diamond walked over to the mini-van and returned a minute later with a green back pack, "There is half a million right here in this bag. This is all I could come up with after everything that happened. I assure you that everything will be on the up and up from now on," Diamond promised.

"Okay, I'm going to work with you, Diamond," Mister Bolivar said. "I'm going to accept this as the whole million that we agreed upon because I hate to have my friends in a hole. I'm also going to give you the same amount of product as the last time, on consignment, for the same price. However, I will require the extra five hundred large at the time of your next payment. Bring that back successfully and we can begin doing some real business," Mister Bolivar announced with a smile. "Does that sound fair or what?" he asked.

Diamond could not believe his ears and thought, *Of course that sounds fair. Is this guy losing his marbles or what?*

"Yes, I think that's pretty fair and attainable, Mister Bolivar," Diamond answered. The drug lord extended his hand to shake Diamond's.

"Call me Simon."

Diamond and Big Mama drove off with one hundred kilos of cocaine. Once Diamond and Big Mama arrived at his safe house, Diamond immediately dialed up his first drop-off. After one ring, Gordo's voice came over the phone. The two street kings agreed to meet up in the parking lot of Maxine Waters Park at 4 P.M., which was two hours away.

After separating and weighing out the product, Diamond looked at his watch. It was 3:49 P.M. Still unsure whether or not he could trust Gordo, Diamond reached into his closet and removed his Heklar and Koch .40 pistol that held a substantial amount more than his favorite gun, the .44 Bull Dog that he kept in his shoulder holster. The fact that the men were meeting at the park gave Diamond even more confidence that Gordo was not planning on trying anything stupid. Plus, Big Mama kept a little .380 semi-automatic Saturday Night Special in her purse, and she knew how to use it well.

When Big Mama and Diamond arrived at the park, they quickly spotted Gordo, who appeared to be by himself and leaning against a dark-blue Chevy Silverado pickup truck. Gordo raised his hands high in the air as soon as he saw Big Mama and Diamond pull into the parking lot. Big Mama drove slowly through the parking lot and maneuvered her minivan, parking it right beside Gordo's truck.

Although Gordo had a big welcoming smile on his face, Diamond still felt slightly leery since this was the first time he would see the *Vatos Locos* boss face to face since their last transaction that had not turned out so well. Diamond knew he had done wrong, but at the same time, he knew that money talked. *After all, why would a man who is about to get ten kilos of pure cocaine with more to come in the future try anything crazy?* Diamond's rationalization of the situation managed to put his mind at ease, so after Big Mama parked the van, he hopped out of the vehicle to meet with his old business associate.

"What's up, Dee?" Gordo exclaimed with a smile.

The men shook hands, while Gordo glanced into the minivan and spotted Big Mama who was looking in his direction with her hand inside her purse.

After an awkward moment of silence, Diamond spoke, "Well, let's hurry up and do this so we can get the hell up out of this parking lot. See the grocery bag in the backseat?" Diamond asked.

Gordo nodded his head affirmatively.

"Well, go ahead and check it out. Make sure everything is on the up and up and grab it."

At that moment, it seemed to Diamond that the federal agents began to appear out of thin air. They emerged from behind parked cars and surrounded the trio from every angle, "Freeze!" one of the agents screamed at the top of his lungs, realizing that Diamond was looking around for an escape route. With five guns pointed at him and a chopper now hovering overhead, Diamond decided to surrender. He followed Gordo's lead and dropped to his knees with his hands behind his head. That's when he heard the sound of Big Mama's van starting up.

"Freeze!" several agents yelled while running toward the vehicle. Big Mama threw the van into reverse as unmarked federal vehicles continued to speed down the street and into the parking lot from both directions. Big Mama reluctantly put the van back into park and twisted the ignition switch backward, turning the van's engine off. She lifted her hands up at the command of the federal agents who now had her entire van surrounded.

Diamond and Big Mama were placed in the backseats of separate cars. The only thing they could do now was sit handcuffed and watch as the federal agents went through the van with a fine-tooth comb. Big Mama cringed when she saw a female agent emerge from her backseat holding the brown grocery bag.

While Big Mama was watching the federal agents search her van, her man was busy watching something that he found a bit more interesting than the inevitability of the pigs finding his guns and drugs. Diamond stared at Gordo, whose hands were still cuffed behind his back, but who was now on his feet in the middle of a conversation with two middle-aged federal agents. Diamond tried hard to read the lips and gestures of the three men but failed to surmise the basis of their conversation. Just the fact that Gordo was talking to the feds was in itself enough for Diamond to smell a rat.

The young agent who had handcuffed Diamond opened the driver-side door and entered the vehicle, "We'll have you at the station in time for dinner. I hear they're serving chicken down there tonight," the young White agent taunted. On the way out of the parking lot, Diamond managed to make eye contact with Gordo.

Gordo quickly thought to himself, *If looks could kill, I would be on my way to the city morgue instead of Cabo San Lucas.* The Mexican street boss had to snicker at this thought.

Chapter 65

In the middle of a deep, dreamless sleep, Sergeant Curtiss Bookman's phone rang, waking him up at 4:15 A.M. There was no doubt in his mind as to who was on the other end of that phone. Bookman hesitated for a moment, almost deciding not to answer the phone at all before he shook the notion off. *After all,* he thought, *how worse could this shit get?*

He was already feeling the pressure mounting at the station. It would not be long before Peter Kinbrew told the truth about their ordeal. Plus, Bookman believed that Marcos Felix, who had already been reassigned to another ride-along, was snitching on him. The sergeant had done his best to complete every mission that the mysterious Asian man on the other end of the telephone had sent him on, and, as a result, he felt that the asshole should at least respect his efforts.

Bookman removed his new cordless phone from its charger and put it to his ear, saying nothing for a moment.

"I can hear you breathing, Sergeant, so I know you are there," the voice proclaimed in a pestering manner. "Is it not impolite to answer the telephone without the proper greeting, Sergeant?" the man asked.

Gritting his teeth in anger, Bookman fought to keep himself from snapping. The sergeant was aware that any display of emotion would be counterproductive at this juncture.

Bookman spoke in a calm and collected voice, "Yeah, man, it's me. How can I help you now?"

"Well... truth be told, Sergeant Bookman, you are really of no more use to me, as you have failed miserably in completing the most important task I asked of you," the voice proclaimed.

Bookman paused for a moment to gather his thoughts, *This shithead hasn't called me for no reason, so it's probably that he needs something. Maybe it isn't too late after all.*

"So where do we go from here?" Bookman asked.

"Well, Sergeant, that choice will be left strictly in your hands, but may I suggest Cuba. I hear the weather is very nice there this time of year, and they do not extradite U.S. fugitives from that country."

Bookman's heart dropped at that last statement. The man was not playing fair, therefore, Bookman knew he had to think of something fast.

"Look, man," Bookman said, ready to make his final attempt at getting this monkey off his back. "I've got over one million dollars saved up, and it's all yours if you will just give me the tape and get the hell out of my life."

The only thing this statement managed to accomplish was to cause an eruption of obnoxious laughter on the other end of the telephone. After a good laugh, the voice once again began to speak, "I appreciate your offer, Sergeant; however, I must say thanks but no thanks. Your petty cash is of no interest to me at this point. I do believe that you have played this little game of ours by the rules, so I feel it my duty to warn you that it has come to an end. Last night, I addressed a box containing the master tape that you so desperately seek to a man by the name of Benjamin Cody and sent it express mail to the 77th Precinct of the Los Angeles Police Department. You don't have much time left, Sergeant Bookman." The line went dead.

Chapter 66

At 3 A.M., Psycho Twin felt helpless as he lay in his hospital bed. Although he had done a good job of hiding his pain from his brother and best friend, he had felt this way since the moment he found out that he would more than likely live out the rest of his days as a paraplegic. The teenager rested the back of his head against the soft hospital pillow and stared at the serene flower-covered wallpaper while daydreaming about the day he had been sentenced to life in a wheelchair.

He could still hear the loud pop of the .38 along with the silence that had followed. He could still feel Gina's body fall on top of his and hear the sound of her voice speaking words that fell upon his ears as no more than a distant echo. Tears of rage began to roll down Psycho's cheeks as he thought about the possibility of Smiley leaving this hospital alive. The news of his twin brother Sicko's arrest had thrown a curve ball in his plans. And now with Lil Ricky also in jail, the teenager's feeling of helplessness was quickly growing into one of sheer hopelessness. It would have been no problem for one of his partners in crime to come see him, and then, on their way out, to walk a few rooms over to drop in on Smiley to pay him a visit with a silencer-equipped 9mm. But now that Sicko and Rick Rock were both in the slammer, Psycho Twin was still dead set on taking Smiley out, even if it meant doing it himself.

Psycho lay in his bed for a while, daydreaming in an attempt to come up with a plan that would leave his arch enemy dead, but the plan should also avoid landing himself in the penitentiary in the process. He thought about having one of his home girls bring him a pistol but decided that a gunshot would be too much noise, and there was no way he was going to tell one of those gangster bitches where he kept his real artillery, because that would also lead them to his money and drugs which was all he had left at this point. He thought about stabbing Smiley to death but quickly came to grips with the fact that this was something much easier said than done.

Psycho pushed himself up off his pillow and used his strong arms to maneuver himself above his wheelchair at the side of the bed as the nurse had taught him to do. With a hard push, he landed perfectly in the wheelchair. He began to look around the room for anything he could possibly use to kill Smiley and yet still remain low-key. After glancing around the room for a moment, Psycho wheeled himself over to the area where the cabinets were located. One by one, he began to open cabinets. The first one he opened had nothing but a bunch of clean sheets, towels, and pillow cases. This gave Psycho the idea of smothering his enemy to death with a pillow, but then he looked down at his legs and laughed at this idea.

The next cabinet held a few cleaning supplies, a bottle of Liquid Drano, and a stack of bedpans. Once again a bulb lit up in the young gangster's head. He could use the Drano to poison Smiley. He dismissed this idea quicker than the last, thinking to himself, *How in the hell will I manage to drop this shit in his food and water without anyone noticing? And even if I did, how much of this shit will the dumb-ass eat before he spits it out all over the place?*

The next cabinet contained a bunch of cardboard boxes with labels on the side. Psycho began reading the labels; Hand Sanitizer, Double-ply Toilet Paper, Disposable House Shoes, and Latex Gloves. *No murder weapons here,* Psycho thought to himself.

When Psycho reached the last and final cabinet, he placed his fingers around the handle, closed his eyes, and whispered a brief prayer to no one in particular, "Please let there be something up in this motha fuckin' cabinet that a nigga can use." He opened up the cabinet's double doors and was once again disappointed. This one held a few large electronic machines, and he had no idea what they were used for. He also found a large, round, plastic container with a bunch of glass thermometers inside.

Once again, Psycho's eyes became busy scanning the room. It was at this point that a big wolf-like smile spread over the teenager's face. Mounted to the wall right beside the door was a large, red, plastic box with the words BIOHAZARD written on the side of it in bold, black letters. The memories of nurses using

243

syringes to shoot morphine into his body or drawing his blood and then carefully dropping the needles into that box quickly surfaced in Psycho's brain. He rolled himself swiftly to the big, red box and reached up, using his hand to feel whether or not there was an opening wide enough for him to fit his hand inside in order to remove some of the needles.

"Bingo!" the young killer said. He removed two soiled, needle-equipped syringes from the box. He then rolled back to his bed and placed them under his pillow just in case a nurse happened to come in.

Next, Psycho wheeled himself back to the cabinet where he had found the cleaning supplies and removed the Liquid Drano that had sparked his interest only moments earlier. He removed one of the bedpans and then placed the bottle of Drano and a few other cleaning products in it before pulling the bedpan out of the cabinet and placing it on his lap.

Psycho decided to do one more once-over of the remaining cabinets to make sure he did not miss anything. When he came to the cabinet that held the latex gloves, he punched one of the boxes open and removed a few pairs of gloves.

When Psycho opened the final cabinet, he glanced at the same thermometers he had seen only minutes earlier, but this time they triggered a memory from long ago, before he and Sick Twin's mother had become strung out on drugs. It was late at night when their mom had come home from work and caught the two of them in the bathroom playing with a silver liquid-like substance that had oozed out of a thermometer they had broken. Psycho remembered vividly the whipping he and his brother had received that night and how his mother had screamed, "Boy, this ain't no damn toy! That shit will kill your dumb asses!" Psycho carefully removed five thermometers from the container and dropped them into the bedpan sitting on his lap.

Next, he quickly wheeled himself back to his bed and removed the two needle-equipped syringes from beneath his pillow and dropped them into the bedpan with the rest of the items. He glanced at the clock on the wall, which read 3:58. In two minutes, the nurse would be walking in for the hourly check, so Psycho placed the bedpan underneath his bed so that it was out of view and then used his strong arms to pull himself back into his bed. He pulled the covers over himself and closed his eyes to pretend sleep. Less than two minutes later, he heard the squeaking door being opened followed by a few footsteps before the door closed again.

Once Psycho was sure the coast was clear, he climbed back into his wheelchair and reached under the bed to retrieve the bedpan. With the bedpan back in his lap, he wheeled himself to the bathroom and closed the door.

In the seclusion of the bathroom, Psycho began to feel as if he were some kind of mad scientist as he decided what chemicals to use. After deciding against the ammonia and floor wax, the teenager thought that the mercury and Ajax, along with a nice dose of Liquid Drano to help mix everything up, would be enough to do the trick.

First, he removed all of the items from the bedpan and placed them on display on top of the bathroom sink before putting on a pair of latex gloves. The first thing Psycho elected to use was the powdery Ajax. He shook about four tablespoons of the cleaning agent into the bedpan and then eyeballed it to make sure it would be enough. Next, Psycho began to carefully break the glass thermometers in half, allowing the metallic substance to ooze slowly into the bedpan on top of the Ajax. He noticed that the mercury did not soak into the Ajax the way he thought it would, but he was sure the Liquid Drano would cause everything to jell just right. After dumping the mercury from all five thermometers into the pan, Psycho was sure to dispose of the broken glass fragments by flushing them down the toilet.

"Now it's time for my final ingredient," Psycho said to himself, and with a sinister movie villain laugh, "Muhuhuhahaha," he felt like Doctor Frankenstein himself as he dumped about a cup's worth of Liquid Drano on top of his concoction, causing the pan to release a pungent smoke into the air making his eyes water and his throat itch.

"Yeah, that's what the fuck I'm talkin' 'bout, baby," Psycho said to himself after clearing his throat and wiping his eyes.

He began tilting the bedpan from side to side for about three minutes, allowing all of the substances to mix together properly. Now it was time to get down to the real business. Psycho removed the two soiled needles from the sink top and held them up toward the light, examining them the way a real doctor would. Next, he squeezed all the air from each syringe, and, one by one, he dipped the tips into the bedpan and drew his magic death potion until each syringe was filled to capacity.

Now, the young gangster felt his heart begin to race. With the deadly dose of poison, he was anxious to hit the man who had ruined his life. After thoroughly rinsing out the bedpan and drying it with toilet paper, Psycho flushed his latex gloves, along with the rest of his trash, down the toilet and then placed the cleaning products back inside the bedpan and wheeled himself out of the bathroom. He put on another pair of clean latex gloves and grabbed a towel from the counter before returning to the cabinet where he had found the cleaning supplies. He carefully wiped each item off with a towel before placing it back into its previous spot. After that, he wiped each and every cabinet he had touched along with the biohazard box to ensure there were no fingerprints that could come back to haunt him if left behind. Psycho thought about how Lil Ricky had often gotten on his case over the years about learning how to cover his tracks, *"One mistake could be a nigga's last,"* Rick Rock would always say. Once Psycho was sure there was not one shred of evidence left behind, he wheeled himself to the room door. He twisted the handle and slowly pulled the door open to prevent the loud creaking sound that it made every time someone opened it. With the door slightly ajar, he stuck his head out and got a good look at the empty hallway outside of the door.

"One, two, three, go," Psycho whispered to himself and then wheeled out into the hallway and made the right turn toward room 307. He made it to his destination without a hitch and quietly opened the door. He was relieved when this door failed to squeak the way his door did.

As soon as Psycho entered the room, he immediately spotted his victim laying in the hospital bed sound asleep. Psycho felt his heart rate increase once again. Now, it felt as if his heartbeat was loud enough to hear if someone came within ten feet of him.

"Ain't no turnin' back now," Psycho whispered to himself in an effort to muster up the courage to go on. He began to slowly wheel himself in the direction of his sleeping target. After what seemed like a wheelchair marathon, Psycho Twin found himself at Smiley's bedside, face to face with his enemy.

"This is *really* gonna help ya punk ass sleep," Psycho whispered as he lifted the full syringes from the seat of his wheelchair.

Psycho's first instinct told him to take one syringe in each hand and shove them into Smiley's neck simultaneously, squeezing the contents of both of them into the sleeping *cholo's* body; however, after a brief moment of rationalization, he decided against this method. He would have loved to just stab his victim in the neck with the deadly cocktail, causing him a violent and painful death, but Psycho could see this plan turning into an intense struggle that could possibly end with his being wheeled away in handcuffs.

He turned his attention from Smiley to the IV stand that stood next to the bed. After making sure that Smiley was hooked up to the IV, Psycho came to his final decision. He wheeled himself to the IV stand and inserted the first needle into Smiley's IV tube. With no time to waste, Psycho quickly squeezed the contents of the first syringe into Smiley's IV tube, pulled it out, and then shoved the second needle in and repeated the process. Once his second syringe was empty, Psycho removed the needle and placed both syringes beside his hip on the seat of his wheelchair.

The young killer knew that he should be on his way out of the room, but he just could not help himself; he had to sit and watch for a moment to find out whether or not his masterpiece would work. After about thirty seconds, Psycho jumped with surprise when he saw Smiley's body jerk. Psycho began backing his wheelchair toward the door with his eyes fixed on his victim. All at once, Smiley's body began to shake violently, and Psycho could hear the steady beeps of the heart monitor machine begin to speed up at an alarming rate. Psycho turned his wheelchair around as fast as he could and raced for the door.

On his way down the hall en route to his room, the teenager heard a female voice yelling over the loudspeaker, "Code red, room 307!"

Psycho made it back to his room and closed the door just in time to hear the sound of several pairs of footsteps racing past.

247

Chapter 67

After Lil Ricky's arrest, he had been transported straight to Los Angeles County Jail. Usually, an arrested person would be detained at the nearest substation pending arraignment, however, Lil Ricky's asthmatic condition mandated that he be transported straight to Men's Central Jail where there were medical facilities that were adequate in the treatment of his condition.

Rick Rock faced his first heartbreak only minutes after he arrived at the county jail. When he went to the classification window, he went through the usual motions of answering questions about his work history, gang affiliation, sexual preference, and other personal questions. At the end of the interview, the county jail worker handed Rick Rock a pink paper with his charges printed on it. The first thing he noticed was the section of the paper titled BAIL AMOUNT. The teenager shuddered at the sight of the words 'No Bail' typed next to his bail amount. He was well aware of the possibility of this happening, but he had hoped that he would be able to make bail before his parole officer was able to place the hold on him. Next, Rick Rock focused on the charges, CHARGE 1) 187/A, CHARGE 2) 187/A, CHARGE 3) 187/A, CHARGE 4) 187/A, CHARGE 5) 187/A, CHARGE 6) VEH.10851. Lil Ricky was charged with five First Degree Murder and one count of Grand Theft Auto.

After being processed in, the teenager was escorted to 2400 module and assigned to cell 13. He was happy to see an unoccupied telephone when he stepped into the four-man cell. After introducing himself to the other occupants in the cell, Rick Rock picked up the phone and immediately dialed up the number to Stormy's apartment. When he got no answer, he hung up the telephone and redialed Stormy's number. Once again — no answer.

Chapter 68

When Sergeant Curtiss Bookman hung up the telephone after his latest conversation with the mysterious voice, he knew that the jig was up. Instead of going into a panic, Bookman came to grips with the fact that it was time to turn the page and begin the next chapter in his life. The crooked sergeant always knew there was a possibility that all the dirt he was doing on a day-to-day basis would one day catch up and bury him alive. As a result, Bookman had spent the last fifteen years preparing for a situation such as this.

He had started off in the late eighties by accepting protection money from drug kingpins with the agreement that he would do whatever he could to keep them out of jail. The protection business had evolved into extortion, drug trafficking, and all-out robberies of big time drug dealers. The result was now a two million dollar nest egg that Bookman planned on using to fund a permanent vacation in a faraway land.

After hanging up the phone, Bookman wasted no time getting on the move. The sergeant quickly got dressed and then ripped open the box springs under his mattress and retrieved the two million dollars that he'd kept hidden there. Next, Bookman grabbed a suitcase from the floor of his hallway closet and tossed a few changes of clothes into it along with the cash. After that, he grabbed his wallet from the top of his dresser. Bookman removed his drivers license, credit cards, and all other forms of identification from his wallet and threw them on the bedroom floor. After that, he opened one of his dresser drawers and pulled out a drivers license, Master Card, and passport, all with his photo on them, under the name Lionel Rookard. Then he placed these new IDs in his wallet. After downing a triple shot of Jack Daniel's rum, Bookman walked out of the house without bothering to lock the door behind himself.

On his way to the airport, Bookman used the Internet option on his cellular phone to book his flight. He knew he would save himself a lot of time and anxiety by avoiding the long ticket lines at Los Angeles International. After a fifteen-minute freeway drive, Bookman found himself pulling onto the circular road of LAX while looking for the Delta Airlines terminal. Once he found his destination, instead of finding the nearest parking space, Bookman parked his Cadillac into the loading area and hopped out. He hastily removed his suitcase from the backseat and then slammed the door shut, abandoning his Caddy in the 'No Parking Zone'.

The soon-to-be fugitive walked into the doors of Delta Airlines and headed straight for the airline's WILL CALL window. He handed an elderly White man his passport and fake ID and then waited as the airline employee punched a few keys on his computer. It was music to Bookman's ears when the noise from the printer began. Soon, his ticket popped out of the machine. The airline worker handed him the ticket and informed him that his flight boarded at 8:00 A.M. Bookman glanced at his watch; it was 6:58 A.M.

* * *

The time was 7:15 A.M. when several police cars sped onto Sergeant Curtiss Bookman's street, coming to a screeching halt in front of his house. Detective Richard Houston's car was the last to drive up, parking right in Bookman's driveway. While several officers positioned themselves in the sergeant's front yard, others went through the gate leading to his backyard. Once the house was surrounded, the call was given over the radio and Detective Houston began knocking hard on Bookman's door. After ten seconds went by with no answer, the detective twisted the door handle, and to his surprise the door opened.

With guns drawn, five officers stormed into the home along with Detective Houston. After searching every room in the house, it became apparent to the cops that their suspect was not around. Detective Houston approached the door that accessed the garage and opened it. Bookman's Cadillac was nowhere to be found. Just then, the detective had an idea. He quickly got on his walkie-talkie and radioed in to dispatch. The detective ordered the dispatch operator to go into her computer and find out the license plate number to Bookman's car and then put out an All Points Bulletin on that vehicle. Next, Detective Houston gave the officers an order to thoroughly search the sergeant's home for evidence and contraband. Fifteen minutes later, the dispatch officer radioed back to the detective informing him that the vehicle he had inquired about had just been towed from the loading area of Delta Airlines at Los Angeles International Airport. Richard Houston immediately contacted LAX security and ordered them to delay any flight with a passenger on it by the name of Curtiss Bookman. After that, the detective set out on his way to the airport.

Driving on the freeway in excess of one hundred miles per hour, it took the detective less than ten minutes to reach the airport. He pulled his car into the exact spot where Bookman had parked an hour earlier, hopped out, and ran into the terminal.

* * *

Once Bookman had retrieved his plane ticket, with an hour to kill, he went straight to a small airport restaurant for breakfast and coffee. As a result of the severe anxiety that he was now experiencing, the rogue sergeant found it impossible to eat the pigs in a blanket he had ordered. Instead, he just sat around and watched the restaurant door while nervously taking sips from his cup of black coffee. Bookman could not help thinking about the possibility of a bunch of cops storming through that door to arrest him at any minute. He was relieved to finally glance at his watch and find that it was now 7:50 A.M.

With no time to waste, the sergeant tossed a tip onto the table and headed out the door, sure that by the time he reached Delta Air Lines it would be time for him to board his flight. Five minutes later, Bookman arrived at his destination and stepped into the line.

It was like a thousand-pound weight being lifted off of his back when the sexy female voice began talking over the loudspeaker moments later, "Flight 169 non-stop from Los Angeles to Seychelles now boarding."

Following the lead of the people in front of him, Bookman handed the man in the Delta Airline uniform his ticket and stepped onto the plane.

He walked to his assigned seat on the plane, deposited his suitcase into the overhead compartment, and sat down. When Bookman saw the last passenger board and the flight attendant pull the airplane's door closed, he could not believe how good his luck had gone in pulling off his escape. He relaxed and began daydreaming to the sound of the jet's engines. He wondered how difficult it would be to find a good cocaine and marijuana dealer once he arrived in the Seychelles Islands. He knew it would be no problem to drop his dirty money into a Swiss bank account and never have to worry about paying a dime of taxes on it. Once he got to the Seychelles, he would ditch his fake identification right away and retrieve a new one there in order to get established.

Suddenly, Bookman's daydream was interrupted in mid-thought by the sound of someone pounding against the outside of the plane's door.

The sergeant's heart began to thump hard and fast when he saw the flight attendant approach the door. Everything inside of Bookman told him to tackle the flight attendant and hold her hostage until the plane took off. He watched in horror as she released the latch and began lifting the plane's door open. Bookman closed his eyes and whispered a two-second prayer.

He knew the Good Lord was on his side when he saw the flight attendant help the little-old, wrinkled-up White man, who appeared to be at least in his mid-nineties, onto the plane. Once the little-old man was safe in his seat, the flight attendant once again pulled the plane's passenger door shut. After a brief speech from the captain over the plane's loudspeaker regarding weather conditions and the estimated time of arrival, Bookman felt the plane begin to move. Two minutes later, the plane was airborne.

Chapter 69

After Diamond went to his arraignment and found out that he had been classified as a flight risk and denied bail, he knew he had to come up with a plan. The first thing he did was demand a speedy trial. The street veteran knew that there would be no benefit in dragging his case out while giving the district attorney's office more time to build a case against him. Next, Diamond made arrangements for Big Mama to be bailed out. He needed someone he could trust on the outside to handle his business. Outside of his nephew, Rick Rock, Big Mama was the only person Diamond trusted. Finally, Diamond got in touch with his old friend, Wild Bill Mansfield. Diamond remembered the last conversation he had engaged in with Wild Bill, when his old buddy had told him about his wife's father being a high-powered lawyer. After forcing Diamond to promise not to reveal to the lawyer where he had heard about him, Wild Bill gave Diamond the phone number to the law offices of Joseph Trigilio.

When Diamond got in contact with the attorney, the first thing Mister Trigilio said was, "Due to my full caseload, I am unable to take your case at this time."

Mister Trigilio had a sudden change of heart when Diamond asked, "How does one hundred and fifty thousand dollars cash upfront sound to your caseload?"

Chapter 70

Three days after his arrival at the Los Angeles County Jail, it was time for Lil Ricky to go to court in order to be arraigned on his charges. He was rudely awakened at 3:00 A.M. by a nasal voice yelling his name and booking number, along with the names and booking numbers of at least twenty other inmates. On his way out of the module, Rick Rock was handed a bag with his breakfast in it, consisting of peanut butter, a small carton of milk, and a box of cereal with the label CRISPY RICE. He and the rest of the men were led in a long line to a downstairs holding tank where they would wait to be put on a bus to their respective courts. After a three hour wait in the packed holding tank, Rick Rock's bus driver arrived. Ten minutes later, he was on the bus, shackled up, and on his way out of the county jail parking lot.

When Lil Ricky strolled into the holding tank at Compton Courthouse, he was happy to see his friend, Sick Twin, laid out asleep on a concrete bench. Rick Rock immediately walked over to where his homeboy was sleeping and put his face right next to the sleeping twin's ear.

"I'm gonna kill you, nigga!" Rick Rock yelled right into his buddy's ear. Everyone in the holding tank laughed out loud when Sicko quickly rose up and threw up his guards.

"Damn! You scared the shit outa me, blood!" Sick Twin said while rising to his feet to greet his best friend with a hug.

"That's what you get for bein' up in here slippin' like that, lil nigga."

"I got ya lil nigga right here hangin' low," Sicko said while clutching his manhood.

"Step over here into my office," Lil Ricky commanded while leading Sicko to a secluded section of the holding tank. Once the two teenagers were out of earshot of the other prisoners, they did not

254

waste any time getting down to business, "How in the hell did we get charged with this bullshit?" Rick Rock inquired.

"How in the fuck should I know, nigga?" Sicko answered. "Hell, we had on all kinds of wigs and gloves and all dat other shit," he continued.

"Yeah, and plus we was in a G-ride, blood," Lil Ricky agreed.

"They ain't got shit on us, Rick Rock. We just gotta ride this case out for a few months," Sicko promised.

Lil Ricky nodded his head in agreement before he spoke again, "Alright, homie, we gonna see what they got on us today, 'cause it don't make no sense to pay for some lawyers if they ain't got shit on us, *but*," Lil Ricky paused for a second to place emphasis on what he was about to say next, "if these White folks *do*, by some chance, have some solid evidence, then we both gotta have paid lawyers, 'cause I ain't fuckin' with no state-appointed or no county public defenders."

"Don't you mean, county public pretenders?" Sicko asked with a snicker.

Before long, the holding tank door opened, and a handsome, young, African-American bailiff stepped halfway into the room and announced as he began reading from a sheet of paper, "The following people are going to court on the fourth floor, department nine. I need Moss and Pittman to step up."

The two young gangsters stood side by side so the bailiff could handcuff them together. After they were chained up, the officer escorted them to an elevator and then up to the fourth floor.

When Lil Ricky and Sicko were being led into the courtroom, they spotted several family members and friends sitting in the spectator seats, including both of their mothers.

"Order in the court," the bailiff announced. "The Honorable Judge Henry Rudolph presiding."

"Thank you," the judge responded.

Lil Ricky looked the judge over to find that the man had a Santa Claus appearance, with a pair of kind eyes sunken deep inside his pudgy, rose-colored face.

"Today, we're going to do the preliminary examination for case number CV135169 A and B, the People of the State of California versus Patrick Pittman Jr. and Carnell Moss. Is counsel for both of these men present?" the judge asked while glancing around the room.

"Yes, Your Honor. Jeremy Burgess, Los Angeles County Public Defender here, representing Mister Pittman," announced the young White man.

"And Christian McDanial, Los Angeles County Alternate Public Defender here for Mister Moss," the grey-haired Black man proclaimed.

"Are both parties ready to proceed?" the judge inquired.

"If I could just have a moment to consult with my client, Your Honor?" the young White lawyer requested of the judge.

The judge gave him an affirmative nod without speaking.

Both teenagers sat in their chairs, perplexed as to why they had not met their lawyers until now. Just then, the young White lawyer approached Lil Ricky, while the Black man walked up to Sicko.

Lil Ricky's lawyer leaned over and began whispering in his ear, "I'm sorry that I haven't had a chance to talk to you before now, but it's been one hell of a week. Basically, all we're doing today is finding out if they have enough evidence to bound you guys over to trial. The DA is saying that she has a witness ready, but that's all she's giving up right now. So here's the deal; we can see what they've got today and get the show on the road, or I can ask for this to be put over for a week or so, since I haven't had a chance to talk to you. I say let's do it today since the evidence they have today will be the same thing they have next week."

The lawyer waited for an answer as Lil Ricky consulted with Sick Twin. After a brief whispering conversation with his homeboy, Lil Ricky turned back to Mister Burgess, "Let's do it," Lil Ricky said.

"We are ready, Your Honor," Mister Burgess informed the judge.

"Well, let's proceed then," the judge said. "I assume that both defendants are aware of the charges they are faced with in this case, so is it safe to say that we can waive the formal arraignment reading of the statement of rights?"

"Yes, Your Honor," Mister Burgess answered.

"So waived, Your Honor," Mister McDanial responded.

"The People are represented by Deputy District Attorney, Chantal Hathman. Are the People ready to proceed?"

"Yes, Your Honor," the DA answered.

"You may call the first witness," the judge informed her.

"Your Honor, the People would like to call Mrs. Olga Ocasta to the stand," Chantal Hathman announced.

Sick Twin's jaw dropped when he saw Gina's grandmother walk into the courtroom. All the young gangster could do was sit and watch in shock as his nephew's great grandmother approached the witness stand.

When she reached the stand, Olga Ocasta was told by the court's clerk to raise her right hand, "Do you solemnly state that the testimony you are about to give in the matter now pending before this court shall be the truth, the whole truth, and nothing but the truth, so help you God?"

"Yes, I do," Olga answered in her heavy Spanish accent.

"You may be seated," the court clerk said before sitting back down herself.

Lil Ricky and Sicko both held their breath as they watched the DA approach the witness stand, "Mrs. Ocasta, I'd like to direct your attention to October 23 of this year, a couple of weeks ago, at somewhere around 5:00 P.M. Do you remember where you were that night?"

"Yes," Olga Ocasta answered, "I was at my home with my granddaughter, my great grandson, and my granddaughter's boyfriend," the old woman proclaimed.

Sick Twin was shocked at the way that the old Mexican lady could just sit there and lie on the stand like this.

"And Missez Ocasta, can you give this court a play by play recollection of what you saw and heard on that day in question?" the DA asked.

Everyone in the courtroom watched as the old lady's eyes filled with tears and she began to give her choked-up recollection of the dreaded day's events, "Me and my granddaughter and her boyfriend were all at my house. Adam was holding the baby and feeding him his bottle when we heard a loud 'Boom, Boom, Boom,' on the front door," Olga explained, while giving an animated demonstration of what she had heard and making a hand gesture as if she was banging on a door. Her Spanish accent grew heavier as she got deeper into her story, "Adam looked out of the peephole and then he turned around and started yelling at me and Gina, saying, 'You guys take the baby and go upstairs right now!' So that is what we did. When we got up the stairs, we heard a 'Bang, Bang, Bang' like a gun and more 'Boom, Boom, Boom' sounds against my door, so Gina and the baby went into my closet, and I crawled under my bed. That is when I hear the sound of footsteps coming up my stairs." Olga Ocasta's tears were now pouring from her eyes as she relived the nightmare. "I heard Gina open the closet and yell for Adam, but it was not Adam who walked into the room!" Olga screamed as the tears poured down her face.

The deputy district attorney stepped a little closer to the witness stand and began consoling her witness, "Mrs. Ocasta, I am so sorry about this terrible, terrible loss that you have had to endure, and I thank you so much for your strength and courage through all of this. I know how hard it's going to be for you to do this."

The DA then asked, "Can you please tell the court whether or not you see in this courtroom the person who walked into your room that day?"

Without hesitation, the little old Mexican lady pointed at Sick Twin. "It was heem!" Olga screamed. "He shot my Gina and killed her!" Olga Ocasta put her head down and began to bawl uncontrollably.

"Let the record show that our witness has identified Mister Darnell Moss," Chantal Hathman instructed.

Olga Ocasta's positive ID of Sick Twin and the fact that several witnesses had seen two suspects that day, along with Lil Ricky's being caught red-handed trying to ditch the getaway car, was enough for the judge to bound both of the teenagers over for trial.

Chapter 71

It did not take Gordo long to climb back to the top of the *Vatos Locos* pecking order after he orchestrated the downfall of his old friend/turned enemy. The Mexican street don was surprised at how easy it had been to oust Diamond while gaining his throne back at the same time. When Gordo thought about it, he realized that the outcome had been inevitable. It was a simple matter of supply and demand economics. The projects demanded massive amounts of drugs on a weekly basis, and it did not matter who was supplying that demand as long as that individual had the resources to keep the beast fed. Gordo was now the only man around who could handle the workload, therefore, the hustlers did what came natural to them and followed the money.

Diamond's arrest, paired with the project peace treaty, had made it easy for Gordo to implement his plan. The first thing the crafty street boss did was lower his drug prices for every hustler on the dark side of the projects. Although his new prices would cut his profit margin in half, this was fine with Gordo, because not only would it mean a higher turnover rate, but it would also act as an incentive to help the Black gangsters turn a blind eye to the claims from Diamond in the near future that Gordo was working with the feds. The Mexican boss knew it would be impossible for Diamond to prove he had set him up, because there was no paper trail of court transcripts, sworn statements, or the like. It would be Diamond's word against his, and the man with the money usually held the trump card in a situation such as this. Gordo operated by the Golden Rule: He who has the gold makes the rules. And now, every minute that went by was fortifying Gordo's position as street king while simultaneously weakening Diamond's.

It was 10:00 A.M., and Gordo was just waking up with a hangover when he got the phone call. He picked up the phone on the third ring and pushed the talk button, *"Ola,"* Gordo said into the phone in a low and scratchy voice.

"Well, hello again, my friend!" the voice loudly exclaimed into the phone, causing Gordo to have to temporarily hold it away from his ear.

The street don quickly picked up Detective Montenegro's voice and asked, "Yeah, what's up, man? How have you been?" Gordo attempted to feign happiness in hearing from the pig who was on the other end of the line.

"Aww, hell, just another one like the other one, *comerada*. I'm just calling you to personally thank you for your help in busting that *pinchi* super fly *negro*, Diamond," the detective proclaimed.

Gordo thought for a moment in an attempt to figure out the detective's angle before he spoke again, "Yeah, well... that sword cut both ways, homes. It helped me out too, so you don't gotta call me to thank me and shit like I did something heroic or something, *esse*," Gordo informed the cop.

The detective busted out laughing at Gordo's cynicism, "Well... whether it helped you out or not is beside the point. The point is, we helped each other, *carnal*. It's impossible for one member of a team to win without everybody on the team winning, so you deserve credit for playing your part. On that note, I'm gonna let you go, but promise me that if you need anything — you won't hesitate to call."

Gordo felt like a fish out of water in this conversation and just wanted to end it as quickly as possible, "Yeah, I promise, *vato*," Gordo answered. He hung up the phone with a strong feeling of anxiety, so he headed straight to the kitchen for a beer.

Chapter 72

The Los Angeles County Men's Central Jail is such a miserable place that inmates and cops alike often joke that a call from MCJ to hell would be a local one. If there was not a gang stabbing happening, a rape being committed, or a race riot going on, then the sheriff's deputies were savagely beating someone in one of the jail's many cold hallways.

Lil Ricky had been in the county jail for close to a month now, and he was doing everything he could to mentally prepare himself for his trial, which was scheduled to begin in less than one week. Ever since Rick Rock had found out that the district attorney's office was seeking the death penalty in his and Sicko Twin's case, he had been under a tremendous amount of pressure. He had already retained private counsel for himself and Sicko, so he knew that outside of that there was not much more he could do.

After saying his morning prayer and reading the day's daily bread, Lil Ricky was just laying back on his bunk and staring at the graffiti-covered walls while daydreaming about the upcoming week. He had yet to decide whether he would take the stand and speak for himself or simply allow his attorney to attempt to create reasonable doubt in the minds of the jury.

Lil Ricky was imagining himself on the stand being grilled by the DA when his daydream was interrupted, "Patrick Pittman, Denver 13, get dressed for visiting!" the voice blared through the PA system. Rick Rock jumped off his bunk and removed his blue jumpsuit from beneath his mat. It was an old county jail trick for a prisoner to place their jumpsuit neatly underneath their mat and sleep on top of it. That way they would wake up to a freshly-creased outfit.

Rick Rock shook the lint from his jumpsuit and slid it on along with his shoes. Two minutes later, the cell gate rolled open and he headed to the control booth to retrieve his visiting pass. A young Hispanic deputy handed Lil Ricky his pass and he was off. On his way down the hallway en route to the escalators, Rick Rock wondered why his home girl had arrived so early for their visit today. Usually, Midget would get there around 5 P.M. when the second wave of visits began.

When Lil Ricky arrived at the visiting room, he understood why Midget always came late when he saw how long the line was in front of the visiting room. After a fifteen minute wait, Lil Ricky handed the visiting officer his pass and was instructed to go to "G" section, booth #15. He was happy he had been assigned to the last booth on the row out of view from the deputies. This guaranteed the young gangster a peep show from his home girl who always wore a short skirt with no panties on underneath along with a blouse with no bra. On his way to the visiting booth, Rick Rock felt the bulge in his pants begin to expand at the thought of his self-proclaimed "Homie-love-a-friend's" tits pressed against the glass for his eyes to feast upon. On his way to booth fifteen, Rick Rock looked through the two-inch-thick glass windows of each cubicle he passed while admiring all the different shapes, sizes, and ethnicities of the women who tortured themselves every weekend to come up to the county jail to see their men.

When he arrived at booth #15, Lil Ricky's eyes grew as wide as a racoon's and his mouth dropped open. There sat Stormy with a big smile on her face. At first sight, Stormy's presence caught Lil Ricky by surprise, and he had to admit to himself that she was looking extra fine today with her tight, blue denim jumpsuit hugging her every curve to a T. It did not take long for the young gangster's mind to flash back to reality. The reality was that Stormy had not visited him or even answered his calls since he had been arrested.

Before he sat down and picked up the phone, Lil Ricky intentionally changed the expression on his face from surprise to anger so Stormy could see. He could not wait to hear his supposed-to-be girlfriend's excuse for the reason she had been missing in action for so long. The two young adults picked up their phones simultaneously and pressed them to their ears.

For a few seconds, they just sat and stared at one another without saying a word before Stormy broke the silence, "Hi handsome."

Stormy's smile was contagious and Rick Rock could feel his heart beginning to melt just looking at her. He quickly fought it off and got right down to business, "Hi, handsome?" Rick Rock asked with disdain in his voice. "I ain't heard from you, seen you, or nothing else the whole time I been locked up, and you got the audacity to pop up on a nigga with your tight-ass superhero costume on and some lipstick and think shit is gonna be all peaches and cream. Who you think you fuckin' wit? Some ole punk-ass tender dick or somethin'?"

At that moment, Lil Ricky noticed something in Stormy's eyes that he did not like. He was sure that the young suburbanite White girl would be crying her eyes out by now after the brief tongue-lashing; instead, he looked into her eyes to find that she was wearing a look of pure defiance.

Once Stormy was sure that Rick Rock was finished, she remained quiet for a brief moment in order to allow him to bask in his own words before she responded, "First of all, you know I have a record deal. I do believe that I told you about it the last time I saw you, which was over a month ago. In the meantime, I have been all over California and even took a trip to New York City working with different producers in the recording of my album. This month has been so stressful and I have been under so much pressure that I just needed someone to be there for me to talk to and just hold me to let me know that this dream would not turn into a nightmare."

The tears finally began to roll down Stormy's cheeks as she spoke, "But where was my man when I was going through all this, Mister Rick Rock? I'll tell you where; he was in the streets doing who knows what with who knows who. And then when I did get in touch with him, I get cursed out like a dog. So you're darn right I haven't been available to you, Ricky, because what's good for the goose is good for the gander."

The teenage girl looked satisfied with what she had just said and did not show the slightest bit of remorse.

Rick Rock was in shock. He could not believe the way he was being talked to by this little girl he had picked up and rescued like a stray puppy. Rick Rock stared into Stormy's eyes and thought for a moment, *It's time to tell this little heffer about herself. If it wasn't for me, the bitch would've never seen the inside of a studio. And now she got the nerve to be getting' at a nigga like she Beyonce or some damn body. If it wasn't for me, this bitch would still be in my uncle's whorehouse carryin' a mattress around on her back.*

With his intentions fully aimed at cursing the young girl out, Lil Ricky opened his mouth but was only able to come up with three words, "I'm sorry, Baby."

As difficult as it was for him to swallow his pride, the young thug had come to the conclusion that it would be foolish to run a young woman off who had the potential, and now thanks to him, the connections to become a multimillionaire. When Stormy failed to respond to his apology, Lil Ricky continued, "Baby, I know how hard it must be doing everything for yourself, and I realize now that I should have been there for you. Once I get out of this mess, I promise to be a better man for you. Please just believe in me, Baby."

Lil Ricky looked into Stormy's eyes and realized that the tears were once again beginning to well up inside of them. A second later, the tears began to roll down her cheek one after the other. Before Lil Ricky knew it, Stormy dropped her head and began to speak without looking him in the eyes, "You don't understand, Ricky. The reason I came down here was to face you like a woman. While you were running the streets, J Star was the only man who was there for me. He told me that by the time you get out of prison, cars will be flying!"

Tears continued to pour down Stormy's face, while Rick Rock was so upset that he felt like crying himself. For a minute, Lil Ricky stared at Stormy sitting on her stool with her head down, unable to look him in his eyes after her stunning revelation. After a minute, Rick Rock let out a small chuckle, hung up the visiting phone, and walked off the visiting row without another word, leaving his ex-girlfriend sitting there with her head hanging.

Chapter 73

Diamond liked what he saw when he walked into the attorney room of Los Angeles County Federal Jail to find his lawyer waiting for him. At first sight, Joseph Trigilio managed to surpass every expectation Diamond had for his super-high-priced attorney. The custom-tailored Italian suit equipped with gold cufflinks along with the dark and handsome features of the man who was wearing the suit, paired with all the things that Diamond had heard about him, quickly managed to squelch any reservations he may have had about hiring him.

Diamond had also done his homework on Mister Trigilio prior to sending Big Mama to his office with the retainer fee. If he was going to pay $150,000 cash upfront with more to fork out later, there could be no room left over for future buyer's remorse. Diamond had Big Mama do a Google search on the law offices of Joseph Trigilio and then print up everything she found and mail it to him. When the mail arrived, he had been expecting a standard-sized envelope that a regular letter would fit into, but what he received instead was a large manila envelope packed full of papers. With every page that Diamond flipped, he became more and more confident in his representation. On top of the hundreds of cases the man had won and the unheard of plea bargains he had negotiated, there were several published cases that set precedents in courtrooms all across the United States. Big Mama had also printed up the newspaper clippings she had found on the Google search concerning the post conviction relief that Mister Trigilio had succeeded in securing for the defendants in every single case that he had ever lost in open court.

The things Diamond enjoyed hearing most about his lawyer were what his old buddy Wild Bill had told him, "Oh, he's one ruthless son of a gun, brother," the biker had said in his deep Hulk Hogan-like voice, "That fucker will do anything and everything he's gotta do to win a case. He's worth every dime, dude," he had promised.

There in the attorney room, without regard for the jail's rules, Mister Trigilio reached over the table to greet Diamond with a firm handshake and then instructed him to take a seat, "I'm going to be brutally honest with you, Mister Pittman," Mister Trigilio said. "With your record and the amount of drugs recovered in this case, you are looking at a hell of a lot of time, my friend."

"So much for small talk, huh, counselor?" Diamond joked with a smile on his face. The seasoned attorney failed to find humor in the street veteran's statement. He stared at Diamond with a look of pure intensity in his eyes.

"Look, Mister Pittman, I'm not here to make small talk with you, because frankly there is nothing small about the money you are paying me nor the time you're looking at, for that matter. Let me put this in perspective for you, Mister Pittman. They've charged you with one count of 11370.4(A)(3), possession of a controlled substance exceeding the amount of ten kilos. Now that charge alone carries a mandatory ten years. That was the good news. The bad news is they've decided to hit you with the Habitual Criminal Act. What that means is that for each prison prior, each time you've been to prison, they will enhance your sentence by five years. You have three prison priors, so that will come up to fifteen years on the priors, which will run consecutively with the ten years for the crime itself. You do the math, Mister Pittman. So on that note, we can shoot the shit later, but right now we need to come up with our game plan."

Chapter 74

"**D**arnell Moss — I repeat — Darnell Moss, get dressed. You have a pass."

It was a quarter past noon, and Sick Twin was sitting in his cell in the middle of eating a bologna sandwich when the voice came blaring over the loudspeaker. He followed the order, got dressed in his county blues, and then waited five minutes before the voice came back over the intercom, "Watch the gate. The gate is opening. Inmate Moss, step out."

Sick Twin walked out of his cell and headed to the deputy's podium where he was given a white piece of paper and told to report to "Booking front".

"What the fuck?" Sicko asked himself out loud, aware that a pass to booking front was never a good thing. It usually meant one of two things; either a person's codefendant was planning to testify against them and requested a separation order which would guarantee that they would never end up in the same place at the same time in the county jail, or it meant that a person was being rebooked due to added charges from crimes other than the ones they were currently in jail on. Sicko knew that Lil Ricky was the last person he ever had to worry about snitching, so it had to be the latter of the scenarios.

After the long walk to booking front, Sicko approached the desk and informed the deputy on duty who he was.

"Oh yes, Mister Moss," the young Hispanic deputy announced with a smile, "Boy, we have been waiting for you."

"Should I be worried?" Sicko asked.

"Well, it all depends, Mister Moss," the deputy replied, "If you have proof that you were on vacation in Hawaii at the time of these four murders earlier this year, then you're in luck. If not, I hate to say it, but you assed out, bro."

"Four murders?" Sicko asked, "You fuckin' wit me, right?"

"Unfortunately for you, I'm not," the cop answered as he handed Sicko a sheet of paper containing a list of his new charges. "All I can tell you is you are being charged with four 187(A)s. Those are first degree murders, and you're also being charged with one count of 664/187(A). That's attempted murder in the first degree. You are scheduled for arraignment in Compton court tomorrow morning," the deputy informed Sicko.

The young gangster took a moment to reflect on all the dirt he had done over the past year.

"Well, can you at least gimme the dates that the murders happened on?" Sicko asked in an attempt to get a better idea of what he was faced with.

The deputy took the piece of paper back from Sick Twin, analyzed it, and then pointed at the date printed beside each charge, "They all took place on July 13 of this year," the deputy informed him.

At that point, Sicko felt a thousand butterflies in his stomach and his knees went weak, as the teenager had a brief flashback of the day that had just come back to haunt him.

Chapter 75

At 7 A.M., the big grey and black bus rolled down the steep driveway and up to the entrance of the underground parking garage of Ronald Reagan Federal Courts Building and stopped in front of a large metal gate. The bus driver immediately honked the horn two times and then waited as the gate slowly rose high enough for the balding White man to drive into the parking garage, carefully swing his bus into a tight parking space in front of the court's entrance, and turn the ignition off.

Five minutes later, with their ankles and wrists shackled, Diamond and thirty-seven other men were led off the bus. All the men were taken into the courthouse through the underground entrance and then led to a long hallway where a line of officers awaited. The officers patted each prisoner down and then removed their shackles. After that, all the inmates were separated according to ethnicity and placed into their respective holding tanks where they would wait until it was time for their court sessions to begin.

Diamond was one of the last prisoners to step into the crowded graffiti-filled holding tank. By the time he found a spot to sit down on the long, dirty, concrete bench, an officer reopened the large steel door and shouted his name, "Inmate Pittman!"

"Yeah, right here," Diamond responded, standing up to alert the cop as to who he was.

"Step out; you have an attorney visit," the officer announced.

That statement was music to the ears of the street veteran, and he quickly made his way to the door, put his hands behind his back interlocking his fingers, and followed the officer. Diamond had been in touch with Mister Trigilio every day since the first time the two men had met, and he quickly found out that the renowned attorney was truly game for trying any strategy that could potentially prove useful in winning his case.

Diamond was escorted through the door of a small room located right outside the courtroom and then chained to a counter positioned directly in front of the thick, glass window. He took a seat on a small metal stool and watched as the young, Black bailiff left the room, closing the door behind himself.

Less than a minute later, the door opened on the other side of the window that separated him from the attorney room, and Mister Trigilio strolled in with his briefcase in hand.

"How are you holding up, Mister Pittman?" the snappily-dressed lawyer inquired as he took a seat and smiled at Diamond through the glass window.

"Well… to be honest with you, sir, I've seen better days," Diamond responded. "I'm losing a shitload of cash every second I'm stuck in this can. My lawyer is costing me an arm and a leg, plus, when they served me my breakfast tray this morning, I found out that green eggs and ham really does exist. Other than that, I guess I'm doing halfway decent."

"I'm sorry to hear about your problems, Mister Pittman, but 'halfway decent' trumps 'halfway indecent' any day, and I'm pleased to inform you that I do have some good news for you today."

"Now you're talkin', counselor," Diamond responded with a new sense of optimism written on his face. "I'd love me some good news."

"Okay, well here goes," Mister Trigilio said while lowering his voice and leaning in closer to the air holes at the bottom of the window, "I had a long conversation with that certain person who we spoke about last time I talked to you, and we've got the green light to proceed with the defense that we discussed," the lawyer said. Diamond closed his eyes tight in a display of emotion. A tear ran down his face as he sat in silence for a moment.

"So… do you think it will work?" Diamond asked, breaking the silence after a full minute.

"Barring any unforeseen occurrences, I can't see why it wouldn't, Mister Pittman," the lawyer assured him. "I must warn you, though, that the DA is going to fight this thing tooth and nail, so if I were you, I wouldn't count on being out of here in time for lunch, but in the end, you will definitely come out on top if everything goes the way I think it will."

"Well, what about bail?" Diamond asked.

"As I told you before, Mister Pittman, I'm going to try to get the judge to set bail for you, but unfortunately, you have a history of jumping bail, so she isn't going to be very eager to release you to the streets pending trial, and even if she does, it will probably be some astronomical amount," Mister Trigilio warned.

"Well... that's better than nothin'," Diamond responded. "I know a guy, so just get her to set bail and I'll take it from there."

"See you in court, Mister Pittman," the lawyer announced, as he stood up and removed his briefcase from the floor. He nodded his head at Diamond and then stepped out of the attorney room.

An hour later, Diamond was led into the courtroom in handcuffs and instructed to sit down next to Mister Trigilio at the defendant's table. The bailiff removed his handcuffs, strolled up to the side of the witness stand, and began speaking in a loud voice, "All rise!" Then, the bailiff announced as the Black, middle-aged woman judge walked into the courtroom, "The Honorable Judge Jeanine Pearson presiding. You may be seated," the bailiff added after the judge sat down.

"Thank you kindly," the judge said as she glanced at the stack of papers sitting on her desk. "Today, we are here for the preliminary hearing in case number F-82498, The United States versus Daniel Pittman. Are all parties present in this matter?"

"Yes, Your Honor," the deputy district attorney answered.

"The defense is present, Your Honor," Mister Trigilio said.

"Okay, so let us proceed," the judge instructed and flipped through a few pages. She then again began to speak, "Mister Pittman has been charged with possession of cocaine exceeding the amount of ten kilos, and conspiracy to traffic a controlled substance was just added this morning, correct?" the judge asked and then looked down at the DA for an answer.

"That is correct, Your Honor. Due to the large amount of cocaine recovered in this case, we felt it necessary to add the conspiracy charge to the list," the DA responded.

"Okay, and I see that the People are also seeking the Habitual Criminal Act in this case. He pleaded not guilty to these charges, so here we are. Mister Bowley, is the People's first witness ready?"

"Yes, Your Honor. At this time, the People would like to call Federal Agent Melvin Sanders to the stand," the DA announced. Everyone in the courtroom watched as the short Black man approached the witness stand. The court clerk swore in the witness and directed him to have a seat. Deputy District Attorney Hezekiah Bowley walked up and stood next to his witness, "First of all, good morning to you, Agent Sanders," the DA greeted.

"And the same to you, sir," the agent responded.

"Agent Sanders, on October 13 at about 1:00 P.M., where were you?"

"I was on a stakeout in the City of Los Angeles around the Watts area," Agent Sanders replied.

"And can you please explain to this court what the reason was for this stakeout?"

"Yes, sir. We had reason to believe that a large drug transaction was about to take place."

"Okay, and will you please explain to this court why you had a reason to believe that a drug transaction was about to occur?"

"Yes, sir. We received that intel from a CI," the agent responded.

"And for those of us who do not understand cop language, will you please tell us what CI stands for?"

"Confidential informant."

"Thank you, Agent Sanders. Now please apprise the court as to whether or not this stakeout resulted in any arrests."

"There were two arrests made as a result of this particular stakeout."

"Please disclose to this court the names of those two people and the reasons for their arrests."

"We arrested a forty-two-year-old woman by the name of Radmillia Jearman on charges of possession of cocaine. Miss Jearman was sitting in the driver's seat of the van where we recovered an excess of ten kilos of cocaine. And the other arrest was a forty-four-year-old man by the name of Daniel Pittman. We observed Mister Pittman ride up in the passenger side of the van and then exit the vehicle in the parking lot of Maxine Waters Park."

"And finally, Agent Sanders, do you see either one of the aforementioned people in this courtroom today?"

"Yes, sir, I do. Mister Pittman is sitting right there in the defendant chair."

"Let the record reflect that the witness has identified the defendant. Thank you, Agent Sanders," Mister Bowley said. "I have nothing further at this time, Your Honor." The deputy DA walked back to the prosecution side of the table and sat down.

"Mister Trigilio, would you like to cross-examine the witness at this time?"

"Yes, Your Honor, just briefly," Joseph Trigilio answered as he approached the witness stand. "Agent Sanders, a moment ago you said that my client was in the parking lot of Maxine Waters Park when he was arrested, correct?"

"Yes, sir."

"Okay, and was my client in possession of cocaine or any other controlled substance at the time of his arrest?"

"Well... not exactly but—"

"That was simply a yes or no question, Agent Sanders," Mister Trigilio informed his witness.

"No, sir, he did not have any drugs on his person," the agent answered.

"Okay, and did you at any time witness my client touch or make any contact whatsoever with the drugs that were recovered in this case?"

"No, sir, I did not."

"No further questions at this time, Your Honor." Mister Trigilio made his way back to the defense table and took a seat next to Diamond.

"Does anyone else have any questions for this witness?" the judge inquired.

"No, Your Honor."

"No, Your Honor."

"In that case you may be excused," the judge informed the agent. "Who's next, Mister Bowley?"

"Your Honor, the People would like to call Agent Holley Francisco to the stand," Mister Bowley announced, and the attractive Hispanic woman made her way to the witness stand and raised her right hand to be sworn in.

Once she was sworn in, Mister Bowley approached the witness stand and got right back down to business, "Good morning, Agent Francisco."

"Good morning," she replied.

"Agent Francisco, how are you employed?"

"I'm a senior criminologist with the Federal Bureau of Investigation's Scientific Services Department, also known as the crime lab."

"And what are your duties there?"

"I perform a myriad of services, but my specialty is the identification, weighing, and repackaging of controlled substances."

"Could you please give us a brief summary of your educational background, experience, and training?"

"Sure," the agent responded. "I have a Bachelor of Science in Forensics from Dominguez Hills University. I have been employed with the bureau for over six years and have been in my current position for the last four years. I have received training on the job with respect to the methods and theories of analysis with regards to controlled substances."

"Your Honor, the People would like to introduce exhibit-A at this time," Mister Bowley announced as he walked up to the prosecution table to retrieve his evidence exhibit. He walked back up to the witness stand with what appeared to be an oversized Tupperware container and handed it to his witness. "Agent Francisco, at this time I will ask you to describe the contents of this container," the DA requested.

The agent took the large rectangular container from Mister Bowley and ripped off a piece of paper that was taped to the side of it.

"This little piece of paper right here is what we call a CIC, or Contraband Identification Card," the agent announced while holding the card up for the judge to see. "This card is what we use to describe the contents of recovered contraband before we send it to the evidence lock-up." The agent then turned the card around and began reading from it, "This particular card tells me that the contents of this container tested positive for cocaine base that weighed out at ten thousand, seventy-three grams. That's just a smidgen over ten kilograms."

"No further questions for this witness, Your Honor," Mister Bowley said as he took his exhibit back from the agent's grasp and headed to the prosecution table.

"Mister Trigilio, your witness," the judge announced.

"Thank you, Your Honor," the handsome, dark-haired lawyer responded as he walked up to the witness stand. "Just real quick, Agent Francisco, was the container that Mister Bowley just took back to the prosecution's table the same container that the drugs were in when they made it to your office?"

"No, sir, it was not."

"Well, in that case, can you please describe to the court the container that the cocaine base was in when you received it?"

"Sure. It was wrapped inside five individual plastic bags that were all wrapped inside a large, brown grocery store bag."

"Okay, and can you enlighten us as to what happened to those bags — the plastic and the grocery bags?"

"They were all discarded at the time the contraband was transferred into one of our formal containers."

"Okay, and were any of the original bags dusted for fingerprints before they were discarded?"

"No, they were not."

"And with all you have just told us about the contraband, in your professional opinion, with everything you have just told us about your education and expertise, is there any way that you can prove that those drugs belonged to Mister Pittman?"

"Not at all. My job is to strictly analyze the contraband, not to pin it on any particular person."

"Nothing further, Your Honor," Mister Trigilio announced with a look of satisfaction on his face.

"You may step down," the judge informed the witness. "Are there any more witnesses?" the judge asked.

"Not at this time, Your Honor," the deputy district attorney answered. "The People do have several more witnesses prepared to testify; however, I am confident that we have presented enough evidence here today to take this matter to trial."

"Well, let me be the judge of that, Mister Bowley," the judge warned. "Mister Trigilio, do you have any more witnesses?"

"Yes, Your Honor, I do," Mister Trigilio responded, to the surprise of the DA. "At this time, I would like to call Miss Radmillia Jearman to the stand. She is out in the hallway."

Assistant Deputy District Attorney Hezekiah Bowley stood silent as the bailiff walked out of the courtroom and returned a minute later with the Black woman. Big Mama made her way up to the witness stand and took a seat.

"Good morning, Miss Jearman."

"Good morning," Big Mama replied.

"Miss Jearman, I'd like to direct your attention to October 13 of this year at about 1:00 P.M. What were you doing at that time?"

"I was sitting in my van in the parking lot of Maxine Waters Park."

"And can you tell this court the reason for your being in that parking lot at the time and date in question?"

"Yeah, me and my boyfriend had not been getting along all week, so we was just sitting in the park trying to talk things out."

"Miss Jearman, did anything out of the ordinary happen while you were sitting in that parking lot?"

"Yes, my boyfriend had got out of the van to smoke a cigarette 'cause I got asthma, and not even two minutes later a bunch of cars just swooped into the parking lot out of nowhere. Next thang I knew, I was handcuffed in the back of a police car on my way to jail."

"Can you explain to the court your reason for being arrested on that day?"

"Yes, I was charged with possession of a controlled substance and conspiracy to distribute."

"And can you tell us the reason you were charged with those particular crimes?"

"They found a bag full of cocaine in the backseat of my van."

"Can you tell this court whether or not you knew about the bag in question?"

"Yeah, I knew the bag was in my backseat, 'cause a friend had given it to me to drop off to another friend, but I didn't know what was in the bag."

"That's very unfortunate, Miss Jearman, and my heart goes out to you," Mister Trigilio said in a sincere gesture. "To your knowledge, did my client Mister Pittman know what was in that bag?"

"No, he did not," Big Mama answered.

"In fact, did my client even know that the bag was in the backseat of your van?"

"There was no reason for him to be paying attention to the backseat of my van, so the answer to your question would be — no."

"No further questions," Mister Trigilio announced and headed back to the defense table.

"Mister Bowley, would you like to cross-examine Miss Jearman?"

"No, Your Honor, but I would like Miss Jearman's testimony to be stricken from the record under U.S. rules of court 4709, which states in part that an opposing party in litigation must be afforded adequate notice of all witnesses prior to the witness' testimony in open court. I was not given any notification whatsoever that this witness was scheduled to testify."

"Mister Trigilio, what is your stand on this?" the judge inquired.

"Well, Your Honor, it seems that Mister Bowley has forgotten to read the first four words of section 4709, which are 'Aside from extreme circumstances'. Your Honor, the first time we gained knowledge of Miss Jearman's willingness to testify was this morning when she showed up in this courtroom. I believe that qualifies as an extreme circumstance."

"I've made my decision on this," the judge announced in a stern voice. "I'm going to allow Miss Jearman's testimony. Mister Bowley, you have been doing this long enough to know that the proper time to enter your objection to the admissibility of a witness' testimony would have been prior to that testimony. You knew that you had not been given proper notice of Miss Jearman's plans of taking the stand, yet you sat there and allowed her to testify. so as far as this court is concerned, you conceded to this witness."

The judge turned to Big Mama, "You may be excused, Miss Jearman. That said, I believe there is a lot more to this case than what we've heard today, therefore, I find that there is sufficient evidence to send this case to trial and let a jury sort it out. Let's set a date."

The judge watched as the court clerk checked the docket calendar.

"The next available trial date is December 18, Your Honor," the clerk informed the judge.

"Are any of the parties opposed to beginning the trial on that date?"

"That date will be fine, Your Honor," Mister Bowley said.

"We don't have any objections to that date, Your Honor," Mister Trigilio answered, "but I would like to address the court regarding one final issue if I may before we adjourn."

"I'm listening, Mister Trigilio."

"Your Honor, in light of Miss Jearman's testimony before this court today, I believe that these charges should have been dropped; however, we do respect this court's decision. We are confident that we will beat these charges in trial, and we thank the court for giving us the first available trial date. Your Honor, all the defense asks is that bail be set in this case. My client has a solid defense and is also rooted in the community. He has been out of prison for many years now, and his last failure to appear was over seven years ago."

"Do the People object to a bail being set?"

"Yes, Your Honor," Mister Bowley responded. "The People would ask that this case remain a no bail. Over the years, Mister Pittman has had several failures to appear and has jumped almost every bail he has ever made. Now that he is facing well over twenty years in prison, how much more incentive is that for him to skip town?"

"Both of you have a point," the judge said, "but Miss Jearman's testimony, paired with the fact that Mister Pittman has been out of the system for seven years, causes me to be a bit more inclined to give him a second chance. Bail is hereby set in the amount of $350,000. Court is adjourned."

Joseph Trigilio winked at Diamond as the bailiff led the street veteran out of the courtroom in shackles.

Chapter 76

Gordo had been up all morning preparing for his Mexican vacation. All the lights were out; the house was in order; the suitcases were packed, and he was just about to walk out of his front door when he was interrupted by the ringing of his telephone. The *varrio* boss almost decided not to answer the phone, but when he thought about the possibility of missing out on some money, which he could not afford to do at this point, he changed his mind and picked up the phone. "*Si?*" Gordo said into the phone in an impatient voice.

"*Ola, senor!*" the cheerful voice at the other end of the line spoke. The sound of the man's voice caused Gordo to become nauseous. He recognized Detective Montenegro's voice from the first word he spoke.

"Detective Montenegro, what a nice surprise," Gordo lied. "It's real good to hear from you, aye, but I was on my way out the door, so I'm going to call you back later on, okay?"

"Not so fast, *amigo*," the detective announced. "I'm sorry to tell you, but whatever plans you have will have to wait because I need to talk to you about something very important," the cheerful voice that the detective had begun the conversation with had suddenly become demanding.

"Let's make this quick, detective. What is so important that you have to hold me hostage on the *telephono*, homes?" Gordo asked, beginning to feel slightly irritated.

"Well, since you are in a rush, I'm going to come right out with this without sugarcoating nothing," the detective announced, hinting to Gordo that there was bad news ahead. "That thing we had you do with the Diamond guy a while back just backfired on us, Gordo."

"Wait, whaddaya mean, 'backfired'?" Gordo asked, getting defensive. "With all due respect, I did my part, homes, so whatever happened after that ain't my problem or my business."

After this announcement by the Mexican street don, there was a moment of silence.

Then the detective responded, "Let me make this clear to you, *amigo*. You are big bad Gordo only in your *varrio*. To me, you are Hector Torez, and about a month ago your door got kicked in and Hector Torez' ass got busted with over ten kilos of coca. Well, let me tell you something, Hector; if you think we flushed all that dope down the *tocador* when you walked out of that federal jail, then you've got another thing coming, aye. As a matter of fact, we still got all that coca along with the reports by several federal officers who say they caught you red-handed with that and the scale. And guess what else; we have up to one year from the date of your arrest to file that case."

The detective paused for a moment to allow Gordo a chance to speak. When the *Vatos Locos* boss failed to respond, the detective went on, "Now I hate to hold this over your head, Gordo, but we're dealing with a slick *miyathe* here. He has got his old lady trying to ride the case for him—"

"And I guess that's where I come in, right?" Gordo interrupted.

"The only thing we need you to do is take the stand one time to testify that you were in the parking lot to buy cocaine from Diamond on that day. We already have a video tape with him getting out of that van to talk to you and everything, but without your testimony, we have no case now that this woman is claiming responsibility for the dope."

"Okay, well... you've got his old lady then," Gordo responded. "She is taking responsibility for the coca and there is your conviction. That's what it's all about, isn't it? As long as you guys get your conviction, who cares who takes the fall?" Gordo inquired.

"I care, god dammit!" the detective responded. "The woman has no prior drug convictions, and on top of that, she has already created a defense for herself. She will get no more than a five-year slap on her wrist at most. This man, on the other hand, is the leader of a gang that is responsible for the deaths of more cops than I care to count, the leader of a gang that is on the top tier of our public enemy list, and dammit, a gang that is responsible for killing a shitload of Mexicans in the last few months. I take that personal, homes, and so should you when three of your brothers were victims of his. You can't sell your soul for money, *carnal*. You and your *varrio* couldn't stop this guy by yourself, so now we are going to try this a different way, because the last thing we need is for that son of a bitch to gain more power than he's already got. Now here's the deal; I'm going to guarantee you pure immunity in this case and for the bust a month ago for this one testimony. I'm going to have the paperwork drawn up, and whether we convict this asshole or not won't have any bearing on your deal. As long as you get on that stand and tell the truth, you will come out squeaky clean. Sure, the *miyathes* in the projects are going to be a little upset with you that their daddy is gone, but it's nothing that a little cash can't fix, right? Other than that, you're getting off scot free. The trial starts in a week, so I will need you to get over to my office before then to sign this agreement."

When Gordo hung up the phone with detective Montenegro, he immediately began unpacking his suitcases.

Chapter 77

Rick Rock and Sick Twin had already been on trial for two days when Lil Ricky walked into the Compton Courthouse holding tank at 7:00 A.M. It had taken an entire day and a half to pick their jury, and after seating five Blacks, three Hispanics, three Whites, and one Asian, the teenagers were more than satisfied with the jury their lawyers had selected.

After the jury selection was completed, the prosecution had only managed to call one witness before the day ended. The first witness Deputy District Attorney Chantal Hathman had chosen to call to the stand was a representative of the Los Angeles County Coroner's Office. This had proven to be a crafty move by the veteran DA, because although the witness' testimony had not directly incriminated the two defendants, the shock value of the exhibits that had been presented had been enough to gain the undivided attention of every juror.

When Mrs. Hathman called her witness Mister Joel Madson, instead of walking directly up to the witness stand, he drug a large overhead projector to the middle of the courtroom and then rolled out a large white screen and stood it up ten feet away from the projector. Mister Madson then instructed the DA on how to use the device and took the stand.

With a simple click of the hand, one by one, Deputy District Attorney Chantal Hathman had flashed the life-sized photos of the dead bodies of each victim laid out in the exact spot where they had fallen. Every photo Mrs. Hathman flashed onto the overhead screen was more graphic than the one before. The jury let out a gasp with the introduction of each photo, all of which showed Hispanic men laid out on the ground in the middle of large puddles of blood. The only difference between them were the locations of their gunshot wounds. With the introduction of each image that the DA flashed onto the screen, Mister Madson read a paragraph from the autopsy report describing the cause of death.

District attorney Hathman had saved her knockout punch for last. What had proven to be the most powerful photo in the lineup was the image of Gina's lifeless body laid out on the floor of the bedroom. The photo showed the beautiful young girl on her back with her right eye wide open staring into space. Her left eye was where the bullet had entered and penetrated her brain. The clever district attorney knew that this final image of the teenage girl with one eye open and the other blown in by a bullet with blood flowing from the socket would be lodged into the minds of each and every juror for the duration of the trial.

* * *

It did not take Lil Ricky long to spot his homeboy when he walked into the courthouse holding tank. Now that they were on trial, the bailiff would bring them their suits every morning for them to dress up before they walked into the courtroom. Sicko Twin's bus would always drop him off an hour earlier than Lil Ricky's, therefore, he was already dressed in his three-piece, navy-blue suit with the gold buttons when Rick Rock entered the holding tank.

"Whaddup, Sugar Free?" Lil Ricky said as he approached his homeboy who had traded his signature French braid look for a neat ponytail that hung all the way down his back. The ponytail, along with the three-piece suit, gave Sicko the look of a smooth and dapper pretty-boy pimp. When Sicko failed to laugh or even smile at the joke, right away Rick Rock could tell that his good friend was not in a playful mood.

"Nigga, I know you ain't lettin' these White folks get the best of you, not my nigga Sicko, blood," Rick Rock taunted in an effort to brighten up his homeboy's mood.

"Na, blood, it ain't like dat. A nigga just don't feel like playin' right now," Sicko responded.

"I feel you, homie. I'm just tryin' to laugh to keep from cryin' up in this bitch," Lil Ricky admitted.

"I need to holla at you about something, my nigga, so let's step to the back for a minute," Sick Twin informed Lil Ricky.

The two young men walked to the rear of the holding tank where they could have some privacy. Once they reached the back of the tank, Sicko got right to the point, "I'm finna take this case, Rick Rock," the teenager announced. Lil Ricky was caught off guard by the statement and could not believe his ears.

"What the hell you mean by that, my nigga?"

"Nigga, I mean exactly what the fuck I said. I'm about to get on the stand and say that I did everything and you didn't have nothing to do with it," Sicko announced. Lil Ricky stared at his friend as if he were an alien.

"Now why in the hell would you do some ignant-ass shit like that when you know damn well deez honkeys is tryin' to give us the death penalty?"

"Shit, life in prison, death penalty, what's the difference?" Sicko asked. "These motha fuckas got me, Lil Ricky. They got me on these murders, and on top of that, they got me for the shit that went down at Gordo's spot, so either way it go, I'm through wit money."

"Darnell, shut dat shit up, blood. I ain't about to let you do this when we both got action at beating this case," Lil Ricky insisted. "Plus, you couldn't take the whole case even if you wanted to when all the witnesses sayin' that it was two people."

"Lil Ricky, I ain't as dumb as you think I am. I know what I'm doin', homie," the teenager announced. "They got me dead bang on the Gordo shit with my DNA on that cigarette. That's a death penalty case by itself. It ain't no sense in us both being on the row, nigga, so just—"

"I don't wanna hear this shit, Sick. Fuck! What you goin' through feelin' sorry for yourself and shit, but we are riding this thing out together — win or lose."

Right when Lil Ricky made his final demand, the holding tank door opened, "Moss and Pittman, let's go," the bailiff stood in the doorway with Lil Ricky's suit in his hand, "Get dressed quick, because we're running late."

Every seat in the courtroom was full, just as they had been since the two teenagers had started trial three days earlier. Just like in the Nickerson Gardens projects, the courtroom was visibly segregated according to ethnicity. The family and friends of Lil Ricky and Sicko were situated on one side, while the other side of the courtroom was where the family and friends of their victims sat. Following a small riot in the hallway outside the courtroom between the two parties, the judge had assigned five sheriff's deputies to be present at all times in order to keep the peace until the trial ended.

"Order in the court," the bailiff announced prompting every spectator in the court to prematurely end their conversations. "The Honorable Judge Margaret Johnson presiding."

The judge thanked the bailiff and began the court's daily formalities, "We are on the record in case number CV135169 A and B, the People of the State of California versus Patrick Pittman and Darnell Moss. Are all parties present in this matter?"

"Yes, Your Honor. Good morning. Fay Warren here representing Mister Pittman who is present," the attractive, middle-aged Black woman responded.

"And Joey Davis here for Darnell Moss," the light-skinned, gray-haired Black man announced.

"Chantal Hathman here for the People," the DA announced.

"And are the People ready to call their next witness?" the judge inquired.

"Yes, Your Honor. At this time, the People would like to call Darnell Moss to the stand," Mrs. Hathman proclaimed.

Lil Ricky was stunned by the announcement from the DA, since he and Sicko had already come to an agreement before trial that neither one of them would take the stand. As a result, he quickly turned to his lawyer and asked in a loud whisper, "What the fuck is going on here? Aren't you going to object to this shit or something?" he asked.

The nonchalant demeanor of the lawyer, as his partner in crime approached the witness stand, made Rick Rock even more hot under the collar. While sitting next to the angry teenager, Fay Warren used a finger to motion for him to lean over so she could whisper in his ear, "Look here, Mister Pittman," the lawyer began.

285

"My job is to do what I believe is in the best interest of my client, and I promise you that Mister Moss taking the stand right now is going to turn out in your best interest. There has been some agreements which have taken place between all concerned parties that you don't know anything about because your friend up there did not want you to know." Fay Warren promptly lowered her voice after the witness had been sworn in, and the DA began her line of questioning.

"Mister Moss, I'd like to direct your attention back to October 23 of this year. Do you remember that date?"

"Yes I do," Sick Twin answered.

"And can you tell this court where you were at about 5:00 P.M. on that date?"

"Yes, I can," Sicko replied. "I was in the Nickerson Gardens housing projects."

"And did anything out of the ordinary happen on that date and time in question?"

"Yes, it did," Sicko answered.

Lil Ricky could not believe his eyes and ears. Tears began to roll down his cheeks as he attempted to wake himself up from this nightmare. There, on that witness stand, was one of his two best friends in the whole world, a friend who he had retained a high-priced lawyer for and was prepared to either go free or go to the lethal injection chamber with. Whatever happened, they were supposed to face it together, but instead, his homeboy was about to sacrifice his very life.

"Mister Moss, at this time, I am going to ask you to give this court a detailed description of the events which took place on that day and time in question," Mrs. Hathman requested.

"Well, I don't know how much detail you're looking for, ma'am, but here goes nothing," Sicko announced before turning his head so that he was looking Lil Ricky directly in his eyes as he spoke, "It's like this, me and my homeboy, Little Smokey, decided to go put in some work on the *Vatos Locos* because they had just killed one of our friends the day before that," Sicko proclaimed.

"And is Little Smokey a monicker?" the DA inquired.

"What's a monicker?"

"A monicker is a nickname, sir. Is Little Smokey a nickname?"

"Oh, yeah!" Sicko exclaimed. "Little Smokey is the name of my homie who is resting in peace."

"Your Honor, the People would like the record to reflect that the aforementioned Little Smokey has been confirmed as Percy Washington, a known member of the Bounty Hunter gang who was murdered a couple of weeks ago."

"So recorded," the judge announced, "and you may proceed," she informed Sicko.

"Yeah, and like I was sayin', me and Little Smokey decided to go put it down on the VLs, so we drove on over to they side of the projects, then hopped out the car, and just started shootin' all the *cholos* we could shoot. I do believe y'all saw the results on the big screen, high definition TV yesterday," Sick Twin proclaimed and then began laughing as if he had just told a hilarious joke. At that moment, an old Mexican woman in the spectator's seats began to wail out loud and had to be escorted from the courtroom by one of the deputies before Sicko could continue testifying.

"Mister Moss, this is not a circus; it's a court of law," the judge scolded. "Now I'm aware that you don't have much to lose at this point, young man, but I am going to ask you, for the sake of those victims' families, to at least exercise a little bit of self-control on this witness stand. Can you handle that, young man?" the judge asked in a stern voice.

"Yeah, I guess I can respect your court," Sicko replied. "as long as I ain't gotta show no remorse, 'cause I ain't got none of that," the young gangster announced while staring to the side of the courtroom where the family and friends of his victims were sitting.

"That's fine," the judge said. "Now, let's proceed."

When Mrs. Hathman was sure that the spectacle was over, she continued her line of questioning, "Mister Moss, let me get this correct; you are admitting before this court that you and Mr. Washington killed all those men we saw on that screen yesterday?"

"Yes, ma'am, that's what I'm sayin'. We killed all the men you showed on that screen yesterday."

"Thank you," the DA replied, "and can you tell this court what happened next?"

"Yup," Sicko answered. "After we spilled all them, we kicked in the door to a house where we knew another VL named Smiley was at."

"Your Honor, the People would like the record to reflect that the aforementioned Smiley was confirmed as Adam Garcia, a known member of the *Vatos Locos* gang who is also deceased at this time."

"So ordered," the judge replied and then gave Mrs. Hathman the okay to continue.

"Mister Moss, will you please tell this court what happened after you and Mister Washington kicked in that door?"

"Little Smokey ran through the bottom floor of the house lookin' for Smiley, and I went upstairs lookin' for him, but he wasn't there. While I was upstairs, I found his girlfriend tryin' to hide in a closet, and the big screen told y'all the rest yesterday," Sicko announced.

"So, are you admitting before this court that you also murdered the girl who was on that screen yesterday?"

"Yeah, I'm admitting that I murdered the girl who was on that screen yesterday," Sicko announced with his signature evil grin.

"Your Honor, the People would like for the record to reflect that the defendant has just admitted to the court that he personally murdered Gina Hernandez."

"So recorded," the judge replied.

"And I have no further questions for the defendant at the moment; however, all concerned parties have agreed to a change of plea in this matter. Mister Moss is going to enter a plea of guilty in all five of the murders in this case, and in exchange, the People are going to drop all murder charges against Mister Pittman and have him enter a plea of guilty to the charge of grand theft auto. And we are offering Mister Pittman a four year deal of which he will serve half, along with the credit for the time he has already served. In regards to Mister Moss, there has been no deal made with respect to his sentence, so that will be left strictly to the discretion of this court, Your Honor."

"I see," the judge said. "Mister Davis, are you sure that this will be the best thing for your client, seeing as this will more than likely result in his being sentenced to death?"

"Well, You Honor, I have tried with every fiber in my being to persuade Mister Moss not to do this. He has been advised several times of the consequences and everything else," Mister Davis went on, "however, there are no mental health issues with regard to my client, therefore the final decision ultimately rests in his hands."

"Very well then," the judge announced. "I am prepared to accept his plea."

"Your Honor!" Fay Warren interrupted.

"Yes, Mrs. Warren?" the judge asked.

"I would like to exercise my right to cross-examine the witness at this time."

"Well, I don't see any reason for it, but it is your right, Mrs. Warren, so the witness is yours."

"Your Honor, this is a death penalty case, so chances are that the witness won't be around in the event that the State decides to refile murder charges against my client."

After explaining her reasons for cross-examination, Rick Rock's lawyer turned to Sick Twin, "Mister Moss, just for the record, did my client have anything at all to do with the murders you have just admitted to?"

"No, ma'am, he did not," Sicko answered.

"And did he have any knowledge that those murders were about to be committed?"

"No, ma'am."

"And to your knowledge, was my client ever in possession of that stolen vehicle before the murders were committed?"

"No, he was not. I would imagine that he stole the car from the place where we parked it after we did our thang in it."

"And last of all, was my client aware that the stolen vehicle had been used in those murders or any other crime at the time he stole it?"

"No, ma'am, there's no way that he could've been aware."

"No further questions," Fay Warren said, and she walked back to the defense table and took her seat next to Lil Ricky.

"Okay, I trust that we can accept the pleas now and get this thing over with?" the judge inquired. When she received no answer, she continued, "Mister Moss, as to count one, do you plead guilty to the charge that on or about October 23, 2008, you committed the crime of premeditated murder against Armondo Espinoza in violation of penal code 187(a)?"

"Yes," Sicko replied.

"Okay, and do you admit that pursuant to the amended information that you personally used a fire arm under penal code 120.22(a)?"

"Yeah, I do," Sicko answered.

The judge repeated the same questions to Sick Twin concerning four more victims, and just like the first, he pled guilty to them all. After the judge accepted his pleas, she accepted Lil Ricky's plea to the charge of grand theft auto and sentenced him to two years as the district attorney had promised. Sick Twin's sentencing was postponed for a week so that the judge would have time to review his criminal history before she made her final decision. At the end of the court session, Rick Rock walked out of the courtroom in handcuffs with his head hanging in despair, while Sicko exited right behind him with his head held high, still sporting the same sinister smile that he always kept on his face.

Chapter 78

It was 9:55 A.M. when Diamond exited the 405 Freeway and drove down the Avenue Of The Stars off ramp in Century City. He had been out of jail on bail for only a week when he received a call from Mister Trigilio telling him that they needed to meet at his office as soon as possible to have a discussion about some new developments in the case. Diamond had argued against the meeting, saying that he had urgent business matters to take care of in the streets and that they should talk about whatever they needed to discuss over the phone. That was when Mister Trigilio took his time to slowly explain to Diamond the importance of meeting in person and cautioned him about the danger of talking over the phone, two things which he believed he should have never had to explain to a so-called street hustler.

Once Diamond took the time to consider what Mister Trigilio was trying to get across to him, he realized that the savvy lawyer had a point and had agreed to meet up with him at his office the next day.

When Diamond pulled up to the security booth in front of the gates of the high-rise building where Mister Trigilio's office was located, he was promptly approached by a security guard who asked for his name and the name of the person he was there to see. After a brief conversation on his intercom, the security officer pulled the lever activating the lift gate in order for Diamond to pass through. After passing through the gate, Diamond realized that the beautiful all-glass high-rise building that he'd seen from the main street was even more impressive up close. The street veteran found himself admiring the flawless landscaping as he drove toward the parking lot. The outside layout of the building was perfect, surrounded by freshly-trimmed hedges and well-kept flowerbeds.

Diamond parked his car in the closest available space and walked up to the building's entrance. In the foyer, he passed by a waterfall with a large statue of an angel in the center. Diamond's Stacy

Adams clicked against the dark-gray granite floor as he approached the elevator where he pressed the shiny, gold button with the upward-pointing arrow. When the doors slid smoothly open, he stepped into the elevator and pressed the button for the top floor.

It did not take Diamond long to locate the suite with the plaque over the door, which read, 'THE LAW OFFICES OF JOSEPH TRIGILIO'. When he walked into Mister Trigilio's office suite, he quickly found out where all the money was going that he was paying his top-dollar lawyer. Mister Trigilio's office was plush. The first thing Diamond noticed when he walked through the door was the one-hundred gallon salt-water fish tank containing a variety of tropical fish and other sea creatures, all built into the long wall in the lobby. He then looked straight through the office to the large glass window that yielded a paramount view of the city.

"Mister Pittman?" the attractive fortyish secretary inquired.

"Yes, ma'am, that's me," Diamond answered.

"Please have a seat and Mister Trigilio will be right out," the secretary instructed. Diamond followed the woman's instructions and sat down on the soft, black, leather couch. A minute later, a door opened and Mister Trigilio emerged.

"Come on in, Mister Pittman," the attorney invited. "Would you like something to drink? Water, coffee?"

"No, I'm okay," Diamond answered as he strolled into Mister Trigilio's office.

Just like everything else in the building, the lawyer's office was notably luxurious. The floor was a dark-gray-colored marble and was polished to the point where Diamond could look down and see his reflection. To one side of the room was a fireplace constructed of lava rocks with a tinted-glass covering so that all that could be seen through the glass was an orange flame. Displayed on the wall above the fireplace was a medieval weapons collection consisting of several different varieties of swords, shields, and maces. At the other side of the room was a wall-to-wall bookshelf containing what appeared to be every law book ever written.

"Have a seat, Mister Pittman," the attorney requested. Diamond sat down in one of the high-backed leather chairs that were positioned in front of Mister Trigilio's neatly-kept desk when he noticed the life-size self-portrait of the lawyer hanging on the wall behind him. Directly under Mister Trigilio's self-portrait was a shiny, golden plaque with the words '*VAE VICTIS*' engraved on it.

"That's a nice portrait of you, man," Diamond complimented. "I've always wanted one of those."

"Well, thank you, Mister Pittman. I myself find it a bit pompous, however, my daughter gave it to me as a Father's Day gift, so I figured I'd better display the darned thing," Mister Trigilio stated while looking at the portrait as if for the first time.

"So, what does that say on the plaque up under it? Is that Greek or something?" Diamond asked, dumfounded.

"Actually, I don't even remember *what* it means," the lawyer replied. "It's just some Latin gibberish that one of my professors gave me back in law school — live long and prosper or something. I just thought it would compliment the portrait nicely. But at any rate, I know you're a busy man, Mister Pittman, so let's get down to business," Mister Trigilio announced, changing the subject.

"Instead of insulting your intelligence with the old good news bad news cliché, I'm just going to get right to the point. The district attorney is attempting to back us into a corner. First of all, he has offered the first plea bargain," Mister Trigilio announced.

Diamond immediately began to shake his head at the very mention of a plea bargain and asked, "Now why in the hell would I cop a plea when I got an airtight defense? That would be ass backwards; wouldn't it?"

"Well... not exactly, Mister Pittman, and if you care to hear me out, then you might understand why I say that."

"Oh, I'm sorry. Go ahead," Diamond apologized.

"Well, as I told you before, you are looking at close to thirty years in federal prison if you, by some remote chance, are found guilty in this case. The DA has offered ten years, which is a third of what you would end up doing if found guilty. Now, along with this offer came a couple of unpleasant surprises," the lawyer announced. "First of all, they are prepared to give Miss Jearman a deal for two years if she agrees to change her preliminary statement—"

"Ha, ha, ha!"

Mister Trigilio was rudely interrupted by Diamond's laughter.

"Sorry, Mister Trigilio, but I had to laugh at that," Diamond proclaimed. "If I don't trust another damn soul in this world, I trust Miss Jearman. I know that she would never in a million years do anything to hurt me and especially not for no damn two years. Do Mister Bowley know that they offered her pure immunity the last time we was in a situation like this?" Diamond asked.

"Well that's excellent, and I hope you are right, Mister Pittman, but there is just one last problem," the lawyer warned. "Mister Bowley filed a motion yesterday to add a man by the name of Hector Torez, who was documented as being detained and questioned in that parking lot the day you were arrested, to his witness list. Now, Mister Pittman, we haven't discussed your case much other than your defense and how I will go about placing reasonable doubt in the minds of the jury, but if I had to gamble on it, I would bet my soul against a cuckoo bird's turd that this Mister Torez is planning to testify that he was meeting you in that parking lot to purchase those drugs from you and that he has never met Miss Jearman in this life."

The lawyer added before he allowed Diamond to speak, "But please correct me if I'm wrong, Mister Pittman."

"So that fat Motha fucka is gonna snitch on me, huh?" Diamond asked, talking to himself.

The room remained silent for a moment while Diamond ran scenarios through his mind. After two minutes, he began speaking again, "So, what if I paid this fat blob of shit to disappear for a while until the trial is over?" the street veteran asked while staring at his attorney with a somber look on his face.

"Mister Pittman, I have been a criminal defense lawyer for a very long time," Mister Trigilio announced. "In that time, I have seen this same thing over and over and over again, where a guy says he's going to pay a witness off to not show up or that the guy is a gang member and that prohibits him from snitching. Well, guess what, Mister Pittman? They always show up and they always snitch. You had better believe that Mister Torez is the prosecution's number one priority right now. Chances are they've got some dirt on him, and if he tries anything funny, they will arrest him and drag his ass into that courtroom by his ear. Now, I'm going to be as candid with you as possible and I will speak slowly so that you can understand what I'm about to tell you, Mister Pittman. The best prosecution witness is no prosecution witness at all. Now I'm not telling you this for any reason except as an example in what would happen in a perfect world. I am prepared to fight this thing regardless of any evidence they are prepared to present, and I am confident that I can dismantle the testimonies of Mister Torez, Miss Jearman, and anyone else they put on that stand, but without Mister Torez, we are fighting a toothless tiger. Without him, we'll run circles around the prosecution. Miss Jearman gets a couple of years for possession, and Mister Pittman tries not to let the door hit him in the ass on his way out of the federal courts building — case closed," the lawyer promised while staring his client in his eyes with a persuasive look on his face. The hint was as plain as day, and Diamond understood exactly what his attorney was suggesting without him having to state the obvious.

"Toothless tiger, huh, counselor?" Diamond asked while standing up. He gave the attorney an affirmative nod to let him know that he'd caught the drift and began walking toward the door. Once Diamond made it to the office door, he turned to face Mister Trigilio who was still seated at his desk, "Well, I guess I will talk to you in a few days," Diamond announced. "Right now, I gotta go pull some tiger teeth."

Mister Trigilio smiled and gave his client a quick wink before he walked out the door.

Chapter 79

Diamond was suffering from a slight feeling of helplessness as he drove out of the parking lot of Mister Trigilio's office building. The street veteran knew exactly what he needed to do to ensure victory in court and maintain his freedom, however, he also knew that his task at hand was more than just a notion. After all, he had just finished spending four straight months trying to take out the prosecution's new star witness, but to no avail. Gordo had always been a reclusive man who could rarely be caught hanging out in the streets, and now that the *Vatos Locos* boss knew that he was going to be testifying on behalf of the prosecution, there was a big chance of him turning into even more of a hermit.

Diamond was also a bit skeptical about his lawyer's claim that Gordo was preparing to testify against him in court. Setting him up to get busted with the dope was something that could be denied and was also impossible to prove, but if Gordo were to take the stand and snitch in open court, Diamond knew that it would most certainly mean the end of the truce, thus the end of the *Vatos Locos* gang. After jogging every scenario possible through his mind while traveling on the freeway en route back to Watts, Diamond concluded that his best bet would be to follow the advice of his lawyer. The only dilemma he was faced with now was how he was going to go about pinpointing his target.

As soon as Diamond reached the projects, he immediately went to work attempting to find out any and every location where he might be able to catch Gordo. He started off by questioning street hustlers that he knew were still doing business with the VL boss regularly. Diamond managed to get a few leads this way on several locations where Gordo had been known to frequent, but for the most part, the small time dealers told him that Gordo always sent his henchmen to conduct his business transactions, something that Diamond was well aware of.

Next, the street veteran began asking the all-knowing dope fiends whether or not they knew where he could track down the VL boss. Diamond's logic in this endeavor had a lot to do with knowing the nature of a dope fiend. He knew that crack had no loyalty to any particular race, creed, or gang, and that birds of a feather flocked together. He was correct in his assumption that the Lil Tijuana dope fiends interacted with Dark Side dope fiends but dead wrong in assuming that he could get any solid leads about a big-time drug dealer from a small-time drug user.

Following a great deal of brainstorming and labor, Diamond finally realized that the possibility of hunting Gordo down was remote at best. As a result, the street veteran decided that the only way he could find the VL boss would be to smoke him out of his hole. The first thing Diamond decided to do was get in touch with an old acquaintance of his by the name of Spanky. Spanky was a thirty-nine-year-old member of the *Vatos Locos* gang and a well-known project rival of Gordo's. As a career criminal, Spanky had done time in more than half of the penal institutions in California. At a young age, he had joined a powerful Mexican prison gang and risen up in the ranks over the years by engaging in acts such as smuggling drugs into prisons and for also being handy with a shank while participating in several large-scale race riots involving Mexicans and Black inmates. He had spent most of his time in jail doing time in high-security housing units due to his assaults on Northern California Mexicans known as *Nortenos*, on African-Americans, and on anyone who dared to go against the grain within his own gangs. This is why Spanky believed he should be *Llavero*, boss of the *Vatos Locos* gang.

He believed that Gordo was a fat, lazy coward who gained his position strictly through his genius of keeping money flowing throughout the *varrio*. Although Spanky settled for second in command, it was well known in the projects that he had a large crew of homeboys who would be quick to take his side if it ever came down to a civil war. As a result, Diamond always maintained and even cultivated a personal relationship with the VL second in command. It was well known that Spanky's crew had been the ones doing most of the killing during the VL and Bounty Hunter war;

nevertheless, Diamond's main target throughout the war had been Gordo. When Spanky answered his cell phone, he was happy that it was Diamond at the other end. *"Diamante! Odalay, vato?"* Spanky exclaimed into the phone.

"Whaddup, Spank?" Diamond greeted him.

"Nada, right now, homes. I'm just trying to stack some *fedia* real quick for me and my *hina* to get our down payment on this townhouse."

"A townhouse, huh? It sounds like you tryin' to do big thangs, *essay,"*

"Na, it ain't like that, aye. I'm just tired of having my little boy in the projects. I want better for him than what I had growing up."

"So, what's up with your boss?" Diamond asked. "He ain't tryin' to help you out on nothin' or what?"

"Now you know damn well that drunk ain't no boss of mine, homes," the Mexican man replied, noticeably agitated at the statement. "Any lame that ain't never been to *la penta* can't tell me *nada.* And plus, I would rather rob a fucking Brinks truck than ask that sucker for something."

Diamond laughed at this statement, because he knew that Spanky was serious since he had been to prison for robbery on more than one occasion, "Ain't you gettin' a little up in age for that type of shit, Spanks?"

"Aye, homes, that's all I know. My hustle has always been getting mines the fastest way possible."

"Well, maybe it's time to change all that, Spanky," Diamond suggested in an effort to soften up his mark to his latest request.

"And just how am I going to do that, Diamond? Tell me something good, homes."

"Well, I'm pretty sure you know what the problem is. Or should I say, who the problem is?" Diamond said.

"Yeah, homes, but you know how our shit goes in Lil Tijuana," Spanky replied. "That fool is *Llavero,* and until I have a good solid reason to take his ass down, I gotta kick back, aye?"

"Bingo!" Diamond said. "That's why I'm calling you today. When our homeboys was out there blasting on each other, it was a whole bunch of foul shit going down from your side of the park and—"

"Wait, hold on one second, homes," Spanky interrupted. "I ain't never been down with ratting or killing innocent people. That was that fat punk Gordito. He couldn't stand the heat after he lost his brothers, so he panicked and started having scandalous shit done. But you already know it, Diamond; my little circle wasn't doing none of that bullshit. We were bringing it straight to you *vatos!*" Spanky proclaimed. "That fat-ass *rata* gave cowards like himself a way to help by doing lame shit. He knew his ass was on thin ice, so he did what he had to do. I don't respect that fool at all, homes, and it's a damn shame that his little sister is downer than he is."

"Hey, Spanky, do you think I don't know who is who in my neighborhood?" Diamond asked. "Look, man, I believe that your time to shine has come — if you want it. You can't just sit back and allow your crew to be the dirty-broke enforcers who do all the killing while Gordo collects all the money. That motha fucka is in violation all the way around, and guess what?" Diamond added for emphasis. "He is about to kick off another war between us, and you know that's going to mean a whole bunch of funerals on both sides. I know y'all don't want that just like my homies don't want that, so we gotta act quick," Diamond said.

"But I don't understand, homes," Spanky said. "What has he done to kick off another war?"

"It's not what he did; it's what he's about to do," Diamond answered. "I want you to meet me somewhere so I can prove to you firsthand what I'm talkin' about. Will you do that?" Diamond asked.

"Yeah, homes. Just give me the time and place and I'll be there," Spanky replied.

Diamond gave the *Vatos Locos* second in command the address to the law offices of Joseph Trigilio and told him to met him there at 6:00 P.M. sharp, at a time he knew his lawyer would be finished with court for the day. After confirming their appointment, the two men hung up the phone.

Chapter 80

Psycho Twin had been out of the hospital for only one day. After his stay in MLK, he had been transferred to Rancho Los Amigos Hospital in the City of Downey, where he was supposed to spend several months in rehabilitation, physical therapy, and learning how to cope with everyday life while in a wheelchair. It had not taken long for Psycho to figure out that Rancho Los Amigos Hospital was not the place for him. The only thing the hospital had managed to do was fuel the teenage paraplegic's cynicism. He found it hilarious how the Black, Hispanic, Samoan, and every other race of gang bangers could all of a sudden have a change of heart and begin holding hands and singing "Kumbaya" once somebody shot the hell out of them and put their asses in a wheelchair. Now, all of a sudden, these hard-core killers were all getting along despite the fact that they had all been out to murder one another out on the streets. That had become Psycho's favorite saying in rehab.

When it was time to play wheelchair basketball, he yelled to both teams, "You motha fuckas wasn't playin' basketball on the streets!" When it was time to play table tennis, Psycho yelled, "Y'all punk asses wasn't playin' no fuckin' Ping-Pong on the streets!" When it was time for group counseling, Psycho refused to go and yelled to everyone who was wheeling toward the circle, "Y'all wasn't going to no counseling on the streets. If you was, then ya punk asses wouldn't be in them wheelchairs right now!"

Psycho found this bunch to be even worse than the kids who had come to youth authority back when he was in prison and had all of a sudden found God. As far as he was concerned, the Bible and Quran were the two biggest hiding places in jail. No matter how many drive-by shootings a sucker did on his rivals, no matter how many enemies he killed, all one had to do was come to jail and become a Christian or a Muslim, and that was the end to all their problems. It was the perfect way to avoid the inevitable hand to hand combat that came with representing your turf.

After only one week in the rehabilitation hospital, Psycho had enough, and, likewise, the people in the hospital were all fed up with the bitter, young gang banger.

The first thing Psycho did when he arrived back in the projects was call the great grandmother of his son. He knew that he was in for a battle when Olga Ocasta told him that he would never see her great grandbaby again and not to call her home anymore or she would call the police. Instead of blowing his top the way he usually did, Psycho realized that due to his paraplegic state, he had to learn how to use his mind to get things done instead of his gun. After Mrs. Ocasta had hung up the phone on him, he called her back after taking a few minutes to get his gumption together. Once again the great grandmother of his son answered the phone after only one ring.

"*Ola?*" the old lady answered.

"Mrs. Ocasta, please don't hang up on me again until you hear what I have to say," Psycho begged into the telephone. "Listen, I know how hard it is for you right now after what happened to Gina. I can't express to you how sorry I am about that, but I need you to know that I didn't have nothing to do with what happened. I'm sorry about all the pain you are going through, but I loved Gina and you know she still loved me, so there is no way I would've ever did anything to hurt her."

Psycho paused for a moment when he heard the old Mexican woman sobbing at the other end of the telephone, "Now Mrs. Ocasta, you know deep down in your heart that Little Adam is my son. I always want him to have a relationship with you, and I plan to let him spend as much time with you as you want. Please don't make me go through the courts to get custody of him when we can behave like adults and handle this on our own. I know that the best place for him is with you, and I don't ever want to have to take Little Adam away from you, but you have to let me spend time with my son. He needs his father just like he needs his great grandma." Psycho was amazed at how easy things were when he used his mind. Mrs. Ocasta agreed to let him see his son anytime he wanted as long as he agreed to never take him away from her.

Chapter 81

The late-night telephone call from Spanky had taken Gordo by surprise, informing him that there would be an *encuentro de comite*, a meeting of all the leaders of the *Vatos Locos* gang, the following morning at Chito's house. The VL head honcho found this to be slightly peculiar because not only was he the one who usually called all the meetings, but he had just left Chito's apartment only a couple of hours before he got Spanky's call and Chito had not mentioned anything about a meeting. Nevertheless, Gordo had found out the time the meeting was to be conducted and promised to be there.

Gordo arrived to Chito's apartment at 9 A.M., an hour earlier than the meeting was scheduled to begin, in order to pick his good friend's brain with regard to the reason why this meeting had been planned at his apartment. Gordo had no idea why his pesky comrade Spanky had called this meeting, but he knew he could count on his good friend Chito to give him a heads-up.

Gordo walked slowly up to the door of Chito's apartment and knocked softly. A full minute passed with no answer, so he began to think that Chito was still in bed. Once again he began tapping on the door, this time a little bit harder, in order to wake up his homeboy. After another full minute, Gordo heard the latches begin to unlock from inside the house, and then the door opened.

"*Esse*, Gordo!" Chito announced in a loud voice before he opened the door wide enough for Gordo to enter the apartment. Gordo was dumbfounded when he walked into the apartment to find that he was obviously the last member of the panel to make it to the meeting.

The *Vatos Locos* boss strolled into the living room of his sergeant at arms to spot four more of his high-ranking comrades. Choppper and Negro were both sitting on the long leather couch drinking from plastic cups. Neither of the two gang members acknowledged Gordo when he walked into the room. Sitting on the love seat drinking from a forty-ounce bottle of Budweiser was Picaro who also failed to make eye contact with the VL boss when he walked into the room. Spanky, who was standing when Gordo entered the room, walked up to him and extended his hand to greet him with a handshake. Chito made his way back into the room and removed the gallon of Jose Cuevo tequila from the remote control table and poured a cup.

"What's up, Gordo?" Spanky asked while shaking his hand.

"I don't know, *esse*; you tell me. What's this all about, aye?" Gordo asked while looking around the room.

"First of all, homes, we will get down to business in due time, but first things first. What are you drinking, *vato*? We got beers in the frij. We got a fresh bottle of tequila right there on the table. The ice is—"

"Fuck that shit, homes! I don't want *nada* right now until I find out what you *vatos* are up to!" the *Vatos Locos* boss exclaimed, losing his cool.

"Okay then, Mister *Llavero*, for the first time in your life you don't want something to drink, so let's sit down and have this meeting," Spanky said with a tinge of sarcasm in his voice. Gordo watched Spanky sit down on the couch between Negro and Chopper. Chito sat on the arm of the love seat next to Picaro and motioned for Gordo to have a seat. The chubby gang leader took a seat in the La-Z-Boy chair and folded his arms over his chest in a gesture of authority and defiance.

When Gordo looked around the room at his homeboys, he quickly realized from the posture of everyone in the room that he was about to be the main subject of this meeting, and as a result, he immediately began to regret the fact that he had not brought his gun. Gordo knew that if worse came to worse, he could always count on his good friend Chito, but he was also aware that his being unarmed placed him and his homeboy at a huge disadvantage, because there was no question as to whether or not all the other men in the room were armed.

"So, what's this about, *esse*?" Gordo asked while looking his adversary Spanky in the eyes.

"What's it about?" Spanky responded. "I'll tell you what it's about, homes; this is about one simple question. Are you or aren't you planning to rat out that fool Diamond in court?" Spanky asked in a "gotcha" type manner.

"Is that what this bullshit-ass meeting is about, *esse*?" Gordo asked with a disgusted look on his face. "You *vatos* called me to this sorry-ass meeting to question me about a fucking dirty Black tire piece of shit *miyathe*?"

"Aye, homes, it's not about helping that fool. What it's about is your word, *esse*," Negro announced. Being the only Black man in the room, Gordo's comment had slightly offended the "Blacksican".

"Yeah, *pedo*," Spanky agreed, "it seems like you don't remember, but the last time we had a meeting right here in this same room, we agreed that there would be no more snitching no matter what happens, and that's what we're sticking to, homes."

Gordo didn't like being grilled and began to grow more and more furious with every comment made by his subordinates.

"Hey, Spanky, it's obvious that this meeting ain't about me, *esse*," Gordo proclaimed. "This is clearly about your jealousy and envy for me. It's a well known fact around here that you want the keys, homes, so if you wanna handle something, then we can do it however you want, aye," the VL boss challenged.

"Wait! Wait! Hold on, *esse*," Spanky responded. "I already told you what this meeting is about, Gordo. We just got our asses handed to us on a platter trying to go to war with a gang that's ten times bigger than us. I was all the way with it, homes, because it was for a good reason. I was willing to ride until I died, homes, but I wasn't never down with the snitching and shooting at little girls and old people and shit. But that shit was working for you, so I just said what I had to say and kept the line moving, *esse*. But then you called a truce!" Spanky exclaimed. "All three of your *hermanos* got dropped, but you called the truce, Gordo. That's when all the killing stopped and we had our meeting and said that there was never going to be any ratting or killing innocent bystanders no more. That was when you gave that big-old speech about being ashamed of how you went about handling your business and all that soppy shit. I even think I remember you shedding a couple of tears," Spanky announced, causing everyone in the room other than himself to break out in laughter. "Well, am I lying or what, *esse*?" Spanky asked.

"Hell na, you ain't lyin', Spanks," Picaro answered.

"So, back to the question, Gordo, 'cause you're trying to make this about me when it's really about everybody in the *varrio*. Are you preparing to get on the stand and testify against Diamond or not? It's a simple question," Spanky asked, while he and everyone else in the room stared at the VL boss awaiting his answer.

Gordo thought for a minute and then shook his head before speaking, "The answer is no, homes. I don't know where you *vatos* got all this shit from, but I ain't ratting on nobody," Gordo proclaimed.

"Is that your final answer, homes?" Spanky asked, prompting another round of laughter from the other men in the room. "Are you telling us right to our faces that you haven't talked to nobody about going on the stand in no case involving Diamond?"

"That's what I'm telling you *vatos*!" Gordo said while standing to his feet. "Now, I'm about to get the hell out of here before you guys piss me off with these accusations."

At that moment, every other person including Chito stood to his feet. Spanky reached into his waistband, drew a 9mm pistol, and pointed it at Gordo's face.

"I think you need to sit back down until the meeting is over, homes," Spanky demanded.

Gordo could not believe his eyes. The VL head honcho made a mental note to have Spanky and everyone else in the room killed as soon as possible and sat back down.

"*Dispensar*, homes. I thought it was over, aye," Gordo said while staring down the barrel of Spanky's gun.

"Don't even trip, *esse*. We're almost finished here," Spanky announced. "I just wanna get this straight. You're telling us that you don't got any plans to snitch on Diamond in no case and you haven't talked to no one about going to court, that basically you don't even have any idea about what we are talking about, right, homes?" Spanky asked.

"That's what I'm telling you, Spanks," Gordo replied. "I don't know what you *vatos* are talking about, so whatever that *miyathe* told you is a straight-up lie, *esse*!"

"Wrong answer," Picaro said while getting back to his feet and drawing his pistol. Every man in the room followed Picaro's lead with the exception of Chito who went to lock the front door of his apartment. Spanky tucked his weapon back into his pants and bent down to reach underneath the long couch. He quickly brought his hand out and was now holding two pieces of paper.

"Hey, homes," Spanky said, "while we were having that war, I hated how you handled that shit with the ratting and killing of innocent people, but I chalked it up and stayed out of your way because the *varrio* was in trouble and I figured you were just doing what you thought you had to do, but now I'm realizing that this is what's really in your heart, *esse*," Spanky announced while holding up the two pieces of paper. "You ain't *nada* but a coward-ass *rata*, Gordo."

Spanky walked up to Gordo and handed him the motion that the district attorney had filed for him to testify along with a copy of the subpoena with his signature on it. Gordo glanced at the papers and realized that he was busted.

He looked back up to see Spanky pick the gallon of tequila up from off the table. Spanky walked over to the La-Z-Boy chair and held the bottle out toward Gordo. He refused it.

"Hey, homes, you better take this fucking bottle!" the tall, muscular Mexican demanded while redrawing his pistol and pointing it back at Gordo. Gordo took the bottle of tequila from Spanky's grasp and stared at his accuser as if he did not know what to do next.

"What are you waiting for, you fucking drunk! Drink it!" Spanky demanded.

Gordo followed his order and put the bottle to his lips. He took a swig before pulling it back away from his face.

"I said drink that shit, *esse!*" Spanky yelled, "and if you bring that bottle back away from your face without the whole thing being empty, I'm gonna blow your brains all over the back of that chair."

Spanky cocked the hammer on his pistol to let Gordo know he meant business. Gordo quickly followed the man's order by turning the bottle upside down over his mouth. The captive street king took swallow after swallow until the entire bottle of tequila was empty before he removed it from his mouth. Gordo began to feel dizzy and nauseated. The room began to spin right before his eyes, and his homeboys were now just a blur as he fought to keep his composure.

"If you throw up one drop on the homie's carpet, I'm going to plug your sorry ass," Spanky warned.

"Why are you guys doing dees to me?" Gordo mumbled, not knowing if the words even made it off his lips. He felt himself losing consciousness but could not fight it until he was awakened by a hard slap to the left side of his face. Gordo regained his focus and realized that he was now surrounded by the three men hovering over him. He could hear the distant sound of hyena-like laughter as the men took turns striking him about his head, neck, and body.

"Chito!" the desperate man yelled with slurred speech, but he received no answer from his old buddy who had been assigned by the new *Llavero* to watch the front door. Gordo flashed in and out of consciousness with each hit that he sustained. He felt someone holding his legs apart and kicking him hard in the testicles, and a hard punch to his jaw made a cracking sound that only a broken bone could.

The beating went on until Gordo could no longer feel the hits. He could still hear the distant sounds of the taunting and laughing for a few more minutes before everything went blank. When Chito walked back into the room, he had to fight off the tears when he spotted his old friend laid out in the middle of a puddle of blood and vomit. Gordo's eyes and lips were swollen closed, while blood was still gushing from several wounds on his face. Chito felt guilty for allowing this to happen, but he knew that if he had tried to intervene it would have also meant the end of his life.

"You *vatos* gotta help me get rid of this fucking body, aye," was the only comment made by Chito about the situation.

"Go and get some blankets, *esse*," Spanky said. "I got the shovels in my trunk."

Chapter 82

"Inmate Pittman, what's your last two?" asked the green-jumpsuit-clad correctional officer after stopping in front of cell 141 in Ironwood State Prison's B2 block. It was 5:50 P.M. when the cop appeared at Lil Ricky's door with the evening mail.

"Forty-eight!" Rick Rock responded, accepting the envelope that the correctional officer handed him before moving on to the next cell. Rick Rock glanced briefly at the return address on the front of the envelope and was happy to see that his uncle had written to him. He sat back down on his bunk, removed the letter from the envelope, and began reading:

Dear Lil Ricky,

Watts up, Baby Nephew? I hope all is well as can be expected on your end considering your current address. I won't tell you how much fun I'm having out here 'cause I don't wanna stress you out. The good thing is that you will be home very soon. It doesn't even seem like it's been nearly two years since you left. Oh, and I don't know if you've heard, but your boy Psycho just took a deal for five years after fighting that robbery case all this time. I know he didn't want to do any time at all, but he is actually lucky to be doing only five years. Your Auntie Big Mama has been out for a few weeks now. We went out to Las Vegas and tied the knot last weekend. Yeah, ya uncle finally caved under her pressure and made it official. She moved in with me, so I don't know how that's going to work out. So far, so good, though. Well, anyway, you know how ya uncle feels about this writing shit, so I will end this one. I put a thousand more dollars on your books to last you until you come home, and I also sent your boy Sicko another gee to last him a few more months. I mean, damn! How much shit can a nigga buy on death row? You know it's a small thing to a giant though, baby nephew. Anyway, keep that head up and I'll see you soon.

Love always,
Uncle D

Lil Ricky slid the letter back into its envelope and looked up at his television just in time to see the *Tyra Show* come on. Tyra Banks walked down the stage to the sound of all her screaming fans in the audience. She quieted them down and then began to speak, "We have got a very nice surprise for you guys today, yall," Tyra announced. "We've got multi-platinum artist Stormy Love in the house performing her brand-new hit singles 'Replace you' and 'You don't know me' from her self-titled sophomore album!" yelled Tyra, as everyone in her audience began screaming as if they had lost their minds.

Lil Ricky still felt sick to his stomach every time he saw Stormy on television or heard her on the radio. It had been a little over a year since Stormy's debut album *The World By Storm* had come out, and just as the title said, it had taken the world by storm. It seemed as if every inmate in Rick Rock's cellblock owned a copy of *The World By Storm*, and the CD could be heard blasting from many of the convicts' radios.

Lil Ricky had never told any of the other inmates about his history with the singing phenomenon, because for one, he was trying to forget about it, and two, they would not have believed him anyway. He quickly reached out and changed the channel to *Oprah*, prompting his cellmate to complain, "What the hell you doin'? Didn't you just hear Tyra say Stormy was comin' on? That's my wife, blood!"

Lil Ricky had to catch himself. He came very close to telling his cellmate to get his own TV if he wanted to see that black widow slut, but being the generous person that he was, he simply turned his television back to the *Tyra Show*, "My bad, homie," Rick Rock answered. "I guess she *is* pretty good, isn't she?"

Made in the USA
Las Vegas, NV
16 April 2022

47602064R00174